Rest at Journey's End

Also by Steven Muenzer

Farewell Berlin

Rest at Journey's End

STEVEN MUENZER

Alexander Press • St. Paul, Minnesota • 2017

On the cover:

Eiffel Tower, Paris, photo by Steven Muenzer

This is a work of historical fiction.

The author acknowledges the following for background and story ideas:

Herman Mahlerman, *The Fugitive*, Pageant Press, Inc., 1967.

Editing & Layout

E. B. Green Editorial, St. Paul, Minnesota

Manufactured in the United States of America

10 9 8 7 6 5 4 3 2 1

Library of Congress Control Number: 2017932367

To Jeanne

now and always

Rest at Journey's End

Up lad: when the journey's over
There'll be time enough to sleep.
—*A. E. Housman*

History . . . is a nightmare from which I am trying to awake.
—*James Joyce*

What sweet thoughts, what longing led them to the woeful pass.
—*Dante Alighieri*

PROLOGUE

Grim-visag'd comfortless Despair.
—*Thomas Gray*

On the train to France, near the Belgian border, August 1939

Rosa screamed, then fell to her knees next to Sonny. She cupped his face in her hands and began to cry. Minutes earlier, Sonny had whispered into her ear: "In Mons, we catch a local to Hautmont, the last stop in Belgium. Then into France at St. Remy du Nord."

She had squeezed his hand. "What could possibly go wrong now?"

Then he left for the men's toilet, in the next car. He pushed through people in the corridor, then onto the platform between the cars. He grabbed the door handle to steady himself and pushed. Something was wrong. He felt sudden movement. Someone grabbed him from behind, pinning his arms. Then a blow to the side of his head, and he crumpled like a house of cards. The lights were out.

The cop and the conductor raised Sonny to his feet. They dragged him into the station, his feet scraping along the platform. Rosa and her parents—Robert and Elise Fischer—trailed anxiously behind. Sonny was taken into a small office. They were told to wait outside.

Sonny, yielding to gravity, slumped in a chair. His head felt as if it had been stuck with an ax. Each movement sent its blade deeper. He heard an unfamiliar voice—German. He searched for the source. Straining to focus, he saw a face, lips moving. Slowly he understood just how untenable his position was. Stripped of passport and visa, he was an illegal refugee, again. Not only would he be denied entry to France, but also he would be arrested, jailed, deported.

In late December of the previous year, Rosa Fischer had arrived in Antwerp with her parents. Sonny Sander—or so said the name on his passport—arrived several days later. Sonny and Rosa had met on 9 November 1938—or Kristallnacht, the horror visited upon German

3

Jews by the government. Rosa's father was arrested with many thousands of other Jewish men and sent to the Sachsenhausen camp. Weeks of anxiety ensued.

Sonny was part of a group that supplied forged documentation to Jews. The day before Rosa's father's release, a Gestapo lieutenant had accosted Rosa, intent on rape. He died for the transgression—Rosa and Sonny killed him. And more Gestapos had died during Sonny's last days on German soil. Sonny and Rosa married in Antwerp on 3 April 1939, but the need for Sonny's greater distance from Germany grew imminent . . .

"What happened?" a voice asked.

Sonny did not answer. The question was repeated.

"Water . . . please." Sonny's throat was parched.

A glass appeared. Sonny drank, then licked his lips and took several shallow breaths. "Going to toilet . . . grabbed from behind . . . hit on head."

Reflexively, his hand went to his empty pocket, and he grimaced: "Stole papers . . . money."

"Another one," the German-speaking cop said.

"What?" Sonny asked.

"Robbers—usually attack older people."

Sonny groaned. "Wife . . . I want to speak to my wife."

He heard someone speaking in French.

Then Rosa sat in a chair next to him. Her big dark eyes filled with sadness and concern. "To come this far . . ."

"I'm all right." His voice was hoarse. "Papers, money . . . gone."

"What are we going to do?"

Sonny shook his head and winced. Rosa squeezed his hand.

"You go," Sonny started then gasped. "Ah . . ."

"Sonny!"

"I'm okay. No papers . . . can't cross border . . . go with your parents.

"No!"

"You must."

She was silent but for quiet sobbing.

"I'll get there . . . Write Sammy at the little café in Antwerp with an address in Paris. I'll find you. Promise me you'll go.

Part I

Not die here in a rage, like a poisoned rat in a hole.
—*Jonathan Swift*

1

Camp Wortel, Belgium, November 1939

Lying on his bunk, hands clasped behind his head, Sonny let his gaze follow the geometric pattern of the wooden joists to the peak of the roof, pointing heavenward. Light bulbs dangled from long cords along its length, unlit in the dim light of midafternoon. Shadows, hazy outlines, milled about the bunks.

A caged man, Sonny shut them out, wanting to be left alone. His mind's eye saw Rosa hunched on the platform, tears staining her cheeks, hands drawn into fists, railing against injustice, receding until she disappeared from view.

"Get far away from Wortel—find Rosa." He banished all thought but that of escape. His saw three choices: to despair, to walk away and never be seen again, or to wait for something to happen. The first was hopeless, the second risky, the third inertia. Sadness overwhelmed him; his melancholy was staggering. But he vowed never to surrender. He would live, escape, and find Rosa, his raison d'être. He wrote letters to her, kept them under his mattress, ready to mail.

Still, as incarcerations might go, this one seemed relatively benign. The camp was not exactly a prison. No barbed wire encircled it. There was no locked gate though the "guests" were not at liberty. The keepers threatened severe punishment for attempted escape— threats were enough.

Like something in a fairy tale, Camp Wortel had been dropped into the forest years earlier and been forgotten. Near the Dutch border, 35 kilometers northwest of Antwerp, it was hidden on the outskirts of the town of Wortel. Illegal refugees—overwhelmingly Jewish—filled the camp. Similar camps dotted the countryside like mushrooms sprouting after a spring shower.

Impenetrable forest darkness enveloped the camp—demons seemed to lurk in the shadows. Sonny had heard them at night. At the gate, a circle of three guards, rifles slung over their shoulders, smoking, talking, occasionally laughing, posed no immediate threat of intimidation. This was Belgium, not Germany's Sachsenhausen or Dachau.

Forty guests—not prisoners—were housed in each of the king's five old army barracks. Peeling paint and broken windows evidenced long neglect of the long, low building. Bunks, 20 to a side, lined up in rows like new recruits in basic training; toilets and communal showers, shared by the 200 men, were in another building. The camps were segregated by gender: husbands separated from wives and children, boys over the age of 16 with the men. Democracy reigned—guests governed themselves. An elected leader represented the camp to the director and government officials upon periodic inspection. Aided by an elected council, he oversaw the camp's daily operations, assigned mundane chores—food prep, garbage detail, recreation. Lifting the guests' spirits required a morale team.

Government leaders feared the cascading numbers of refugees. Police departments cried, "Law and order!" Corralling refugees into camps solved problems real and imagined. The government could control the refugees, remove the foreigners from the streets, keep them from public sight and thus out of mind. Perhaps most importantly, the government could be seen as in charge—not welcoming refugees to Belgium. Jews, especially, were nobody's favorite—a classic understatement. Xenophobia was ascendant. Fear trumped rationality.

Sonny had caught a break in Mons. He might have been arrested and deported to Germany, but sympathetic cops released him for return to Antwerp. Then weeks later, on 1 September 1939, the war began. *Blitzkrieg!* Poland bombed into submission.

On his way to see the man who had forged his papers, Sonny had run into a cop—literally. "Excuse me," he said absently in German—a mistake.

"Wait!" the cop said in Flemish. "Papers! Show me your papers."

Fate had turned against Sonny again. Was this the end of the line? His youthful, hopeful façade, his belief that every possibility was open to him had begun to crack when his parents died. It crumbled with Hitler and was crushed to dust on Kristallnacht. Now he felt stomped upon.

At times, Sonny's blood boiled, threatening to scald his sanity. Struggling to stay afloat and frantic for Rosa's safety and whereabouts, he flailed for his next breath. Despair nipped at his heels like an angry little dog. But self-pity was the refuge of the forgotten and hopeless, and he fought against it. He could not wallow in the muck of defeat. That could only lead to death.

Some could not cope, he knew. On a Saturday, the Sabbath, he had heard commotion in the yard after morning services. Word quickly spread—a man was missing. An escapee? A search party found him hanging from a tree. Tired of waiting . . . despondent . . .

Thomas Minsk (surname like the city in Ukraine) sat on the bunk next to Sonny's, talking nonstop: "Hitler's waiting to take vengeance on France . . . everybody knows that! Damn Soviets dealt with the devil, Stalin's mortal enemy . . . Can you believe it? We going to sit here and wait?"

Sonny's young friend was right. When Hitler turned west, he would trample Belgium and Holland in a flood of man and machine. But not France. Sonny had to get out and get there now.

Thomas was 22 years old—Sonny's age when he started smuggling. Thomas came from Heidelberg, home of the oldest university in Germany, but he had never attended the school. In better times he would have—he was that smart. But he talked too much. He looked barely out of his teens, so Sonny called him "Kid," and it stuck.

Sonny tuned Kid out, didn't want to hear it . . . again. Kid was just trying to make sense of the maelstrom. No surprise he was having trouble. Like everyone else, he had to feel his way through, experience it and hope he would make it out the other end. There was no other way through Hitler's war—life was like that. Kid wouldn't say anything new, and if he did, Sonny would hear it later.

His mind clear of chatter and clutter, Sonny thought of Rosa. His eyes closed, he saw her standing on the railway platform, tears streaking her cheeks. Three months had passed, and still it seemed like yesterday. Every night—beautiful, scared, alone—she arrived. He would feel her body next to him, mutter something, and reach . . .

Was she safe in Paris? Why hadn't he received a letter? Did she miss him? When would they reunite?

The days dragged as if he were crawling on his belly. From sunrise to nightfall he read, heard endless talk of people left behind and where they'd go, given the chance, the remote possibility . . . There was little stimulation.

Everyone—Kid, the Berlin lawyer Victor, teacher, tailor, the Orthodox alike—had left someone behind. Memories kept them going; dignity and hope gave them strength. Most fought the blues, but some wallowed in self-pity. The lawyer was no better off than the tailor, the doctor no better than the warehouseman. For some, that hadn't sunk in.

"What's to become of us? Why me?" Sonny had no answers, only hope. "Hell! Life isn't fair, or we wouldn't be stuck in this shitty camp," he had told Kid more than once. "Be careful. Complaining leads to despair."

"What else is there?" Kid said.

Kid's voice in his ear, Sonny glanced around the half-full barracks. Victor sat on his bed, reading. The teacher from a small town in northern Germany was talking to some Orthodox guys. What had each of them endured? Had any of them killed anyone?

Kid and Victor were the only friends Sonny needed. Friendship meant expectation, responsibility. Friends might slow him down when the time came. He didn't want too much of that.

Thin and wiry, with strong Semitic features, dark eyes and full mouth, Kid exuded energy. Deprived of an education, he had read widely to compensate. Capable of discussing a range of topics, he usually did so ad nauseam. He had been forced to work at whatever he could—buying and selling, as Sonny had done.

Incarceration and separation from his family had made Kid insecure. He had emigrated from Heidelberg in the summer of 1939; his parents and younger brother arrived several months later. Their plans to meet in Brussels never materialized, and Kid was arrested. Scared and alone, adrift, he needed someone like Sonny.

Victor Glazer was 42 and self-assured bordering on arrogant. Cynicism replaced what probably once had been a sarcastic sense of humor. Still, his eyes twinkled when he laughed his rich baritone. Physically unimposing, Victor was short and slightly overweight. He had practiced law during the Republic, after 1933 representing Jews, often for free. He had been at Wortel when Sonny and Kid arrived in late September. Sonny and Victor, fellow Berliners, bonded rapidly.

On the second day, the three of them went for a walk. Victor's short legs churned to keep up. Sonny slowed. Kid listened—a rare occurrence. They threw out the names of family, friends, and associates, searching for connections.

Victor had lived in the West End for years but had family in Mitte. At least once he had been in the warehouse where Sonny worked, had purchased a book. Did he remember the man who had sold it to him? Was his name Joseph?

He shook his head. "Can't remember."

They continued the game, names vaguely familiar, until Sonny recalled that Mina's grandfather was a lawyer. "You know the lawyer Peter Cohn?"

"I did," Victor answered, his smiled fading, "and met his wife once, heard she died. His daughter married a KPD official by the name of . . . ?

"Dix, Helmut Dix," Sonny supplied.

"How do you know?"

Sonny explained his smuggling enterprise in broad terms. "We provided documents for Dix, his wife, Grete, and Peter. His daughter, Mina, stayed and fell in love with my best friend. They're in England with Dix."

Victor nodded his approval. "Impressive. What's your real name?"

"Sigmund Landauer."

"Hmm . . . Landauer. Landauer . . ." Victor put a fingertip to his lips, considering. Finally, he said, "I remember a Simon Landauer."

"My uncle." Sonny smiled at bittersweet memory.

"Killed himself, didn't he?"

"Ja." Sonny looked away, recalling the gentle misanthrope. "How well did you know him?"

Victor shrugged. "An acquaintance. I'd say hello . . . hear him tell a joke."

They wandered in silence through the grove of trees, golden leaves crunching under foot, no gremlins in sight.

"How did you get here?" Victor asked.

"Bad luck, like everyone else," Sonny started.

"Bullshit! Everyone's got a story."

Sonny laughed, looked at Kid, back to Victor: "Got that right."

Sonny told them about Mons and his separation from Rosa. They stopped behind a big evergreen. The gray gloom of the sky dulled the landscape to two dimensions with no depth, as if a wall were blocking their path. It was chilly, not cold.

"What about you?" Sonny asked.

Victor shrugged and instead of answering asked Kid, "How did you get here?"

"Bad connections," he said.

"Rather terse," Victor said, smiling.

"Not much to say. Missed meeting my family. Got arrested. Now it's your turn."

Victor exhaled a long sigh. "I was caught in a sweep and arrested, though I held legitimate documents, passport and visa, even an identity card—for all the good it did."

"When did you get here?" Sonny asked.

Victor stifled a laugh. "Came to this lovely locale in September . . . arrived in Belgium, in December last year." He swept his arms in a grand gesture, a master of ceremonies acknowledging applause.

"Family?"

He shook his head. "Not married, no children. Family spread around Germany, America, God knows where."

"What about Kristallnacht?"

Victor grimaced and lowered his gaze.

"Where?" Sonny asked.

"Sachsenhausen."

No more questions. They returned to the barracks.

Everyone worked. Jobs were assigned—very democratic, or maybe Communist ideals in practice. Sonny's team cleaned the dining room. Kid and three other guys cleaned the barracks. Victor liked to cook and volunteered.

Being surrounded by 39 snoring, coughing, talking men was a challenge. Cliques formed; men chose sides by commonality—hometown, profession, social or economic status. The pious gathered like bees to a hive. Leaders rose to the top, transcending clique, and ran the camp—someone had to. The rest took orders, running the camp smoothly if not efficiently. Sonny had no patience for power and left that to others.

When a mate fell ill, another did his chores. Fostering an attitude that they were all in it together made it easier for everyone. Several doctors attended to medical needs though supplies were minimal. There were loners, outsiders, malcontents, and surlies. Some were unbalanced, unsuited to cooperative living in close quarters. Anger might flare like a struck match. A guy felt crowded, shoulders brushed, then fists flew. Fights were rare, but occasionally two jokers had to be separated.

Let them brawl, Sonny figured. An occasional fight released anger and anxiety—so long as they didn't harass others. Fear, boredom, and close proximity bent some to aberrant behavior. Too many had seen the inside of Sachsenhausen, Dachau, and Buchenwald. They never involved the guards in their scrapping.

The lives of the refugees were worth little in the eyes of Europe. Most of the men wanted only the love of a woman and the chance to make a living, raise a family, and pray to God in peace. Each kept his meager belongings—clothes, and personal items stuffed in a suitcase, box, or bag—under his cot. Memories and mementos of a former life, sacred and inviolate, were what they shared. Theft was rare.

Life at Camp Wortel continued in tedium: Do your chores, walk the grounds, repeat. Books were few and dog-eared, passed around with pages falling out. One day, a kind guard brought a soccer ball for the men to kick around. Meals were more than food—a social gathering for a chat with friends.

While some men prayed, others met in small groups. Complaints of dismal present, wrenching past, and uncertain future pushed them to talk, rarely to action. Everyone knew flight was a long shot. Escapes were plotted, most of them fanciful. Still, the hunger for action was real.

Rumors spread of another escape plan. Several days passed, the rumored time to come with morning cloud cover. The sky darkened into midafternoon, and a light rain fell—not too much for a stroll off the grounds. At dusk, three men slipped quietly into the woods.

Several days later, the inmates were ordered to gather. A frowning inspector stood next to the camp director. He spoke in German: "Three of your fellows violated rules. They were apprehended only five kilometers away. They await deportation. You have been warned.

Do not attempt escape—you will not succeed!"

Sonny took that to heart. He would bide his time. He needed documents and a plan. He had neither—yet.

Then to Sonny's bemused surprise, he was awarded a pass with transport to Antwerp. Passes were occasionally granted—further evidence of Belgian enlightenment. So on a chilly November day he flashed his pass to a disinterested guard and walked to the road, thumbing his nose at the forest gremlins. The bus stopped at the square opposite Antwerp's railway station.

Sonny headed to Sammy's Café. Perhaps a letter awaited. Jostled on the narrow medieval lanes, he heard Yiddish words . . . comforting. He sat restlessly at a table in the back of the café.

Sammy set a plate on another table and walked over. "Where you been? You look terrible."

"Thanks."

Sammy shrugged. Sonny told him about the cop and asked whether a letter had arrived.

"Matter of fact . . . " Sammy went into the kitchen and returned with an envelope with a French stamp canceled in Paris.

Sonny's heart pounded as he ripped it open. He read: "Sonny, I miss you desperately. Can't stop thinking about you. Come, now . . . Love, Rosa." A name and address were printed at the bottom. Rosa was safe, and now he knew where she was! Staring at the letter, his hands shaking, he returned it to the envelope and put it in his pocket.

"Good news?" Sammy asked.

"What? Oh!" Sonny nodded, then mumbled, "Rosa made it to Paris. I have to find a way there."

Getting to Paris consumed Sammy's thoughts. He could not recall what occurred at Sammy's Café after that . . . On the street, he shivered in the cold November air as it roused him from stupor. He scurried to the bus station. Escape was all he thought about.

He wrote another letter to Rosa, then tore up his cache of letters. She was safe in Paris. He knew where she lived. His relief was beyond measure. How would he get there?

But back at Camp Wortel, the days dragged on. Sonny was no closer to Paris, no closer to Rosa. His spirits sagged. Religious guys had their prayers. He stared longingly at the open gate, remembering what had happened to the three guys disappearing into the mist.

2

Camp Wortel, Spring 1940

Europe was between peace and war, Poland vanquished, Hitler on hold. "What's he waiting for?' Kid asked.

"How the hell should I know?" Sonny answered. He was tired of the false quiet, the stress of not knowing. Everyone was on jagged edge with this phony war.

A new guest had been assigned to Sonny's barracks. He sat on his bunk, head hanging forlornly, as if he were alone. At least 60 years old, he wore a well-tailored but torn jacket and scuffed leather brogues. His hooded, bloodshot eyes took in the long room as if surprised to see men around him. A hooked nose split his thin face; his hair was short.

"What's your story?" someone asked. They waited respectfully for him to speak.

Finally, he sighed and said, "Police arrested us—my wife and me—at the French border, took our papers. Don't know where she is." He stopped and looked down at his hands, lying inert on his lap. His voice lowered to a bare whisper. "What have they done with her? What will happen to us?" He went quiet.

"When?" another asked.

Without looking up, he answered, "Got to Brussels on forged papers from Cologne, some time before . . ." He waved his hand as if the date were irrelevant. "Left Brussels by train for Paris on . . . 10 April, the day after Hitler invaded Norway." He shook his head. "Doesn't matter. "

"Norway?" Sonny was perplexed. Everyone talked at once.

"Quiet!" Victor shouted above the din. The place went still. "Tell us about Norway."

15

"Norway?" he asked, confused. "I'm in prison, my wife is God knows where, and you ask . . . "

Victor cut him off. "Ja, I know. We're all stuck in this shit hole. We know nothing about an invasion of Norway."

"They keep us in the dark," Sonny interrupted.

"Tell us what you know," Victor continued, then sat next to him. "It's tough . . . we're in this together."

Their eyes met. Victor nodded encouragement.

"All right." His voice was flat, his eyes straying to the window. "Germany invaded Norway the day before we left, on 9 April. British and German ships battled near the port of Narvik—several sank. Both sides want Sweden's iron ore. Control Norway and you can get it out. Last I heard, Germans are in Norway, Brits aren't."

Two days later, after breakfast, guests were assembled in the yard. The camp director dropped a bombshell: "Camp Wortel will be closed."

Men murmured. One shouted, "We going to be released?"

Guards quieted the men. The director ordered them to gather their belongings and reassemble in an hour. The men wore what clothing did not fit inside the suitcase, satchel, or box at each one's feet. The anticipation of release was powerful. Hope trumped all. Quietly, they waited.

When instructions came, the groan of dashed hopes spread to a dull crescendo: trucks would transport them to southern Belgium, to another camp, near Marquain.

No reason was given for the move, leaving only speculation and rumor. Experience from the Great War suggested the Germans would attack through the Low Countries—Holland and Belgium—then south into France. Wortel lay in the path of likely attack. Or was there another reason?

"Where the hell is Marquain?" Kid asked.

His answer came the next day: Marquain lay on the strategic highway between Tournai in Belgium and Lille in France. Sonny was to be imprisoned less than 10 kilometers from the French border, less than 50 kilometers from where he'd last seen Rosa. He had memorized the name and address in Paris. He carried her letter in his pocket. Had she received his?

The thought of proximity brought renewed hope.

Barbed wire crowned the fence, circled the compound, but an open gate was left unguarded. As at Wortel, the standing order was that no one leave the camp. But within days of their arrival, six guests took an after-dark stroll through the gate. The next day the director, who spoke only French, announced that six men had been transferred for deportation to Germany. Lesson delivered again.

———

Early on the morning of 10 May, two gendarmes with rifles, bayonets attached, stood guard at the locked gate.

"Fiction's over—we're prisoners," Victor observed, looking out the window.

"Something's up. Let's visit the guy with the radio," Sonny said.

A crowd had gathered inside; the rest stood outside his window. Agitated men talked one over the other. Hearing was impossible.

"Quiet!" someone yelled.

"Shut up," shouted another. Surprisingly, it worked.

"German troops crossed the border into Belgium," a voice called from inside.

For an instant there was hushed silence as if the men had taken a collective breath. The only sound was the crackling of the radio, their minds threading that single declaration into their own situation. They were tethered and had no escape route; it was like having hands clasped to their throats. Anticipation of a worse fate suddenly struck, fueling an explosive din. Men cursed. Some wept.

The news, an uncontrollable virus, quickly spread. Panic gripped the camp. Men turned to their cliques for support. Sonny huddled with Kid and Victor. Others turned inward.

"Funny how news of the German army coming our way sends Jews into a frenzy," Victor dryly noted.

Kid ignored him and asked Sonny, "Now what?"

The memory of boot-stomping storm troopers marching in perfect formation, singing insane songs of hatred through deserted streets on Kristallnacht, rushed back. Sonny was scared to his bones.

"Sonny!" Kid said.

Sonny returned from his unnerving flashback.

"What the hell do we do?" Kid repeated.

"Damned if I know."

Kid's question was answered several hours later. "Father of the

Refugees," the solemn director called himself, addressing them in French. He droned gravely of his responsibility to the men, promising to protect them, then ordering them to dig trenches for shelter against air raids—and confiscating every radio.

"When will the Wehrmacht get here? Where the hell is the BEF [British Expeditionary Force], the French army?" Kid, back in the barracks, babbled.

Victor seemed unconcerned.

"Doesn't anything get you excited?" Kid's anger seized an outlet.

"A knife at my throat."

"Germans may arrange that," Kid snapped.

"What the hell . . . " Victor sputtered.

"Kid, knock it off!" Sonny commanded. "Let's think this out."

"What's to think? We're sitting in the Wehrmacht's path, locked up tight, no place to go. So tell me, what's to think?"

"Kid's got a point," Sonny admitted.

"Of course," Victor agreed. "We pay the price for shortsighted Belgian policy, refusing Brits or Frenchmen onto Belgian soil—until now, when it might be too late." He waved an arm in the air. "We don't know a goddamn thing!"

"Stuck in the middle," Sonny muttered.

So it went, the arguing, speculating, and bantering. Though on one crucial matter they agreed—the need to get out of the way.

Squadrons of bombers flew in formation high above the camp toward destinations in France. *Rat-a-tat-tat,* antiaircraft guns fired into the sky, seemingly without end. Wailing sirens sent the men scampering to trenches under cover of foliage along the forest line. Bombs whistled and exploded. An occasional bomber left a trail of black smoke in its wake. The men waited for each bomber to land in a furious explosion—and cheered when they did!

The first night, just before dawn, they clambered onto the roof of the barracks to glimpse the conflagration. Orange and red glowed spectacularly against the black night sky—a kaleidoscopic show, woefully tragic yet awe inducing and thoroughly frightening. Tournai glowed in the distance, like a gigantic Roman candle.

Sleep was impossible. Lying in bed, fully clothed, the guests heard air-raid sirens droning like gigantic cicadas and ran to the trenches to huddle in fear. Confusion and panic, the fear of an errant bomb, gripped men and guards. Stuck in the camp, they were like goats staked for a lion. Flight trumped risk of capture.

BEF green trucks filled with valiant soldiers and pulling artillery, streamed along the road adjacent to the camp.

"Finally!" Sonny exclaimed.

Morale rose, but they received no news. Food supplies were desperately low. They lived on a few potatoes a day. Rumor was that the director's telephone calls to Brussels went unanswered. Several days passed. Then columns of motorized conveys rolled by in increasing number—in the wrong direction.

"What the hell? They're moving toward France!" Sonny's optimism turned sour.

"Regrouping for a counterattack," Kid said hopefully.

"Or retreating," Victor murmured.

"You think?" Kid was incredulous.

Observing troop movements, listening to rumors, dealing with food shortages and piercing sirens became the tortured routine: Dash from the barracks to the trench, then back, then again. Jagged nerves, rubbed raw, flared to angry confrontation. Fights ensued.

On 18 May, in the middle of the night, the camp was roused from fitful slumber.

"Prepare to move," came the director's order. They would flee to France at daybreak.

"Now we know for sure—the Brits are retreating," Victor said.

The following day, 19 May, at 2 AM, the order to assemble came. Confiscated belongings, including documents, were returned. Nearly 200 men began the march south. The camp director, accompanied by his family, led the way, promising to get them into France.

His words of reassurance, the sudden prospect of freedom, brought eerie stillness, as if the men had been rendered mute. Silently, the men queued for a portion of the remaining food, then passed through the gate. Marching in loose formation, they reached the French frontier in an hour. Told to wait, the director and several guards walked to the border crossing.

He returned in 30 minutes. Anxious, the men gathered around the director. He spoke, but his frown told them the answer. Victor translated: "We are denied entry. The British army retreats. No civilians allowed into France at this time."

Military trucks pulling artillery, staff cars, tanks, and disheartened soldiers on foot streamed past them and over the border. Advancing Germans had pushed the British and French armies from Belgium. Sonny could hardly believe it.

Like the BEF dejected and demoralized, the men retreated—but back to Marquain, toward the German advance. As they neared the camp, they saw black smoke slowly rising. The camp had been leveled. Men scattered and disappeared into air like the smoldering from the charred remains. Luggage was abandoned. Sonny, Kid, and Victor followed the director, deciding to stay together.

"He knows where to go," Sonny said.

About a hundred of their fellows agreed. Walking northwest along the border, they reached the crossing to Roubaix. Then the director and his family disappeared among the throng of refugees.

"Every man for himself," Victor said acidly.

Refugees flooded the French border. Only French citizens were allowed to cross. Trains were closed to civilians. But when word spread of a nearby, unguarded crossing. Sonny and his friends joined an anxious group finally reaching a row of trees along a canal.

"France is just across," someone pointed. "A stone's throw."

A village sign announced "Estaimpuis." They entered.

"Only Belgian citizens can cross," someone yelled. "Don't bother."

"Maybe tomorrow," another said.

Dejected and fatigued, they returned to the village.

Belgian peasants, heading south, streamed past. "Ne pas passé?" they asked.

"Oui. For you."

Twilight darkened the sky to soft gray then black, ending a day of frustration. Familiar Marquain faces appeared. The 200 had dwindled to a handful. No new information; they parted. Another group took its place, excited by rumor of an open checkpoint at Cornet, a tiny village in the direction of Tournai.

They ran for 20 minutes. Cornet was empty, and the border was open. Sonny's little band joined the line of refugees. The French village of Baisieux lay on the other side. Movement stopped, the hopeful voices stilled. People circled an official in the center. He questioned everyone, then eyed the three suspiciously.

"Papers," he demanded.

Rejected again! Whipsawed, like a ball bouncing between walls, Sonny felt the pain of it in his head. A knot stuck in his throat as if the ball were lodged inside.

They remained in Belgium. Being surrounded by so many other refugees brought no solace. They swarmed tiny Cornet like ants to a honey pot. Some broke windows to enter empty houses and barns. Most slept in the fields, shivering in the night air, waiting for morning. Artillery fire and bomb blasts punctuated the night, making rest impossible. Men and women hugged the ground or each other, making smaller targets as if that would save them from a bomb. Tension crackled like the live electrical wires dangling to the ground.

Sonny could not sleep.

"We're doomed," Kid's plaintive voice emerged from the darkness.

"Don't cave. We've just begun."

Dawn brought more shelling, ever nearer.

Sonny stretched his aching body. Cattle grazed in the field. Wagons overflowing with people and belongings moved slowly south.

Sonny's meager French made Kid and Victor indispensable. Word spread quickly that the German army had met little resistance from the Belgians, French, or British. That was obvious by the flow of humanity.

Moving northwest along the border, the trio was never alone, always looking for a crack to wiggle through, like a fish darting this way and that. Villages were eerily empty.

Kid walked to a cottage, away from the road. "Door's open."

"Wait!" Sonny knocked. No answer. He knocked a second time—again, nothing. They went inside and rummaged for food.

"Hey!" Kid shouted. "Bread, jam, butter in the larder."

They ate quickly, in silence. Sonny looked at Kid, then at Victor. So far they hadn't slowed him down. Instinct told him to travel alone, but he needed one of them to translate. Which one? He let it go—for the time being.

They left the house to the rumble of artillery fire—ever closer. Immediately, they encountered a group of German refugees and shared information. A man warned, "French squads patrol, looking for spies and saboteurs, arresting refugees—be careful."

"Arrests?" Kid's voice raised several octaves.

"Spies sent by the Germans," the man responded, and they separated.

"Like we don't have enough trouble," Victor moaned.

"Let's go," Sonny said.

"Where?" Victor asked.

Sonny scratched his neck.

"Anywhere the squads aren't." Kid's voice cracked with strain, his hands rubbing his thighs.

"And where the hell would that be?" Victor spoke with exaggerated deliberateness.

"You tell me!" Kid shot back.

"Stop bickering! That gets us nowhere," Sonny chided.

Neither spoke or looked at the other. Then Sonny pointed and said, "Same direction we've been going . . . toward the sea."

"About the same time the Germans get there," Victor answered, sarcastically.

Kid started to respond, but Sonny cut him off and shot back, "No! Back to Roubaix, try again . . . bigger town, get lost there. Can't be more than five kilometers."

A shell whistled dangerously close, exploding, shaking the ground.

"Shit!" Kid exclaimed.

3

Northern France, 20 May 1940

Stray dogs roamed Roubaix's streets. Cats scurried into alleys, leery. Except for fleeing refugees, the town was nearly empty. Most important, there were no cops.

"Look!" Kid pointed, eyes wide.

Several hundred meters away, a squad of soldiers approached from the north.

"Wrong helmets—not Germans." But even as he said it, Sonny was unsure.

"Brits," Vincent said.

"Still, we don't want a confrontation—let's get out of sight."

Vincent and Kid disappeared into an alley. Sonny retreated to the nearest doorway, a men's haberdashery. A suited mannequin, arms open in perpetual welcome, stood rigidly on the other side of the glass. Twenty-five soldiers, give or take, moved warily in two single lines, one on each side of the street, their rifles at the ready. Smoke rose in gentle circles from cigarettes dangling from the corner of several of their mouths. Sonny was barely concealed.

"Mind you look for snipers," one of the soldiers said.

Hearing English, Sonny breathed easier. He had learned some English in Berlin from an American friend.

In the lead was a young officer with a confident stride. He had rolled his sleeves to the elbows. Sweat stains marked his shirt, and on his shoulder was a patch with the number 44. With rifle across his chest, pistol on his right hip, and helmet pushed back on his head, he moved his eyes side to side, scanning both sides of the street.

Boots scraped on the pavement, echoing on the otherwise empty street. A dog barked and jogged beside the soldiers. One patted its head. Sonny was more intrigued than frightened. They passed so near, his outstretched hand might have touched another outstretched in a moment of fellowship. Then the young officer's eyes met his in a momentary squint, examining, processing. Sonny must have passed the test because the officer nodded and broke contact, never breaking stride.

Sonny closed his eyes. A youthful face, serious and purposeful, appeared on the screen behind his eyelids. Brilliant green eyes, like oriental jade, glowed. They were eyes he might never forget.

Kid and Vincent left the alley. They watched in silence as the platoon moved out of sight.

"Let's get the hell out of here," Vincent said.

"They were no threat," Sonny mumbled. His first close encounter with soldiers gave him a vicarious sense of the conflict. Close but removed, energized and frightened at the same time. Green Eyes had an ally. He just didn't know it.

Moving quickly, they rounded a corner and stopped. A crowd of several hundred people gathered, waiting. "No buses, none arrived—no drivers," a man told them. They would walk nine kilometers, over the border to Lille.

British military, civilian wagons, automobiles, and people clogged the roads. It seemed as if Belgium had been lifted at its north end, sending inhabitants, refugees, and the BEF careening to the border.

At the Lille city hall a group had gathered, so the trio turned away. But they had been seen, and within seconds they were surrounded.

"Spies, spies . . . !" Spittle flew as they screamed, faces contorted in anger. The circle drew tighter, the small mob rising to a frenzied pitch. Someone waved a revolver.

"No—not spies." Kid screamed, unheard through the din.

Victor tried desperately to convince the man facing him that they were refugees, escaping Germany. He wasn't buying it—no one was.

Backed into a tight triangle, Sonny felt a hand grab and pull on his jacket. Hot, stale breath struck his face. Sonny winced. "Stop!" Then in French, "Stup."

Heads turned. Sonny, taller than his captors, saw a soldier, maybe an officer, wading into the group.

"What the hell's going on?" he asked in French.

"They're spies," one of the Frenchman shouted.

"No!" Sonny, Kid, and Victor shouted in unison.

"Come with me!" He led them to his truck and out of danger. Then he dropped them at the police station in Seclin, five kilometers deeper into France. "You're on your own . . . can't deal with you."

"What's going on?" Victor asked.

They spoke in French. No reply.

"Are we in danger?" Kid asked.

"From the Germans or the French?" the officer forced a laugh. "Hell! We all are." His smile turned ironic, and he gave a vague salute before returning to his convoy.

The harried police chief pushed them outside: "Go . . . leave my town."

Victor pointed to a poster on the side of a building. It showed a man with a finger to his lips above the caption "Don't give away secrets." He read it, then said, "Everyone's a damned spy."

Kid shrugged. "I'm hungry. Got any money?" The question was a revelation.

Victor shook his head.

Sonny jiggled the few remaining francs in his pocket. The sadness of his separation from Rosa rushed back. "I've got a few francs left."

They entered the first tavern they encountered and froze in the doorway. Drunken French soldiers filled the place. But they ignored the three men.

"No wonder they're losing," Victor whispered.

"Damn demoralizing," Sonny added.

"Let's eat," Kid said.

They ordered and ate heartily. Beer made them drowsy. Sonny paid and still had francs in his pocket. "I've got to go outside before I fall asleep," he said.

A stranger confronted him, demanding papers. Sonny showed his internment identity card, proof of refugee status. Scowling, the man ignored it, grabbing Sonny by the lapel and shouting, "Boche! Spy!"

Another mob formed and set upon Sonny—hitting, kicking, and shouting obscenities at the supposed spy. Even some women joined the fray. Anger and frustration had them abusing the outsider in their midst. He tucked his legs to his chest, folded his arms over his head, closed his eyes, and waited. Then he felt his body being pulled. Had he died? Was he no longer earthbound? No, two British soldiers were dragging him by his arms. When safely away from the mob, they raised him to his feet.

Sonny was rubbing his neck and the side where he'd been kicked when Kid and Victor found him. They had been safe in the tavern.

"What happened?" Kid asked.

Sonny quickly explained.

Then a young corporal commanded, "Come with me," and led them to the nearby British command post. Flanked by the two soldiers, a woozy Sonny entered the makeshift office, Kid and Vincent trailing behind. A British officer and a French policeman were inside.

"Filthy boche!" The Frenchman exclaimed, striking Sonny on the side of his head.

Sonny nearly lost consciousness but stayed on his feet. The startled British officer stepped between them and berated the gendarme. They argued and the Frenchman abruptly left the room screaming, "C'est moi la police [I am the police]!"

The British officer watched him leave without comment then turned to Sonny. "Didn't I save your ass in Lille and drop you in Seclin?"

In a daze, and Sonny remained silent.

Impatient, the officer asked the question in French.

"Oui," Vincent intervened, "thank you a second time,"

"So . . . are you spies?" he asked.

"No," Kid and Vincent denied in unison.

"We're Jewish refugees, running from Germany. We're on your side," Vincent said.

"I'm thankful you won the fight for our custody," Kid added.

The officer smiled ruefully. "Not for long . . . you're free to go."

They hesitated, then Sonny, his head clear, asked in broken English, "Why you retreat?"

He shook his head and would not answer.

"Please, let us travel with you. We won't get in the way." Kid begged in French. "It's not safe out there."

Laughing, the officer said, "That's for damn sure. Now get the hell out of here! And stay out of trouble. I don't want to see you again."

The midday sun beat down. The road radiated heat like an oven.

Skin scorched, throats parched, stomachs growled, sapping strength. A sign indicated five kilometers to Wavrin. Traffic sent the dust rising, like swarms of mosquitos, clogging throats and nostrils. They plodded, one foot in front of the other.

"He wouldn't answer my question," Sonny said.

"They're getting steamrolled," was Victor's glum reply.

"What day is it?" Kid asked. "Twenty-first . . . second?"

"Hell . . . who cares?" Victor murmured absently.

"We left Marquain on the 18th, no the 19th, so . . . " Kid silently calculated. "It's only the 21st. How can that be?" he moaned.

"Feels like I've been through the wringer," Sonny said, glumly. "Prey to enemy and friend alike, slaves to fate—a cosmic joke." But he didn't laugh.

They walked in silence until Kid asked, "Where are we going?"

"How the hell do I know?" Victor snapped.

"Deeper into France," Sonny answered, "have to get to Paris."

"What does it matter? If locals don't kill us, Germans will." Victor's cynicism grated.

"You're a big help," Kid shot back.

Tired of their bickering, Sonny walked ahead, letting them work it out. He saw a church spire, rising above fields and forest—the small town of Wavrin. At the outskirts all was quiet, cottages looked deserted. They turned onto a dirt road and nearly collided with two French soldiers. Unlike the drunken soldiers, these men looked battle hardened. They stared at one another for a several beats.

"Come," one commanded, rifle raised. He led them into town, the other following at the rear. No accusations or threats.

They were taken inside a building in the center of the village, now a French Army garrison. It had probably been the office of the village council. An officer sat, examining a map. Without looking up, he asked brusquely, "What?"

One of the soldiers explained.

"Talk fast," Sonny said under his breath. And that's what Victor and Kid did, simultaneously.

The officer put up a hand, "One at a time."

Victor quickly explained.

The officer sighed and looked bored, as if he'd heard that story before. He conferred with another officer, then ordered the soldier:

"Take them away."

"Where?" Kid asked. No answer.

"What's going on?" Vincent asked. They were ignored.

"Are they going to shoot us?" Kid whispered.

They were led to an abandoned building damaged by bombs and told they could spend the night. Kid and Victor pumped the soldier for information. He shook his head.

"You moving into battle or retreating?" Again nothing. Events had moved so quickly, the worst seemed possible. But there were no threats or accusations.

Then Kid, always hungry, asked, "Any food?"

"Wait." The soldier returned in 10 minutes with three plates of food.

"Smells like food—a good sign." Kid shoveled some into his mouth, raised his head to take a breath. "Not bad."

"Delicious," Victor said sarcastically.

They ignored him.

"Nice knowing not every Frenchman wants to kill us," Sonny noted with relief.

"Where do we go tomorrow?" Kid asked.

Victor grimaced. "Always the same damn question." He was increasingly prickly, hard to take.

"It's important and bears repeating." Kid didn't back down.

"Who needs a French mob? You'll kill each other," Sonny quipped.

Victor's eyes narrowed. He spoke slowly: "Kid is getting on my nerves."

"Go to hell!" Kid closed on Victor.

Smaller and no fighter, Victor flinched. Sonny got between them.

"Then leave!" Kid shouted.

"Exactly what I intend to do," Vincent countered.

Blessed silence fell, but crackling tension between the gruff Berlin lawyer and callow young man put Sonny on edge. Ignoring them was difficult, but he tried. Then, absently, he gave voice to his thoughts. "If only we knew where the Germans were heading, we could go the other way."

"You being ironic or just obvious?" Victor asked.

Sonny hadn't realized he'd spoken. "I . . . of course, it's obvious."

Victor's mouth turned ugly. "What's the damn point?"

"We've got to do something—if the Brits and French are retreating, the Germans are close behind. We can't outrun them."

Kid's nod was emphatic. "We're stuck in the middle of a massive military catastrophe."

"God save me from simple minds," Victor said. "First thing tomorrow, get a briefing from the commander, find out where the Wehrmacht is—if he knows," Victor snarled, his words biting. "You deserve each other." He left.

Kid watched Victor warily. "What's with him?"

"Pressure got to him, that knife at his throat . . . "

Darkness finally fell, and they lay on the hard floor. Kid was quiet, thank God. Sonny closed his eyes and waited for sleep. When finally it came, Rosa returned in a dream. A tear fell onto her cheek, but she managed a smile. Dark hair framed her beautiful face. She wore the bloodstained dress. He held the brick, dripping crimson . . . then he was running breathlessly through a labyrinth with Rosa was at the other end . . . every turn wrong . . . faces from the past leered, cried, laughed, were frozen in death . . . a French mob had hold of him . . . he was desperate, searching for escape, sweat stung his eyes . . . He woke with a start, exhausted.

They left early. Victor walked ahead. At the outskirts of the village, a friendly soldier gave them a tin of meat. "Good luck!"

"Merci."

Victor waited. When they caught up, he said, "I'm going alone." Neither tried to change his mind.

"Which way you going?" Kid asked.

"Don't follow me!"

Kid tried to suppress a laugh but failed. "Just wanted to know so I can go in the opposite direction."

Sonny laughed at Kid's needling. Victor left without a word. They hadn't told him about the meat.

The road was clogged, but Sonny and Kid were at liberty, moving. Military personnel had priority, shunting cars, carts, and people out of their way. Abandoned vehicles—broken down, out of gas, or hit by a bomb—littered the side of the road, relics of broken lives.

Children carried dogs, cats, even cages with birds. Mothers and grandmothers held infants. Farmers led cattle and horses, too precious to leave behind. A man on a bicycle wove his way through a group of black-habited nuns reminding Sonny of the penguins he had seen at the Berlin Zoo. People looked hungry, dirty, anxious— Sonny's smile faded. Scared and fatigued, he heard horns honking and men yelling, tempers flaring.

Progress was slow. An occasional airplane buzzed low, but no bombs fell, not yet. Germany had made quick work of Poland—had the same happened to Holland and Belgium? Not France—that was unthinkable.

Sonny and Kid joined a group of refugees, about 20 men—there might be safety in numbers. Some were from Marquain. A tall, dark fellow, their leader, did the talking, which was fine with Sonny. He decided to stick around at least for a while, to see how it went. Men joked and laughed nervously—it was their way of dealing with a dire though not-yet-hopeless situation. Kid got in on the jokes, cracking wise, something he was good at. Sonny thought the humor forced, a bit off kilter.

Walking in the hot sun, their throats parched, the men watched their humor evaporate. Someone pointed to a farmhouse at the edge of a village.

"Water?"

A woman who must have seen them coming met them at the door. North of 40, she smiled, wearily. The leader spoke in fluent French. She thought they were Belgian, which he did not contradict. She pointed toward the back of the house, to the well.

After drinking their full, the men sat in the shade of the trees and rested. The warmhearted woman brought them bread and jam. They talked. She lived alone. Her husband was gone—in the army . . . dead? They thanked her for the food and water and departed.

They had barely resumed their trek when a man claiming to be the mayor of the town confronted them. Several armed men backed him up. His interrogation was all too familiar

"Spies! Spies! Strangers, spies, provocateurs roam northern France. Do you not know that?" His face reddened.

"We are refugees . . . refugees!" their leader pleaded. "Enemies of the Germans."

"Where do you come from?" he asked, eying them with hostility.

"Germany, some from Poland, elsewhere."

"So you are Germans."

"Enemies of Hitler!"

"You are spies! I caught a spy the other day. My duty is to be vigilant—for France, for the safety of the republic. We are at war! You are all under arrest—move! If you run, you will be shot."

They were taken to the main square, in front of the town hall. At least 35 refugees were already there, familiar faces from along the trail, Victor among them. Neither Sonny nor Kid made eye contact.

Another local official waded through the pile of documents. He opened a passport, a visa, an identity card, placing them in one of two piles. The process took half an hour. German nationals were ordered into one group—Poles, other nationalities, and stateless people without papers into the other.

British troops mingled at the edge of the crowd. Refugees were corralled to the side of the building. Without much notice a group of six Tommies formed a line facing the refugees.

"Firing squad!" someone shouted.

An unnatural quiet descended, as if everyone had been muzzled. Disbelief, shock, resignation mingled with overriding fear. Kid's face turn ashen . . . Sonny put a hand on his shoulder. But his eyes stayed on those conscripted to shoot them. Young Brits moved from foot to foot, gazing at the ground, reluctant, uncomfortable. Rifles remained at their sides. Sonny had been at war longer than any of them. They didn't look like cold-blooded killers—but neither did he.

Then a voice broke the silence. It was one of the soldiers. "Habt nisht ka moire mer shiesst nit so schnell [Don't be afraid. One doesn't shoot so quickly]."

"Yiddish?" Sonny murmured. Rationality was the first victim of war, but this was madness. He'd heard Yiddish almost daily since he was a kid, though he never spoke it. He understood what the soldier had said. He searched for the speaker. "Who?"

"Second from the left," Kid said.

No older than Kid, the man looked as scared as the men he faced. Sonny smiled. An airplane buzzed low overhead. Circling above the crowd, the pilot tilted its wings in salute, showing the plane's French markings, and flew away. It was surreal, surely an insane cabaret act—the pilot overhead, facing death from a young Brit who spoke the language of European Jewry.

Sonny couldn't die, not in this carnival sideshow. Sure, he had left a few dead behind. Was it his turn now? No! He knew where Rosa lived. He wouldn't die . . .

Trapped, he saw the faces, the streets, the warehouse flashing past—scenes passing too rapidly to decipher. He had done all he could—at least he had tried. Regrets were for those in control of their lives. A forced laugh escaped his lips, something like a grunt. Stay or run—a simple choice. That he could control anything in his life was pure fantasy. All he wanted was to get to Paris . . .

"This is crazy," Kid muttered, then laughed cynically.

Sonny heard Kid's voice, then the cheering crowd.

The pilot's swagger had brought joy to the townsfolk. They applauded, some yelling patriotic slogans. For the moment, the condemned were forgotten. In the confusion, Sonny saw several refugees slip into the other group and maybe away. Sonny grabbed Kid's arm and gestured with his head to move.

"Go," he whispered. "They're distracted."

The threat of imminent death receded. Presented with a choice . . . run.

Part II

Alone, alone, all, all alone;
Alone on a wide, wide sea.
—*Samuel Taylor Coleridge*

4

Paris, August 1939

Rosa wanted to love Paris. From the Seine to Montmartre, from wide tree-lined boulevards to the dark meandering alleys, to its charming sidewalk cafés, fabulous gardens with extravagant fountains, museums, and the Eiffel Tower poking through the rooftops, she wanted to absorb it, breath its culture and life. But she was consumed by loss.

On 16 August, standing on that God-forsaken platform, she had watched Sonny's face, distorted through the dirty glass of the railway car, his bloodshot eyes staring at her, lips moving: "I love you." His face was a mask of dejection, an image impossible for her to shake.

Lives tightly entwined . . . broken, gone, like breath's vapor on a mirror. Crushed by disappointment and despair, she gasped for air, then placed a hand to her mouth and felt something soft—Sonny's handkerchief.

"Here . . . clean your hand with this," he had said, handing her his handkerchief, then walked to the next railway car.

Their plans for a new life had ended in a flash. Glued to the platform, in a dingy railway station in a Belgian provincial town, Sonny's scent in her hand, she licked salty tears from her lips. What would become of him . . . her . . . them? Could he ever find her, even look for her? Write to Sonny's friend Fritz in Plombières, to Sammy in Antwerp, then hope.

How could this be? And why? Who could she ask—her father, mother, a rabbi, a cop, a philosopher or derelict? They were as clueless as she, because there was no answer, not one that would satisfy her. In the off chance there was an explanation, a shorthand answer, her bet was on evil. Evil and wickedness stood center stage—the world was full of it! How to navigate that world was her challenge. She would figure it out on her own or not at all.

"Click . . . clack," steel wheels rolling on steel track grew faint. An arm rested softly on her shoulder. Her father's voice, trying to comfort, sounded mechanical though he meant to be sympathetic. Her mother's arm was around her waist. They led her to the Paris train . . .

Paris was hot. The streets around Gare du Nord were crowded. Travelers hurried past, coming from and going to places unknown. The steel elegance of the Eiffel Tower poked skyward in the distance. Rosa had sleepwalked off the train, her parents one at each side. Abandoned, cheated, emotionally spent, she dried her tears.

A woman emerged from the flow of humanity. She stood before them and spoke in French. Elise and Robert stared blankly. Rosa shook her head, her French rusty. Then, magically, the woman spoke German.

"My name is Francine Dreyfus . . . no, not that one, a different family." Clearly scripted, she smiled warmly. "Welcome to Paris. There is an office in the Marais, the old Jewish Quarter—we call it the Pletzl, little place—in the old center. Former home of the aristocracy, now filled with thousands of Jews and a thriving garment district."

"What is there?" Robert asked.

"Go to the Jewish agency on Rue de Rosier." She gave them an address and directions. "A new government program retrains refugees." She searched their faces for a response. "I strongly recommend taking advantage . . . agricultural jobs are in the south. Refugees are not popular in Paris; arrest and deportation remain an unfortunate option." Her words came rapidly. She was a woman in a hurry.

Robert and Elise exchanged glances.

"What is there for us in Paris?" Rosa asked.

"Next to nothing," Madam Dreyfus answered, her smile ironic. "Go to the agency . . . information is there. Walk too far south, you're at the River Seine; too far east, you've wandered into the Place des Vosges. I must go . . . good luck." She left to greet the next refugees.

They turned into an alley that emptied onto a narrow street.

Buildings blackened with grime, the soot from years of burning coal, like most of the ones they had seen thus far. Still, the city exuded unmistakable charm. Hesitant, unsure of where to go, they stopped on the crowded pavement.

"S'il vous plait, ou est Rue de Rosier?" Rosa's French was sufficient to frame the question.

A woman pointed.

"Merci."

They passed a tailor's shop, a second-hand clothier, hat maker, furrier, grocery, butcher, and bakery, Orthodox Jews, refugees, and the rest. Some looked poor and hungry, others prosperous and well fed. The street was teeming with life—like Berlin's Hirtenstrasse.

"Ach, there!" Robert pointed to a sign reading "Rue de Rosier."

They entered the small, shabby office. A fan at the corner of a cluttered desk whirred hot air, riffling papers on a desk with little effect. Noise from the street below came through the open window. Opposite sat a pleasant-looking young Frenchman, younger than Rosa. Leaning forward, his eyes lingered on her. She didn't notice.

"Bonjour. Welcome to Paris. My name is Michel Riccard," he began in German. "I'm with the Jewish Council of Paris, and you are . . . ?"

Robert made introductions then explained their situation.

Michel made sympathetic noises. "Awful . . . alas, a story too often told these days." He looked at Rosa. "I hope you will be reunited, soon."

"Merci."

Wasting no time, he explained the new program. "France's problem is a lack of workers and a surplus of refugees, two problems begging a solution. You would be employed but first housed, most likely in Chelles, 15 kilometers east, for training. After that you could be working . . . where needed." He shrugged and smiled at Rosa.

Rosa moved her head slowly from side to side. "What if I want to stay in Paris?"

"Do you have proper papers?"

Robert nodded. "We have visas."

"Visas expire whether valid or forged, making you subject to arrest and internment, even deportation. Though after Kristallnacht that horrible fate is more remote. Besides, there are no jobs in Paris."

Michel stood, signaling the meeting was over. "You needn't decide today, but don't delay." He bid them good-bye.

"We need a place to stay." Elise said.

Michel led them down a corridor to a wall with a bulletin board. On it were bits of paper with names and addresses. "These people provide short-term shelter. Make arrangements directly with them."

They looked at the board filled with names and addresses, trying to make sense of one or the other. Finally, Robert removed one. "This will do: Jean Friedman, 32, Rue du Roi de Sicile, second-floor front."

"Puis-je vous aider?" asked the man at the door.

"Oui," Rosa answered then stammered, "Ah, ah..."

He smiled, then said in German, "Can I help you?" He was tall and thin, about 60 years old, with a full head of gray hair above vaguely Semitic facial features.

"We came from the Jewish center. Your name was on the board."

"Ja, ja, please come in," he beckoned.

They entered.

"I am Jean Friedman, as you already know. Welcome to my humble flat. My wife, may she rest, and I raised two children here. There is room for all of us. My children are grown. Catherine lives nearby with her husband and young son. They operate a small grocery on Rue de Rosier. My son, Alain, performs his patriotic duty in the army. I welcome the company."

"Your German is excellent," Robert noted.

"My parents came from Alsace after the War of 1870. They spoke German to me as a child. I was born in Paris. Now tell me about yourselves."

They did . . .

To Robert, the man said, "You persevered through terrible misfortune. I congratulate you." Then to Rosa, "I am sorry about your husband. Stay here until you decide what to do."

"Thank you," Elise said.

"What do you know about the retraining program?" Robert asked.

"A new program. The government finally faced reality."

"Should we accept?"

"That is for you to decide." Friedman shrugged. "In Paris, there are no jobs for Frenchmen, let alone for thousands of Jewish refugees. Thanks to the maniac across the border, the country has been flooded with refugees. Many Frenchmen sympathize with Hitler, others will do anything to prevent another war, and still others want you to be gone. Thank God cooler heads prevailed."

Then there was silence. Rosa sat on a divan between her parents, her eyes consuming the comfortable room. Two open windows overlooked the street below; curtains hung lank in the hot, still air. Shelves filled with books next to the worn, leather club chair in which Monsieur Friedman sat. Framed photographs hung on the wall next to the door, too many to focus on one. Her gaze strayed to several framed prints hanging on the other wall above an ebony cabinet.

"Do you like them?"

"Excuse me?" Rosa said, surprised by the question.

"The prints," he replied.

"I don't know," she said, unsure.

"You're not alone. The sad one by Andre Fougeron, *Martyred Spain*, provokes rather then comforts. The colorful one is a poster by Fernand Leger, signed by him, called *L'Esprit Nouveau*—new spirit. That image was a famous magazine cover—you may have seen it. If you like art, you will love Paris." His gaze left the Leger and returned to Rosa, his smile comforting.

Rosa nodded, unsure of what to make of the art or of Monsieur Friedman.

Elise broke the uncomfortable silence: "This is a very nice room."

"My wife had excellent taste. She worked for years at a little gallery on Rue de Rivoli, near the Louvre."

"What is your work?" Robert asked.

"Retired independent businessman—a little of this, a little of that."

Rosa laughed then covered her mouth. "I mean no disrespect. My husband, Sonny, used a similar phrase to describe his work." She looked down at her hands, slowly raising her gaze to meet Monsieur Friedman's eyes.

"It's good to laugh. It pleases me that I remind you of your husband."

Rosa held his gaze.

"What exactly did you do?" Robert inquired further.

Friedman flicked his wrist absently. "Buy and sell, a little here in the garment district, a little in the art world. Whatever brought in a few francs. I still dabble from time to time." Then he changed direction. "Do you speak French?"

"Un peu [a little]," Rosa answered.

Friedman's eyes twinkled when he smiled, something that seemed to come naturally. "And you?" he asked Robert and Elise.

"Unfortunately, no."

"Then it will be impossible to novelty work.

5

Paris, August 1939

"Treachery!" . . . "Dagger to the heart of the Alliance!" . . ."Hitler free to do his dirty work!" the newspapers screamed.

On 23 August 1939, the Nazi–Soviet Non-Aggression Pact shook France to its core. Hitler and Stalin agreed not to wage war against each other, for now. Each tyrant had a free hand to make mischief—Hitler in Poland, Stalin in Finland—without fear of intervention by the other. War seemed inevitable. France mobilized its army, calling almost every able-bodied man to duty.

One week later, on 1 September 1939, Germany invaded Poland. Two days later France and Britain declared war on Germany.

For years, the right-wing newspapers had bellowed: "Why should France give a damn about Danzig? Worry about Communists—not Fascists. What's a Polish port to France? It's not our problem. War-mongers on the left want to send France into the abyss."

Suddenly everything changed—now France's solemn duty was to fight and die for ideals that previously had not been of concern.

The posters were omnipresent: a man with finger to lips urging silence, a long, bony finger warning Parisians to be wary of foreigners, a vast underground of German spies. The phrase *fifth column* had entered the lexicon during the Spanish Civil War, and now it became widespread, was taken seriously. Shop windows, kiosks, empty walls, virtually any available vertical space, exhibited posters.

Fear, uncertainty, and doubt spread through the city like thunder-heads foreshadowing a storm. Blackboards appeared at railway stations and on government buildings, outlining evacuation itineraries. Each arrondissement (district) had a host destination in another part of France. A trickle of Parisians at first and in greater number later, left the city, though no full-scale exodus occurred. The French police arrested any undesirables—refugees and Communists—and sent them to internment camps. Jewish, German, or Russian—it mattered little without proper documentation. Roland Garros, a large tennis stadium in Auteuil, was converted into a detention camp.

For years the French government and press had demonized Germany for the Great War and the needless slaughter of French manhood. Vengeance, in the humiliation of Germany through smothering reparations, was the Allies' peace term. Would the Great War's legacy be Satan's revenge on France?

Parisians feared a German night stalker had crept in, grabbed them by the throat, and left them dangling in mid-air. Slowly the grip loosened. Parisians gasped, then cringed, waiting for the other shoe to drop. "Uneasy quiet before the storm," became a common refrain. Others thought and hoped that Hitler had been satisfied and there would be no war.

What raged, or more precisely what did not, became drôle de guerre—the phony war.

That everything and nothing had changed became clear when Rosa's feet touched Belgian soil. Anxiety and mistrust do not disappear overnight. Hitler's Reich taught Rosa to be wary. Kristallnacht brought terror. She retaliated and survived, though scars remained.

Berlin was a distasteful memory—forget it and move on. Her grandparents had died when she was young; two friends had left for America. And she had worked in her father's store from age 12, though that had ended. In 1935, a customer denounced her father and his business withered like roses denied water and died. She was 22, and she begged her parents to leave Germany.

Life had become increasingly intolerable. Feeling choked and desperate, she made a cynically, conscious decision to snare a man. That ended badly. Then Kristallnacht's orgy of violence quaked the earth beneath her feet. A knock on the door brought salvation— Sonny pulled her from the abyss.

After November 1938, she thought her previous life shallow and empty. She had merely existed, neither suffering nor flourishing. Then love came for the first time. She and Sonny planned a life. They were happy!

Then another quake had toppled her. Dangling by the thinnest of rope, she had watched him pull her to safety. He had rescued her before—why not now? She had to believe. Everything and nothing had changed after Sonny came into her life.

She was alone—that truth came hard. Alone she would grapple with the days and months to come, cling to her lifeline of hope, regardless how thin it might be. Optimism was free, like air and wind—all she had in the swirl . . .

Two days before Germany attacked Poland and four days before France declared war, Rosa's parents left Paris for Chelles. Wisely, they chose legal status to live and work in France rather than be trapped in Paris.

Rosa declared, "I won't leave Paris without Sonny at my side." They argued, but she was steadfast.

Letters arrived from Chelles. Her father was learning farm-implement repair, her mother cheese making and baking. Rosa could not visit them; it was too dangerous for a refugee with a forged visa. Then in early December, her parents' training complete, they were sent to Sare, a village in Aquitaine in southwestern France—to work in a vineyard and winery . . .

"What are your plans?" Jean asked Rosa, the day after France declared war on Germany.

Apprehensive, she bit her lip, fearing he wanted her gone.

"What's the matter?" Jean looked alarmed.

"Should I leave?"

"No . . . no," he shook his head. "Stay as long as you like—there's plenty of room."

Relieved, she exhaled but said nothing.

"We need to talk."

Rosa sat where she had the first day. Jean leaned back in his old leather chair and smiled warmly, putting her at ease.

"Relax, my dear, you're at home. My question, again: what are your plans?"

Frowning, she glanced at the wall. Her eyes went to her favorite photograph, *Latin Quarter* by André Kertész. It was both simple and complex—of intersecting vertical and horizontal lines, flat and articulated surfaces, walls and roofs, chimney cylinders, shades of gray. A wrought-iron fence enclosed a small rooftop deck; a man sat with a newspaper on his lap. Behind him, another man stood in a doorway, partly obscured. Their heads were slightly bowed, oblivious to the viewer—two isolated figures in the 20th-century urban maze.

Tearing her gaze from the rooftops, she sighed. "I . . . I don't know. Wait for Sonny, I suppose."

"You must do something besides wait." Jean spoke to her softly. "There's nothing here." His hand swept in an arc, taking in the room. "But help in the kitchen . . . clean the flat. Then what?" His shoulders rose in an exaggerated Parisian shrug. "Walk the neighborhood, talk to people, look at the pretty sights—be a tourist?" He smiled. "Young men follow you with their eyes."

"No, they don't," Rosa protested.

"Why deny it? Be French—take it as a compliment."

She shook her head.

Realizing Rosa's conundrum, he said, "Acknowledging reality doesn't make you disloyal to Sonny."

"Reality?" Rosa laughed harshly. "Reality is war, internment camps, not some guy in the street leering at me. What do I care? My husband is . . . " she stopped. "I'm sorry. You don't deserve this."

"It's my fault for being flippant." He moved to the divan, placing a hand softly on her shoulder. "It's my nature. You deserve better of me."

"You've done more than enough for me already."

"Perhaps," Jean acknowledged. "I have a modest plan."

"Plan?" Rosa muttered, perplexed.

"Soon your visa will expire. You need an identity card to walk the streets unmolested by police. There are rumors of arrests, especially here in the Marais."

Rosa nervously kneaded her hands as if purging the anxiety. "Will they come for me?"

"No, my dear," Jean reassured her. "But to be safe, stay inside until I get an identity card and, perhaps, a passport."

"You can do that?"

"Connections . . . " He tapped the side of his nose with his right forefinger and nodded. "I simply need a photograph."

Rosa was about to speak, but Jean said, "There's more."

"Bad news?"

He shrugged, then smiled. "I don't think so. With a new identity, you will need a new history. Staying here . . . people may talk." He frowned in disgust. "'Who is she? What's she doing with Jean?'" He pointed out the window. "Marais is filled with illegals. Most of my neighbors don't know you, and some may not be sympathetic. Loose tongues create problems with police."

Rosa considered. "Hmm."

"You are my niece from Alsace—come to stay with her uncle."

Rosa relaxed then smiled demurely. "Whatever you say, Uncle Jean."

He winked. "That's a good niece."

"By the way—what's my name?"

Jean laughed. "Rosa Friedman—my brother's daughter."

"You have a brother?"

He shrugged. "Ernst. Haven't seen him in years."

———————————

Ten days had passed since France declared war on Germany, nine since Rosa joined her new family. Jean nervously paced the flat, mumbling, cursing. Frowning, he stopped, straightened a picture, stepped back, and straightened it again. Manic, he moved in circles, like a caged animal. Rosa had never seen him like that.

"Damn! I don't like it. Newspapers report an attack on the 5th Army in a place called Schweix at the Maginot—Alain's in the 5th."

"What happened?" Rosa had heard much about Alain.

"Don't know. He's stationed somewhere near there. Letters are censored. He writes QQPEF. That's all he can say."

"Q . . . Q . . . P . . . ?"

"Q-Q-P-E-F—Quelque Part En France—somewhere in France," Jean answered impatiently.

Rosa put a consoling hand on Jean's arm. "He's probably all right." She couldn't think of anything else to say.

Jean's forced smile came out as a grimace, and he became uncharacteristically quiet, distracted. A spider's web of worry lines spun over his forehead.

Several days later, a letter arrived.

"He's safe but cannot say more—that's enough," Jean told Rosa, smiling broadly, banishing worry from his face.

Later that day, he handed Rosa an identity card and passport. Her photograph and prefect of police stamp were affixed to the card, looking official. Rosa Friedman hailed from Strasbourg in Alsace.

She examined the document, then said, "Thank you."

"They should work."

"*Should?*"

"Why not?" Jean shrugged.

Rosa stared at the card. "Rosa Friedman . . . Friedman . . . Have to get used to the name."

"Fischer . . . Friedman . . .no problem," Jean said, cheerfully.

Rosa's lips moved silently as she repeated her new name. Then she asked hesitantly, "What are your plans . . . about leaving Paris?"

He shook his head. "No plans. I am nervous, like everyone."

"Rightly so," Rosa agreed.

"Some left . . . most will stay. I shall rely on our magnificent French army, the Brits, and Maginot. Besides, where would I go? My little family is here."

"What if Catherine and Jacques take René and leave?" Rosa asked.

"Abandon the store? No! But you could join your parents in . . . " Jean's face went blank.

"Sare in Aquitaine."

"Sare." He repeated and nodded absently. "My memory . . . " He waggled a hand in the air.

"I found it on a map." She pointed to the bookcase. "It's tiny, a speck. Sonny would never find me there." She paused. "Please understand . . . I can't leave Paris. We planned on Paris. I have to stay . . . as long as I can."

"I mentioned Sare as an option— if things worsen. Stay as long as you desire."

"Thank you."

"Do you miss your parents?"

Rosa hesitated. "They have each other."

"That's not what I asked."

"I love them dearly, but I have to be on my own." Conflicted, she grimaced. "Yes, I miss them . . . kind of."

"I understand. Now, the rest of my plan."

"What . . . pray?"

Jean laughed. "No . . . maybe later. Now that you're legal." He cleared his throat. "Catherine and Jacques can use help at home with little René and in the grocery. Your French improves by the day. If you agree, you may stay here free—room and board. I will also pay a small wage—we will work that out." He waited for a response. Getting none, he asked, "Is my proposal inadequate?"

"I'm overwhelmed . . . Everything you've done for me is wonderful. Of course, I accept—thank you."

"Good." Jean rubbed his hands together. "And we'll continue our French lessons."

"Lessons?" She was confused.

"We're having one now—our daily conversation."

Rosa's lips curled into a smile. Her eyes twinkled.

"Smiling lights up your face, makes you even more beautiful."

She shook off the compliment. "You are too nice."

"You must be active, optimistic," Jean exhorted.

Suddenly a shy ingénue, she smiled tentatively and nodded, "I try." Changing course, she asked, "My French improves, don't you think?"

"Oui!" Jean clapped his hands, joyously. "I enjoy having the company of a spirited young woman. It makes me feel young. I should thank you."

Rosa kissed him on both cheeks.

"You become more French by the day," Jean quipped.

Early the next morning, Jean took Rosa to Catherine's flat on Rue Pavee, near the synagogue. Rosa had spoken briefly to Catherine and Jacques Garnier at the store on several occasions.

Catherine's gaze was direct, her smile warm. Jacques was at the store. According to Jean, Catherine had inherited her mother's sharp intellect, though Rosa found little of him in her features.

"I will leave you to work things out," Jean said as he left.

"He's very sweet." Suddenly uncomfortable, Rosa glanced toward the doorway Jean had exited.

Catherine followed her eyes. "He likes you very much."

They stood awkwardly in the middle of the room. Then Catherine laughed.

"What's funny?" Rosa asked.

She saw Jean in Catherine's shrugging response: "Damn world's going to hell, and we act like strangers, waiting for a bus."

Rosa smiled. "Then let's talk."

They did, for the next hour, while René played on the kitchen floor. Rosa learned that Catherine and Jacques had purchased the grocery several years earlier, with Jean's help, giving him a vested interest beyond a parent's concern. Jacques ordered, stocked the groceries, and dealt with customers. Catherine did the books and helped where needed. Occasionally, they hired neighborhood kids to stock shelves and make deliveries, but that cut into their profit. Times were tough and promised to get tougher.

Then Rosa spoke of Antwerp, her parents' decision to work in Aquitaine, and the horrible event in Mons. She concentrated so that she wouldn't lose control. She was more or less successful, but at one point she felt Catherine's hand on hers for support. Catherine asked about Sonny. Rosa told her some but not all.

"What an interesting man!" Catherine responded. "You must miss him terribly. I'm sorry for your predicament."

6

René was a delightful child. Catherine became a new friend. Rosa had a roof over her head, food to eat, money for the cinema, and coffee afterwards. Her nightmares receded, though not completely. Her wants were few, other than . . .

She had silently muttered the words "Life is for the living" so often that she sounded like a broken phonograph—annoying and in need of repair. Waiting was no way to live. She had to act—not stand pat. She had come to despise passivity, but she had no clue as to what to do.

Pushing René in his stroller, Rosa traversed the narrow, crowded streets of the Marais. Haussmann's reach had eluded the Marais, so the neighborhood had not been ruined like the rest of Paris, some said. Its medieval streets and old buildings had been spared, so that they uniquely maintained the ancient atmosphere of Paris. Small shops lined Rue de Rosiers. Yiddish, French, German, Polish, Russian, and a smattering of other languages punctuated the din.

Rosa noticed a couple standing front of the kosher butcher's. They were young, with sad, dark eyes, black hair. Like many couples, they looked alike—lovers, husband and wife, brother and sister? Fresh-faced, innocent, guileless but conflicted by the aura of despondency Rosa had seen in others. They seemed helplessly alone but for each other. Rosa saw some of herself—her fear, her isolation—in them. Her heart ached for them.

Then day after day—same clothes, same pose, standing on the same spot. Where did they come from, where did they go at night, where would they land? Rosa searched for clues not there. Like mannequins, they stationed themselves in front of the butcher.

Should she approach, ask whether they needed help? Did they have someone like Jean?

Then one day the young woman's eyes met Rosa's and held. She stared dully—expressionless, without acknowledgment. Unnerved, Rosa nearly ran into an old man. Forcing her eyes from the young woman, she uttered, "Pardonnez-moi." The young woman smiled with childlike amusement at Rosa's sidewalk burlesque. Pedestrians filled the space between them, and she was gone.

Rosa walked the embankment, on to Ile de la Cité to Notre Dame, then to the Left Bank, the lively 5th Arrondissement, to Luxembourg Gardens in the 6th. Or she remained on the Right Bank and strolled Jardin des Tuileries to the Louvre. Along the way, she perused embankment bookstalls, watched artists working on canvases, chatted with vendors in Les Halles, with mothers and nannies with children in hand.

Rosa's French was vastly improving, though she feared her German accent would blow her cover. "I am from Alsace, living with my uncle," she explained upon any questioning glance. Within weeks, she and René were accepted as regulars.

Eiffel Tower rose majestically from behind the building here and there along her route. The complicated patterns rendered by the crisscrossing girders of the tower against blue, grey, or white sky were enchanting. The tower's iconic, graceful lines were thrilling, inspiring optimism and possibility.

"You've become a Paris flâneur—strolling about the city, watching, talking, learning," Jean complimented.

René's dark, curly hair and big, bright eyes attracted attention, and so did Rosa. That was unavoidable. Paris was filled with beautiful women and men in pursuit. She could have walked head down, behind a curtain of hair or a cloche pulled low onto her forehead, but she did not. Instead she ignored the advances, disdained flirtation.

Autumn's bounty of rust and gold blanketed the parks and boulevards, crunching underfoot. The air was crisp, not cold. Rosa sat on a park bench in Luxembourg Garden and explained to René. "Trees sleep in the winter, turning leaves from green to gold or red." She plucked a leaf from the ground, closing her hand with a crunch.

"Me . . . me!" René pulverized leaf after leaf to great delight until she was no longer interested. Then Rosa walked past the massive

Pantheon and turned left onto Rue Descartes.

Several policemen stood in a doorway, a car at the curb, its rear door open. Rosa stopped at a distance, avoiding their notice. A terrible foreboding washed over her. Shivering, she knelt and whispered to René, "Something unpleasant . . . "

Then a man exited the building, hands bound behind his back. Another man followed on his heels. The bound man was pushed into the car, and it rolled away. Two uniformed policemen remained.

"That unfortunate man," Rosa thought and straightened, about to leave.

"Mademoiselle!"

She froze.

"Identification . . . s'il vous plaît." The policemen blocked her path, his hand extended.

Rosa fumbled for the card in her pocket. Her hand shook. She steadied and handed the card to him. René stared at the cop and squirmed.

"Rosa Friedman?"

"Oui."

His eyes went from picture to face and back. He traced the contours of her body with his eyes. He moved closer, his smile unpleasant. Rosa instinctively stepped back and raised her hand in lame defense.

"I could take you in . . . " he sneered.

René shrieked and began to cry. Rosa scooped him up in her arms and held him close. He wailed. Rosa frowned at the cop.

Several people stopped to watch. The cop stepped back, his mouth open, but nothing emerged. Nonplussed, he threw Rosa's card at her, turned, and walked away. She hugged René until the cops were out of sight, then retrieved her ID.

Rosa's hands shook. She felt lightheaded and, worst of all, violated. Holding René tightly to her chest, she whispered, "Thank you, René." Then she walked to the embankment and sat on a bench for half an hour to calm down. She had stumbled onto a terrible scene. A man had been arrested. What could she have done differently? Nothing! What if she had been alone? What if it happened again?

That night she dreamt of the cop, that he hadn't backed away, kept coming . . . Sonny's face, slowly receding through the train window, had replaced her nightmares of Oranienburg. Now, the sour taste of French hostility intruded.

Life could never be normal until Sonny reappeared. But what was normal—lover, children, career? Meeting Sonny as she had was not normal. What was normal to the young couple on Rue de Rosier? Not living on the street as stateless refugees, holding the lies of false documents! Luckier than most, she had been saved by Jean's kindness. Then why did she hurt so much?

By mid-December 1939, almost five months after Rosa arrived in Paris, a comfortable routine had set in. She loved her new family— little René, Jean, and Catherine—they felt real and sincere. And she loved Paris—subversive, beautiful, dingy, rich, poor, crowded, provocative, and more—its allure legendary and true.

A letter arrived. Her spirit soared. Sonny was alive and well— interred in a place called Wortel. Jean brought the atlas, and they finally located that tiny town north of Antwerp. Rosa immediately wrote a letter addressed to the camp.

"He'll know where I am. All I have to do is wait," she told Jean. That he was imprisoned did not dampen her optimism.

Rosa passed the cold winter afternoons with René in the warmth of the Louvre, distracted by works of famous, long-dead artists. *Mona Lisa*—her inscrutable smile, eyes watching, seeing all—was Rosa's immediate favorite.

"She is sublime," Jean agreed. "But don't be dominated by her. Look further to less well-known pieces and new experiences."

Exploring deeper into the vast museum, Rosa became enchanted by a massive and elaborate sculpture: *Psyche Revived by Cupid's Kiss* by Antonio Canova, an Italian. Rosa admired its grandeur and refined sensuousness. Cupid's wings lay at rest, a quiver at his waist, supporting the prone Psyche's head. His other arm supported her breast. Their heads were close, as if to kiss. An undulating sheet, carved from marble, was loosely draped over Psyche's lower body. In Greek mythology, Psyche ignored the warning and looked inside a jar. It held the "sleep of innermost darkness"—not beauty—and Psyche was rendered "a corpse asleep."

Rosa was moved by the magnificent sculpture's immediacy and

power. Holding René, she circled Cupid and Psyche, admiring the work's beauty, elevated by its spirit. Where was her cupid?

That night, in the quiet of her room, street noise as background, Rosa held Sonny's handkerchief to her face and cried softly—for herself, for Sonny in the camp, for her parents toiling in a God-forsaken corner of France, for the young couple, the man arrested, and for all unfortunate refugees . . .

"Tell me about yourself," Jean gently probed.

"Not much to tell," she said, which was largely true, with several glaring exceptions. "Kind parents, though for years, I'd wanted them to take me from Germany. They hadn't the means, but that didn't stop my anger. I was selfish, unfair to them. I *hated* Germany. My two friends were nice . . . they left for America. Boys flirted . . . I played hard to get."

"Not too hard," Jean teased.

"They were immature." Rosa shrugged. "I passed reasonably unscarred."

"And school?"

She made a sour face. "Didn't like it much—it showed." She talked about working in her father's kitchen-supply store near Alexanderplatz and how it had ended.

Days later, during another French lesson, Jean started, "Tell me how you met Sonny."

"Kristallnacht—that horrible night—Sonny appeared at my door," she murmured, took a breath, and slowly exhaled. "Father hadn't come home. Rumors ran through our building of Jewish men arrested, synagogues burned, and businesses looted. I smelled smoke. Mother and I stayed inside, afraid to leave. Our neighbor, Frau Milberg's husband, was also missing. She sent Sonny to check on us. He knew the Milbergs' son and did him a favor, checking on his parents. I opened the door, and my anger erupted." She closed her eyes as she spoke.

"My anger knew no bounds—father missing, probably arrested, stuck in that Nazi hellhole. I took it out on Sonny." She smiled. "He didn't seem to notice."

"He was smitten."

She nodded at the memory. "He stood in the middle of the room, facing me . . . my mother off to the side," she motioned with her hand, "calm, confident, promising to find Herr Milberg, then to return and find my father."

"Remarkable," Jean said softly.

"And he found Herr Milberg. I was impressed."

"When did he tell you he was a smuggler?"

Her brow wrinkled in thought. "First or second visit. We had time to talk. He kept coming back, like one of those yo-yos."

Jean laughed.

"It took about a week to find out that my father was in Sachsenhausen."

"Where is that?"

"Oranienburg, near Berlin—a hideous place." Rosa shivered at its mention. "I knew he was imprisoned but not where. Then to know officially was devastating. Weeks passed before he was released—another ordeal." She cringed but kept her eyes on Jean.

"What?"

Rosa shook her head. "Another time."

"Fine . . . continue."

"Mother was in a terrible state. I was alone, vulnerable . . . Sonny never took advantage. Then he told me he sent Jews over the border with forged papers. I was . . . amazed, didn't believe him at first. I'd been waiting for him, and he found me. I can't put it into words in French."

"Try."

She looked at the photographs for inspiration. "Hope . . . that I might have a future . . . a million butterflies dancing . . . boulders lifted from my shoulders."

He smiled. "Very poetic."

"No way was I going to let him get away. It was like," she considered her words, "the bitterness of life suddenly tinged with possibility—my lucky break . . . is that the right word?"

"Maybe serendipity?"

Rosa shook her head, not understanding.

Jean spoke in German.

"Entdeckung—serendipity of discovery . . . serendipity," she repeated and smiled.

"Sonny had a circle of friends, but he was lonely. I don't think he was looking for a lover, not that night."

"But he found one."

"Oui. He was good company, bringing little presents—bread, chocolate, whatever. Always helping me—and Mother—get through the horror of father's imprisonment. That was our courtship." She shrugged. "So . . . I fell in love with him."

"I wish I could know Sonny."

"So do I. Here . . . now—more than anything, Sonny is the thread that keeps me whole. I need him. I can't navigate underground. But I have to hold it together until we're reunited." She stood. "I want to show you something."

Rosa returned with a handkerchief, neatly folded, in the palm of her hand. "This, our wedding photograph, the letter—and memories, of course—are all I have of Sonny. He gave this to me just before he was attacked. I won't wash it until we're reunited." She held it under her nose. "At least I can smell him, until . . ."

"Show me the photograph," Jean said softly.

Rosa was smiling brightly into the camera, dark eyes wide with happiness. Sonny's arm was around her, his profile to the camera, mouth a half-smile, one eye looking at her intently. On Sonny's other side, Mina's shoulder was barely visible.

"You look radiant. Sonny's harder to read. Still, I can tell he is a handsome man. And I see that he might be mistaken for a gentile."

"We were so happy . . . never happier in my life," Rosa said softly. Then she looked down. "Sonny loves me . . . I love him. He'll find me . . . someday."

"He will—and soon."

Rosa smiled at Jean. "Maybe I'm selfish, but I want to live on my terms . . . regardless how difficult."

Jean sat next to Rosa and took her hands in his. "I fear life will soon be difficult for us all." Then he clapped his hands together. "Still, we must eat. Let's have dinner."

7

Paris, December 1939

Through December's dark cold, Rosa and René strolled the Louvre in the warm company of the planet's most beautiful art. Rosa's route always included *Psyche Revived by Cupid's Kiss*. She inhaled its aura, dreaming, hoping . . .

"I see you with the little one every day," a man's voice said from behind her.

Rosa turned. The smiling young man held a drawing pad; his eyes full of mirth. He had Sonny's everyman good looks.

"You must love Psyche and Cupid."

"I do." Her eyes went to his pencil and pad.

He followed her gaze. "I study at École des Beaux-Arts and draw art made by famous dead men."

Rosa laughed.

He waved at the sculpture with a sweep of his pencil-holding hand. "A critic complained of no singular view of the vitality of Canova's embracing figures . . . viewer runs around, looking from all angles, keeping from getting lost."

Rosa frowned. "Too academic . . . I just love it."

"Agreed. That's the drivel I read in school."

Conversation moved to the *Mona Lisa* and the Louvre's endless and exhausting collection. Then the young man knelt next to René and asked, "Who are you?"

"René."

"I'm Paul Masson." He shook René's hand then looked up. "And you?"

"Rosa."

"A pretty name."

"Thank you."

"Is Rosa your mama?"

"No!" René shook his head.

"It's complicated," Rosa said, leaving it at that.

"I detect an accent . . . German?" Quickly he added, to soften the blow, "Your French is good."

"That a problem?" Her tone was slightly defensive.

His lyrical laugh made Rosa smile. "Should it be?"

"No," she answered and walked away.

"Bye . . . bye," René called.

The following days found Paul nearby with pencil and pad. He waved, walked over, and chatted amiably. He seemed to have no motive beyond conversation . . .

Two days before the New Year, Paul extended an invitation to a play on the coming Tuesday, at a small theater in Montparnasse.

Rosa hesitated.

"My girlfriend's in it. You'll like her."

"Maybe . . . "

"Show up . . . there'll be plenty of room. It's very avant-garde . . . experimental, and all that." He gave her directions to "an old warehouse."

"Never been to Montparnasse," Rosa said.

"Then you must come. Studios are cheap, perfect for struggling artists—like me. Montmartre has its charms, but it has grown stale. Hope to see you."

———————

Alain arrived in Paris on the last day of 1939, Sunday, for week's leave. At 18, he was a taller, youthful version of Jean, with the same good looks, ready smile, and outsize personality. Drafted in early August, his plans for university were on hold.

Jean hugged his son then stepped back for a good look at him. He began peppering him, rat-tat-tat with questions: "How's your health? . . . You eating? . . . How's morale? . . . Conditions on the front?"

Laughing, Alain held up his hands to thwart the onslaught. "Father . . . let me catch my breath."

Rosa cleared her throat. Jean, already excited, became flustered, realizing his omission. He made introductions. Alain and Rosa laughed. Jean explained Rosa's situation.

Alain's expression moved from surprise to understanding. "Welcome to the family!" He kissed Rosa's cheeks.

"What's going on?" Jean demanded. "Brits crossed the channel the day after the declaration of war. How large a force?"

"Don't know, but I've heard that if you drew a line from the coast at the Belgian border east to Germany, you couldn't spit without hitting one. I haven't seen them. Rumors are they're a pain in the ass. Thousands bored stiff—no war to fight, so they drink and fornicate." He nodded to Rosa. "Pardon my language."

She smiled and shook her head. "Where are you stationed?"

He shook his head and smiled back. "Can't say . . . but I serve under a guy who looks a lot like Jacques."

Jean whispered to Rosa, "Family joke—Jacques looks like Colonel De Gaulle."

Rosa and Alain sensed immediate rapport and talked late into the night about their lives, hopes, and disappointments.

"We're at a crossroads," Alain observed after Rosa had told him most of her story, "German barbarians or muddle on, seeking a better way."

"Oh! Before I forget . . ." Rosa told him of the invitation to the play. He eagerly agreed to escort her "for a bit of culture."

Montparnasse was familiar territory, and Alain found the old warehouse with a minimum of misdirection. A side door opened onto a large open space with no seating and no stage. Muted voices seeped from behind a large curtain hung in a corner. About 30 people milled about, waiting.

"Rosa!" Paul suddenly appeared, then saw Alain. "My God! What the . . . ? It's good to see you."

"Paul! You're my cousin's Louvre friend."

Confused, Rosa listened to feverish questions and answers, bringing them up to date. She gleaned they had gone to school together but not seen each other for months.

"Annette's in the show . . . I'm helping—got to go."

They agreed to meet after the performance.

For the next hour and a half, actors—young men and women—walked, skipped, and ran through the empty space, pantomiming, speaking or shouting lines, creating hilarity. The physical humor made Rosa laugh, though the dialogue was difficult for her to understand. Still, she greatly enjoyed what she took from it.

They met outside and walked around the corner toward a little café on Rue Delambre. "Over there," Paul pointed, "the Dingo Bar, where Ernest Hemingway drank, and l'Hôtel des Ecoles, where Man Ray's career began."

Rosa had heard of Hemingway but not of the man with the funny name.

Annette Dufy exuded youthful confidence. Chestnut hair, a swath falling into her forehead, framed her big, expressive eyes. Baggy pants and a loose sweater hid her petite frame.

Rosa liked Annette immediately, sensing her natural stage presence. They congratulated her on her performance.

"Merci . . . merci . . ." Annette bowed slightly. "Pure farce, fun to perform. I'm still a student. I act whenever I can. Now the stage, but it's the cinema I want." She looked at Alain, then at Paul. "No talk about the war, army duty, or anything unpleasant," she ordered.

Both men laughed and answered in unison: "Agreed." Alain saluted.

For two hours they talked and laughed. Rosa told most of her story, despite its unpleasantness. By late into the night, actually early the next morning, they had drained three bottles of cheap wine and become close friends. Annette and Paul never questioned Rosa's pedigree. She was good company, Alain's cousin, and her story was compelling.

Walking the nearly empty, winding streets of Montparnasse, Annette and Rosa leaned against each other, arms intertwined, immune to the cold. Alain and Paul walked behind them. Rosa was having too much fun; she didn't want it to end. For the first time since Mons, she felt completely at ease. A gust of wind blew against her face, banishing anxiety—for the moment at least.

"What are you going to do?" Annette asked.

"Probably what I'm doing . . . long as I can."

"Then?"

"Don't know and tonight I don't care." Rosa burped then giggled.

Annette laughed. "Want to make extra money?"

"How?"

"Pose at Paul's school—you have the figure," she said casually. "I do."

"Maybe." Rosa changed the subject. "Why isn't Paul in the army?"

"No unpleasantries!" Annette shot back.

"Oops . . . forgot."

"Ask him if you want to know!"

Alain and Paul's muffled voices were barely audible.

"Paul's a talented artist," Annette said, her outburst forgotten.

"I've seen his sketches."

"He's wading through the 'isms.' Now the surrealists—you know Salvatore Dali?'"

"No . . . should I'"

"No!" Annette's tone was derisive. "Spaniard . . . leaves me cold. Paul played with African art—masks are wonderful, but he doesn't like the colonial connection."

"Oh." Rosa frowned.

"Too esoteric?"

"Big French word!"

Annette laughed. "Sorry—too *obscure*."

"Ah!"

"Your French is quite good." Then Annette tripped on a cobblestone, but Rosa held onto her. Annette laughed then shouted over her shoulder, "To the flat—show your paintings." To Rosa: "Not far . . . Rue Cels . . . other side of the cemetery—Baudelaire's eternal home. You'll love it."

Six flights up a narrow staircase, Rosa was breathing hard, calves burning at the top. Paul unlocked the door to a small, old-fashioned, low-ceilinged garret, defined by the roof's low angles. The kitchen was tiny and the bathroom smaller yet—but there was one. A double door opened onto a small balcony in the Parisian style, as in the Kertész photograph—*Latin Quarter*—that Rosa loved. She stared into the dim night, rooflines barely visible, lights glowing here and there like fireflies.

"So intimate, romantic, charming," Rosa gushed. "I love it! I want one!"

On the Métro from Montparnasse to the Marais, she asked Alain, "How can two young students afford a flat, even one touching the sky?"

Alain laughed. "Parents with money. Not sure about Annette's father. Paul's father is a lawyer and politician . . . planned the family exodus, booked a flat in Marseille. Part of Blum's Popular Front, interior ministry—I think. Then out when the government fell."

"Blum's a Jew?"

Alain nodded.

"Amazing, considering Germany's cesspool."

"First Jewish prime minister, something to be proud of. He was a Dreyfusard and follower of Juan Jaures, the socialist leader. Juares's assassination pushed Blum to the front of the line. Hitler's rise emboldened French fascists—our dirty little secret," Alain whispered. "That threat was real, forcing Socialists, Radical Socialists, and Communists to quit squabbling. They formed a coalition, and voilà: Popular Front." Alain waved his hand with a flourish.

"Democracy finally delivered real change in '36—like Berlin before Hitler—fighting in the streets. Hell, we've been fighting the revolution since 1789. Finally, the workers had a voice. Half a million people turned out in Paris, marching past the Mur des Féderés."

"The what?"

"Wall commemorating workers killed in the Paris Commune in 1871. We got the 40-hour week, paid vacations, better wages, right to strike. Unfortunately, it was too good to be true and didn't last. Inflation sent prices skyrocketing, wages went . . . poof!" He blew air from between closed lips. "Automobile workers struck and Blum's government . . . poof." He exhaled, again.

"What's the government now?"

"Paul Reynaud—Prime Minister . . . leader of the Democratic Republican Alliance, career politician . . . opposed Munich."

"But England . . . " Rosa noted.

"I know—let Hitler loose in Czechoslovakia, but we agreed."

Rosa's response was an exaggerated sigh, long and drawn out.

"Got that right, cousin."

"Very well informed for a lowly private."

"What I lack in rank, I make up for with information no one gives a damn about. I'm interested in politics . . . the 'art of the possible' according to Bismarck—imagine quoting him!"

"What will you do?"

"Study history at university when this . . . ends."

"Give Hitler a black eye if he turns on France."

"I plan to, personally."

"Why isn't Paul in the army?"

"He will be . . . soon. Makes Annette sad, doesn't want to talk about it."

"Don't blame her. Do many unmarried couples live together?"

"Not common, but not so out of the ordinary, especially in Montparnasse."

"They make a handsome couple."

Alain took Rosa's hand and squeezed. "Like us, cousin."

8

Paris, Winter 1940

Winter darkness brought cold, snow, and sustained anxiety. Alain resumed his post; Parisians braced for war; Sonny was not in Paris.

Annette became a great friend and confidant. Together she and Rosa frequented the Montparnasse avant-garde art and theater scene. Rosa felt her spirit strengthen.

Hundreds of kilometers away, near the Spanish border, Rosa's mother and father receded to Rosa's fond memory. Knowing they were safe was enough. But the pain of separation from Sonny was sometimes more than she could bear. Theirs was an intimacy built upon the foundations of life and death—love, loss, uncontrollable rage, reciprocated hate, and predatory, animal instinct . . .

Clenching her fists so tight her knuckles hurt, Rosa found her eyes filled with tears, but she refused to cry. "Be strong," she murmured, then wavered. Sonny, the "go-to guy," would know what to do. Was he still in that awful camp? Intersecting lives, faint lines drawn on paper, disappeared, fading in the sunlight. Rosa wanted to break the recurring theme into a million pieces.

————————

They sat in the little café on Rue Delambre near Hemingway's bar and Man Ray's hotel. Late afternoon sunlight glistened like diamonds through their wine glasses, dancing on the red-checkered tablecloth. Paul had been drafted. The café was nearly empty.

Annette knew Rosa's story, about Sonny and the letter, but she sensed that Rosa kept some things close—everyone did. Fixing her eyes on Rosa's, Annette asked, "What awful secrets are locked inside? Not good to hold them in."

Rosa fingered her wine glass, nervously. "We need secrets."

"Big ones eat you up."

Rosa nodded. "You're wiser than your years."

A man walked by, their eyes met, he smiled. Rosa looked away.

"Only Sonny knows . . . " she shook her head, "no, some of his friends know. One's in England, the others in Germany.'

"Tell me."

"I have to be sure . . . " Rosa looked around. A couple talked quietly; a man read a newspaper. She had kept her secret corked inside for so long, and she yearned to tell someone. She hadn't told Jean; a woman might be easier. " . . . that you trust me."

Rosa's eyes slowly met Annette's. She nodded. "That bad?"

"Worse."

Rosa searched Annette's eyes, saw her friend's sincerity and concern. "Everything shattered on Kristallnacht," she said.

Then Rosa took Annette on the train to Oranienburg that day she had gone to get her father from the Sachsenhausen camp: "Sonny followed at a safe distance, my hidden protector. We couldn't be together, his false identity was Christian, and I'm a Jew." She looked down, took a deep breath, fear jabbing her like the prick of a needle. Blood drained from her face, turning her skin alabaster—like Psyche and Cupid.

"Drink." Annette handed her a glass of wine. "Good, take a few breaths." Annette put her hand on Rosa's. "You all right?"

Rosa nodded, then told Annette everything. "'Work makes you free'—that's what it says above Sachsenhausen's gate." She shivered. "But they wouldn't release Father until the next day, so I walked back alone, looking for Sonny. Suddenly, someone grabbed my arm from behind. I thought it was Sonny." She shook her head from side to side. "It wasn't. He was a tall, limping man, Gestapo . . . didn't know it then. He dragged me by the arm into a cold, empty warehouse. Where was Sonny? There was a mattress on the floor. I knew what he wanted. I saw a knife, its blade stuck on the table. He taunted me and his laugh was . . . horrible." Her eyes hardened.

"But he underestimated me. I grabbed the knife and plunged it into his chest." Her chin rose defiantly, her voice calm and steady. "Then Sonny was standing next to me. I had had no idea he was there. There was blood on my dress. He told me he had been hiding behind a pillar, my protector. He had cracked the man's skull with a brick, but the knife was already in him." Rosa licked her lips then muttered, "Sonny was like a ghost."

"Oh, my God," Annette intoned.

Rosa nodded. "Sonny said we couldn't leave his body, that they'd find it. So he set the warehouse on fire, calling it a 'fantastic funeral pyre.' I was in shock." Rosa shed no tears and stared icily across the table at Annette, her veneer peeled away.

Annette fell back under the gravity of the story, her eyes wide. A chair scraped on the floor, there were unintelligible mumblings, people passed. The door opened, and the couple left the café.

On the street, Annette hugged Rosa. They stood, leaning against each other for several minutes, then walked arm in arm, silent. Finally Annette blurted, "Of course, I'm shocked . . . and sad and angry." Then a mean smile worked its way onto her crimson lips, and she whispered, "To tell the truth, I feel a vicarious thrill."

"Don't," Rosa commanded. "It's . . ."

"Prick got what he deserved. I'm honored to know you."

"It's a terrible burden," Rosa started, then emitted a hollow, mirthless laugh, "and funny, in a way—how you change in a flash." She snapped her fingers. "Into someone you don't recognize. Sonny's friend Emil said that by the time this is over I'd wish I'd killed more."

"I understand why Sonny looms so large."

Nothing more was said of Oranienburg, but the telling brought change in its wake. Rosa's inner demons quieted. She had expelled the stale, dead air inside her, a measure of inner calm and peace filling the void.

Annette also changed. She deferred to Rosa, sought her opinion, and confided in her. Rosa welcomed the change and rather enjoyed it—at first. The emotional barriers between the two friends dissolved. But when Annette's gaze held an exaggerated sense of wonderment, bordering on awe, the hero worship went too far. After several weeks, Rosa clasped Annette's upper arm, said "Stop! Your adulation is oppressive. You act like I'm a saint."

"Well . . . you are—Saint Rosa," Annette's joke held truth.

"No!"

"You should have told Alain and Paul. They could use your kind of courage."

Rosa's head shook, vehemently. "I don't want to talk about it."

"You brought it up." Annette said, cheerfully. "You want to go to a party tonight? It should be very interesting."

"Where?"

"You'll see. Meet me at the station on Boulevard Montparnasse and Avenue l'Observatoire at 8."

Rosa spotted Annette's chestnut hair, partially visible beneath a man's hat, jauntily askew. Her eyes dropped to the tailored jacket and culottes. They kissed cheeks: "Interesting outfit."

"You like it?"

"Must be the rage. Looks great on you."

Annette laughed. "Open your coat. Let me see." She looked at Rosa's dress, tailored to her body. "You look splendid."

They linked arms and walked.

"I was married in this dress," Rosa said softly.

"Then it's very special." Annette squeezed her arm.

They walked past Val-de-Grâce, a massive Baroque, dome-topped, church used for the present as a military hospital. A big tri-color flag hung limp in the still night air. As they talked, puffs of vapor emerged, then dissipated, like too many hopes and dreams.

"Where we going?" Rosa asked.

"Not far."

After several turns, Annette stopped in front of an elegant old building. "We're here." She looked up. "Remember, nothing is as it seems."

Rosa frowned, perplexed, but before she could respond, a couple, apparently a man and a woman, breezed by, into the building. Annette and Rosa followed their voices several flights to a landing where a door stood open. Conversation punctuated by laughter heralded a good time for all. The lights were dim, the faces obscured. Rosa and Annette sliced through the crowd. A tuxedoed waiter appeared, hoisting a tray of drinks.

Annette grabbed two, handing one to Rosa. "Cheers!"

Rosa leaned in close. "Was that a man or woman?"

Annette smiled enigmatically. "No men here."

"The couple at the door . . ."

Annette shook her head.

Rosa fingered the lapel of Annette's jacket and understood. Smiling, she said, "You're corrupting me."

"Moi?" Annette laughed, then whispered, "You, with the checkered past?"

Rosa shrugged and looked around the room. Several women wore slacks similar to Annette's, a uniform of sorts, though most wore dresses. Music floated softly from a phonograph perched on a table next to a baby grand. Several couples danced slowly. All seemed normal but for the lack of men.

"So glad you came," said a voice, husky from smoking.

Rosa turned. A short, well-dressed woman, with a stunning string of pearls dangling above impressive décolletage, kissed Annette on both cheeks.

"I wouldn't have missed your party for the world," Annette cooed.

The woman smiled warmly at Annette then glanced at Rosa. "And who is this beauty?"

"Agnes Capri, my friend Rosa . . . "

" . . . Friedman," Rosa supplied.

Her eyebrows rose in mild amusement, or surprise, or both. "Friedman?"

Rosa nodded, nonplussed.

"Same as mine—changed it for the stage and became Agnes Capri—voilà. Better, don't you think?" Agnes waved a hand, deflecting the possibility of answering.

"Where are you from?" she demanded. Her eyes fixed on Rosa, crooked smile pasted on, white teeth showing—she was a shark in pearls.

"Alsace. I'm staying with my uncle in the Marais."

"Ah . . . the accent."

They spent several minutes, parsing the spelling of their surnames. Agnes, or Sophie-Rose, spelled hers, " . . . mann."

"We'll talk later," she commanded, "now, *enjoy*—while we still can." Her lyrical laugh softened her eyes. Then she abruptly turned and walked away, leaving a trail of expensive perfume.

"She likes you," Annette said.

"How could you tell?"

"She wants to talk to you, silly."

"Who is she?"

"Singer—owns a cabaret on Rue Molière bearing her name." Annette put an arm around Rosa. "I smell opportunity," she sang. "Don't let it slip away."

Rosa shrugged, amused. "How do you know her?"

"She came backstage, piled heaps of praise, then invited me to the party. Imagine that?"

"Of course. You're a wonderful actress."

"You *are* a dear." Annette demurred, feigning modesty. "She also operates 'le Petite Theater.' Do I sense a part in a new play?"

"Good for you."

"If there's anyone left in Paris to attend the theater."

An earthy growl, meant as laughter, escaped Rosa's lips. Putting a hand over her mouth, she asked, "Who are these people?"

Annette scanned the room. "Artists, wives of well-known and unknown men . . . I don't know. Social circles over my head." She leaned close to Rosa. "Agnes caused a sensation on an Easter Sunday several years ago when she sang, "Our father who art in heaven . . . stay there!'" This time Rosa's laughter was full of mirth. Soon both women laughed so hard they fell onto each other, tears rolling down their cheeks.

"I'll have what they're drinking," someone said.

Annette, knowing how to play an audience, sang, "Our father who art in heaven, stay there!" Then sang it again.

Laughter. Several women sang back. Soon the refrain reverberated through the flat. Women pressed against Annette and Rosa, hugging, laughing, kissing. After several minutes they ran out of steam, and the party returned to the pre-singing din. Rosa hadn't had this much fun since . . . she couldn't remember.

"Who are you?" Women wanted to know. They threw names about, none remembered. Then they were alone again.

"Great fun! I'm hungry." Annette headed to the next room, Rosa in tow. A table displayed an assortment of luscious hors d'oeuvres. Filling plates and glasses with wine, they retreated to a corner.

Giddy from the evening's energy, Rosa felt she belonged in Paris with Annette, at Agnes Capri's party in the company of Parisian sybarites. The camaraderie delighted her. Sonny was not displaced in her heart . . . still, bubbles of guilt found their way to the surface.

They sat at a small, round, bistro table in a corner, surrounded by lively chatter, peels of laughter, and background music. Hot from the press of gyrating bodies in the room, Annette fanned her face with her hand. Open windows invited a chill, evening breeze.

They had barely sat down when Agnes appeared. "My dear, you know how to get a party boiling."

"Great fun, isn't it?" Annette agreed.

"Oui. Come to the club on Monday at 6 PM. I have plans for you." She turned to Rosa. "I may have something for you as well."

"Fantastic!" Annette exclaimed to Agnes's back.

"What was that about?" Rosa asked.

"Have to find out, won't we—on Monday? Now, forget it and have a good time."

Agnes's offer swirled in Rosa's head. Annette made sense—a part in a play. But Rosa couldn't act, sing, and her French was barely fluent. Rosa felt a hand grab hers and pull her from her chair.

"Let's dance," Annette chirped and led her to the other room.

Several couples danced, or flailed, to a syncopated rumba tune. Annette threw herself into the music while Rosa watched, amused.

"Just move to the rhythm," Annette shouted.

"What's it called?" Rosa asked when the music stopped.

"'*El Manisero* [peanut vendor].' Isn't it fabulous? It's all the rage."

Rosa nodded. Someone put Gershwin's *American in Paris* on the phonograph.

"Too . . . for dancing," someone shouted.

"Something slow," another shouted back.

Then a woman sang in English: "'Summertime and the living is easy, fish are jumping and the cotton is high . . . '"

"Better!"

The light further dimmed, and more women coupled, dancing slowly. Rosa waited, unsure of what to do. Annette's tongue flicked as she licked her lips. A slow smile curled onto her mouth. She moved close, put her arms around Rosa, and moved rhythmically from side to side, her feet planted in place. Her body was hot, slowly swaying, and their breasts pressed together.

Annette put a hand on Rosa's neck, gently pulled until their lips met. Her breath tasted of wine and caviar. She let go and laughed: "Welcome to my Paris!"

9

Paris, Winter 1940

Through the evening, women streamed in and out of the flat—army reinforcements to the front—creating an illusion of boundless energy. Too much wine, gaiety, and noise, bodies jostling, perspiration and perfume dulling the senses—all part of a night to remember. Only long past midnight did the frenetic pace of the evening's revelry slow.

Rosa and Annette walked toward the subway, energized by the night chill. Passing autos and their soles on the empty pavement made the only sounds. Agnes's invitation had washed away in the wake of Annette's remarkable dance. Rosa's closest friend in Paris, maybe her closest friend anywhere, had crossed a line. Rosa couldn't purge it from her mind. But did it matter? Was this the real Annette? Rosa felt confused, adrift.

Ghostly shadows cast by dim streetlights added to the muddle in her head. Not knowing how to start, she blurted, "Do you love Paul?"

Startled, Annette looked at Rosa for several seconds. "Of course."

"Then why . . . ?"

Eyes bright and with another slow smile, Annette asked, "Did you like it?"

Rosa's silence was no answer.

"If I scared you, I'm sorry."

"Well . . . a little."

"In the company, the moment felt right—I wanted to kiss you. I may be young, but I'm no fool." Annette felt for Rosa's hand and held it.

Rosa stopped but left her hand in Annette's. "I . . . can't do this."

"Do what—feel affection toward another woman?"

"In that way."

"All right." Annette's tone conveyed more than her words. "Paul's gone . . . Sonny's somewhere in a camp. I'm lonely . . . you're lonely." She moved closer. "I experimented once, haven't made it a habit . . . and you're so lovely."

Rosa slowly shook her head back and forth. "I'm not . . . that way."

"Those women acted so naturally," Annette shrugged.

"You did it before," Rosa reminded her.

"The other girl came on, like I did with you."

"Did you resist?"

Again, Annette slowly shook her head. Her gaze wandered. "Don't know how you'll respond until . . . Forget it. I got carried away in the moment. Call it an experiment."

"A failed one!" Rosa exclaimed.

Annette nodded. "Some at the party . . . they're like kitchen doors in a bistro—swinging both ways."

Rosa laughed.

"We're close friends, right? Nothing changes that." Annette needed reassurance.

"We are." Rosa was not angry or flattered, just confused. Annette fancied herself avant-garde, but Rosa did not. "I know little about you."

A man walked past, interrupting them. He slowed, looking them over, but kept going.

"What's to know? I'm a struggling actress . . . "

"Tell me what I don't know," Rosa interrupted, impatiently. "What about your parents?"

"They're boring. I'm boring."

Rosa laughed. "That you are not!"

"Next to you, your life, mine seems so . . . banal, uninteresting."

"I'd take yours in a minute," Rosa countered, then shook her head. "You think this is romantic . . . stateless, separated from Sonny, waiting for . . . ?"

"The world to blow up."

"Exactly! I make a good story for someone to write about—not live. Now, answer my question," she demanded.

Annette's face screwed in concentration.

"It can't be that hard," Rosa said testily.

"I want to get it right," she protested. "Okay, I'm a young, unknown actress, barely surviving, trying to make it, learning how to play the game . . . alone." She paused.

"Keep going."

Annette nodded. "We're at war, lovers gone, Alain gone—they're all gone. I look at what you've gone through, your poise . . . like you've stepped out of a novel."

"No," Rosa moaned. "You're turning it back to me."

"That's how I feel." Her arms extended, pleading for her to be understood.

"All right." Rosa sighed, frustrated with her friend. "For you it's fiction, 'all the world's a stage' . . . for me, reality."

They walked, still holding hands, neither speaking.

Rosa broke the silence "Where do your parents live? What does your father do?"

Annette frowned. "In a big flat in the 15th, near Pont Mirabeau. Days after the war started they left for Bordeaux." Her affect was too flat; she was trying hard not to care. Her voice softened. "I miss my sister."

"Must be nice to have a sister. What's her name?"

"Jeanne . . . " Annette stared into the distance, seeing what Rosa could not, "had long curly hair when very young, like an angel in old church paintings." She sighed and spoke softly. "She's sweet and lovely."

"Like you." Rosa squeezed her hand.

Annette snorted. "Okay, forget the sweet part." She laughed.

"Why didn't you leave with them?"

"Give up acting? Never!" Annette shook her head violently. "They tried. I have to act; it's who I am. So I moved in with Paul" She tightened her grip on Rosa's hand. "We don't get on; they object to my friends . . . what I do . . . I failed them." Then Annette's anger spilled out. "To hell with war and stupid politicians!"

"Where does your father's work?"

Annette frowned. "Some big company," she waved dismissively, "made a lot of money." She stiffened. "My parents' departure is of no consequence."

"How do you survive?"

"I'm not above taking his money," she said bitterly. "He won't let me starve—the fate of all actors and artists in his mind."

"Not far off the mark."

Annette frowned at Rosa. "Don't you start in."

"Could we be any more different?" Rosa observed.

"Are we?" Annette asked. "We're both alone . . . a powerful connection. Both strong—you for sure, but so am I, in my own way."

Rosa nodded. "Living on your own and staying, even if you take your father's money. That's two."

"That's enough. I admire your strength. You exude . . . " she paused, "dignity...strength."

"You already said strength," Rosa teased.

"You're so damned modest! There's a difference." Annette curtsied and took a bow.

Rosa chuckled.

"Third! Most important: we like each other. Friendship trumps everything."

Just ahead was the Métropolitain's fanlike wrought-iron entrance, perched like a giant insect. Two lamps glowed eerily off-white, lending a surreal atmosphere to an extraordinary night.

"Spend the night at my place," Annette offered, her tone hopeful. "Its empty . . . lonely."

"No, I better go home."

They embraced and parted.

———

It was Monday, several minutes before 6 PM. Rosa waited at the corner of Rue Moliére and Avenue de l'Opera, in the shadow of the Palais Royal. *Cabaret* and *Theatre* appeared in big letters on the building across the street. She was lost in thought about what a well-known entertainer could possibly have in mind for a no-talent, illegal refugee, who couldn't sing, dance, act, and wasn't who she claimed to be. Sonny would be amused . . .

Voices from behind surprised Rosa. She turned to see two gendarmes. Her eyes met those of the younger cop. Stiffening, she managed a thin smile. Nearly brushing her shoulder, he returned her smile and put a hand to the brim of his cap.

"Bonsoir, Mademoiselle."

She shivered as they walked past, leaving Rosa behind, holding her breath.

"Exciting isn't it?" Annette's familiar voice calmed her. "Ready for an audience with her majesty?"

Rosa laughed nervously.

"You all right?"

"Just nerves. You look splendid."

Pirouetting, Annette asked. "You think?" She wore a short blue dress showing her legs to advantage and matching shoes. Her hair curled attractively behind her ears.

"Of course."

"You look lovely as usual."

"Same old rags." Rosa shrugged as she walked into a cabaret for the first time. It was empty but for tables, chairs, and a stage. A zinc-topped bar lined an entire wall. Rosa heard Annette's voice.

" . . . an appointment with Madam Capri." Annette stood near the bar.

A man holding a trumpet in one hand, sheet music in the other, looked them over. His shirtsleeves were rolled over his forearms; a faint smile graced his lips. His hair was streaked with gray, the color of concrete. Rosa pegged his age at too old for the army. He nodded, squinting, a cigarette dangling from the corner of his mouth. He jerked his head, sending ashes floating to the floor.

"This way, ladies."

He led them to a narrow corridor past the stage and pointed with his trumpet. "In the back." Then he gave a little toot on his horn, heralding their arrival.

They passed the kitchen, the door to a dressing room. At the end of the hall, a door stood ajar. Agnes Capri sat at a desk framed in chrome, studying a sheet of paper.

Rosa and Annette exchanged glances, waiting for each other to do something.

Agnes, sensing their presence, turned her head. "You're here. Come in." She stood to greet them.

They entered.

Agnes Capri held a cigarette in one hand, paper in the other. Her cream-colored jacket with matching long skirt and blue silk scarf tied loosely like a man's tie were très à la mode. The office was small but tidy. Agnes sat in a chair with the same motif as the desk and pointed to two leather club chairs. "Sit, ladies."

She crushed the cigarette in a big crystal ashtray, looking each up and down for what seemed an eternity. Pointing to Annette, she said, "You're the actress." It was a statement, not a question.

"Oui," Annette agreed.

"I'm terrible with names."

"Annette Dufy."

Agnes nodded, affirming Annette. "Your play was avant-garde fluff, but *you* were good."

"Merci."

"I'm always looking for young talent. We're doing *Lysistrata*. I want you for the lead."

Annette's face lit up. "The ancient Greek play?"

"Of course . . . what else?"

Annette blushed but managed, "When do we start?"

"It opens in three weeks—Friday, third of May. Our take on the coming war." She tossed her head as the trumpet player had. "Talk to Frankie, the stage manager. He'll tell you all you need to know."

"When . . . ?"

"Frankie knows all." She dismissed Annette with a wave of her hand. Then she turned to Rosa. "You're Friedman . . . from Alsace."

Rosa nodded, continuing the lie.

"Is it Mademoiselle Friedman?" Her question tinged with sarcasm.

"Rosa."

"Rosa . . ." she repeated, "what shall I do with you?"

"Didn't think there was anything needing to be done with me," Rosa shrugged, despite having wondered the same.

Agnes laughed. "Snap! I like that."

"You beckoned . . . I came."

"True enough." Agnes leaned back in her chair, holding an unlit cigarette in front of her mouth, making no effort to light it, staring at Rosa. "Where in Alsace?"

Jean had told her a little, very little, about Strasbourg, so she answered, "Strasbourg."

"La Petite France is an enchanting district—medieval streets and bridges. I sang at Emile's a couple years ago. You know it?"

Rosa shook her head.

"Never mind. Strasbourg's beautiful in spite of the Germans."

Agnes laughed. Rosa did not. She wanted to change the subject.

"Jews flee Alsace in droves. Where did you live?" asked Agnes.

Rosa's mind raced. "Ah . . . in . . ." she stammered, "near the river in the old Jewish Quarter."

"What's the name of the old synagogue? I took a peek inside, hadn't been in one for years."

Rosa looked at Agnes as if she had asked her to explain Einstein's theory of special relativity. She bit her lip then confessed, "I don't know . . . I'm not from Strasbourg. I'm from Berlin."

Agnes's eyes narrowed, then she nodded. "Your real name?"

"Rosa Landauer—no, Sander." She was flustered.

Agnes frowned. "Don't know your name?"

Rosa blushed but said nothing.

"And your papers?"

"False—Friedman is my Parisian adopted family. My husband's name is Landauer, but he uses Sander, the name on his papers."

"A dangerous game . . ."

"No game." Rosa shook her head, slowly back and forth. "I have nowhere to go."

"I'm sorry. You have no worries from me." Agnes offered Rosa a cigarette.

"No, thank you."

"You're Rosa Friedman, maybe a distant cousin." Agnes lit the cigarette, keeping a steady gaze on Rosa. "How does that sound?"

"Nice," Rosa answered, hopefully.

"What can you do besides stand and look pretty?"

"Like a department-store mannequin?"

Agnes threw her head back and laughed heartily. "You're making me laugh. That's good." She inhaled deeply and blew a flume of smoke from the side of her mouth. "Got any special talents?"

"Hmm," Rosa considered. "Can't sing, dance, or act, if that's what you mean."

"More's the pity," Agnes said, without sarcasm.

"Are you going to offer me a job?"

"Don't know yet. Where's your family?"

Rosa told her an abbreviated story of her parents in Sare, of Sonny in the internment camp.

"Damn Nazis!" Agnes cursed and took another drag. After a few seconds, she said abruptly, "Stand up. Walk to the door and back."

Rosa hesitated, then did as instructed.

Agnes took another drag from her cigarette, appraising Rosa as if she were modeling a Chanel creation. Then she stood next to Rosa, making a circular motion with her hand. "Turn."

Rosa turned in a circle. "Did I pass?"

"Very attractive. You'll turn heads . . . you carry yourself well. You can work in the club."

"Doing what?" Rosa laughed.

"Hostessing, welcoming patrons—the face of Agnes Capri's Cabaret . . . do whatever else needs attending to." Agnes described her duties more fully, then: "Have you heard from your husband?"

"One letter. He knows where I live." Rosa's stomach muscles tightened.

"So maybe he'll come." Agnes' eyes softened. "You want the job?"

Rosa felt conflicted, even disloyal. "I already have one—a nanny for my adoptive family in the Marais. I . . . we have an arrangement. I can't give it up."

"This is evening work, late into the night. Would it interfere?"

"Maybe not."

"Tell me tomorrow, no later."

. . . Rosa waited on Rue Moliére for Annette.

"What an opportunity!" Annette exclaimed. Then she prattled on about the play, the theater, and her part. Finally, she asked, "What happened after I left?"

"I told her," Rosa said.

"What?" Annette asked, bewildered.

"That I lied about my name . . . I'm not from Alsace."

"She won't tell anyone—will she?"

Rosa shook her head. "She was sympathetic and offered me a job"

"Wonderful!"

10

Paris, 10 May 1940

The late spring brought warmer weather, much to the Parisians' delight. Couples holding hands paraded along the Seine Embankment and Champs–Élysées. Colorful blooms lured birds and bees to Luxembourg Gardens, the Tuileries, and ubiquitous window boxes across the city. Sidewalk cafés overflowed. All things considered, it was a glorious time to be in Paris.

Still, there was the uneasy quiet of the phony war. In January, the Belgian military had cancelled all leaves. What did the Belgians know? People hungered for information. What they got was the prediction of imminent attack by bloviating wireless and newspaper commentators, who were like little dogs nipping at theirs heels.

"What the hell do they know?" Jean complained.

On 9 April, tiny Denmark had surrendered to Hitler just hours after Nazi troops penetrated the border. That same day the Germans invaded Norway, fighting a naval battle with the British over a port in Norway—Narvik. Germany lost the battle but nevertheless gained a foothold there.

"Steel for the war machine," Jean said.

"What's next?" Rosa asked, chewing nervously on her lip.

Jean shook his head. "Whatever it is, no reason yet to panic . . . "

After hectic rehearsals, *Lysistrata* opened on schedule. A short, favorable review in *Nouvelle Revue Française* was gratifying, but like a bit of chocolate, it left the actors wanting more. Colette—former music hall performer turned novelist and reigning cultural icon—appeared backstage. She praised Annette's performance in a royal paean, grazing her cheeks with kisses. Her presence guaranteed a full house for weeks.

Alain wrote that he was fine, missed everyone. They were "not to worry" but to "send food."

Jacques, Catherine's husband, informed Jean that he had purchased an automobile, a 1935 Peugeot 202. "It was in an accident, so he got a good deal . . . says it runs will," Jean told Rosa.

"They going to make a run for it?" Rosa asked.

Jean chuckled. "You sound like an American gangster." He shook his head. "No plans for the present. A safety valve, according to Catherine."

"What about the store?"

"Shutter it, if they have to. Hope it won't come to that." His smile faded. "Jacques is an old Communist, Catherine a Jew . . . prepare for the worst."

" . . . And you . . . me?" Rosa asked.

Jean did not answer.

———

Despite these hiccups, the routine was comforting—the Jewish butcher, the fresh-baked baguettes perfuming the air, the crowded Marais walkways. Rosa glanced toward the butcher shop, shielding her eyes from the reflected sunlight. The young couple she had watched earlier was not there.

Momentarily addled, she continued toward the Seine, pushing René in his stroller through the crowd. She noticed a face in profile that looked familiar. Then she realized it belonged to the sad young woman by the butcher shop. She was alone. Rosa maneuvered closer and walked next to her.

"Mademoiselle," she said softly. "Excuse me."

Dark eyes flickered nervously, unwilling to meet Rosa's.

"You speak French?"

"Oui, some." Her affect was flat, her accent German.

"I know you . . . I mean, I've seen you."

Confusion fought fear, until fear won out. The woman's eyes widened as she turned away.

"Please . . . " Rosa spoke softly, "stop."

She did.

"Pardon my intrusion. We've never spoken. I've seen you with a young man on Rue de Rosiers . . . one day our eyes met. You even laughed. Today, you weren't there . . . now you're alone . . . "

The woman's mask cracked like dried paint, revealing the girl beneath the veneer. Tears filled her eyes.

Little René cried too. Rosa held him in one arm, wrapping the other about the young woman. Overwhelmed, Rosa searched for refuge. A small café at the end of the alley looked promising.

Rosa ordered two cups of coffee and found a table at the back of the café. René sat on her lap.

"I'm Rosa. The little guy is René."

He smiled at the young woman.

Shivering though the café was warm, the woman still avoided Rosa's gaze. "Jenny," she said in a barely audible voice, smiling weakly at René.

"Jenny . . . who was the young man?"

After several seconds, she answered, "My brother."

"Where is he?"

Bloodshot eyes finally met Rosa's. "Don't know . . . I watched the police stop him . . . he ran . . . we had a meeting place." She shook her head. "He never came."

Jenny and Max Wolf had left Germany days after it declared war in September '39. Originally from Dessau, Jenny's father had been arrested on Kristallnacht and sent to Dachau. Weeks of frantic inquiry led only to the discovery of his death. How he had died she did not know. Her mother, distraught and already emotionally unstable, took an overdose of sleeping compound. Jenny was orphaned at age 19, Max at 20.

Jenny had studied dance at a Berlin conservatory until the dismissal of her teacher and all Jewish students. Max was denied university admission. The final indignity: Nazis had appropriated their father's business. They had taken everything dear but for a small legacy. Max used it to purchase passports and French visas. They arrived in Paris in January; their visas were to expire in July.

"The Jewish Agency put us in an empty flat in the Marais . . . with other refugees . . . near here. I was a maid for a Jewish family."

"You were lucky . . . work is scarce."

She nodded. "But they left, and we ran out of money . . . don't know what to do. I am sick about Max—he's all I have."

"Why did he run if his visa was still valid?"

She shook her head. "It's forged. He got scared."

"I understand."

Jenny's sad eyes briefly met Rosa's as her head shook from side to side. "No, you don't."

"But I do," Rosa said. "Let me think." Jean . . . Agnes . . . Annette . . . Rosa exhausted her list of possibilities. "Can you stay at the flat? Is it safe?"

"I can . . . whether it's safe . . . ?" Her voice trailed away.

Then Rosa had an idea. "Are you a good dancer?"

Jenny's forehead creased with surprise. "Why?"

"Might be a job, a long shot. Are you a good dancer?" Rosa repeated.

"Yes . . . yes, I am. I wanted . . . want to be a dancer."

"I work in a cabaret. Meet me at Agnes Capri's tonight at 7:00." Rosa gave directions . . .

. . . Jenny was waiting in the foyer when Rosa arrived . . .

"Do I look like I run a Jewish refugee agency?" Agnes sighed, her smile wry. "I got enough potential trouble having you here . . . now you bring me a kid." Then, tapping her pen impatiently on the desk, she said, "What the hell! Let her audition." As Rosa left her office, Agnes added, "She better be good."

Later that evening, Agnes beckoned Rosa and said, "She's a little short, needs a haircut, but she's a good dancer . . . I'll use her in the chorus."

Max remained missing . . .

. . . In the wee hours of Friday in the second week of May, Rosa bid Agnes "Good night." She had spent all day with René, then worked past midnight on her feet, and she was bone tired. But stars lit the sky like a million pearls, and the fresh air infused her with newfound energy. Rather than take the Métro, she decided to walk

Rosa crossed Vieille du Temple onto Rue du Roi-de-Sicile. Cars were parked there as usual, but something seemed wrong, out of place. She hesitated, then saw a police car, engine running, double-parked in front of No. 32. Quickly she retraced her steps to the alley. Hiding at the corner of the building, she watched, remembering, "People have loose tongues . . . create problems. Some gentile neighbors may not be sympathetic . . ."

She felt queasy and chewed on her lip. A man, not in uniform, exited the building. The car door slammed, and he drove away. Rosa tasted blood. She had bitten her lip, though she felt nothing. After several deep breaths, she ran to the building and up the stairs. She found the door ajar, Jean in his old leather chair, looking small and ghostly pale. She closed the door. Jean took no notice of her presence—as if he were in a trance. She knelt beside him, speaking softly.

"Jean, I saw police—what . . . ?"

His head slowly lifted until his eyes found hers.

Rosa held his hand. "Jean . . . tell me."

Stirred from his reverie like a man roused from deep sleep, he spoke slowly. "Looking for a young woman . . . accent . . . coming, going . . . " He shook his head, still dazed. "Can't stay—not safe." His composure slowly returning, he forced a thin smile.

Rosa stared, her mind churning for an answer to a question not yet posed.

He shrugged. "Your papers won't hold up. I said you're my niece from Alsace to explain the accent. 'No problem,' the cop said. You have to report to the station with your papers. He was firm but sympathetic."

"Sympathetic . . . right! Straight to an internment camp for permanent residence." Trouble had finally found her. She would deal with it, but she worried about Jean. "I brought you trouble. Harboring an illegal is a crime . . . I'm sorry."

Jean got to his feet, scratched his neck, and looked around the room. "I'm going to miss this place." His eyes washed over his gallery of framed art, taking inventory. "Have to get those to an old friend for safekeeping—until this blows over."

Now in control, he immediately retrieved boxes from his cellar storeroom. Carefully, he began to wrap and pack the paintings . . . Coming to the Kertész rooftop photograph that Rosa loved, he said, "I want you to have this—to remember me."

"I don't need anything to remember you."

"Take it." His tone suggested she not argue, that she be gracious.

She stared at the photograph, then kissed him on the cheek. "Thank you!"

Jean called Catherine, waking her. "There was a little trouble. We're all right. We have to leave for a while." He listened to Catherine, then said he would call again later.

"Where do we go?" Jean asked, staring at Rosa, gears meshing.

A glint came into Rosa's eyes . . . "Annette," she muttered.

"Of course! First, we deliver these." Jean dialed a number and waited. "Marcel . . . Jean Friedman . . . I know it's late . . . this is important . . . "After several minutes back and forth, Jean replaced the receiver. "Now to Place de Vosges. Marcel's a friend and art dealer I trust. Not a Jew, actually not anything . . . he'll protect these for me."

"How do we deliver them?" Rosa asked.

Jean rubbed his chin, making a sound like cat claws on carpet. "Jacques's new car!" he exclaimed.

He called Catherine again and asked for Jacques. "Oui . . . oui . . . I know it's late. I'd like a spin in your new car . . . now . . . I know . . . *very* important . . . I'll explain." He disconnected.

Rosa stuffed her few clothes, a toothbrush, Sonny's handkerchief, the wedding picture, and letters into her satchel. She carried the Kertész wrapped in brown paper. In 15 minutes, the battered Peugeot double-parked in the spot the squad car had filled, waiting.

"Hope it runs better than it looks," Jean observed.

"Middle of the night—beggars can't be choosers." Jacques looked ragged, like a man roused from his bed. They quickly loaded the boxes into the boot, then drove into the still night. An hour later, Rosa and Jean sat in Annette's Montparnasse garret, explaining their visit.

"Stay as long as you like." Annette yawned.

"Thank you," Jean said.

Annette waved her hand, carelessly.

Rosa sighed. "Jean, because of me . . . "

He interrupted. "No! You're not to blame. I took you in because *I* wanted to—end of story. I could never have thrown you out like . . . like . . . "

"Dirty bathwater," Annette supplied, then yawned again.

Jean smiled and nodded.

Rosa wrapped her arms around him and hugged tight. "I love you!"

"We are in a spot of trouble," Jean noted over Rosa's shoulder.

"Yet again." Annette winked at Rosa.

Jean eyed them suspiciously, pursed his lips, then said, "Again?"

"Always on the move," Rosa replied quickly as she frowned at Annette. "Gypsy in me . . ."

. . . The next day—Friday, 10 May 1940—started sunny, though it was no ordinary day.

"I cannot survive underground," Jean sighed, "haven't thought this through."

"You don't have to—go home. I couldn't sleep, so I thought about it. I'll go missing. Tell the police I left Paris. There's no proof of your involvement."

"I lied about our family status," Jean countered.

Rosa frowned. "There is that."

"Let's get coffee and croissant," Annette suggested. "Before you both go off the rails."

They had just sat down in the café when a man rushed in. "It . . ." he gasped, catching his breath, then shouted, " . . . started!"

"What?" A man at the next table asked.

"Invasion . . . what else?" the man replied.

"How do you know?" asked another.

"Wireless—Germany invaded Holland and Belgium!"

Everyone spoke at once, several shouting. They ate quickly and returned to Annette's flat.

"I have to go to Catherine," Jean said.

"I'll go with you," Rosa said.

"Stay here, disappear," Annette insisted.

"It'll be chaos," Rosa pointed to the roofs of Paris, "and we're going to Catherine, not Jean's flat."

On the Métro, the gravity of the crisis struck, like a blow to the gut. That the expected had finally occurred made it no less jarring. People talked, if at all, in hushed voices. Sadness fought with anger and fear for primacy, each taking the lead but failing to hold on.

Visions of armies locked in battle, Sonny caught in the middle . . . Alain and Paul on the battlefield . . . Paris endangered. Rosa recoiled in a sudden spasm of fear. She had to do something, but what? Seek Jean's counsel . . . his reassurance. But he seemed as helpless as she.

Catherine met them at the door. Jacques's ear was to the wireless. A tinny voice was barely audible. Jacques raised a hand for quiet. René ran to his grandfather. Rosa waited, catching her breath. She needed a piece of Sonny, but the handkerchief was at Annette's.

"We're figuring out when to leave," Catherine said quickly.

"When to leave?" Rosa silently repeated the words, then, like a needle skipping on a record, again. Stunned by the suddenness, it's portent, she rubbed her temples, trying to catch up to events. René cried. She wanted to comfort him, but she was frozen, used up.

Catherine was talking. " . . . walking through Quai des Tuileries, pushing René. People stared across the river at Quai d'Orsay [the Foreign Ministry] . . . Police everywhere, directing traffic. Something was going on. I had to get home. Jacques was here. He'd closed the store."

Rosa felt nauseated again. Annette, her very best friend in the world—energetic, cute Annette with her dreams of greatness—would not abandon her. Tonight, she would talk to Agnes. An outline of a plan formed in her mind. She regained control.

News was sketchy, incomplete. German tanks and parachutists were moving into Holland and Belgium. The French Army and the British Expeditionary Force (BEF) crossed into Belgium to meet the Germans. Jean was sick with worry for Alain, somewhere along the Maginot Line.

The room was quiet, except for the crackle of the wireless, voices from the street below, and a distant siren. Rosa felt the room closing in on her. Suddenly panicking, she nearly ran out the door, but she seemed rooted to the floor, immobile. She sagged, muscles aching, under the burden of the previous year and a half—Oranienburg, Kristallnacht, separation from Sonny, now war. "Impossible," she muttered. Had she tipped over into the abyss? She felt trapped, sinking deeper. Her breath ragged and uneven, she waited—for what?

Jean faced her, his lips moving.

Rosa couldn't hear him.

"Are you all right?" he asked.

"What?" She was breathless, confused.

"Of course, you're not. None of us are. Catherine talks of leaving. I don't know what to do. What about you?"

She shook her head, unable to answer . . .

That evening, Agnes Capri's Cabaret overflowed with Parisians thumbing their noses at Hitler. Fortunately, Rosa was busy the moment she arrived at the club. Three shows—at 8:00, 10:00, and midnight—began with Agnes leading the crowd in a rousing "Marseillaise." For an hour and a half, the audience ate from her hands. Between songs she toasted: "Long live the Third Republic! Our leaders Reynaud . . . Gen. Gamelin! Our valiant British allies!"

The audience responded with fervent shouts, "Boche can go to hell!" and "Kick the snot out of the Germans!" Those present tried too hard, pressing every button to show how little the war would affect them. Rosa felt undercurrents of fear and anxiety cutting through the false gaiety. She was scared.

It was past 3 AM when Rosa left the club. Later in the day, there would be three more shows. She was glad the cabaret closed on Sundays and Mondays. Annette had wandered into the club after the final curtain to watch the last set. Rosa fell into a chair next to her, exhausted.

Agnes joined them, carrying a bottle of champagne. Antoine—or Tony, the guy with the trumpet—followed in her wake with four fluted glasses. Everyone else had gone. Agnes poured, then raised her glass.

"Vive la France!"

They drank.

Agnes looked from Annette to Rosa, "What are you going to do?" It was the second time Rosa had been asked that in less than a day.

Annette spoke first. "Keep acting."

Agnes nodded to Rosa. "And you?"

"Don't know." Rosa hesitated as the thought of unfolding tragedy to the north resurfaced.

"Your uncle?" Agnes winked. "Is he leaving?"

"He says no, not with his son at the front. But his daughter's family will leave."

"Don't know how long Tony and I will stay. While I'm here, you both have jobs. Otherwise . . ." she shrugged, " . . . the theater might continue, but the club—who knows? Drink up. See you tonight."

Reality soon pierced the collective mantle of denial. Censorship denied the public any real news. Newspaper stories informed the hungry readers only between the lines. Rumors, like rising floodwaters, ran rampant.

Shrill air-raid sirens disquieted the night and disturbed busy days.

Eyes reached heavenward; ears tuned to the drone of impending doom: Run to the nearest shelter. Wait for the "all clear." People complained of the infernal noise.

The French Army, according to rumors, was moving along the coast from Belgium to Holland with no resistance; in the Ardennes, small French tanks were performing well against bigger German tanks. The Dutch queen was fleeing to England. A German soldier had parachuted into Place de la Madeleine. So it went. Truth was an early fatality of war.

Jean returned to his flat, unmolested by police. He listened politely to neighbors and nodded, silently discounting each rumor. His paramount concern was the safety of Alain.

"It's getting worse: police arrest German émigrés and hound Communists. Never mind that I'm a Frenchman—it's time to go," Jacques told the family on the evening of 13 May. "Catherine and I leave tomorrow."

"Come with us?" Catherine pleaded to Jean. Then to Rosa, "Join us."

"Thank you, but," Rosa's head shook back and forth, "I can't, not yet."

Jean closed his eyes and ran fingers through thinning hair. They waited.

"Father . . . ?"

"I need time to think."

"There is no time! We leave early in the morning," Jacques said.

"What?" Jean, distracted, gazed into the distance, toward Alain.

Jacques repeated his statement.

"And the store?" Jean asked, avoiding an answer.

"Close . . . reopen when Boche are beaten," he answered, impatiently. "We need to know—both of you."

Jean looked from Jacques to Catherine. "I will telephone tonight."

Rosa walked with Jean to Rue du Roi de Sicile. Neither made a move to part. He pointed to a little bar on Rue des Écouffes. "Let's talk over wine."

They sat in the corner, Rosa's back to the door. Jean ordered a carafe.

"Too early to leave. The French Army will fight valiantly— Germans will never set foot in Paris." Jean spoke with conviction.

"And you?"

"Don't know." Rosa clung to the miracle that Sonny would work his way south and find her—as he had in that decrepit warehouse in Oranienburg, conjured like a coin from behind a child's ear. She smiled wanly.

"The army performs well, according to newspapers and the wireless. No bombs fall on Paris. Bookstalls remain open. Life goes on," Jean observed, optimistically. "People should be as afraid of leaving as of staying. Here they have jobs."

"The city's quiet, like a cemetery . . . " Rosa murmured.

"Except for the endless stream of cars bearing Belgian license plates. Mattress and birdcage strapped to the roof, a dog's head emerging from a basket. Comical, if not so terribly sad."

Rosa sipped while Jean drank.

"Abandon my beloved Paris? I'm torn."

"More beloved than your daughter, grandson?" Rosa countered.

"No," he answered without hesitation.

"Separated from Alain, now René and Catherine . . . months, maybe longer?"

Jean rubbed his eyes, his brow furled. "My world is imploding."

Rosa's world had already imploded. "Leaving home is hard."

"You wanted out. I don't."

"True," Rosa admitted.

"What will you do?" Jean asked.

"Sonny needs time to get here. I may be naïve, but that's what I believe."

"Take care."

"Don't worry about me—I land on my feet."

"I must worry about my adopted daughter."

"Niece," she corrected.

"What the hell's the difference?" He drank, staring at Rosa, until the carafe was empty, then muttered, "It's that kind of night."

"You'll regret not going."

He nodded. "You're right. Please . . . come with us." He spoke softly. "We're Jews, you're German—Nazis are coming!"

"You're a lovely man." She shook her head, tears on her cheeks. "The army will stop them—I'll take my chances . . . live with Annette. With chaos in Belgium, Sonny may be on his way."

Disbelief covered Jean's face. His mouth opened.

She raised a hand. "Don't say it. I have to believe . . . " Her voice trailed away.

He raised a hand in surrender. "Very well. I must pack a few things." He leaned back in he chair and nodded. "My art is safe. And you'll be with Annette."

"You'll be back soon—I'm sure of it."

He looked at her without speaking, eyes narrowed.

"What?"

"There are . . . things you haven't told me," Jean said.

Rosa's eyes widened, feigning surprise.

"Annette gave it away. And you're not a very good actress."

She sighed, then said, "We live with secrets—some deeper, more awful than others . . . they define us." Suddenly, she wanted to tell Jean about Sachsenhausen, Oranienburg, the Gestapo lieutenant, and his death. She did, weeping at the end of her story.

Jean, lips tightly closed, remained silent, shocked. At the end, he rested a consoling arm around Rosa. They sat silently, then left the bar

11

Paris, early Tuesday morning, 14 May 1940

At 6:20 the battered Peugeot stopped on Rue Cels in Montparnasse. Rosa waited on the curb. Annette watched from behind.

Rosa hugged René and whispered, "I will miss you."

"I love you." Catherine hugged Rosa.

Jacques kissed Rosa on both cheeks.

Jean stood awkwardly, not knowing what to do or say. Rosa wrapped her arms around him, resting her head on his shoulder. "I will miss you most of all."

"Be careful," Jean said.

"Promise you will telephone me at the club in three days." Rosa handed a card to Jean that read: "Agnes Capri Cabaret, reservations —Anjou 25.26."

Three days later, on Friday, 17 May, Rosa was summoned to the telephone at the club. Catherine was at the other end, calling from Saumur, a pretty town between the Loire and Thouet rivers, 320 kilometers from Paris. "Miss you! Have to be quick. There's a long queue. Petrol is scarce . . . lucky to have gotten this far. We're stuck here, at least for a while."

"I miss you. Any problems?" Rosa asked.

"Not for us. A German plane, flying low, dropped bombs—not on us, thank God." Catherine laughed nervously. "I love you. Jean and René send their love, Jacques too." The line went dead.

Rosa stared at the receiver in her hand, realizing the hole they had left in her life.

On Saturday, the blue sky over Paris seemed normal, but something was off key. Rosa ventured from the flat, refusing to remain cooped up. A crowd gathered at the corner. She investigated.

At the center a swarthy man held court.

"He's a Belgian Jew." Rosa heard a woman say.

" . . . parachute hunting . . ." Rosa pushed closer, " . . . first parachute's a dummy filled with dynamite, mustn't touch it." He waggled a finger in the air. "No . . . no . . . but the second, there's the prize. I saw a fellow strangle a German pilot with his bare hands."

The crowd, wide-eyed, uttered nary a sound while he spoke. When he finished, there was scattered applause. Several men slapped the fellow on the shoulder.

"Good news!" someone shouted.

At the club, a man told the story of a German pilot shot down, his right arm and leg broken. Still, he fired his machine gun, killing refugees until finally he was subdued, dead. Rosa was terrified. There were rumors of poison candy dropped at Gare d'Austerlitz, of Germans crossing the Meuse River at Sedan, of French deserters appearing in Paris suburbs, and of Germans breaking through the Meuse—none verified.

Then the *Herald-Tribune* reported 750,000 French troops encircled, or about to be, and blown-up bridges over the Somme River in northern France preventing the French Army from moving south. More news, none of it comforting, trickled from the front. Rosa's dream faded with each German advance and the diminished hope of Allied victory. Even Annette pondered leaving.

Increasing numbers of Belgian and French refugees passed through Paris.

Agnes Capri's Cabaret filled with Parisians, partying as if there were no tomorrow. Others, fearing the morrow, wanted out of Paris. Train stations were mobbed, tickets impossible to obtain, roads often impassable, petrol scarce for anyone so fortunate as to have an automobile. Intrepid souls bicycled or walked out of Paris. Much of the city was an empty glass, lying on its side, knocked over by the last patron hurrying out the door. Reports of lost battles, retreat, and the encroaching enemy created citywide anxiety, disbelief.

Rosa worked far into the night—in the kitchen, setting up the clubroom, seating guests, serving… the days quickly passed.

On Monday 27 May, Tony disclosed terrible news, "The wireless reports the BEF is being evacuated from Dunkirk."

Rosa had never heard of the place.

"I'm hopeless at geography," Agnes said.

"North, on the coast, at the Belgian border. England has abandoned us . . . Germans are also on the coast, 50 kilometers south of Dunkirk at Boulogne . . . Belgium fell."

The next day at Annette's flat, Rosa listened to Prime Minister Reynaud's speech to the nation. "Times are dark and grave!" he intoned, somberly urging France to continue the fight.

His words played over and over, a carrousel of desperation, gargoyles circling in a devilish funeral dirge, Nazi storm troopers astride. What did it mean? His saying it made it true. Despair burrowed deep, fueling a downward spiral.

If Belgium had capitulated, had Sonny escaped? . . . or been captured? Rosa ran from the room and fell onto the bed, crying. Grabbing a pillow, she hugged it tight, lying there until it was nearly time to leave for work. Tears dried, numbness supplanted fear, then her mind cleared. She would plan for her future. No one else would. She descended six flights into the early evening, resolving to be strong. No more tears.

On 3 June, a German air raid demolished houses on Rue Poussin in Auteuil, littering the 16th Arrondissement. Avenue de Versailles was littered with glass . . . the big block of flats near the bridge was badly damaged. There were shattered windows . . . people injured, some dead—thankfully none in Montparnasse.

It was late. Agnes, Tony, Annette, and Rosa, sober conspirators, sat around a table planning their next moves.

"We're driving out of Paris in a few hours," Agnes said.

Annette and Rosa exchanged worried glances.

"I told Frankie—he'll tell the others. He can keep the theater going. It's up to him."

Tony spread a map on the table and pointed to the coast. "We're heading to Bordeaux, then Marseilles, on to Algeria."

"You're both welcome to join us," Agnes offered.

"I . . . I . . . " Rosa stammered.

Annette jumped in. "I already talked to Frankie—I'm staying. The play must go on and all that."

"Your parents are in Bordeaux."

"Oui but no . . . thank you." Annette shook her head.

"Rosa?"

When she didn't answer, Agnes repeated, "Rosa . . . you coming?"

In the three short weeks since Rosa had spurned Jean's offer, the situation had deteriorated. There was no percentage in staying, especially for Rosa. She worried about Jenny, a young woman she barely knew, who would be alone without her Max.

"Jenny?" Rosa asked.

"I'm afraid she's on her own," Agnes said. "Sounds harsh, but I can't do more for her. We asked the two of you . . . now you."

Rosa felt her head nod, heard herself say, "I will . . . thank you." She had to take care of herself, as did Jenny. Still, she felt wretched.

"Be here at dawn," Tony said.

Rosa packed her few belongings, then talked with Annette until it was time to leave.

"I have to see Jenny, to tell her I'm leaving," Rosa said.

"No time—I'll tell her."

"The club's closed. She might not come."

"Tell me where she lives."

Rosa told her. Then she scribbled something on a piece of paper. "Give this to her. It's where my parents live. I hope to get there."

"I'll do my best," Annette promised.

They embraced, vowing to meet "after the craziness ends." Abandonment was a recurring theme for Rosa: Sonny, her parents, two girlfriends, Mina and Otto, Jean, Jenny, Annette . . .

. . . Rosa sat in the back seat of a comfortable sedan, gazing at the empty space Jenny could have occupied. No mattress strapped to the roof, no birdcage, and no barking dog. They carried a minimum of clothes and food for three to four days, bottled water, and a case of wine.

"One must be civilized, or all is lost," Agnes had sniffed. Rosa had money for several weeks—but after that?

Tony had consulted a road map and planned to use side roads, avoiding main arteries. Petrol would be a problem, though not until later. When they had settled in the car, Agnes informed Rosa, "You're my niece—better for all of us." She turned in her seat to face Rosa. "Name's spelled different, but that's all right. My father changed it; yours didn't."

Rosa nodded. "My family grows ever larger."

By first light, Tony had skirted Versailles, driving past the aerodrome then south. By midmorning they reached Chartres, out-skirting the city and its gothic cathedral, saving time and gasoline. The plan was to make Le Mans, 185 kilometers from Paris. Damaged and broken-down automobiles, wagons, and carts littered the roadside. Congestion slowed traffic to a snail's pace then the road opened, only to close again, like a flirting tease.

The amiable companions conversed—about Agnes's career as a singer and operator of club, theater, and cinema, about her rela-tionship with Tony, her music director and lover of 10 years, and about Tony's life before Agnes and the comfortable life they had left behind.

"Who doesn't have regrets? I'll come back," Agnes predicted.

"Of course you will, darling. Better than ever!"

"I'm weary of hearing myself talk." Agnes turned to Rosa: "How did you and Sonny meet?"

Rosa gave her the basics.

"Was it as bad in Germany as people say?" Tony asked.

"Worse!" Rosa told them of her father's arrest, about Sachsen-hausen and Oranienburg, omitting her abduction and the dead Nazi.

"How did you get out?" Agnes asked.

"Sonny and his friends ran a forged documents ring. Hundreds of Jews got out because of them. He got us out."

Agnes's eyebrows rose in surprise. She stared at Rosa, seeing her differently. For Rosa, it was a familiar response.

Tony glanced at her in the rearview mirror and said, "Your husband must be quite a guy . . . wish I knew him."

"A terrible break at the border," Agnes offered sympathetically.

Rosa stared silently out of the window at the French countryside.

"Police roadblock," Tony announced. They had reached the outskirts of Le Mans. "Checking papers."

Rosa passed her first test. The cop motioned for Tony to proceed, and he drove into Le Mans. Traffic was heavy, cars honked, angry men yelled through open windows at other drivers, children cried, and dogs barked. It seemed forever until they reached the hotel.

Cash, discreetly placed in the hotel clerk's palm, secured a room for the night. Food remained in the larder, and they ate well in the company of fellow Parisians. Several recognized Agnes and stopped to say hello and commiserate.

The group left early the next morning, after Tony found petrol, though at an exorbitant price. The driving day would end somewhere in the Loire Valley, the next day in Bordeaux. Two hours into the journey, Rosa heard a whining overheard. The sound grew louder.

"Plane!" Tony shouted, turning off the road onto the grassy verge.

Rumors of strafing warplanes had put them on edge, but they had seen none. Instinct sent Rosa to the floor. Within seconds, she heard a terrible explosion. The car rocked from side to side. Deathly quiet settled. No one spoke for long seconds.

"Everyone all right?" asked Tony.

First Agnes, then Rosa said, "Oui."

Several vehicles passed them slowly.

"Let's go," said Tony. Within a minute, they saw the wreckage of a mangled sedan flipped onto its side . . . two bodies in the ditch. Petrol dripped from under the car, pooling on the pavement. Tony stopped. The overpowering pungency of petrol fouled the air. The constant scraping of a slowly turning wheel, like a phonograph record after the song has ended, was the only sound.

"We've got to help," Rosa exclaimed. She ran from the car.

"Careful," Tony warned. "The car might explode." He followed Rosa.

Agnes watched from a distance. Cars passed.

The were two bodies, bent at unnatural angles . . . four arms and legs askew . . . a man's face covered with blood . . . the woman's face down . . . neither moved. Rosa felt ill.

The wreckage—mangled steel, broken glass, and a growing pool of petrol, smoldered. There were suitcases, ripped open, clothes strewn—the remains of two lives. Only minutes before, a man and a woman, full of life, had planned their future . . .

Tony peered inside the empty car. "Poor buggers didn't have a chance."

Rosa fought revulsion and knelt next to the dead woman. Rosa had killed a man, but this was different. Sonny had felt the Gestapo man's neck for a pulse. She placed two fingers on the woman's carotid artery—feeling nothing but fading warmth of her skin. Hair obscured the woman's face. Rosa's hand hovered. Then she pulled back the woman's hair to reveal smooth skin, undamaged by the bomb. One dark eye was dull, lifeless. Her lips formed a perpetual grimace. Rosa scanned the area and saw a purse. On the ground lay scattered remnants of a life—lipstick, handkerchief, billfold, keys, and a small leather case labeled Passeport—within reach.

Passeport? Passeport! Reflexively, Rosa grabbed the case, knowing she had to take it.

Tony described the scene to Agnes.

"I'm scared. Let's go," Agnes implored.

"Rosa," Tony called out. "Nothing we can do for them . . . Let's go."

"Sorry . . . so sorry . . . you don't need this anymore . . . " Rosa touched the dead woman's arm and muttered, "Thank you."

They drove in silence. Rosa mourned for the young couple. It might have been Sonny and her, Jenny and Max, Annette and Paul...

"Damn Germans," Agnes said in a lament.

Rosa had secreted the passport under her blouse to examine at later. She felt queasy, desperate to put distance between her and the dead woman, so young, lying in the ditch, her life torn . . .

That night in the small town of Parthenay, they found the last room in a small inn. Rosa stood in the shared bathroom down the hall, nervously fumbling with the strap closure on the leather case. Inside was the passport and identity card for Rita Daurat, 28 Rue Raffet, Auteuil, Paris.

Something familiar about the address, she frowned. Auteuil? Then she recalled that Auteuil . . . Rue Poussin . . . had been bombed. They had escaped, only to be found. Poor Rita and . . . what's his name.

Rosa held her breath, then gasped upon seeing the photo. A young woman with dark hair and dark eyes stared at her. Their ages were close enough, but Rosa didn't think she resembled Rita. Holding the photograph up to the mirror, she looked from her image to Rita's. Smaller eyes, closer set, nose straighter, lips not quite as full. Not dissimilar—still, she would need to have her photograph inserted.

Now to hide the documents, but where? Next to her body or . . . her gaze fell on the small suitcase, lying open, and to the lining. She set to work.

Part III

I am amaz'd, methinks, and lose my way
Among the thorns and dangers of this world.
—William Shakespeare

12

Northern France, mid-May 1940

Sonny grabbed Kid's arm and took a step away from the rifles, not yet raised against them. Other eyes remained skyward, on the slowly disappearing, showboating French flier. He would be gone in seconds. The panic of imminent death dissipated. Still, time was running out . . .

A command, unintelligible to Sonny, rang out. Soldiers stiffened. An officer appeared. Sonny closed his eyes, waiting for bullets to rip his flesh.

"No!" someone cried.

Sonny exhaled, felt his body relaxing, nearly losing control of his bowels.

"Stop!" boomed the command in English. A voice of authority penetrated the din, quieting everyone. The crowd parted like the Old Testament's Red Sea, forming a corridor. Angry eyes above a strong, jutting chin, set for confrontation, marched through. Taller than the others, the officer carried what looked to be a riding crop in one hand, his helmet in the other.

Scowling, he stopped, hands on his hips, and surveyed the situation. "Damn it!" he bellowed. "What the hell's going on? Who gave the order for a firing squad?" His face reddened to that of a ripe apple. "I came to fight Germans, not execute civilians!"

He shouted at the mayor, this time in French. "You overstep your authority. Explain yourself!"

The mayor puffed his chest, rose on tiptoe, and thrust his chin defiantly. But he was all artifice, and he stuttered, "Spies . . . all spies . . . sent to defeat France . . . " His voice trailed away.

The officer spoke slowly to the mayor, as if he were a child. "How

99

can they all be spies? Absurd, crazy! No firing squad today or any other day while I'm in charge."

Head bowed, the Frenchman silently endured the harangue.

The officer turned to the formerly condemned. "It's hard for all of us, but I can't do anything else for you . . . I'm sorry." He spoke to them in English, his face showing compassion, concern. "You are free to go, but you must report to the French garrison at Marquillies, several kilometers west. When you get there, your papers will be returned. Good luck."

Blank but grateful faces stared at him.

"Do you understand?"

No, of course, they didn't. Few knew English. After huddling with a junior officer, the man in charge ordered the Yiddish-speaking soldier to interpret. Relief was palpable. Sighs and nervous laughter greeted his words.

Again, Sonny had been pulled from the fire and wished well. How many more times would there be? Better to hear that than . . .

Their brush with martyrdom past, Sonny, Kid, and the others started the slow walk to Marquillies. Shuffling unsteadily, feeling a disheveled mess, Sonny was unaware of where he was. It was a strange sensation, of feeling like his entire body had fallen asleep, numb from head to toe.

"That British officer is my hero," Kid said.

Sonny's mind churned . . . He thought about the hero business. War ground up young men and spat out heroes. All across northern France were arms and legs bent and broken, eyes unseeing, mouths in grotesque grimace—their deaths a testament to human failure. People needed myth—heroes . . . But to die for nothing is to not have lived. And what the hell was a hero, anyway?

Finally he said to Kid, "It wasn't our time to die. Can't prepare for the moment anyway." His gait lengthened. He felt stronger.

Kid was quiet for a change. The sun beat on his face, his body pushed to the side of the road by rolling tanks then trucks. Cheating wasteful death was . . . ? He was weary of defending himself, having done nothing to deserve punishment. If there was a spy among them, he didn't know or care. To slaughter 40 innocents was obscene.

They reached the first houses of Marquillies in 30 minutes.

"What day is it?" Sonny finally spoke.

Kid frowned, his fingers moving as he counted off the days. "Ah . . . 23 May, maybe Thursday. I think."

Sonny nodded. "That all?"

They stopped on the side of the road, letting others walk ahead.

"I close my eyes, and that guy talking Yiddish has a long beard and, not a rifle." Kid sighed. "They weren't going to shoot us—right?" He sounded unsure.

Sonny shrugged. "Fooled me."

A row of houses divided by a narrow street led into town. Waiting in the road were a French officer and several of his staff: "You are my prisoners . . . in the custody of the French army." He spoke plainly but with authority. Thick through the chest, of average height, he had intelligent eyes that said, "I know what I'm doing. Don't cross me."

Sonny was suspicious though relieved by the absence of hostility.

"Maybe our luck has changed," Kid remarked.

"We'll see," Sonny replied laconically. His mind went blank, washed clean by a retreating wave, a pleasant change of pace.

A sergeant and several privates, using rifles as prods, assembled the group into two loose columns, collecting the remaining documents in a basket. Sonny and Kid's had ben taken earlier.

The headquarters was a handsome two-story structure in the center of town. Sonny sat cross-legged in the courtyard, Kid next to him. The soldiers took the marchers inside, one at a time.

"What's happening in there?" Kid asked.

"Hell! I don't know. We're all spies." Sonny's cynicism boiled over. "Let them play their damn games. It's their country."

"At least we're not up against the wall again."

"Not yet," Sonny sneered.

The group shrank. "Where did they go?" Sonny wondered aloud.

"Maybe they let them go," Kid said, far too optimistically.

Sonny snickered. Then they fell silent. A light breeze blew through the courtyard; a sparrow flitted from ledge to ledge; a yellow butterfly landed on a flowerpot. The tranquil scene was comforting. War had not yet visited this little town.

Kid's name was called, then five minutes later, Sonny's. He was escorted into the building. Rooms ran along each wall. A large marble staircase at the center rose to a second floor with balconies around the perimeter. He figured this was the city hall. He heard voices. He was lead silently up the stairs. They turned right at the top and walked to the other end. The soldier knocked softly on the door.

"Entrez."

The door closed behind him. Alone with the officer and another man, he smelled a faint scent of aftershave hanging in the air. The walls were bare. A big desk, with graceful, curving legs, and two chairs were the only furniture, centered in the room. On the desk were documents, money, jewelry. The officer sitting there smiled.

"Do you speak French?"

Sonny shook his head from side to side. "No."

The other man acted as interpreter. "My name is Captain Favier." He nodded his head slightly, a pleasant smile fixed on his pleasant face. "What is your name?" His eyes never left Sonny's.

"Sonny . . . I mean Sigmund Sander." Sonny looked at the captain when he answered.

Captain Favier broke eye contact to thumb through the documents. "No papers, but this . . . internment card?"

Sonny shook his head. "No."

"Empty your pockets. Place everything on the desk. Leave nothing in your pockets," he warned. "You would regret it."

Sonny took out his last francs and Rosa's letter and placed them on the desk. Both men stared at the paltry sum, then the captain extended his arms toward Sonny, his palms up in the universal gesture "Is that all?"

Sonny nodded. "That is all."

"Unfortunate," the captain said under his breath. He shook his head sadly, then opened the envelope and took out the letter. Nothing else was in the envelope, so he returned the letter to Sonny.

Favier wrote in a ledger and without looking up said, "Go."

"Bastard fleeced us good," Kid complained.

"Pawns in a game of greed and cynicism, nothing but clothes on our backs and blood in our veins. We're better off left to chance than to have our future in his hands." Sonny's anger seethed. "Thought it couldn't get worse. Hell, forget it—one day at a time."

A soldier gestured with his rifle for them to follow.

"Line us up . . . ?" Kid sounded scared.

They walked for 10 minutes to an old schoolhouse. The soldier pointed, "Your home."

Sonny, Kid, and three others were ordered into a room with 24 Frenchmen. There was barely enough room for them to sit—another five seemed impossible. One window looked out over a playground where, only weeks before, children had skipped and laughed. Body odor and urine perfumed the air. Thankfully, the circulation was enough to keep them from fainting. They staggered tentatively into the room, smiling sheepishly.

A staccato "Quiet!" quelled groans of protest. The guard locked the door behind him. An uncomfortable silence ensued. Hostility pulsed through the room. Forty-eight eyes dissected the new arrivals in a thorough going-over. The new men huddled in a corner on the floor. Knees pulled to their chests, they avoided eye contact, trying to disappear for fear of antagonizing their cellmates.

"Poor sods." Kid interpreted.

The tension broke. Several of the men produced stale bread and bits of fruit and shared it with the newcomers. "Who are you . . . where did you come from . . . what news of the war?" The questions fired.

Kid summarized his and Sonny's travels and travails. Then he asked the other three for their stories and translated. When he had finished, Kid asked, "What brought you here as guests of the good captain?" His hand swept the room.

Some laughed.

"Good captain, my ass," hissed a short man, with small, round, glasses and a high forehead. "He loots from all who pass his way, probably sharing with his two lieutenants and the high-ranking NCOs. There's enough to go around."

"You're Frenchmen—why prisoners? What have you done?" Kid asked.

"Nothing. We're Communists," said a fellow with a gravely voice. "They've wanted to get rid of us for a long time. After the Nazi–Soviet pact, they seized the opportunity to outlaw the party." He spat on the wall in disgust.

"Everyone knew war was coming . . . The Soviets pulled a fast one on us," a sad voice said.

"We're agitators, and we want more. The right saw an opening and got rid of us. We could be fighting the Boche, but instead we're under arrest."

Angry silence set in.

"Ask him whether women were arrested," Sonny said to Kid.

"Oui . . . refugees like you. See! Communism works. This jail doesn't discriminate—not only Jews are here." He laughed. "Women are in another part of the building. We see them whenever they let us out of this hole."

Another voice: "Not content with money and jewelry, Favier took a pretty young thing. Spoils of war, no doubt his rationale. She's German, can't be older than 19—a refugee like you, probably a Jew—goes everywhere with him. Handpicked her as his," he paused, "concubine."

An angry voice: "Whore."

"She doesn't have the freedom to say no," said another.

"Probably enjoys her privileges, eating better than us," the angry voice offered.

"Captain can spend the night with me," said a big, bearded fellow, arching his eyebrows suggestively, pursing his lips.

"Pierre, we should pay the captain to spend the night with you." They laughed.

13

Northern France, end of May 1940

Caged and cramped, Sonny felt tested by the cacophonous chorus of snoring men, others talking and shouting in their sleep, by the knee or elbow against his body that made his first night nearly impossible.

At sunrise they were ordered into the courtyard. Their heads were shaved, beards shorn as well—baldness was the badge of captivity. It was a minor humiliation after what Sonny had experienced previously, but he feared indefinite incarceration.

Food was the next concern. Meals were irregular—twice a day, when they were lucky. Scraps from the French mess in the courtyard delivered in a bucket—a potato, maybe a bit of meat, a slice of bread. There were plates and spoons but no knives or forks—too dangerous.

Nearly all of May drained from the calendar, which meant Sonny and Kid had been there a week. The monotony of prison life had barely set in. On the seventh night, before Sonny completed his troubled journey to the edge of sleep, a blast obliterated the quiet. It sounded nearby.

Jarred awake, Sonny raised his antennae. A second blast shook the building, shattering the window, sending shards onto frightened men. The fear of being trapped under the collapsed building prompted their restless stirring. Distant blasts continued.

"Help! Let us out," some shouted.

The crash of artillery subsided, quiet returned, and the men calmed. They brushed the glass away. Nobody had been injured. Morning soon arrived.

"Get the prisoners into the yard," ordered the captain. A truck arrived, women corralled onto the back before it drove off. Favier was all military discipline and cold determination, his false smile and easy manner conspicuously absent. He held up his hands for quiet.

"German artillery disrupted our night. We leave presently. I warn you it will be arduous and difficult. Don't ask questions. I cannot answer them." He saluted and left his subordinates to organize the prisoners, who never saw Captain Favier again.

Sonny leaned against a building, scanning the courtyard. His gaze passed over an old man, bent and crooked. He stood with effort in a corner of the yard, weakened by his incarceration, his face pale and pasty. Loose skin hung from his throat. Small half-moon bags clung below his dull, yellowed eyes, filled with melancholy and a millennia of misery. He was a grandfather separated from family, nearing the end. Sonny started toward the old man to help. A rifle butt in his side intercepted him.

"Ah," Sonny groaned and stopped. His eyes remained on the old man. The rheumy eyes seemed to say, "Forget me—I'm dead."

Two guards, on either side of the old man, walked him slowly from the yard, out of sight. An eerie silence ensued. Had the others felt that, too?

Sonny heard a rifle shot, like a blow to his chest, and recoiled. His knees buckled. Witness to an execution impersonal and cruel, he'd seen it all but the final act. Message delivered: no stragglers.

Everyone heard the shot. "What . . . who?" Kid asked, not having seen the old man, and Sonny explained.

The old man's image haunted him. In a surreal landscape of leaf-less trees and faceless men with rifles, his eyes burned like coals. "Old man, I tried. Please know that," Sonny cried in silent torment.

Word quickly spread of the old man's fate. Scared and intimidated, the prisoners formed two columns—with guards at front and rear. A barrel-chested sergeant in a white turban commanded these colonial troops, black-skinned Moroccans. He had small, squinting, hard eyes, and a bushy mustache beneath a big Gallic nose. He was both ominous and ridiculous—a hippopotamus in a funny hat.

The Goumiers of the North African colonial regiment were unique in Europe. Silent and erect, they possessed an intimidating glower that became their prisoners' nightmare. Unable or unwilling to speak French, they administered the sergeant's orders with callous discipline.

"Move quickly, quickly," the sergeant ordered, "or risk a Goumier baton."

Water was scarce, parched throats and thirst their constant companions. Speech was difficult, but speaking was forbidden anyway. The Goumiers ladled limited water rations directly into their wards' mouths. Their progress was painful. Blisters sprouted like mushrooms in damp soil from their endless walking in disintegrating shoes. Diesel engines whined, and men shouted. The noise was incessant. Civilians walked, pulled carts, or filled automobiles jockeying for position. Military convoys slowly passed, pushing the walkers to the side of the road. Forlorn and dispirited soldiers, many wounded, some seriously, obviously were in retreat. Sonny searched for signs of where they were going, but he learned nothing.

They were ordered to march in rough columns, without regard for sick or elderly. Laggards would be shot. Only the urge to survive kept them moving—blisters, hunger, thirst, and weakness be damned!

Along the way, more unfortunates swelled the group to more than 50. Sonny plotted, dreaming of escaping south to Paris and Rosa at 32 Rue du Roi de Sicile or to the coast.

The sun beat them down, draining moisture from their bodies until they were bone dry. Heavy coats were shed on the roadside. Nighttime made them wish they had kept them. Occasionally given an army ration of rice, they crouched by the side of the road, eating from shared tins.

An old man in a torn, black overcoat too heavy for May's warmth, fell behind, losing ground. He tripped. Kid caught him, his face contorted with exhaustion. His head shook as he gasped for air. "No more," he murmured.

"Get up. You've got to move! You can do it," A companion exhorted.

Driven past exhaustion, he lost the will to live; it had evaporated like a puddle in the midday sun. Sagging to his knees, he waited for the *coup de grace*—he was ready to die.

A cruel nod from the turbaned sergeant gave the order; then he spat. They watched in horror. With a face as blank as his victim's, the Goumier shot the old man where he knelt, leaving his body to decompose. No tears were shed, no prayer said. The group shuffled away, eyes to the ground, one foot in front of the other, shoulders sagging. Another elder's death, a monstrous, murderous act infused to the landscape, familiar as the trees and sun.

Unable to protect the weak, Sonny was wracked by guilt, and he turned inward, away from the others. He felt drained and useless, his mind a muddle. All that was left for him was to bide his time, look for a crack, and then run—alone or with Kid.

They walked another hour when a woman, one of a group that had joined them en route, tripped and fell. She clutched her painful ankle, unable to stand.

The group stopped, holding its collective breath. A young woman, apparently her daughter, fell to her knees, comforting her mother. Locked in an embrace, both wept—one no longer able to walk, the other refusing to do so. Abandoning her mother was out of the question—that would be the worst of crimes.

"Move! Float on the air if you can," Sonny silently begged.

Eyes locked on the terrible tableau.

"Come . . . come, you can't help her. Save yourself," said one of her group, placing a hand on her shoulder. "Remember the old man."

She did not stir and would not hear. She had retreated to another world.

Others pleaded: "Let us help them."

Their words were German, incomprehensible to the sergeant. Kid made their case in French, convincingly, saying all the right words, conveying the proper sympathy. Who would not feel moved?

The sergeant's eyes narrowed as he spoke. "They might be spies—all of you spies. You are my prisoners. I have orders. I would shoot all of you should the order be given. It's not my doing—dirty Boche started another war!" Spittle flew from his sneering lips.

Riveted to the awful scene, Sonny's instinct was to intervene. He watched the faces of the Moroccans nearest the mother and daughter. Goumier eyes darted side to side, unsure, as if to say, "These are women."

Maybe . . . Time stopped—everyone waited. Surely the sergeant would spare the two innocents. Nothing mattered but a mother's embrace—he had to see that. An older man, still vigorous, leaned over mother and daughter, talking to them, imploring the daughter to come along.

"Move," the sergeant screamed, then spat again.

The group hesitated. Several Moroccans raised batons. The group moved. All eyes were glued to the women.

Seconds ticked. Sonny was paralyzed. A Goumier pushed him hard, and he nearly fell. Birds chirped in a nearby tree. Sunlight reflected off the leaves. A hot breeze brushed his face. Then it became still. Sonny turned toward the women.

Kid caught his arm and whispered, "No."

The end came quickly—two rifle reports. Sonny's head jerked spasmodically, tears stinging his eyes. He had wanted to help lift them to their feet, provide comfort to the mother, get them moving, keep them alive. He wanted to rip the rifle from the murderer's hands, turn it against him. His frustration and anger were unbearable.

"Alle, alle," broke through his rage.

The old lady sat on one leg, with the other splayed. Pain creased her face with the terrible hand life had dealt. Deep circles ringed the eyes unable to shed more tears. Her mouth hung slack. She panted. A daughter's arms enclosed her mother. Nothing else in the world mattered. The mother's lips moved, but Sonny could not hear.

"Leave. Save yourself. You have a future, a husband to meet and marry, children to raise, memories to build," he imagined the mother saying.

Why hadn't she gone? Sonny would be wracked forever by the question.

Moving slowly, all eyes were on the two figures, arms entwined, embracing in a final act of love, slumped in death on the side of a road somewhere in France. It was a sight so wrenching, so diabolically cruel . . .

Sonny memorized his captors' dark faces, thick lips, and broad noses, some lighter, with Caucasian features. They melted into one African image, impossible to identify. Kill the sergeant, that one monstrous face—hard, squinty eyes, bushy mustache, big nose— etched like a marble sculpture onto his memory. The monster must die! He was caught in a netherworld of banal evil, where a stumble or false move could mean a bullet to the head. Defensively, Sonny shut down his emotions, and indifference settled in. His subconscious took control, and he backed off, black fog squeezing out his humanity.

At nightfall they stopped at an abandoned hospital. Men were locked in one big room, women in another, until morning. Goumiers guarded the doors so that no one might wander into the dark. The inmates talked in hushed voices in the crowded room, searching for a lifeline, for reassurance. They encouraged their mates to be strong and fight the demons.

"Don't let the beasts steal your soul."

"Surely, the end must be in sight," said another.

"We're headed for the coast," said Alon, one of the French Communists. "Probably Dunkirk."

"How do you know?" Kid asked.

"Saw the sign for Bailleul, 40 kilometers, give or take, from Dunkirk. Soldiers are headed that way."

"We'll be trapped," Sonny murmured.

"And pushed into the sea," Kid expanded on the possibility.

"We can still walk, they haven't shot us, there's hope," said the short Communist with the round glasses and high forehead.

Agitated, they talked at once. Hope appeared, clearing space through the fog of despair. They were alive and would go on.

At sunrise there was pounding on the door. "Alle . . . alle!"

The men groaned and cursed.

The soles of Sonny's boots had worn away, exposing bruised and battered feet to the rough road. The black ruptures oozed red, like overripe tomatoes. Every step burned. He ignored the pain and pushed on. He had seen French mercy and thought little of it.

They started on a road they thought led to Dunkirk. British troops gave curious glances as they passed. A group of French soldiers, enlisted men, apparently separated from their units, did not pass. Nobody seemed to be in command. They loitered curiously, hostility rising, circling the refugees. Then one of them asked, "What's with the funny hat and the black fellows?"

The sergeant raised his rifle, apparently fed up with the rabble. This cued the Goumiers. They raised their rifles too, ready to be part of the action. "North Africa Corps and if you don't like it . . . "

"Don't want no trouble. We're headed for Dunkirk. Brit troops were ordered there," one said. The stragglers backed away, hands outstretched in peace.

"Dunkirk," Sonny muttered.

The sergeant waited several minutes before giving the order to move.

After half an hour, Sonny heard a faint buzzing and swatted at invisible insects. Within seconds, however, the volume increased, and explosions came in quick succession—boom . . . boom! Sonny ran into the ditch at the side of the road just ahead of another explosion. Face down, hands covering his head, he felt the debris raining down on him. Silence.

Voices pleading for help broke the deadly stillness. Kid was not in the ditch.

"Kid!" Sonny said urgently. He scanned the bodies on the road. Kid lay next to one of the French Communists. Sonny ran to him, then froze at the sight of a bloody gash on the side of Kid's head. He grabbed his arm and shook it.

"Kid . . . *Kid* . . . We've got to run."

No response. Sonny felt light-headed, his throat constricted. He fought the urge to vomit, taking in air in deep gulps. He stared at his friend and companion, waiting for him to pop up and ask, "Now what?" Kid just lay there immobile, silent, with no cutting comment, no question. He wasn't supposed to die. "Damn it, Kid!"

Sonny turned to the voices pleading for help. Passing British soldiers slowed. Some helped survivors to their feet. Most kept going. Several prisoners ran away, but some stayed, helping the wounded. Others, like Kid, were dead. The Goumiers had taken the brunt of the explosion, and their bodies littered the ground, black faces streaked crimson in death. Several stirred, still alive.

Then Sonny saw the turban, with no sergeant beneath. He searched among the bodies until he saw the sergeant face down, half on the road, half in the ditch. Sonny prodded him with his foot then spat on his corpse.

A girl stood staring nearby. Sonny had seen her before, part of a small group that had joined them along the way. He looked back at Kid's inert body, soul gone. He turned back to the girl. They seemed to be the only two standing.

She looked away and pointed. "My father . . ."

Sonny followed her finger to a human form. He walked to the body, knelt, and looked back at her. She covered her mouth with her hands and nodded. An anguished sound escaped her lips.

He searched for a pulse, then said, "I'm sorry."

She fell on top of her father and cried.

He knelt beside her. "I lost a good friend," he faltered. "We have to take care of ourselves. Bombs scare me."

She ignored him. He took her hand, but she pulled it away: "I won't leave him like this. Can you leave your friend on the road to rot?"

Now Sonny felt guilty for abandoning Kid. Fear and despair had turned him inward, isolated and alone, and selfish. He knew that was a lame excuse. Because others lost their humanity did not mean he must lose his. Sonny looked at the young woman. She was older than he thought, though still young, in her early twenties. Anguish distorted her features.

"No, we can't." But how to bury her father and Kid? An idea came, and he walked along the ditch.

"Where are you going?"

"Wait. I'll be back." He walked toward an abandoned farmhouse and found a shed. Inside were a wheelbarrow and shovel. He returned with both. "We'll lay your father and Kid on this and find a place . . . "

She nodded.

"Can you help my friend?" She asked several passing British soldiers in perfect English with only a slight German accent.

One helped Sonny load the bodies.

"Thank you."

Two dead men on a wheelbarrow, arms and legs dangling over the side, made for a strange sight. The heavy load listed dangerously, but Sonny pushed it to the edge of the field without incident. The earth was soft, and within minutes two shallow graves became real.

Kid and the young woman's father, arms crossed on their chests, looked dignified in death. His grief fighting for space with anger, made Sonny's thoughts a jumble. "Unlucky Kid," he murmured as he shoveled dirt onto the body.

The young woman fell to her knees and sobbed, heaving painful wails—she might never find peace. Sonny averted his eyes, but his ears could not escape the torment.

Then she stopped crying and shoveled dirt until her father's body disappeared. Her lips moved as she recited in Hebrew the Mourner's

Kaddish. Sonny followed her lead.

Then she faced him. "Thank you. We can leave."

He nodded. "I'm Sonny. What's your name?"

"Rebecca." Her voice was soft and distant.

"I'm sorry about your father."

"And your friend," she replied.

Sonny walked into the woods behind the farm. She followed.

14

Northern France, end of May 1940

The fear of capture and his anguish over Kid's death kept Sonny going. He ignored blisters, aching joints, parched throat, hunger, as they traversed the unforgiving ground. After 10 or 15 minutes, he fell to the ground. One foot bled and hurt like hell; the other merely ached.

Between deep breaths, Sonny stared at his foot and silently cursed. "You all right?" he asked Rebecca.

"No." She sat on the ground, arms hugging bent legs, head resting on her knees.

Sonny took off his shirt, ripped the sleeve, and wrapped his foot with it. He stood and put weight on it. "Let's go."

She looked up. "Where?" Her voice was unsure.

"Dunkirk."

"Where is that?"

"On the coast," Sonny answered. "One of the men saw a sign."

"Which direction?"

Irritated, he clenched his jaw to keep from speaking. Kid was dead, her father was dead, and now he had a young woman to take care of. He rubbed his forehead. Finally, he said, "We find a road and follow it."

"Father said the army was retreating. The Germans are pushing the French and the British to the sea."

"He was a smart man."

"He . . . " she blinked back tears, " . . . was a teacher."

"And your mother?"

She shook her head. "Died long ago."

"Where are you from?"

"Near Vienna. We were in Brussels since . . . July last year."

"I was in Antwerp with my wife, but we were separated. She is in Paris—or was." Sonny rested a comforting hand on her shoulder. "We'll make it." He stopped short of a promise.

She nodded but said nothing.

"First, we figure out where we are."

She laughed softly but bit it off. In that brief moment her gaunt face was attractive in a girlish way. Her eyes cleared, appeared bigger. Her short hair was light brown.

Sonny smiled and looked at the sun, high in the sky. "The sun is no guide. Let's find some Brits."

They walked through small farms separated by fields and stands of trees. The sound of trucks and voices grew louder. Beyond a line of trees was a road clogged with soldiers and vehicles, impossible to avoid. There were refugees in smaller numbers.

"It's safer with them." Sonny pointed to a column of British soldiers. Silently, they fell in behind.

Several trucks pulling huge artillery guns pushed soldiers and civilians to the side of the road. When the noise and dust cleared, Rebecca asked, "Why? My father constantly asked that question."

"The brutality is beyond my understanding. Shooting an old man, then a mother and daughter." Sonny shook his head, wearily. "The image, I can't shake it . . . then Kid . . . your father . . . "

"Kid was your friend's name?"

"His real name was Thomas Minsk. I call . . . called him Kid. He was young like you. I miss him."

"What kind of name is Sonny?"

"My name since I was young."

"What is your real name?"

He hesitated then answered, "Sigmund Landauer."

"I agree—Sonny is better."

He laughed.

"What happened to your wife?"

He told her about Mons and the internment camp. "Her letter got to me. I have her address in Paris, for all the good it does me."

"I'm sorry."

Sonny nodded. "What was your father's name?"

"Ernst."

"And your second name?"

"Sontag."

"Glad to meet you . . . Rebecca Sontag." He smiled.

She returned his smile weakly. A girlish innocence, surely threatened, surfaced.

After an hour they came upon a platoon of battle-weary British infantry on the side of the road eating lunch. Rebecca and Sonny stiffened, their experience with the French too recent, too raw.

A young soldier sitting cross-legged, watching them. "You two look terrible. Where you from?"

"Belgium," Sonny answered before she could say anything.

The soldier nodded as if he understood. "We come from there." He reached into his rucksack and pulled out several cans. He opened them. "Here . . . " holding them out, " . . . come get 'em."

"You are very kind," Rebecca said.

The soldier shrugged. "Got more than we need. We're going home."

"Home?" Sonny asked, confused.

"Soon as we get to Dunkirk." Relief pushed fatigue from the young soldier's face, and he smiled.

"Where is Dunkirk?" Rebecca asked.

The soldier pointed in the direction they were headed. "Not far."

"So that's it," Sonny said between mouthfuls of rations. "They're leaving."

"How?"

"Boats—only one way across the channel."

"Can we go with them?" she asked hopefully.

Sonny and Rebecca stayed close to their benefactor and got another meal and water. A sign said they were near a town named Poperinge. Though how far it was to Dunkirk remained unknown. At nightfall, the soldiers found a barn in which to sleep. Rebecca and Sonny picked a spot outside under an overhang. The same young soldier brought Rebecca a blanket.

"He likes you."

"Why would he like me?"

Sonny smiled. "You're a girl. He's a soldier."

"I'm a woman," she protested. "I'm 21 years old."

"Sorry."

"Never mind. It's not important . . . nothing's important anymore."

"Don't fall into the trap," Sonny scolded. "I nearly did. Everyone's trying to stay alive. Don't give up. That's important."

"Everyone's dead."

"I'm not, the young soldier isn't, and you're not."

She didn't respond.

"Your English is good." Sonny changed the subject.

"I learned it in school, and my father," she hesitated, "spoke English."

"I know little," he said, then sighed from exhaustion.

Sleep came easily. Rebecca curled up under the blanket and fell against Sonny. Her body felt warm . . .

Pop . . . pop . . . They were awakened by the sound of gunfire. The platoon of soldiers ran from the barn, leaving them alone.

"That's too close," Sonny was scared. "Let's get out of here!"

They ran into darkness. A half moon played peek-a-boo from behind clouds, dimly illuminating the landscape. The shooting stopped, leaving it quiet again.

Sonny stopped, catching his breath. "This is crazy. We might be running the wrong way. Let's find a place to hide in until dawn."

"There," Rebecca pointed to a shape in the near distance.

"Looks like an abandoned cottage."

Inside, Sonny rummaged for food, finding none. But there was a working well. They drank until they were full. It was quiet.

Sonny looked longingly at the bed, mentally and physically exhausted from the constant walking, lack of sleep, and the horrors of the days before. He shook his head. "Can't lay down. I'll never wake up."

They sat on the floor, backs against the wall, Rebecca next to him. He closed his eyes. They had barely settled when rifle fire sent them flat to the floor.

"Way too close," Sonny whispered.

"Who?"

"Hard to know . . . " Sonny started then stopped, interrupted by gunfire from both directions. "Getting closer." Then the window above their heads shattered, sending shards of glass upon them. Rebecca was shaking and began to whimper.

"You hurt?" Sonny shook off the glass.

"No."

"First shot came from behind," he offered after lengthy consideration, though only seconds passed. "So, which way?" He asked, not expecting an answer.

"I . . . I don't know." Her voice cracked with fear.

Sonny rubbed his chin. "That broken window must be from a German bullet. Don't ask how I know. So, we go that way." He pointed.

She did not argue. That way did not have a door, so they climbed out a window. They ran, crouching, into the woods for cover. At the edge of an opening they saw the faint outline of another house and several outbuildings.

"Over there." Sonny pointed.

They ran behind a big shed and fell into a depression beyond it. Catching their breath, they looked into the faces of three soldiers. Instinctively, Sonny raised his hands in surrender. Rebecca wrapped her arms around Sonny, trying to disappear.

"What the hell?" The voice spoke in clear English.

"Refugees," Sonny managed to say.

"Thank God!" Rebecca murmured.

"Stay out of our way," the same voice said.

The other two had not spoken.

"Jameson," the same voice said, "to the left, MacTavish to the right. I'll stay here. Don't shoot until you can hit something, and for God's sake, stay alive."

"Second that," one of them chuckled.

"Lieutenant, what about these two?" asked the third voice.

"You German soldiers? She doesn't look it."

Sonny shook his head vigorously. "No!"

"Okay," he said to Sonny. Then to Jameson and MacTavish, "Go—take care."

"Sir." They melted into the night.

To Sonny and Rebecca: "Don't talk, don't move—stay out of my way."

Sonny sensed the voice was that of a young man.

Maddening silence ensued. An animal scurried past in the dark. Sonny's heart pounded against his chest. He sat so still, his muscles tightly coiled like a spring straining to snap. Half an hour or more they waited, for the enemy to make a move.

"Where you from?" the lieutenant asked.

Though startled, Sonny understood. "Ah . . . Berlin."

"Near Vienna," Rebecca whispered.

More silence.

"Was it as bad as they say?"

"For Jews, anti-Fascists, Communists . . . very bad," Rebecca answered.

He nodded, but it was too dark to read his face. Gunshots interrupted their reverie. Sonny jumped as if stung. The peaceful interlude had ended. Rifle raised, the lieutenant scanned for the enemy. Sonny sensed the shots came from the right—MacTavish's position. Silence returned. Tension spiked; it was a familiar feeling, imprinted on Sonny by previous encounters. Strangely that brought him a measure of control for the first time since Antwerp.

Shots from the right—MacTavish returning fire? More shots . . . closer . . . but from the left.

"Ah!"

The lieutenant slumped. His rifle clattered to the ground. Sonny leaned over him. "Where hit?"

"Shoulder."

Sonny looked at the rifle, then picked it up. It was heavy, like the Gestapo sentry's rifle he had fired in Aachen, but they looked the same to him. He pointed the rifle toward the action and rested the stock against his shoulder.

"Pull...trigger...be careful..." The lieutenant's voice was small and far away.

Sonny heard but didn't answer. He was sweating. The pulse in his neck slowed. Rebecca curled into a ball. The lieutenant moaned softly.

Sonny surveyed the area ahead, keeping low. Until now he had paid scant attention to the terrain, other than running from trees to shed. Nighttime was rarely totally dark, and this was no exception. He calculated the house to be 20 meters ahead—open space to the right and the woods from where he had come, to the left a field in which it would be more difficult to hide. His money, had he any, would be on an attack from the right.

He pressed his cheek against the stock . . . It felt cool. He closed his left eye . . . aimed down the barrel to the sight . . . tasted sweat on his upper lip . . . felt his heart pounding. Slowly, he scanned the gap between the house and the trees, back and forth. Nothing. He waited. Emil had taught him to let the enemy come to him, to be patient.

Sonny's senses felt suddenly acute. There were shadows but no movement, no sound—nothing. No enemy to shoot, yet.

"Can you . . . shoot?" The lieutenant's voice was husky, nearly inaudible.

"Ja," Sonny answered tersely, not wanting to be distracted.

A rustling sound came from the right. Stalking . . . stop . . . start . . . rifle fire! Sonny ducked. Bullets tore into the shed. Splinters flew.

"Ouch!" Rebecca blurted.

Sonny rose into position, rifle aimed in the direction he thought the shots came from. "Are you hurt?" he asked.

"My arm . . . blood," Rebecca replied.

"Can you move it?"

"Think so."

"Stay calm. I'll get you out of this," Sonny wanted to believe it himself. He heard the lieutenant speak unintelligibly, probably in shock. Sonny held the rifle as Emil had taught him. "Stay calm . . . take a deep breath . . . wait 'til it's time," he mumbled.

He wiped his brow with the palm of his hand to keep the sweat from his eyes, drew saliva onto his tongue, licked his lips...and waited. Seconds ticked. Life crawled on its belly. His breathing steady, his finger tightening on the trigger.

A twig snapped! His ears pricked to the sound. Footfalls? One . . . no, two Germans hunting. He felt them getting closer. He scanned the area again.

Brilliant muzzle flash—burst of gunfire from the right! Vague outlines, moving fast . . . two crouching forms running toward him, rifles pointed . . . in the clearing.

Sonny saw them clearly, silhouetted against the opening sky. Wanting to kill him . . . Rebecca . . . the lieutenant . . .

Sonny slowly moved the barrel until he found the first soldier's chest . . . 20 meters . . . 15 . . . 10 . . .

Gripping the rifle, he held his aim steady on the target, moving straight toward him. Now! Sonny slowly squeezed the trigger. Boom! It was a deafening sound. His shoulder hurt from the recoil. One German fell, face forward. The second soldier slowed, glancing at his fallen comrade. Sonny aimed, fired again, then squeezed a third round. His ears rang. The second soldier fell. Neither moved.

"Get 'em?" the lieutenant groaned.

Sonny stared at the two motionless bodies on the ground, fewer than 10 meters away.

"Ja . . ." he finally answered.

Rebecca was silent, still curled into a ball.

MacTavish appeared, unhurt. "Lieutenant, what the hell?" Sonny told them. Jameson came. MacTavish told him.

"You're a bloody hero!" Jameson slapped Sonny on the shoulder.

Sonny smiled. Then he turned to Rebecca, "How you doing?"

"I think it's a scratch."

"Get both of you to First Aid," MacTavish said.

Jameson and MacTavish clustered around the lieutenant. One of them had a torch. They surveyed his injury. Lieut. Michael Shannon was fading from consciousness. His face was etched in pain, his shirt wet with blood.

"Very slick . . . you've done that before," the lieutenant said.

"Friend teach me," Sonny said in his broken English.

"Tell me later."

He coughed. "Thanks . . . ." he managed a faint smile.

"That was slick," said one of the soldiers. Sonny later learned it was MacTavish.

The other said, "Right! You're 'Slick' from now on."

They laughed.

"No, Sonny."

"Sonny?" asked the other soldier.

"I'm Sonny . . ."

"Hell! You're Slick," MacTavish said.

The field hospital was in a school several kilometers away. Medics first, then a physician worked on Shannon. The young officer had lost a lot of blood, and his right humerus was a mess, broken near the shoulder joint. Only time would tell how much use he would have of his injured limb. Rebecca's superficial wound was bandaged.

Sonny hung around, waiting. Jameson and MacTavish paced

nervously, made sure Sonny and Rebecca had food and water, assumed the role of protectors.

"How did you learn to shoot a rifle?" Rebecca asked.

Sonny shrugged. "Something I picked up."

Before he could say more, MacTavish appeared and said in his Scottish brogue, "Slick, Lieutenant's knackered but wants to talk."

Sonny saw the number 44 on MacTavish's uninjured shoulder. He had seen that before—where? Shannon's arm was bandaged, and morphine had him circling high above the ground. Then it came to Sonny—the 44—he had seen it when he was hiding in the doorway in Roubaix, watching the British troops pass.

"You going to be okay?" Sonny asked.

Shannon smiled, his startling green eyes meeting Sonny's. He licked his lips as if needing lubrication to speak. "Thanks to you."

"I'm glad," Sonny said, recalling the eyes that went with number 44. "What is the 4 . . . 4?"

"44th Division . . . Royal Sussex Regiment, 2nd Battalion—my unit."

Sonny repeated, under his breath, "4 . . .4 Division . . . Royal Sussex . . . 2nd Battalion."

"What are you doing?"

"Must remember . . . I join . . . 4–4 Division . . . Sussex Regiment . . . 2nd Battalion. I get it. Okay?"

"Perfect."

"Good!" Then Sonny said, "You . . . 4–4, in Roubaix? I remember 4–4 and green eyes." Bits of memory—firing squad, Goumiers, fatal brutality, Kid dead—crowded in, then disappeared.

"What are you talking about?" Shannon looked at him, quizzically.

"I hide in doorway, scared. I see numbers, 4–4, green eyes." Sonny pointed.

"Maybe, don't remember . . . How did you learn to shoot in Germany?"

Sonny gazed into green eyes dulled by drugs, then noticed the red hair. He hesitated, then figured what the hell . . . "In Underground. Smuggle Jews from Germany. Trouble in Aachen . . . I shoot Gestapo captain. Two other Gestapo died . . . and one of us. Also kill Gestapo lieutenant near Berlin."

"How many?" Shannon asked.

Sonny raised his hand, fingers splayed, thumb against his palm. "Four. I not alone."

"You learned to fight in the Underground? Didn't know it was so active."

"We want secret, but . . . " Sonny shrugged.

"I told the colonel. He'll talk to you." He grabbed for Sonny's hand. "I want to see you again . . . in England—if we get out of here. Good luck."

"And you," Sonny said, then left . . .

Shannon wanted to see him in England. Sonny thought about that. All the action had pushed Rosa into the background, but now she was on his mind. So much to tell her. So much he didn't know— was she safe in Paris? She had to be safe, wherever she was. He couldn't think otherwise.

Someone approaching roused Sonny from his thoughts. He figured him for the colonel as several men followed close behind, like goslings. When the officer was near enough, Sonny got to his feet and saluted.

The officer smiled. "No need to salute." He stuck out a hand. "Colonel Smith, and you must be the young man of the hour."

"Men call me Slick."

They shook hands.

"Well . . . it just might stick."

Sonny told him his real name.

"Thanks for saving my men."

"My fight too."

"Shannon told me a little about you . . . in Germany . . . the Underground. Is that correct?"

Sonny nodded.

"There's a lot more fighting to be done. When we get back to England, and we are going to make it, you may be able to contribute. Interested?"

Sonny nodded vigorously. "Ja! Much interested."

"Good! You're in my debt. What can I do for you? Just ask."

"Documents, so we legal, me and friend."

"See to it!" The officer ordered over his shoulder, then frowned. "Can I do that?"

They huddled.

"Do it! Get both names . . . bring the documents here. Feed them. Get fresh clothes and boots for him. See what you can find for the young woman." Colonel Smith turned to Sonny. "Wait here."

"I join now?" Sonny asked. "I ready."

Colonel Smith laughed. "Enlist when you get to England. I'll give you a recommendation. Now get your ass across the channel, like the rest of us."

"How?"

He sighed heavily. "That's the problem at the moment—Jerrys everywhere. Get to Dunkirk . . . show the documents we give you. Get on a boat. Good luck."

Battered and bullied, like a lamb to slaughter, Sonny had survived beatings, firing squad, Goumiers, and Kid's death. Then killing two Germans, saving Shannon and Rebecca, maybe MacTavish and Jameson, and himself. He'd traveled from Roubaix to reunion with Shannon behind a shed. He marveled at life's serendipity. No matter that Shannon had no memory of their brief encounter in Roubaix. *He* had remembered, and that was enough.

Sonny could not fully comprehend the epic battle surrounding him. Great armies were in retreat, numbering in the hundreds of thousands, refugees fleeing in their wake, converging on a speck of beach—victims of humiliating defeat. He thought of the 40 men in his Marquain barracks. How many were still alive? Multiply that by . . . He shivered, then closed his eyes.

Rebecca had listened silently to the colonel. After he left, she asked, "Are we really going to England?"

"If we get to Dunkirk. We'll get on a boat."

"Were we lucky we didn't die back there?" She shook her head, confused. "Lucky doesn't fit. My father would have asked why?"

"Lucky, unlucky, we're still alive but not there yet." He thought of Kid, quipping, "Trapped by the sea, then pummeled by German planes and artillery." He smiled.

A soldier delivered documents, clothes, and boots as promised. Sonny had a new set of British Army battledress and Rebecca a Wrens—army nurse—skirt and blouse, both without rank or unit designation. Each was issued a French identity card, provisional British passport, visa good for 90 days, and a letter signed by Colonel Smith, granting ship's passage for both.

They retreated to separate corners and returned in their new clothes.

"Good," Rebecca nodded after inspecting Sonny. "Like a British soldier."

"You, too. We keep our mouths shut, and no one will notice."

"I'm still dirty," she added.

"Take a bath in England."

Rebecca's smile transformed her face; there was a glint in her eyes not there before. She moved close to Sonny, her eyes fixed on his. They conveyed a message—hunger, desire, madness? He wasn't sure.

Then she said softly, "Thank you for saving my life."

Sonny took a half step back and shook his head. "You'd have done the same for me."

"No." She growled her denial. "I can't shoot, and I wanted to die. You saved me. Now . . . " She left the rest unsaid then hugged him tight.

He tensed and felt uneasy, not wanting this to happen. Her body felt warm against his for the second time. He put his arms around her. They stood, entwined for a long moment. Then she released him, and he dropped his arms. She stepped back, her face flushed. Their eyes met. Neither spoke.

Sonny didn't know what to think. He cleared his throat. "I have to see Lt. Shannon before we leave."

. . . Shannon was propped up in a cot, his right arm hung from a metal contraption. He smiled when Sonny came into focus.

"Slick!" His laugh was hoarse.

"Farewell . . . I see how favorite British officer do."

"Soon your English will be good enough to be misunderstood."

Sonny smiled. "How you are?"

"Like a fox in a snare."

"When go?"

"Soon—and you?"

"Now. I have documents." Sonny showed him the papers and the letter from Col. Smith.

"Good."

"I enlist in 4 . . . 4 when get to England . . . beat hell out of Hitler."

"Good." Shannon looked away, then back at Sonny. "My fighting days are over," he sighed heavily, "but thanks to you, I'm alive. Good luck!"

"Another day in my big life."

Shannon laughed.

"Was it bad?" Sonny asked.

"Germans came so fast we were overwhelmed. Lost too many good men. They pushed us out of Belgium then across France. I'm told, Jerry's on the coast, south of Dunkirk. We're fighting to save the BEF and get off the continent."

"No understand . . . French Army big," Sonny spread his hands apart, indicating size, "BEF strong." He made a fist.

"I know. That'll give the smart set something to analyze later . . . much later. Now, we have to beat hell out of here or be up the creek." He saw Sonny's frown. "Big trouble."

They promised to meet again.

"See you in Dover, Slick," Jameson said, MacTavish standing behind him, grinning like a fool. "Take care of your little friend." He winked at Rebecca.

"What is Slick?" Rebecca asked . . .

The road to Dunkirk was clogged with soldiers. The number of men and abandoned vehicles grew as they moved west. Scores of cars, trucks, artillery, and tanks littered the landscape. They seemed to have sprung from the ground, fully formed, ready for harvest.

Sonny's blistered feet were painful, but at least he had new boots. After three hours they entered a massive parking lot of phantom vehicles, beyond it a canal.

They came upon a British soldier, removing equipment from a truck.

"Where are we?" Rebecca asked in English.

"Basse Colme Canal," he said without taking his eyes from his task. "Dunkirk and Bray Dunes—10 kilometers." An arm jerked in the air and his thumb pointed the way.

"Thanks," Sonny said.

"No trouble, mate.

15

Near Dunkirk, France, end of May 1940

Sonny and Rebecca sat on the bank of the canal called Basse Colme, legs dangling over murky, languid water. Tapping his heels nervously on the side, Sonny watched the detritus of a defeated army—bottles, cans, refuse, and human waste—slowly float past. Rebecca recoiled as she pointed to a bloated corpse stuck on a pile of garbage.

Their destination lay on the other side of the canal—a stretch of beach called Bray Dunes. Chaos born of several hundred thousand men converging on a tiny piece of shore separated by a canal with two bridges created a bottleneck of incomprehensible proportions. A cacophony of roaring and dying engines plus voices raised in command, fear, and incomprehension surrounded them.

Salvation appeared in the form of a waiting armada of motley boats and ships bobbing and weaving off the Dunkirk coastline. If all went as planned, the British Expeditionary Force would escape the Wehrmacht's crushing maw and return to English soil.

Fate had thrown Sonny and Kid together. Intimacy had sprung from the tragedy they observed and barely avoided. They had supported and cared for each other, like brothers. Then fate ended what it had begun. Now there was Rebecca.

"Why didn't you leave me?" Rebecca asked. "You could have left Kid on the road. You would have." Her bluntness jarred him with its truth. He stared beyond the canal toward the beach without an answer.

She followed his gaze and said softly, "Wouldn't have blamed you. I couldn't leave my father like that. I didn't care what happened to me."

"I was scared," Sonny admitted, then looked at her. She had

changed much in two days.

"Only a fool would not have been afraid."

"I have reason to live."

"I didn't, but I do now." She took his hand in both of hers.

"No Rebecca . . . not me," he said softly and pulled his hand away.

"Am I a stand-in for Kid?"

Sonny started to say something, then stopped. Maybe she was right. "You were alone, everyone else dead or running away. My reaction was to help. No more than that . . . " He shrugged.

"You saved me," she said. "You are a fine man."

"And you're a fine young woman. Let's leave it at that."

Her eyes glistened as she laughed, another change. "But . . . "

"No buts."

They were quiet for a while, then Sonny said, "I've been through a lot, as have you." He told her about the firing squad calmed by a young Brit, speaking Yiddish, then about being fleeced and thrown into a cramped schoolroom with 24 Communists.

"Kid and I became brothers. I miss him terribly." He looked at Rebecca. "I wanted to run, but I didn't. I couldn't leave you."

They sat quietly, thinking.

"I'll never understand the brutality. I swore I'd kill that turbaned bastard, given the chance." Sonny's voice went cold as ice. "Didn't have to. He was dead . . . on the road. If he moved or took a breath, I would have . . . clubbed him with his rifle butt or strangled him. Germans took care of him for me. Kid would have appreciated the irony. So I spat on his worthless body."

"I believe you would have."

"I've done it before." Sonny looked at her, so young but no longer innocent.

"Done what?" Then her eyes flickered, and she understood. "What you did last night?"

Sonny nodded.

"Where? When?"

"You really want to know?"

"Of course. We almost died back there. I feel like a soldier . . . sort of."

Sonny's eyes narrowed. "I killed a few Gestapos in Germany." He told her about Rosa and Oranienburg and Aachen. "Had help . . .

don't regret any of it. Losing one of ours was terrible . . . Gestapos got what they deserved."

Rebecca was stunned into silence.

"Two more dead—so what! Saved us and an English lieutenant." He laughed, mirthlessly. "Gets us off the continent."

"You might never see Rosa again." Rebecca sounded almost hopeful.

He didn't hesitate. "I will find her."

"From here it seems daunting, impossible," Rebecca said.

"I have to believe."

"But how?"

Sonny shook his head. "Don't know."

"You must love her very much."

"More than anything."

"How will you find her in this mess?"

He shrugged. "Or I'll die trying."

"Don't say that. It's bad luck. I . . . I thought, maybe . . . " Again her hand found his and clutched it. "I'm so alone, so scare . . . " Her voice faded.

"No," Sonny repeated and stood up, unsure of what to do but needing to do something. "Let's go!"

"Think about us, about me."

"Right now all that matters is getting out."

She moved closer and tilted her head back, inviting a kiss. When he didn't accept the invitation, she hugged him.

Sonny closed his eyes and sighed, fearing he might lose control. He stared silently into the opaque water.

"You saved my life, twice. Tell me you'll think about it."

Sonny didn't answer. Instead he asked, "What will you do?"

"I don't know."

"Your English is excellent—join the army like me."

She shrugged, then pointed to the nearest bridge.

Sonny's head turned toward the troops oozing across the bridge in a slow, constant flow. There were two bridges, one on each side of them, about a kilometer apart. Beyond was a harsh, inhospitable swamp. A breeze kicked up the canal's pungent aroma.

"Ugh," Rebecca groaned.

The road was clogged with more soldiers than either had ever seen in one place. As they arrived, more trucks, sedans, and tanks were abandoned in the fields behind the Canal de la Basse Colme. So far no ground attack, but the Luftwaffe was paying regular visits to the hapless armies. If the Brits and French could maintain control over this inhospitable piece of real estate, they just might . . .

France was lost. Tears were to be shed later. Collaborators and cowards would rise to the surface, like the slowly floating canal scum. Opportunists like Captain Favier waited, ready to do business with the occupiers. Sonny imagined Favier burning his uniform, like his patriotism, then smiling obsequiously: "After all, one has to survive."

When the Germans entered Paris as conquerors, how many French men and women would change allegiance, turn a different shade, like chameleons? So it would go through France.

The bridges spanned no more than 25 meters. Hours drained from the day as the bottlenecks swelled and contracted. Increasing numbers waited, impatiently. Several soldiers jumped into the fetid canal rather than endure the interminable wait.

"Bacteria will probably kill them," Rebecca wryly observed. "How many are there?"

Sonny frowned. "Many tens of thousands. In '39, an Antwerp newspaper estimated 10 BEF divisions in northern France."

"How many soldiers in a division?"

Sonny shrugged. "Maybe 15,000."

"How are we going to squeeze in?" She gestured forlornly.

"Don't know until we try."

They walked to the nearest bridge and took their place, two souls in British uniforms, lost in the crowd. Blue sky touched the horizon on all sides. The hours spent under an unrelenting sun flared tempers. Officers and NCOs walked the line, keeping the peace. Strafing planes had everyone eating dirt.

As the hours passed, the azure sky turned pale, losing its luster. As the sun disappeared, Sonny and Rebecca finally crossed the bridge. The funnel opened. Men spread out, making haste on the final leg of their journey—fewer than 10 kilometers to the waiting boats.

Sonny and Rebecca entered the outskirts of what remained of Dunkirk in near darkness. Most of the buildings were damaged, some flattened by bombardment. Burning rubble turned the air opaque. The thick haze stung their eyes, clogged throat and nostrils. Men filtered through the wreckage to the beach, anxious to be delivered from peril. Few lingered.

Sonny's ears pricked to the sound of planes.

"Cover!" someone screamed.

Men flew into ditches, behind walls, piles of rubble. Sonny fell into a small hole, coiled into a ball, and covered his head with his arms. Rebecca seemed slow to react, then ran for a low wall. A plane strafed on its way to the beach. Nothing!

Sonny released the breath he had been holding. A second plane followed closely . . . Boom! The earth shook violently, showering debris. Something sharp and small collided with his left shoulder.

"Ah!" He moved his shoulder. Nothing was broken, but it hurt. Dust filled the air. He coughed, then raised his head slowly and looked around: "Rebecca."

16

Dunkirk, France, end of May 1940

"Rebecca!" Sonny squinted into a moonlit dystopian landscape. He was scared, again. Voices called for help. Soldiers answered. Some were injured—one faced down, not moving. Please, not Rebecca.

Sonny called her name again. He slowly scanned the area until his gaze fell on a gap in a wall. He took four long strides, then stopped. Her chin rested on her chest, as if she had gone to sleep. She looked calm in repose. Part of the wall had collapsed upon her. He moved the stones and crouched next to her. Her eyes were open. Blood seeped from between her lips in a little stream onto her chin.

"Rebecca . . . get up, we've got to go."

No response. Sonny hesitated then, moved his hand to Rebecca's delicate white throat. His fingertips searched slowly, feeling for a pulse. Her skin was warm. "Rebecca . . . no!" he cried. He put an arm around her and gently shook. "Rebecca . . . " He fell against the wall next to her: "Ah, Rebecca—we're almost there."

Men shouted. Truck engines revved. Sonny wiped blood from Rebecca's chin and tightly pressed his arm around her shoulder that his life might drain into her body. Life was everything, all that mattered.

"Why?" Sonny pleaded, echoing Rebecca's father. First, Kid, his exasperating, chattering, generous, trusted companion—and now Rebecca. He rocked slowly back and forth, as if comforting the living rather than mourning the dead.

"Rebecca, I smell the ocean. Take a breath . . . Can you smell it?" Sonny shook his head, confused and forlorn. "I keep losing people: Father, then Mother, Uncle Simon, Kid. Rosa! You lost your father . . . now you." He stared at Rebecca's face, rigid in the soft, dim light.

"Kid reminded me of Uncle Simon. He was so like him. Maybe that's why I miss him so." Sonny smiled at his insight. "Simon's pain was too great. They found him in the River Spree in Berlin . . . jumped off a bridge." Sonny closed his eyes and thought about Simon and Kid. "You would have liked them."

"Then in Aachen, Günter was shot, killed. Emil and I got all three. And Rosa and I got that asshole in Oranienburg, turned him to ash." Sonny laughed mirthlessly. "Rosa was great." He stared at the barren moonscape, amidst no sign of life. They were alone. Soldiers had carried some of the bodies away. Lights glowed from the distant beach.

"Should have told you about the time the Nazis let the garbage pile up in my neighborhood. And Karl's story about Sachsenhausen." Sonny shrugged. "We had our own parade of horrors. You didn't need to hear more." He sighed.

"Rebecca, it couldn't have worked. I'm sorry," he whispered. Tears rolled down his cheeks. He bent his head and wept for Rebecca, for Kid, the old man, mother and daughter . . . for himself.

He sat for 10 minutes, an hour . . . two? Finally, he gently withdrew his arm from his friend's body and stood up. Leaving Rebecca slumped against a wall in a bombed-out town in coastal France was unacceptable—a lesson she had taught him. He needed a shovel. The moon provided light.

Of every passing soldier he asked, "Shovel?"

Finally, one dropped a folding shovel at his feet: "Don't need it."

He found a suitable patch of dirt and dug a decent grave. He lifted Rebecca and gently lowered her into the earth, then covered her body. Arms dangling at his sides, head down, he slowly recited as much of the Mourner's Kaddish as he knew: "Yisgadal, v'yiskadash shmay rabo . . ." Only two days earlier they had spoken those same Hebrew words.

Several soldiers stopped to watch in silent respect until Sonny had finished. "Who?" one asked.

"Friend."

The soldier nodded solemnly and left. Then Sonny walked in the direction the soldier had taken. He shuffled past empty, bombed-out buildings until he found shelter. He would try to sleep and in the morning find deliverance from hell. But even with his back against a wall, his mind raced. In a world shifting and shaking beneath his feet, why had he survived when the dreams of so many were extinguished? He felt sorely tested, but so were others.

"I give up," he mumbled. He had been ashamed for wanting to leave Kid on the road, for his selfishness. Rebecca had taught him a lesson. Kid's death, and now Rebecca's, weighed heavy.

Sonny gazed into darkness, toward the channel, beyond the unseen jetty. A sudden breeze sent debris against his face. He flinched and closed his eyes: a sailboat's bleached, billowing sail, a dot on the water fighting against the wind, its mast nearly parallel to the water, skimmed across the surface . . .

. . . Chancing a glance from his shop window, the baker caught movement on the water. Smiling, he wiped his hands on his apron and bit into a warm brioche. On the rooftop above, the fiddler, sweat dripping from his brow, inhaled the salty air and gazed beyond the water's edge toward the white flash. He plucked several strings, a musical salute. A wind caught the notes, and the fisherman looked up, saw the fiddler, and smiled. His catch lay on the dock, fishtails flopping—applause. His wife, wrapping his lunch in newspaper, pointed out to sea . . . "Ooh."

Sonny smiled at the vision, then lowered his head, exhausted, his nerves raw. Weary of death, mayhem, and waste—ancient themes never put to rest. He teetered on the edge of a sharp blade. Finally, to sleep and to dream . . .

. . . Streetlight, fluted wrought-iron pole yielding to graceful curving, delicate filigree. Yellow globe, big jaundiced eye, a sentinel watching him, illuminating the street. Two lovers embracing in the gauzy glow, man gently stroking her cheek: they kiss, oblivious to all but each other as lovers often are. Foolish to have remained in this empty, bombed-out hole. Lovers are often foolish . . .

The sky lightened, the sun rising behind him. Sonny rubbed his eyes and stretched. A panorama, jarring and spectacular—opened in the middle distance. Pure anarchy, a nightmare of cinematic fantasy played before him. He gaped. How had he slept amidst the cacophony of screaming men, roaring engines, soaring planes, and bursting bombs? Ships of all sizes, from troop carriers to fishing boats, filled the harbor. They twisted and turned like goldfish darting across a pond. Smaller boats disappeared into swells, reappearing shrouded in white foam, bobbing like corks, waiting. One, then another, moved closer to shore. Troops scrambled onto giant piers created by boards atop trucks, dozens of them, driven or pushed into the water. Men clamored onto boats, then ferried to the bigger ships. One quickly replaced another.

Huge, gray ships filled the long, flat horizon, some at anchor, others leaving, more arriving. He might walk to England from boat to boat, so it seemed. From left to right, Sonny counted 75 boats, more than he had ever seen, then gave up. They would not still. It was like trying to count spokes on a moving bicycle.

Two boats, one moving to shore, another ferrying troops out, collided. Rough water swamped the second boat. Sonny averted his eyes from the boats, looking to the beach filled with scared and disoriented troops. Long, bloated, curving lines of people, expanding like giant pythons, awaited the order to scramble onto boats.

Soldiers too injured to walk lay on stretchers—limbs missing, torsos torn by shrapnel. Had Shannon made it to the beach? According to Shannon, the First Corps had been ordered to form a rearguard protecting Dunkirk's perimeter. It was a suicide mission to keep Jerry at bay: "Brave lads, buying time."

Only a generation removed from the "war to end all wars," young men, barely more than children, were desperate to elude encirclement and capture. Thousands lay dead in the fields and woods, unprepared for Wehrmacht ferocity and speed.

A faint whirring, like a spinning saw blade, grew louder, until it roared. Sonny's eyes followed the deadly ballet of strafing planes, swift and agile, framed by water and sky in delivering mayhem to the beach. With no cover, the troops were easy pickings. They scattered, like rabbits chased by a dog, trapped . . . face down, hugging sand . . . Slowly heads rose, eyes on the sky, felt life within. Then they stood, hoping to make it to the next queue, praying Jerry would miss them.

Slow-moving ships, overloaded with soldiers and hard to maneuver, made fat targets—like throwing a ball at a bottle at a carnival sideshow: win a doll for your sweetie. Thick smoke shrouded the ship. Fire licked the edges of the inferno trapping soldiers in a coffin of molten steel. Men scrambled for lifeboats or jumped into the rough sea, frantically working to keep afloat—facing final reckoning! Hypnotized, unable to avert his gaze, Sonny watched in horror as the massive ship slowly disappeared beneath the choppy, blue surface.

Overcome by his own impotence and insignificance, Sonny shuddered at the massive scale of the tragedy. Disgusted and depressed, he turned from the mayhem. His gaze fell upon a flower-filled window box on the ground, torn from its anchor. Geraniums, blood-red in the early morning sun and set off by small white blossoms, provided a red-and-white, asymmetrical checkerboard. Sanguine beauty? Or open wound against pale skin? He thought of Rebecca. He was dismayed, then cheered, by a sparrow flitting in and out, a yellow butterfly daintily landing on a scarlet petal.

He had been teased by illusion—a pleasant tableau, his refuge from the malodorous fires of war. His senses were clouded, impaired by hunger and thirst. Voices! He cocked his head, then covered his ears to block out the incessant noise. Stench from the fires lined his nostrils; his eyes watered. He tasted soothing salt.

Taking another glance at the window box, he saw it was still there—no hallucination, a small victory. He breathed in the blossoms' sweet smell of summer.

Everything but window box and streetlight had been damaged or destroyed—blown away like a house of cards. Shadows, low on the ground, softened the jagged landscape. Gray, black smoke rose from the debris—shards of glass and pottery, a man's hat, a woman's purse, haphazardly strewn. By midday, the sun's harsh rays would bleach the remaining color, add to the gloom.

The flowers, streetlight, and lovers of his ever-smaller world seemed so real. He willed them to be real—a vision of normalcy. Then the world intruded.

Boats crisscrossed, rocking in the surf. If only the sea was all they fought. Planes droned . . . bombs whistled . . . explosions deafened. The song of the moment ran a discordant tune in his ears.

Sonny scratched the many days' growth of beard on his cheek. His ears ached, his heart caromed in his chest, in time with the timpani beating in his temples. His skin tingled. A shower of dust and debris created a fog-shrouded night—but it was day.

He coughed. How bitter life could be? Surely, this must be hell. Placing a hand to his chest, he felt the thump . . . thump: "Enough!"

Sonny reached into his pocket, felt the documents there, and began the slow trek to the beach.

Part IV

O! A kiss. Long as my exile, sweet as my revenge.
—*Shakespeare*

17

Sare, France, June 1940

Rosa thanked Jules Fabres, then said good-bye to his wife and daughter. Sitting in the back seat of his big car, staring at his grotesque head, made her feel dirty.

Agnes had encountered Fabres, a theater agent and acquaintance from Paris, at the hotel in Bordeaux. Fabres, Celine, and daughter were en route to Biarritz, a resort city on the southern coast. When Celine learned of Rosa's destination, she graciously offered a ride.

"Be wary of Jules's probing hands," Agnes whispered. "Celine must be the only woman in Paris who doesn't know."

A big, intimidating man with an incongruously sensual mouth, Fabres cornered Rosa at the first stop. Alone with her for but a moment, he moved in, thighs touching, his breath smelling of cigarettes. He pawed her rump. "Be our daughter's nanny," he whispered.

Rosa stiffened and turned away, out of his reach. "No . . . thank you," she said, stifling anger, not wanting to lose her ride. "I'm on my way to my parents."

"A shame. We could have had fun." His lewd grin turned to a scowl, and he walked away.

Rosa silently cursed his back.

She waited for the Marseille bus that stopped in Sare, only 25 kilometers away. Several clusters of women, their heads down, eyes averted, talked quietly. They looked disheveled, scared, hungry.

She was preoccupied by the family reunion—had her parents received the letter? Were they still in Sare? Were they safe? Could she stay with them? What was Sare like? The women melted from her thoughts. Fear for Sonny, far away, elbowed its way in, filling her with doubt.

Rosa stood in Sare's town square and took inventory. Pleasant, whitewashed, red-shuttered buildings topped with blood-red tile roofs ringed Sare's small square. The jagged teeth of lesser mountains chewed the sky, forming a dramatic backdrop. A huge mound protruded from the ground like a gigantic egg, dominating the horizon—Mount Larrun, she would learn. Tiny sheep grazed in the distant meadows. If she had to be exiled at the end of the road, this beautiful setting would help. It was a pretty town, a world away from Paris.

A horse-drawn cart slowly passed. Its driver stared solemnly, as if he had never seen a young woman. Rosa smiled. He nodded. A woman exited a shop and headed in the opposite direction. A rising cloud of smoke caught Rosa's eye. It came from an old man, rocking gently, a pipe clenched between his teeth. Rosa walked to him, smiled warmly, and said, "Hello."

"Hello," he answered.

"Please direct me to Domaine Poussard—the winery?"

He pointed in the direction of a road leading from town. Rosa thanked him and began to walk. After more than half an hour under the hot sun, she saw a small sign on the side of the road: Domaine Poussard. She turned onto a narrow dirt track between neat rows of grapevines with ripening clusters of pale green orbs. Farther along, a white house with red shutters and roof like those in town appeared. She knocked on the front door.

A woman, about Rosa's mother's age, answered. "Can I help?"

"I'm Rosa Sander," Rosa said tentatively, "Are my parents here?"

"Rosa—at long last!" She smiled broadly. "I'm Irene Poussard . . . come in . . . come in. Your parents will be thrilled. They live in the cottage at the rear . . . go see them. We'll talk later."

Relieved and slightly overwhelmed, Rosa nodded, then turned.

"There's plenty of work here. Stay as long as you like," Irene added.

"Thank you."

Within five minutes Rosa was hugging her tearful mother, then her father. They sat at a small table in the tiny cottage. No letter had arrived.

"Please speak French," Rosa said. "German is repugnant to me."

"We speak only French here, and it's improved, hasn't it, Robert?"

"Oui. It's wonderful you're here. And Sonny? Any word?"

"A letter from a camp in Belgium. I sent Jean's address. Then the invasion." She chewed her quavering lip. "It's chaos up north . . . roads are clogged. Paris was bombed the day before we left. Some died, and more were dead on the road." Rosa straightened to keep from sagging from the weigh of it.

Silence set in for a long uncomfortable moment. Then her father stirred. "Let's eat."

Rosa told them about Paris—Jean, Catherine, René, Alain, Annette and Paul, Jenny, Agnes Capri and Tony—and her trip to Sare. Rita Daurat remained a secret.

"Stay. The Poussards are wonderful people," her mother said.

"There's no place to go." Her father shrugged. "There's a big detention camp in Gurs, 50 kilometers east, filled with . . . " He stopped midsentence.

She remembered the women at the bus station, then said, "You've fallen through the cracks thus far."

"We feel safe here," her mother said.

"I plan to stay. Irene offered me a job."

"Good. The work is physical. We're well treated, lucky . . . under the circumstances," her father said. He told Rosa about the Poussard family. Dominic and Irene ran the vineyard and winery. Marie, a married daughter, and Anton, her husband, lived in town. Anton was the vintner, and Marie helped Irene. They had no children yet. Javier, their only son, had been drafted into the army and not heard from in a month, creating much anxiety. Anton was exempted from the draft because of a leg injury.

"They don't care that we're Jews . . . " her mother started.

Robert interjected, "Frankly, they need workers. They're good people. We fell into a good situation, and I'm learning to make wine."

"With all that's happened, what more could we ask?" Elise then quickly added, "That Sonny . . . "

"Yes, of course," Rosa snapped, then said, "I'm sorry. I have to make it on my own. I miss him terribly, but I have to be optimistic."

Bedtime was early, shortly after the summer sunset. Rosa looked around the small cottage and frowned. Her father smiled and pointed to the ceiling. "In the loft, there's a bed."

They rose at dawn. Rosa worked alongside her mother, cleaning the house before going into the winery. Later, she weeded the garden. That evening Rosa asked her mother, "What is there to do besides work?"

Elise laughed. "Read . . . talk . . . stroll the farm, read more . . . "

Rosa waited, but there was no more. "I'll go mad!"

Her mother laughed. "You get used to it."

A routine settled in: up at dawn, eat a small breakfast, work until noon. Eat lunch in the big kitchen of the main house. Irene and Dominic, Marie, Anton, Rosa's parents, Rosa, and Alesander and Fermin, the two farmhands, sat around the big table. Work and war, with an occasional foray into the personal, were the topics of conversation. Local newspapers, the wireless, and rumors were the only sources of information. The big story of the moment was the dramatic evacuation of the British Expeditionary Force and a fraction of the French army from Dunkirk.

"Both armies were trapped there," Dominic said as if thinking aloud.

"Pushed off the continent—terrible defeat," Anton noted.

"At least they avoided capture," Dominic responded glumly.

After the table was cleared, Dominic spread out a map of France. He pointed to a spot on the northern coast: "Hundreds of boats crossed the channel. 'A miracle,' Churchill called it on the wireless." He laughed harshly at the terrible irony. Then he pointed to eastern France and the border with Belgium: "We started here." His finger moved along the Franco-Belgian border, then stopped. He tapped at a spot near Lille. "Javier must have been near here . . . "

They heard rumors that the Germans were south of the Marne, of Paris lost, the French army routed—mirroring the news of Dunkirk.

That Sonny might be trapped in the maelstrom—eluding bullets, bombs, tanks, and planes—while she was safe, far from the fighting, was at times more than Rosa could bear. Her stomach churned with anxiety, though the heartache and longing were harder. Sonny, Alain, Paul, and Javier, a young man she didn't even know, were enduring horrors of war, and Jenny was alone in Paris or worse. She felt wretched and guilty for her good fortune.

By the end of June, Rosa had been on the domain for several weeks. Weeding the vegetable garden in the midafternoon sun, she was distracted by barking. Leon, the big, friendly dog, its tail wagging furiously, circled a young man in uniform. Javier had safely returned!

All the family plus Rosa and her parents, Alesander and Fermin, and several close friends, gathered for a celebratory dinner. The food was plentiful, and the Domaine Poussard wine flowed.

Javier was 20 years old, a taller, thinner version of his father. They shared a square jaw and piercing, intelligent blue eyes. Shy, he avoided Rosa's gaze, but his reticence receded with the wine.

Javier had a story to tell, and all were eager to hear it. His unit was transportation, attached to the 2nd North African Division, largely comprising colonial troops. The 2nd crossed into Belgium to meet the German invasion. Wehrmacht armored units, with air and infantry support, struck with stunning speed. Casualties were high. The army retreated.

"The news was equally bleak," said Javier. "Germans reported in Rouen, Paris threatened. We heard Boche crossed the Seine, but where? 'Probably at Pont de l'Arche,' our NCO told us. Control the Seine and the Germans would cut the artery, provisioning Paris. Hundreds of Brit guns, big ones, moved past us on the roads . . . maybe 50 tanks on rail flatbeds. Would they counterattack? Then we heard that General Gamelan ordered four or five of his generals shot, and he committed suicide." Javier looked around the table. "Was it true?"

Heads shook, shoulders shrugged—no one knew.

"Letters from Paris, the few that got through, said people fled in droves. It was worse than bad. We stumbled on a mortally wounded officer in Belgium," Javier's voice, quavered, "'leave me . . . run for your lives!' he pleaded, 'I'm finished. you have family, children . . . '" Javier's face darkened as he drank more wine. "The days melted into one. Suddenly, the sea encircled, trapped us. Hitler bragged he'd be in Paris by mid-June, sign peace on Bastille Day, then march through the Arc de Triomphe!"

"Like a damned peacock," Dominic said.

"On 31 May, we left Dunkirk for Dover . . . indescribable chaos." He shook his head in disbelief. "Tens of thousands of soldiers, hundreds of boats. Amazing! Brits pulled it off. One night on English soil, then back to France, south of Deauville."

"Where is that?" someone asked.

"Near the mouth of the Seine. Word spread that the North African Division would regroup near Bernay, 60 kilometers southeast. We muddled on, but . . . "

He paused and looked down at his hands for a long moment. "Near Le Mans we listened on the wireless to Reynaud's plea to President Roosevelt for support and America's entry into the war. 'Cry of alarm—despair of the vanquished,' my commanding officer called it. Then he said Paris would fall. It was over—our 'invincible' French army defeated. I felt numb."

"All of France heard it," Dominic intoned.

"Morale, what was left of it, crumbled. Men panicked, deserted. Rumors spread that the Germans were fewer than 35 kilometers from Paris. Then we heard on . . . 14 June." He shook his head, "The dates are a muddle . . . Paris declared an open city. I overheard my commanding officer say, 'Boche tanks crushed us. They're everywhere . . . can't stop them.' Some units kept fighting. France is finished unless Russia attacks from the east."

"Forget that," Anton said. "Soviets invaded Lithuania—it was on the wireless."

"On their way to Germany?" Javier looked up, hopeful.

"Stalin taking his spoils," Dominic said.

The room fell quiet.

"Maybe America will fight," Javier said softly, breaking the silence.

"Too late . . . " Anton bit off his words.

Dominic stood, raised a glass, his eyes on Javier. "To France and the Republic: May she be victorious."

"Viva la France!" The toast was joined.

Someone began singing "La Marseillaise." They all sang. Spirits soared. Reality suspended for the moment. Victory seemed possible. But alas, wishing could not make it so. The singing stopped. Hope disintegrated under the weight of reality. France lay on the verge of crushing defeat. The impregnable Maginot line had been breached, the army was in flight, Paris exposed. Reality sucked the air from the room. Silence fell. Eyes averted. Rosa shivered, suddenly cold. She closed her eyes, Sonny's clouded image receding from view. It was always the same. Then, an utterly bleak landscape . . .

"Rosa," someone jolted her from her reverie.

"What?"

"We're clearing the table," her mother said.

. . . After they finished cleaning up, Rosa looked for Javier. She found him by the barn, Leon at his side.

"It must have been difficult," she started.

He shrugged. "Some had it worse."

"You painted a terrible picture of Dunkirk."

"Long strip of sand . . . planes strafing, dropping bombs. Ships, big, small, burning, sinking, coming, going . . . Thousands waiting . . . Confusion, chaos, fear."

Rosa was silent, then said, "Good fortune that you got away."

Javier nodded.

"Were civilians evacuated?"

"I don't know . . " He looked curiously at Rosa, then nodded. "Mother told me about your husband. Maybe . . . "

"In my despair, I fear he didn't."

Javier shuffled uncomfortably.

"I'm sorry, didn't mean to . . ." Rosa stopped.

"That's okay. How did you get here?"

She told him.

"What now?" he asked.

"Staying here. That's all I know."

They were quiet, contemplating what might come next. Javier broke the silence. "France defeated. I never . . . "

"There has to be hope." Rosa's words sounded scripted.

"That the French army will suddenly regenerate?" His tone was bitter.

"No," she admitted, then retreated to a tamer topic. "Poussard? That's French, not Basque."

Javier seemed relieved at the new direction of the conversation. "My grandfather was French. He married into a Basque family—not unusual around here."

"Was he in the wine business?"

Javier nodded. "Grandfather started making txakoli, a dry white wine. Later, my father planted cabernet franc and cabernet sauvignon to go with tannat, a traditional grape, already planted, for red wine."

"How many hectares?"

"Five. A small operation but enough."

"Wine's new to me—I like it."

"Who doesn't? Call me Javi."

————

Routine suited Rosa. Cleaning the winery, helping in the house, cleaning the chicken coop, gathering eggs, and tending the goats, ducks, and geese—the work was physical, repetitive, and dull, except when being chased by a goose, snapping at her backside.

Rosa grew stronger and lithe, shedding weight. Country living and working outside, initially novel, became her new life, Domaine Poussard her home and refuge. She accepted her lot with equanimity and acclimated to the pace of rural life, though not without regret.

Paris—she had just begun to penetrate its elegant mosaic, to see its disparate pieces, like a puzzle, fit together—to appreciate its nuance, energy, and idiosyncrasy. She missed crowded sidewalks, bookstalls, cafés, the Louvre, the club, Jean, Annette, Alain, Catherine, little René, Agnes, Jenny—all of it.

What had become of her friends when the Germans occupied the city? Where were Jean and Catherine, Agnes and Tony? And Sonny?

Javi thawed. Isolated in rural Aquitaine, close in age, alienated by recent experience, he and Rosa quickly became friends. Men no longer interested her, not romantically, save for one.

"Have Basques always been here and in Spain?" she asked Javi.

"Forever . . . before the Romans."

"The Basque language is wonderfully musical," she said.

"Unique. More Spanish than French but still different. Basque brothers and sisters in Spain fought Franco. Some crossed on old smugglers' routes from this side to join the fight. More returned after the war was lost. Gurs is filled with Republican fighters."

Again, the women at the station—had they escaped Gurs in the chaos of defeat? Then a thought struck her. "Do people still cross over the mountain?"

"All the time. Why?"

Rosa shrugged. "Just thinking."

"You want to start smuggling?" Javi joked. "There are paths everywhere."

"In Germany, Sonny provided Jews with forged papers."

"How?"

She told him.

"First Jews I ever met were in the army, beside your parents."

"Good that you took them in. Of course, you needed workers," Rosa parroted her father.

"True. One of the Jews I met in the army was from Toulouse. He talked resistance should the Germans win. I thought he was crazy. How could they win? Now . . . "

"Do you think about it?"

He didn't answer.

"Well?"

He shrugged. "When our unit disbanded, a group of officers and enlisted men, eight or ten of us, talked. One said, 'I can't abide the Germans in charge.'"

"What happened?"

"Nothing, just talk. They came from all over France—the Jew from Toulouse, a couple guys from Paris, Lyon. Guy from Toulouse did most of the talking, said it would be hard on everyone, especially Jews."

"What's new?"

"He predicted the Germans would rape the country, take our grain, steel, labor, whatever they wanted, leaving us with nothing."

"What the Germans have in store for the French and Jews won't be good. Can't trust Nazis. Thank God for Aquitaine. Your family saved us from Gurs."

Rosa was intrigued by the talk of resistance and smuggling routes. Sonny's work had excited and frightened her. Now she was more intrigued than frightened.

"Resistance!" She liked the way it sounded, and she said it again. "Resistance!" She would embody Sonny's spirit, if not his presence.

Defiance, an unwillingness to capitulate, made her feel she was doing something. That she wasn't French made no difference. Then she realized . . . she was Rita Daurat of 28 Rue Raffet, Auteuil, Paris. Rita resurrected—a fitting tribute to senseless death. But, what could she do . . . what?

Another realization, of something as obvious as Mount Larrun, struck her. The Basques and the French must be working the old smuggling trails in sending refugees over the mountain, helping Jews, Communists, anti-Nazis flee into Spain, then to Portugal, on to

England, wherever . . .

Smuggling was Sonny's domain—he'd know what to do. That made more sense than blowing up bridges or killing Nazis, though she had no objection to either on principle, being an old hand at the latter. She smiled. She was no longer tormented by nightmares, at least not that one. Javi was her lone confederate. More were needed to make it work. How? She would become Rita Daurat . . .

Things changed with lightning speed. Reynaud resigned on 16 June. France capitulated. Marshal Phillipe Pétain, the old man, hero of the Great War, addressed the nation by wireless on 17 June, calling for the cessation of hostilities and an armistice. Five days later, on 22 June, the Franco-German Armistice was signed at Rethondes, in the same railway carriage in which a humiliated Germany had signed the Armistice of 1918. The war was officially over.

Germans occupied the northern zone, including Paris; Pétain's Vichy-based government ruled the south at the whim of Nazi overseers. Vichy? Rosa had never heard of Vichy, a spa town in central France. Control of the French coastline, only 10 kilometers from Sare, remained solely under German control.

18

February 1941, Sare

Rosa woke in her new room in the winery. Sunrise was an hour away, and it was dark, cold, and wet. A stubborn chill lodged in her bones. She had escaped the cramped, low, windowless loft for an unused room with wood stove in the winery: "That dirty, junk-filled old room?" Dominic had said. He dismissed her request with a shake of his head. A short but persistent campaign had made him relent.

In cleaning out the room with Alesander, Rosa had discovered in a corner a litter of kittens, suckling at mother cat. They carefully moved the family to another corner of the winery. After they were weaning, she picked the prettiest gray kitten—a male—naming him Emil after Sonny's friend.

Finally, she had a room of her own—and a wall to hang Jean's photograph, *Latin Quarter* by André Kertész. She displayed her wedding photograph on a small table in a small wooden frame given by Irene. Sonny's folded handkerchief lay next to the photograph. If she could not have Sonny or Jean near her, these tokens were of some comfort, at least.

With a shiver, she lit the stove in the winery, eager to warm her hands over the fire. She began brushing out a wine barrel. Warmed by the constant rhythmic motion, she wiped a bead of sweat from her brow. Mindless drudgery provided time, maybe too much time, to think.

Rosa ran her fingers along the staves of the barrel, smooth as polished marble. She rolled the heavy barrel into place and retrieved another. Resting on the bench, she looked out the window that framed Mount Larrun. Clouds obscured the newly fallen snow, glistening like a million diamonds. Instead, she saw gray haze.

Sighing, Rosa found her thoughts drifting to Sonny, their months in Antwerp, free of Nazi shackles, holding hands, wandering aimlessly. Though still haunted by nightmares, she slowly recovered from the twin calamities of Kristallnacht and Oranienburg. It would take time, Sonny had cautioned, and he was right. They had married in Antwerp, and they had been so happy. Mina and Otto were there. Her smile in the photo on the bedside table showed how happy they were together, until . . .

So lost in thought, Rosa hadn't noticed two figures outside the window. She blinked. Javi stood next to a tall man in a long, black coat and black beret—for how long? Gesturing with his hands, the man towered over Javi. She had never seen him before. Javi nodded, listened, nodded again.

Rosa returned to the barrel, but curiosity dragged her gaze back to the window. They were shaking hands. The tall man turned toward the window. Rosa jumped as if he had seen her. A severe pencil line of a mouth below a hawk nose bisected his narrow face. But his dark, penetrating eyes startled her. He turned and abruptly disappeared from the frame, a man on a mission. He was not Basque.

What were they talking about? Why did he look familiar? She knew she had never seen him before. Dismissing the thought, she returned to the barrel. Still, it nagged. As she worked, the images of her mind bled to Berlin, the street outside her flat. Dozens like him walked Berlin's streets. What was a tall Jew doing at Domaine Poussard?

Rosa sat next to Javi at lunch. "Who was that man?" She whispered.

Taken aback, he said, "Hello to you too."

"Right, hello. So who is he?"

"A friend," he answered.

"Don't be coy."

Used to Rosa's bluntness, he smiled. "After lunch."

Half an hour later, Rosa cornered him. "Tell me."

"I told you about the Jewish guy from Toulouse . . . "

"I remember," she said impatiently. "You talked resistance."

"They talked—I listened," Javi corrected.

"Don't split hairs. What's he doing here?" Rosa had a vague idea.

Javi pursed his lips and looked over his shoulders in a paranoid pantomime. They were alone. He leaned in conspiratorially, like the Jew from Toulouse: "He wants me to help."

A knowing smile came to her lips. "I thought so."

"You don't know what he wants."

She shrugged. "Resistance, Underground—whatever the specifics, it must be important. I want to help," she insisted.

Javi sighed. "You won't give me a minute's rest until you know."

"Of course not." Her smile brightened.

"Not a word to anyone—promise?"

Rosa nodded solemnly. "I promise."

"His name is Daniel Meyer. He's here to buy wine for his restaurant in Toulouse—a cover, but true. He wants to set up an escape route through the mountains, use smuggler trails into Spain. He wants my help."

So the Jew from Toulouse came with a plan, Rosa thought. She shivered with excitement. When Sonny had told her he was a smuggler—so matter of fact, so calm—she had the same feeling.

"What will you do?"

"Help him . . . talk to Alesander. He has family on the other side and knows the routes."

"Have you taken any?" she asked.

"No . . . Alesander has."

"I want in."

Daniel Meyer returned the next day. Javier took him to the winery. A bottle of Domaine Poussard Superior—a blend of mostly tannat, with some cabernet franc and cabernet sauvignon—three glasses, a bowl of olives, and bread were on the long wooden table.

Rosa watched them go inside, waited for several minutes, then entered. Meyer stood with his back to her, inspecting bottles of wine. He turned at the sound of the opening door.

"Bonjour, Monsieur Meyer."

His eyes lingered for several seconds on her face, then grazed her from top to bottom. He nodded.

She extended her hand and waited. He said nothing, ignoring her hand, and returned to the wine. "I want to taste it."

They sat on hard benches, Javi and Rosa on one side of the table, Meyer on the other. Javi pulled the cork and poured. Meyer twirled the glass, sniffed, checked the color, and drank. Before he swallowed, he swished the ruby nectar in his mouth.

"Very nice. It will do," Meyer said. "I'll take 10 cases." He lit a cigarette and blew smoke from the side of his mouth. Squinting, he said to Javier. "Why is she here?"

"My name is Rosa." Irritation frayed her edges. "I want to help."

His eyebrows rose, rutting his forehead. "You're German."

"A Jew from Germany—a difference," Rosa responded.

"How did you escape?"

"Documents. Got to Belgium then Paris, now here."

"Be more specific," he demanded.

She told him about Kristallnacht, Sonny's smuggling, his forged documents, getting her out of Germany, then about Antwerp and Mons. "After everything, I hate Nazis . . . they should all die."

"Quite a story."

"I want to help."

"Help with what?" Meyer's eyebrow rose, questioningly, then the rest of his face caught up.

"Javi told me a little."

He reddened under Meyer's glare.

"We're close. Why wouldn't he tell me?"

"How close?" A weary smile came to his lips but not to his eyes.

"Friends." Rosa answered with finality, as if the question were impertinent.

Meyer's smile faded. His opaque, dark eyes scrutinized her. "I don't know you . . . did *not* invite you to this meeting. My business is with Javier, not Javier and *you*—how do I know I can trust you?"

She nodded. "The Poussards took in my parents a year and half ago to work in the winery . . . part of the refugee work program, which made them legal. I arrived in June from Paris, ahead of the Germans."

"They're no longer legal," Meyer said. "And you?"

"Sort of," she answered.

Meyer laughed, without mirth. "A little pregnant, too? What the hell does that mean?"

"I have a passport and identity card that needs . . . a little work."

"Explain."

"I . . . " Rosa hesitated, glanced at Javi, then continued, " . . . have a French identity: Rita Daurat, 28 Rue Raffet, Auteuil, Paris." The memory of her lifeless eyes, her grimace, her skin still warm, came back.

"How?"

"Driving from Paris . . . a German bomb hit her car. We stopped to help, too late. I found her passport and identity card. "

"So you took it?"

She nodded. "My photograph must be inserted. Good forgers are hard to find. I asked Javier for help."

He dragged on his cigarette and exhaled a long, gray plume. "Quick thinking. Who were you with?"

"Why the grilling?" she protested.

"I have to be sure."

"Agnes Capri and her partner. I worked at her nightclub. You may have heard of her."

He shrugged and gestured for her to continue.

"They took me as far as Bordeaux. I got a ride to Biarritz, from there a bus to Sare, and I walked . . . been here since."

He nodded. "Your French is pretty good . . . lose the accent or the passport's no good."

"I'll enroll in language school."

Javi laughed.

Meyer didn't. "I meant work on softening your accent—pass for Alsatian."

"Sure, I'll find a tutor, since we're only on the opposite end of France from Alsace," Rosa answered.

Meyer laughed for the first time, softening his features.

"The man I lived with in Paris passed me off as his niece from Strasbourg."

"You lived with a man?"

Rosa felt her face flush. "Jean's older than my father. He took me in as part of the family. Like I said, I'm married."

"So what if you're married. He's not here." Meyer turned to Javier. "You trust her?"

"Of course."

Meyer rubbed his hands, keeping them warm. Then he tore bread from the loaf, put it in his mouth, chewed it, and washed it down with wine. "Maybe . . . " he mused.

"Maybe . . . what?" Rosa asked.

"I fix your documents . . . you leave, go to Portugal . . . from there . . ." He shrugged.

"Use me. I'll stay . . . help smuggle people over the border—people like my parents."

"How did you avoid Gurs?" His tone was neutral, as if he wanted to know.

Rosa looked at Javi. "Luck, and Javi's family."

Meyer looked from Javier to Rosa. "It's dangerous . . . you get caught and it's Gurs for sure, maybe worse. You willing to risk it?"

Rosa held his gaze and answered, "I will risk everything to help."

Meyer moved his jaw, staring hard at Rosa. "All right, I'll take a chance. We need good people. You can be a courier?" His eyes remained fixed on Rosa.

"Stop staring! You're making me uncomfortable."

With a self-satisfied smile, he kept his eyes fixed on her. "'Stop staring!' Is that what you'd say to a Gestapo agent on a train or a cop in Marseille? 'Stop staring!'" He mimicked her voice.

She flushed a dull crimson.

"Your face is Semitic, but with your looks, it may not matter." He shrugged, then sighed. "I don't know what you have in mind—leading groups over the border, blowing up trains, or what. If I fix your passport and identity card, you can courier papers and money, maybe help at the border. You game?"

Rosa stared back at him and nodded. "I said I am."

"Good." He rested his elbows on the table and leaned forward. "You know the mischief Vichy makes for refugees and Jews?"

"We read the newspaper," Javi answered.

Ignoring that, Meyer started, "Late September, early October, Vichy enacted Statut des Juifs [Jewish Law], defining Jews as needing only two grandparents to be of the 'Jewish race.' Jews are forbidden to hold public office, to work in civil service, army, media, or education. It is a crime to listen to English radio, to speak favorably of de Gaulle. Signs that say 'Enterprise Françoise,' appeared in Marseille store windows, differentiating them from those owned by Jews. Vichy and its overseers are this . . . " he crossed the first and second fingers of each hand, " . . . close. We're being slowly strangled." His tone, though didactic, made sense.

"Run from Germany, only to find it in France," Rosa said softly.

He continued as if she had not commented. "In Bayonne there's a small German garrison, only 21 kilometers north, and the charming port of Hendy, 15 kilometers west across the bay from Spain. Geography puts you in the German zone—you know that?"

"Of course," Javi answered.

"That increases the difficulty and the stakes. There's still chaos, but that'll change. Screws will tighten." He looked at Javier. "Have Germans been to the farm?"

"No."

"They will. Cooperate, but don't overdo it. Act obsequious, and they'll smell a rat. Sell them wine, not too cheap, they may just take it, but I don't think so. Don't give them a reason to give the farm another look." He looked at Rosa. "You and your parents will be at risk." Then, turning to Javi, he said, "And your family for harboring them." He paused. "Your parents should get out."

"They never mention it. I'll talk to them."

"Soon!"

She nodded, then asked, "What's your plan?"

He looked from Javier to Rosa before starting. "Pipeline to Spain to get Jews . . . political opponents . . . British soldiers, fliers, out of France, quickly!"

Rosa and Javier exchanged glances.

"First, we deliver your parents to Spain, then Portugal. Take the heat off Javier. They need safe-conduct permits, identity cards, passports, French exit visas, and transit visas through Spain and Portugal—six documents, any two of which are hard to get hold of, let alone six! Your parents don't need safe-conduct permits or identity cards. Do they have passports?"

"German."

He nodded. "We avoid an exit visa by going over the mountain. That leaves the transit visas through Spain, then Portugal."

"Bold plan. How many you planning to save?" Javi seemed impressed.

"As many as we can. We're looking for more passages . . . no concern of yours. Best not to know. Our window is now!" His fist hit the table. "It could close any time. Spain will issue a transit visa if you hold a Portuguese transit visa and have a final destination overseas—Shanghai, Haiti, Cuba, anywhere. The problem is that the first is impossible, making the second unattainable. We solved that dilemma. A Portuguese consul in Bordeaux, a good man, liberally issued transit visas in defiance of orders. They pulled him but not before we got hold of one. Our cobbler in Toulouse is proficient with pen and printing press. He forged more, same with the Spanish visas."

"Why not a boat from Hendy?" Rosa asked.

Meyer shook his head, "Germans patrol the port a mere five kilometers south. The craggy, snow-covered Pyrenees are a formidable barrier and the Spanish authorities are vigilant. From here the Spanish border provides an excellent route. We like the mountains—fewer patrols on both ends."

"What about simple bribery?" Rosa asked.

"Possible but risky and never simple. Pay a guy, and he still turns you in. Even with proper papers, you might have to pay along the way."

Meyer told them about an American named Fry, headquartered at the Hotel Splendide in Marseille. "Centre Americain de Secours is his agency. He issues emergency U.S. visitor visas for a particular kind of refugee—writers, painters, and intellectuals. His preferred route is Banyuls sur Mer—west of Marseille, on the Mediterranean where France meets Spain—over the border to Portbou."

"We've heard that the mayor of Banyuls sur Mer is sympathetic and helps Fry. No one is arrested." He shrugged. "Germans will eventually catch on. He'll be replaced, and they shut down the route. And it's getting crowded at Banyuls sur Mer. Demand is higher than Fry can accommodate. There are others. We'll help fill the void but with a different route . . . on this side . . . closer to Portugal. We want to be ready as soon as the route's free of snow. That's where Javier, maybe you," pointing at Rosa, "come in."

"We're ready," Javier said.

"Guide set?"

"I have someone in mind."

Rosa turned to Meyer. "How do we communicate?"

"Good question," Meyer smiled.

She smiled back—a good student.

"Mail, using code, and couriers, where you come in." He pulled a paper from his pocket and handed it to Javier. "These are key words—visa, passport, and the rest." Turning to Rosa, he said, "When I get your passport and papers fixed, you'll be our courier. Women make good couriers; they're less threatening. I need your photograph. I'll be back, buying more wine. French love their wine and their women." Meyer flashed a winning smile, transforming his face into someone nearly attractive. He winked at Rosa.

Momentarily nonplussed, she looked away. For the first time, Meyer appeared sympathetic, almost likable, even slightly vulnerable. She recovered, then left to retrieve her documents and photos.

"Here," she said, handing them to Meyer, "Javi arranged for photos. My lifeline. Guard them with your life."

Meyer smiled, wryly. "Good line—our motto: 'Your lifeline. We guard it with our lives.'" He laughed at his little joke.

Not an unpleasant laugh, Rosa thought.

"I'll return soon. When snow's out, your parents go over the mountain."

"What do you think?" Rosa asked Javi after Meyer had gone.

"Damn well better work."

19

Sare, early March 1941

Creeping into Sare, a small convoy, three vehicles decorated with German crosses and swastikas, stopped in the square, making its presence felt. An officer stood, legs spread, hands on hips, conqueror's smirk seeping onto the cobbled streets. Soldiers handed papers to townsfolk. One nailed several broadsides to a post. And another waved to the children. They waved back. People stared, curious.

They stayed 30 minutes, then left. Javi witnessed the scene. After the convoy disappeared, he walked to the square with several others. They read the posters. One warned of spies in their midst; the other announced a meeting.

Someone cursed.

The plans with Meyer were on a low simmer. Soon the snow would be off the mountain. Rosa had not broached departure with her parents.

Several days later, Dominic asked Rosa and her parents to stay after the noon meal. "Notice of a meeting was posted in town. I was summoned with other farmers in the area."

"What does it mean?" Robert asked.

Dominic shook his head. "Don't know. Several of us—another winemaker, Vilar, and a farmer, Laure—talked to the police chief, a fellow named Morand, a good chap. Speculation is that farms will be inspected, crops and wine output monitored. I fear a percentage will be taken for use by the army here or sent to Germany."

Rosa recalled Meyer's warning. Hearing Dominic say it brought it nearer to reality. She chewed nervously on her lip.

"What about us?" Elise asked.

"As usual, don't leave the farm," he said. "You came here legally.

Morand knows . . . names are on a document in a file somewhere."
He shrugged. "Some of our neighbors have refugees working for
them. I don't how many. Someone might talk. You stay as long as
you like."

"Thank you. We have no place to go," Robert said.

Rosa saw an opening but hesitated.

"It's risky, helping us," Elise added.

"You help us in return," Dominic responded. Then he unfolded
papers he had taken from his pocket and placed them on the table.
"These were handed out . . . "

"What do they say?" Rosa asked.

"Propaganda nonsense: Germans are our friends, beware of
people sowing discontent, farmers are the vanguard of the *new*
France. Restricted movement—no visits to the coast." He hesitated,
before continuing. "More restrictions on Jews."

Robert sighed.

"We were supposed to register, but we didn't," Rosa said
defiantly. She was about to say more, but Dominic raised his hand.

"Listen carefully . . . I'll get a few days' notice of an inspection;
that's what we were told. When it comes, you leave. We have an old
hut down the valley. They'll never look there. Alesander will make
sure it's habitable. You stay there until it's safe. That's all we can do
for now."

A week later the notice arrived—inspection to take place the
following Wednesday, 12 March, one week away . . .

Shortly before noon, Rosa heard Leon bark. A breathless Javi
found Rosa at the back of the winery. "Hurry . . . we got to go."

"It's only Monday."

"Surprise! German bureaucrat with two soldiers."

"Where are my parents?"

Javi nodded. "Someone's getting them. Come with me." He went
to the door, Rosa following. Then he gestured for Rosa to wait,
walked outside, and looked around. "Clear—walk, don't run."

They headed for a stand of trees, bordering one side of the
vineyard. Leon led the way. When Rosa got to the hut her father was
there but not her mother. "Where's mother?"

His face pinched and pale, he shook his head.

Rosa squeezed his hand. "She'll come." Words belied her fears.

The afternoon slowly ticked away. Still Rosa's mother did not appear. Robert, stationed at the small window, kept a nervous eye on the approach. Father and daughter said little. Rosa knew well the ordeal of waiting. Sunset came—nothing. Voices were heard. Rosa stiffened.

Within seconds the door opened, and Javi led a tearful Elise into the hut. Robert embraced his wife.

"What happened?" Rosa asked Javi.

"She was trapped in the house. Quick thinking by mother got her into the cellar with seconds to spare. We decided to wait until dark."

Later, when they were alone, Rosa asked Javi, "How did it go?"

He shrugged. "Father and I gave a jerk with a steel rod up his . . . back a tour of the winery and vineyard. He didn't know the difference between txakoli, tannat, and cabernet franc. Just as well. Asked lot of questions."

"About what?" Rosa felt anxious.

"The winery, my army service, whether I've seen any of the men in my army unit."

"You think they know Meyer?"

Javi shook his head. "How could they? They asked about your parents."

"What did he say?"

"Father said they left for Marseille," he shrugged. "That's our story."

She nodded, unsettled. Her parents would have to be told.

"Then he went on about harboring refugees, the penalty . . . trying to scare us, looking for a reaction. Father was great—cool and detached."

The next day after lunch, Dominic told Robert, Elise, and Rosa they needed to talk, again.

Rosa knew what was coming.

Addressing Robert and Elise, he started, "He knew about you. I said you fled to Marseille. I had no choice, had to think of something."

"Marseille?" Elise questioned.

"Not good," Robert muttered with gross understatement.

"The inspection brought the dangers home. And there's something else. This morning I was in town and talked to Morand—

there's a push to round up foreigners. Orders from German command . . . Vichy too."

Robert froze as if turned to stone. Fear flooded his eyes.

"If you're found," Dominic shook his head, "I can't protect you— I might be arrested."

Elise wrapped an arm around Robert's waist to steady him. Suddenly, they looked old and tired, as if time had accelerated.

"You came here legally. Your status now . . . " He shrugged.

"I have the answer," Rosa took the opening.

They looked at her quizzically. Dominic's news frightened her more than her father's reaction.

"What are you talking about?" her mother asked.

"Javi should be here," Rosa said.

Dominic looked wary. "Why?"

"Something we need to tell you—it's important.

He squinted at Rosa, his jaw working. "I'll get him."

He returned with Javi.

"Javi, its time to tell them."

He nodded, then told his father about the man from Toulouse, his plan, and their part in it.

"Why wasn't I told?" Dominic asked.

"Waiting for the right time."

"Right time!" Anger flashed in Dominic's eyes. "I'm waiting."

Javi glanced at Rosa. "Remember when the German asked if I had seen any of my old army unit?"

"It was only yesterday." Dominic was testy.

"I lied." He told him about Daniel Meyer's vague talk of resistance when their unit disbanded, his visit to the domain, and his plan.

"Not enough for the two of you, you involve Alesander and his cousin. Damn!" Dominic cursed. "You put us all in danger."

"Alesander offered. And it's in Saint-Jean-Pied-de-Port, not here," Javi protested. "Nazis plan to find *enemies*, ship them to Germany. I can't . . . won't let innocents be brutalized."

"Don't make speeches!" Dominic snapped.

Rosa had never heard Javi talk like that. She was impressed.

"After surviving the war, you want to be shot for resisting?"

"I have to do something," Javi volleyed.

An uneasy silence ensued. The tension engendered by Dominic's news and Javi's revelations demanded an answer. Feeling the heel of German occupation, was Dominic second-guessing his decision to bring Robert and Elise to the farm?

Finally Rosa said, "You don't have to be involved . . . "

"You and Javi make me involved."

"Hear me out," Rosa said. "We'll get my parents off the farm and out of France. And I have documents that make me a French citizen."

"How?" Dominic asked.

"I'll explain. Please be patient," she said. Then to her parents: "You have passports . . . transit visas through Spain and a visa for Portugal will be delivered. Then you get a visa to . . . say, Cuba. Alesander will lead you over the mountain from Saint-Jean-Pied-de-Port . . . "

"I can't believe this!" Dominic was exasperated.

"Listen . . . please," Javi pleaded.

"We'll talk later!"

" . . . You won't need an exit visa. You have a little money saved for when you get to Lisbon."

Her parents were struck dumb.

"Javi, tell them it's true."

"It's true. Listen, Father, we get Robert and Elise to Saint-Jean-Pied-de-Port and from there into Spain. Danel, Alesander's cousin from Etxalar, it's near . . . "

"I *know* where it is!"

Javi flinched, then struggled to regain the thread of his narrative. " . . . um . . . he'll meet them at the summit and bring them down to Roncesvalles. Robert and Elise report to the Spanish border patrol." Javi faced them. "Show them your visas and then be on your way."

Robert finally found his voice. "Will they send us back?"

"I don't think so," Rosa said.

"You don't think so!" Robert was incredulous.

"You'll have valid transit visas, and you won't be staying in Spain," she responded.

Javi quickly added, "You might have to bribe them. According to Alesander, cigarettes work wonders."

Dominic sighed. "You trust this guy from Toulouse?"

Javi nodded. "I do."

The clock ticked. The only other sound was of five people breathing.

Robert broke the silence. "Dominic, we have to leave. It's the only solution." He turned to Rosa. "When?"

Javi answered, "When the snow is out."

"Will you come?" Robert asked Rosa.

Her hesitation answered his question. She shook her head. "Please don't try to change my mind."

"These papers of yours? Where did you get them?" her father asked.

She explained.

"Oh, my God! That poor woman." Elise put a hand over her mouth.

For the second time in a year, Rosa said good-bye to her parents. This time they were leaving for a destination far away, in a new hemisphere. Their next meeting would be . . . ? Best not to talk of it.

Meyer returned the following week. Javi met him in the winery. Javi told him about the early inspection and the tightening of the screws. Fear made Rosa impatient to get her parents onto the mountain. Their departure was set for 2 April, a Wednesday, but nature would not be rushed. Her second wedding anniversary would come two days after they left.

Rosa's passport and identity card were delivered. She was Rita Daurat, formerly of 28 Rue Raffet, Auteuil, Paris, now Domaine Poussard, Sare, Aquitaine. Rosa still needed a passierschein, or free-movement card, to cross between the occupied zone and Vichy. Meyer brought her one.

"Mademoiselle Rita Daurat, your back story?" Meyer waited for an answer.

Rosa blinked several times, then looked away. She felt foolish.

"What do you know about her?"

"She lived in Auteuil in the 16th A. Just before I left, bombs fell there, killed some people, destroyed a building." She shook her head. "I don't know the 16th, don't even know her husband's name."

"Make it up."

Her faced darkened.

"Be consistent, nothing elaborate, too hard to remember. If cops or Gestapo want to dig deeper, game's over. People know their own story, don't have to think about it. You had friends in Paris."

Rosa nodded.

"Use one for a story. Can't make it up as you go. And your accent, don't talk unless you have to, and then do it carefully," Meyer warned her. Then he left.

After he had gone, Rosa thought of Jean, then Catherine and Jacques, the store . . . Okay, she would say her husband had died, change it to the 3rd A. Rita and Jean lived above the store on Rue de Rosier.

Three days later, a letter arrived from Toulouse signed "Frank." Translating the code, Rosa knew to take a train to Toulouse on Monday, 24 March, then to the café on 42 Rue Montoyol, near the university, at noon—she was to knock three times.

Javi drove Rosa to St. Jean-de-Luz for the early train to Bayonne. He kissed her on both cheeks and left immediately.

Posters of smiling German soldiers holding children adorned the station walls, proclaiming friendship to the French; others warned of spies. German army uniforms sprouted like weeds between cracks of broken pavement in a bad part of town. Several soldiers bowed politely. One smiled and greeted her, "Bonjour, Mademoiselle."

Rosa smiled back, digging fingernails into her palms.

Then: "Identification, s'il vous plais . . . "

Her mouth tightened. How did that look? She tried to relax as she held out her documents and gazed into the middle distance. An ache in her stomach ascended. She took several breaths and tried to relax but couldn't.

His eyes went to her, then to the photograph. He smiled and returned her cards. "Merci."

She faced the window, her body rigid. Small towns, farms, and stands of trees dotted the pretty countryside, but she saw little of it. Fear of further encounters occupied her thoughts . . . Finally the train arrived in Toulouse. Next time would be easier.

Above the door of 42 Rue Montoyol was the word *Café*. The shades were pulled. She crossed the street: Three knocks on the plain blue door. Footsteps, key turning, door open. A woman in her twenties, fair-skinned and slim, faced Rosa. She leaned out, looking right and left. Rue Montoyol hadn't changed since Rosa's knock.

"Bonjour." Her smile revealed uneven teeth.

"I'm Rosa . . ."

Her gaze was steady. "Not here." She walked to the back, waving a hand over her shoulder, indicating Rosa should follow. "Hello, Rosa. I'm Celine, Daniel's . . . lover."

They sat in the small kitchen, facing each other at a table, Celine against the back wall, the rear door to her right. An oven and stove were opposite the wall, a refrigerator to her left. Shelves filled with kitchen paraphernalia lined the wall on the other side of the door.

"Trouble?"

"No."

Celine poured from a bottle of Domaine Poussard. "Cheers! . . . hungry?"

"A little."

Cheese and bread appeared on the table. Rosa ate. There was little conversation. Finally Celine said, "Daniel should be here shortly."

Three knocks on the door next to Celine. Daniel entered. He kissed Celine, then shook Rosa's hand, and sat in the third chair. "You made it."

"Why not?" Rosa shrugged, feigning nonchalance. Sonny told her how scared he had been crossing the border with Emil, the first time. At least, she hadn't seen demons, dancing on the side of the tracks.

"Any trouble at all?" He sounded concerned.

"Not really."

"It's okay to be scared."

She sighed, heavily and fell back against the chair. "That obvious?"

He smiled. "You're rigid as a nun in a whorehouse, and your leg's pumping up and down like a piston—a couple of clues."

Celine laughed, then Rosa joined in.

"Each time gets easier." Meyer took an envelope from his pocket—it contained her parents' documents. "Now, it's up to you and Javier."

She stared at her parents' tickets to freedom—and the mountain trek into unknown territory ahead of them. Much could go wrong.

Meyer must have read her mind. "Get them across safely . . . our trial run. Next time you're in Toulouse, we'll drink to success."

———

After sunset, 2 April

Javi drove 35 kilometers southwest to Saint-Jean-Pied-de-Port. Three passengers alighted. He left and would return at midnight. Rosa met Alesander near the inn, out of sight. His dark, intelligent eyes conveyed confidence.

"I'm coming . . . as far as the summit," Rosa said, almost as an afterthought.

"Come with us," her mother pleaded.

"No." The subject was closed.

Alesander and Rosa carried small electric torches, just in case. This was the starting point of the Camino de Santiago—ancient pilgrimage route over the mountain to the Cathedral of Santiago de Compostela. Alesander knew this oft-traveled route well.

"Single file behind me," Alesander instructed. "It's steep . . . narrow in places—be careful. No talking . . . whisper if you have to—voices carry in the thin air. The journey should take about five hours." He looked heavenward. "There's a half moon, you'll see your way—most of the time."

A long, open stretch from the edge of town to the woods posed an unavoidable risk. They hoped no one would see them, or if someone did that he would not care. Elise and Robert wore sturdy shoes, warm coats, and berets against the cold and wind. And they packed light.

Unused to hiking, especially at such an altitude, they walked slowly, stopping often to catch their breath. They marveled at the beauty of distant mountains and valleys below in the soft moonlight. Teased by the silver light, their eyes fooled their brains with animal-like visions. Suddenly, a new vista opened—as if they had taken blinders from their eyes. About an hour into the hike, they heard faint voices from ahead.

Alesander walked back to the others. "Might be a patrol," he whispered. His eyes swept the narrow trail. "Over there—behind the boulder," he ordered. Then to Rosa: "Go with them and follow my lead . . . understand?"

Slow to respond, maybe a little light-headed in thin atmosphere, she blurted, "What?"

"Listen to what I say . . . you'll know what to do."

166

She nodded, then scampered after her parents.

The voices grew louder. Within minutes, two French border guards appeared. One smoked a cigarette; both carried rifles, loosely slung over their shoulders. They didn't see Alesander until several meters away.

"Whoa!" One exclaimed.

"What are you doing?" asked the one with the cigarette.

Alesander faced the barrel of a rifle and raised his hands. "Walking."

"Bullshit . . . smuggler!"

"No!"

"Let's take him to town . . . it's cold . . . I'm hungry," the other one said.

"I'm with my girlfriend . . . " Alesander started, then quickly, "her parents object to me. Honey, come here!" His voice carried.

Rosa faced her parents. They clung to the other for protection. Their eyes were like bowls of cream, each with a blueberry floating in the middle. Placing a calming hand on their shoulders, then a finger to her lips, she whispered, "Stay still. It'll be okay,"

"We're engaged . . . give us a break," Alesander said, not pleading, not yet.

"Where the hell is she?" one of them asked, his tone incredulous.

"I'm taking her to meet my family in Espinal. Rosa, come here!"

Rosa slowly emerged from behind the boulder.

Dry mouthed, she felt her lips stick to her teeth when she smiled. She stood next to Alesander—tall, slim, and dark—modestly averting her eyes. They made a handsome couple.

He put his arm around her and pulled her close, kissing the top of her head. "See!"

The men looked at each other for a long moment. The one with the cigarette shook his head, a sly smile creasing his face.

"Get the hell out of here!" Said the other.

"Thanks!" Alesander responded, cheerfully. They walked away, his arm still around Rosa.

"Quick thinking," Rosa whispered.

"When you're really scared . . . " He squeezed her shoulder.

Rosa laughed nervously.

As soon as they were out of sight, they separated, stopped.

"Wait here. I'll take a look," he said.

"I'm coming."

They headed back. Muffled conversation came at them from down the trail. The two men stood in the same spot, smoking. Finally, they flicked their cigarettes into the darkness. One glanced back up the mountain.

Rosa and Alesander jumped back. In a few seconds, they were out of sight. Rosa moved.

"Wait." Alesander held her arm.

Nothing stirred—they were gone. Robert and Elise were frozen together, like ancient mummies.

"It's safe." Rosa helped her mother to her feet.

"Great acting!" Robert said, breathlessly. "Scared the hell out of me!"

"Me too," Rosa agreed.

In an hour and a half, they reached the summit. Danel, a shorter version of Alesander with the same mournful eyes, appeared from behind a boulder.

"Remember, when you get to Lisbon write to Dominic at the farm. Note the date of departure and one word, Cuba, or wherever. Nothing else—no names. They read the mail. I'll know you're safe. I love you . . . good luck! Until we meet again." Rosa hugged her parents.

"I love you—we'll miss you," her mother said tearfully.

"Take these . . . " Rosa handed her father several packages of cigarettes, " . . . if Spanish guards give you trouble . . . "

They hugged again.

"Elise, we have to go." Robert pried her from Rosa. Elise was crying

20

Rosa understood Sonny's escapades viscerally. She wanted to bottle the excitement on the mountain. Foiling the patrol was exhilarating—the danger brought her closer to Sonny, in her heart at least. Though she was scared, she wanted more, like an addict after another fix—so long as she survived to feel the high.

Rosa found purpose beyond the waiting. Smuggling refugees was a worthy endeavor and if it helped defeat the Nazis, even a little . . . She could dream.

Alesander took a different lesson from their experience. He needed new routes. Ainhoa, a village over the mountain to Dantxarinea, had the advantage of proximity—it was close to Sare. Bidarray was halfway to Saint-Jean-Pied-de-Port. In Bidarray an old Roman bridge crossed the River Nive to a path up the mountain and into Spain. Rotating routes avoided predictability and lengthened the odds. He hoped.

Six separate groups went over the mountain in April: three refugee groups and three separate groups of British soldiers. The small band guiding them kept busy.

Rosa accompanied a group including children. The airmen and the British soldiers cut off from their units moved south, eluding capture with the help of French soldiers and locals. In Spain, documents were not required.

Spanish authorities delivered soldiers to the British Embassy. Spain and neighboring Portugal were neutral, despite their fascist sympathies. Reeling from bloody civil war, Spain did not want to fight and would not risk angering the British. These groups encountered no problems.

Several days into May, Rosa was summoned to Toulouse, for her second trip.

"Congratulations!" Meyer smiled, broadly. Shades pulled at 3 PM, the café closed after lunch. Glasses of wine and a plate of food lay on the table. "How many groups?"

She told him.

"Great. Tell Javier I'm impressed. Be prepared for more." Meyer raised his glass. "To success."

Rosa felt flattered by Meyer's praise. "Oui. To success."

He drank, then poured more. "I'm part of a little band called the Armee Juive, Jewish Army. That makes you and Javier allies if not members."

"Never heard of it."

"Few have. It's under ground, started by two Jews from Lyon to fight Boche. Discretely, word got around the disaffected Jewish community . . . "

"Wouldn't that be everyone?" Rosa interrupted.

Meyer laughed, easily. "Word spread quietly, or we'd be dead. It's too early for fighting . . . for now resistance means propaganda—leaflets, newspapers, posters—drawing support from people. The good guys—Brits, free French, Soviets—need intelligence . . . we aim to provide what we can. That means codes, radios, money." He shrugged. "There's little in place."

He licked his lips and stuck a cigarette between them. "Secrecy, networks compartmentalized, hierarchically organized, so one cell can't lead to another. Several other groups operate in the south, separately . . . same goals: defeat the Boche." He lit the cigarette and kept it between his lips. Inhaling, then exhaling, he disappeared behind a grayish, blue cloud.

Rosa coughed and fanned the smoke with her hand.

"Sorry," he said, holding the cigarette to the side. "The difference is secondary goals—few care about Jews, so we have to."

Rosa nodded. "So . . . what am I here for?"

Slices of cheese and salami disappeared, washed down with wine. He wiped his mouth. "Your assignment ratchets the dangers up a notch—ready?"

Rosa nodded. "Tell me."

"Maps . . . information on German installations and supply depots need delivering. Get the paper . . . bring it here. I'll hand it to a Brit for delivery to London. They're hiding all over Vichy, waiting to get out."

Images of isolated, fearful soldiers distracted her.

"Rosa . . . you listening?" Meyer asked impatiently.

"Sorry . . . again?"

He told her again.

"When do I leave?"

"Tomorrow. Take the train to Gare de Lyon-Part-Dieu and meet a woman in a red coat at the station." He handed Rosa a ticket. "Leaves at 8:00 . . . arrives around 7:00. Name's Antoinette . . . folded newspaper in her hand. You're close friends. Hug her."

He kept his eyes on Rosa. "Got it?

"I vaguely remember how to hug," she murmured.

"Good! Thought you might be rusty. Whisper in her ear, 'I'm Judah's friend Rita.'"

"Maccabee or the other?" She smirked.

His laugh was equally sarcastic. "You done with the mishigas [silliness]?"

Her eyes twinkled mischievously. She nodded.

"Follow Antoinette's lead. She'll give you papers. Return at once."

Excited, Rosa took several shallow breaths. "Describe her."

"Can't. Make sure you're not followed. If they find papers on you . . . "

"Don't have to tell me," she interrupted.

He nodded. "Good cops watch eyes; they betray."

"I know."

"Can't say it enough." He handed her a piece of paper with an address. "Safe house near here. Memorize the address then give it back. Sleep there. Leave in the morning."

In Narbonne, Rosa switched trains to Montpellier, north through Nîmes, Orange, Montélimar, Valence, Vienne, and finally to Lyon's main station, Part-Dieu. Twice she was asked for identification. The police were polite. One wished her "a nice trip." She smiled at him.

Just before Montpellier, a long, black leather coat with coal black eyes under ridged brows and permanent scowl passed through the car—Gestapo! She averted her eyes. He could have had been a French copycat, suffering Gestapo hero worship. She stifled a laugh.

Smuggling involved waiting when nothing happened—you got bored or cocky then negligent. That's when mistakes happened, Sonny had explained. She would not let that happen.

Inside the busy terminal, the massive clock read 7:43. The train had been late. She surveyed the huge room. Excited, she felt a vein pulsing in her neck. Then the crowd parted, like Moses' Red Sea, and a red blotch appeared in the middle of the room, newspaper in hand. Tall and a little stout, the woman was somewhere in her forties, more matronly than threatening.

Rosa smiled and embraced Antoinette, whispering, "I'm Rita, Judah's friend." Her anxiety evaporated.

"Rita! Good to see you, again." Antoinette's voice was deep, reassuring. "Let's go around the corner, get a bite to eat."

Antoinette led her out of the station and glanced around. Hooking her arm through Rosa's, she began to walk. Several turns later, they stood in front of a café with no name, like Meyer's in Toulouse. Antoinette entered and Rosa followed past several diners, to the small kitchen.

"Wait here!" Antoinette ordered. Her eyes met those of the chef. A young woman washed dishes. Antoinette left through the back door.

The chef nodded at Rosa. The dishwasher stared at her, then returned to a pot. They ignored her, as if her presence was normal.

Rosa leaned against the wall. Ten minutes stretched to 30. She feared trouble, but said nothing.

The chef delivered plates of food to the dining room, then returned. Was that Antoinette's job?

"Thirsty?" He handed Rosa a glass of wine.

Startled, Rosa mumbled, "Merci."

"Hungry?"

She nodded.

He glanced into the dining room, then pointed to a chair next to her. "Sit . . . "

"I'm . . . " Rosa almost said her name but didn't, " . . . waiting for Antoinette."

"No problem. It's not busy—yet. If you're still here, you can cut vegetables, wait tables." He smiled then handed her a plate.

Rosa smiled weakly and took the food. When she finished, the girl took the plate and cutlery and washed it. The chef went to the dining room but did not return. Rosa shot a questioning glance at the young dishwasher, who shrugged as if to say "I don't know anything."

Rosa peeked through the glass into the dining room. The chef was talking amiably to a cop. The cop looked toward the kitchen. Rosa jumped back, afraid to look again.

The girl looked into the room. "No problem—friend."

Rosa wasn't so sure.

Several minutes later, chef returned, carrying empty plates.

"What?" Rosa felt trapped in the little kitchen.

"Constable Moreau, a friend." He shook his head. "No trouble."

After washing the dishes, the girl said good night and left. Thirty minutes later the chef said, "Wait." He left through the back door.

Rosa was alone. She peered nervously into the dark, empty café. Was it a trap? Would the cop return to arrest her? Her breathing turned shallow. Maybe she wasn't cut out for clandestine operations. Thoughts of prison and the cluster of women in Biarritz from Gurs made her shiver. She wrapped her arms around her chest. Stuck in Lyon at night . . . she had to calm down.

The front door opened, then closed. She froze. Antoinette entered.

"Where have you been?" Rosa nearly spit the words.

"Busy!" Antoinette snapped, apologized. "Sorry. I'm worried." She was shielding something.

"Problem?"

"Not sure. Follow me." She started, then stopped. "If we separate or there's trouble, go to the station. Leave."

"I don't know where it is. What's going on?"

"Something's wrong . . . Quickly!" Antoinette was out the door.

Rosa jogged to keep pace. Ten minutes later, Antoinette opened the door of a slightly run-down building. Rosa followed her four flights to No. 21. Antoinette knocked three times, once, and twice more.

Though Rosa was frightened, she smiled at the melodrama. The door opened a crack. Light filled the narrow space, then the door opened all the way. Rosa was not surprised to see the chef.

"Georges . . . Rita," Antoinette said between breaths.

He smiled but said nothing.

Rosa nodded.

Throwing her coat over a chair, Antoinette said, "Paris courier was expected at the cathedral at 4. I waited 30 minutes. He never arrived. After leaving you, I went back." She shook her head.

"Who were you looking for?" Rosa asked.

She shrugged. "Don't know. Same instructions: Woman in a red coat and newspaper."

"Don't like it," Georges said, speaking for the first time.

"Could have missed the train . . . " Antoinette started.

"Or been arrested," he said somberly.

They looked at each other. "First operation with sensitive documents, and it blows up in our faces." Antoinette shook her head.

"Is there someone you can contact?" Rosa asked.

"No. Coded instructions, one contact. How many contacts you have?"

Rosa felt her color rise and didn't answer the obvious.

"Until today you didn't know me, and I didn't know you."

"Let's give it until tomorrow," Georges said.

They looked at him.

"Is there a fallback?" Rosa asked.

They looked at her.

"Next day, same time."

"Then it's too early to give up," Rosa suggested.

"Rita's right," Georges said. "Possibilities are endless, too many to list." He shrugged.

"Let's calm down and repeat the process tomorrow," Rosa suggested.

They agreed.

"Rita, spend the night," Antoinette said.

"Where am I?" she asked. "How do I get back to the station?"

Georges told her, then wrote down the directions.

"Who was that cop?" Rosa asked.

"Like I said, an old friend. He asks no questions. We tell him nothing."

"Okay." Rosa was satisfied. "How are you related?"

"Married." Antoinette frowned. "Less we know about each other, the better."

In the morning, rain kept Rosa inside. She paced. Time dragged. Antoinette played solitaire. Georges lit one cigarette, then another. The air became opaque and soupy; it was hard to breathe. She opened a window and stuck her head out but got wet. She wanted to walk in fresh air and stretch her legs . . . then remembered the trouble her presence had brought Jean in Paris.

"Your French is good, considering." Antoinette's deep voice, coming from behind, startled her.

The rain fell harder. Rosa lowered the window, leaving a crack. "That obvious?"

Antoinette shrugged. "Not so much. What do you think, Georges?"

He took a last drag then stubbed his cigarette out. "Now that you mention it."

"I hate everything German!" Rosa's outburst surprised her. "They should go to hell!"

Antoinette pursed her lips and nodded. "No argument here. Be careful, anger makes your accent stronger."

Rosa nodded, embarrassed. "Otherwise my accent . . . ?"

Cocking her head, Antoinette answered, "Slight, like I said, your French is good. My ear is better than most. Isn't it, Georges?"

He nodded in agreement.

"How many times were you stopped for documents?"

"Twice on this trip."

"And other times?"

Rosa nodded. "No questions . . . didn't say much."

"That's good. You could be a Jew—Spanish women are dark," Antoinette paused, " . . . maybe a North African mix."

Rosa laughed. "I'm a Jew from Berlin, playing at being Rita, a French woman from Paris, instead of being with my husband, who's God-knows-where. Last saw him in Belgium on a train that took him back to Antwerp. Cops could have had him deported, so I guess he caught a break. And I could have left France with my parents and been in Lisbon," her eyes fixed on Antoinette's, while moving her hands in an inclusive gesture. "Instead I stayed for this."

"Hope you find your husband . . . glad to have you with us until you do."

"And you and Georges?" Rosa asked.

Antoinette sighed and looked at Georges, her eyes softening. He met her gaze. Finally, she said, "Our only son was killed the second day of the invasion, somewhere near Maginot. We refuse to collaborate, don't we Georges?"

He nodded. "Whatever it takes. Little things now, later . . . "

"Rita . . . " Antoinette looked away, her face calm in repose, " . . . we all have our reasons."

"I'm sorry," Rosa said softly.

"If we survive, we'll grieve properly," she said. "Surviving is what matters. My advice, for what it's worth, is to stay calm. It's obvious. We constantly tell each other to stay calm. Anger clouds judgment."

At 3 PM Antoinette left for the cathedral. Half an hour later, Georges and Rosa left for the café. It opened at 7:00. Rosa would wait there until 5:00.

Georges cut onions.

"Can I help?" Restless, Rosa wanted something to do—to make time pass and calm her nerves.

He shrugged and returned to the onions, head down, sniffling. "Wash the carrots in the sink. Then slice them thin." He gestured toward the pantry.

Rosa was still preparing the carrots when Antoinette came in, smiling.

"He missed his connection and spent the night in Beaune. Police hassled him, but that's all," she said.

The next day in Toulouse, Rosa and Meyer sat at a table in his empty café, the unopened envelope between them.

"A day late. I was concerned."

"That's reassuring." Rosa's smile barely registered. "Courier missed his train—scared the hell out of us."

They stared at the envelope.

"You going to open it?" she asked.

He nodded. "We have to make a copy in case it's lost or captured." Still, he didn't move.

"It won't bite," Rosa said.

"No." Meyer sliced the envelope with a knife. He removed a map of Paris and a list. He placed them side by side on the table.

The map was torn from an atlas or a tourist book. Paris was

divided into the 20 arrondissements with major streets and boule-vards. Someone had written the numbers 1 to 8 in thick black ink.

"No. 1, near Porte de Clignancourt Métro stop, 18th A."

Rosa referred to the list. "Number 1 has written next to it: 'German tanks stored at old Renault storage lot.'"

"No. 2 has an arrow, pointing off the map."

"Le Bourget—Luftwaffe headquartered at Le Bourget Airport."

They went from map to list, checking them off as they went. At the end they fell silent.

"This is crap!" Meyer exclaimed. "Putting everyone at risk—for this? We got to do better."

Three days later, after dark, a British lieutenant with two enlisted men appeared at Domaine Poussard. Their civilian clothing made their origins unapparent. Only the officer spoke French. Attached to the 1st Armored Division landing in Cherbourg on 20 May 1940, they had reassembled south of the Seine. They had too few tanks, a concern become reality, and were cut off from retreat. They ended in Toulouse. Meyer learned of them from a colleague and sent them to Domaine Poussard, with forged safe-conduct passes—and the enve-lope—in hand.

Harboring refugees was dangerous, aiding British soldiers suicidal. Getting them quickly over the mountain was imperative. They had assured Dominic that no soldiers or refugees would come to the domain, but sometimes it was unavoidable. They would cross at Ainhoa.

"Hope it helps. It's only a start," Rosa said.

By midafternoon the Brits were under a tarp covered with empty crates in the back of the truck. Before they departed, Alesander handed a bag to Davidson. "Pepper—put it on your pant cuffs. Wards off dogs."

He had learned several other tricks. Siesta, early afternoon, was the best time to cross. Sometimes it was best to be shoeless—uncomfortable but quiet. Danger loomed despite their precautions. Anxiety and dread intertwined with the work that was too important to let that affect them. Duty trumped fear.

The springtime brought longer days, sunshine broken by rain showers. Farmers welcomed the warmer days and cool evenings of the foothills. Rosa and Emil had moved into the cottage her parents had vacated. Dominic offered her a position as an apprentice wine maker in addition to her regular duties. She welcomed the challenge. Dominic asked no questions about her periodic absences.

May 1941 was coming to an end when another civilian group arrived. Meyer sent four men and two women. The men waited in Saint-Jean-Pied-de-Port, outside the inn. The women arrived at the domain midmorning and were immediately taken to the winery. Visions of the women at the bus station in Biarritz resurfaced. Now, Rosa hungered for their stories.

"I'm Rita." Rosa extended her hand.

"Lilli." She shook Rosa's hand, then introduced her companion. "This is Anni."

Anni stared impassively from behind Lilli, saying nothing. Her face was immobile, like stone. Lilli talked for both, in German.

Anni from Berlin and Lilli from Vienna were both Jews, arrested in Paris and met at Hel d'Hiv, the indoor bicycle velodrome, near the Eiffel Tower. Within days, the Nazis had herded them onto railway cars for permanent internment at Gurs.

"No physical abuse, though conditions were degrading—little food, no privacy, filthy," Lilli explained. We were a motley bunch: Jews, German and Austrian anti-Fascists, even some Nazis, but they kept to themselves. 'Undesirables,' the unwanted ones, had it the worst—they were segregated, got smaller rations, were probably abused. They had no contact with other prisoners. Some of us threw food over the fence to them. I'm thin, but the undesirables were emaciated."

"What had they done?" Rosa asked.

Lilli shook her head. "Don't know—Communists, suspected spies?"

"I was a socialist in Vienna before Anschluss, so my name is probably on the list that Vichy will hand over to the Nazis."

Rosa winced. "How did you escape?"

"Stole releases. The commandant was actually sympathetic. When he realized France was nearing defeat, he lost interest. One evening several of us flirted, got him drunk, and stole them." She smirked. "I don't think he cared."

"Congratulations. We'll get you out."

"We appreciate the trip over the border. Don't we, Anni?"

Pale and unsmiling, Anni nodded. Her dependence on Lilli, and her unwillingness, or inability, to engage, concerned Rosa. The women hid in the back of the truck.

Alesander waited in Saint-Jean-Pied-de-Port with the men. Rosa made her third trip up the mountain to support the women. Making good time, the group reached the first rest stop in 45 minutes for a five-minute break. Water was passed around. Several smoked. Conversation was muted.

They continued single file, Alesander at the lead, followed by the four men, then Lilli at Anni's elbow, Rosa at the rear. Several minutes later, the boulder behind which Rosa had hidden with her parents loomed into view. The vivid memory prompted sudden fear and foreboding. Rosa still felt uneasy, but she blamed it on the rock.

Small stones crunched under foot, creating a quiet cacophony in a minor key. An occasional whispered exchange passed, like the wind, unintelligible. Clouds like crumpled paper hung in the sky, illuminated by a partial moon. Grand vistas opened as the trail rose before. Soon the trees disappeared, and the trail narrowed—one side was a wall, the other a sheer drop. Delivering people to freedom was exhilarating, unlike anything Rosa had ever done. She inhaled the fresh mountain air with pure joy.

Alesander stopped and held up his hands. He spoke to the man behind him, then each traveler passed the message on in turn.

"Walk carefully. It's steep."

Upon their reaching the second narrowing, another vista opened. Rosa gaped at the indescribable drama of the massive mountain fringed with snow, the laurel on its brow. Suddenly anguished wailing pierced the silence, sending a second chill up Rosa's spine—Anni was on her knees.

"No further," she screamed in German, her head tilted back, arms outstretched, keeping demons at bay.

Lilli tried to comfort her with words to no avail. Anne's screams prevented conversation.

Rosa muffled Anni's mouth with her hand. Anni bit her, not hard, and kept on screaming.

"Make her stop," Alesander beseeched. "A patrol will hear."

"Take her back . . . We'll be caught," one of the men pleaded.

"Shut her up," another said.

"She's sick," Rosa snapped.

"Five of us, one of her." Truth put matters in perspective.

Rosa knelt and exhaled softly a soothing "Shhh . . . " in Anni's ear.

Anni's eyes closed. She quieted, and Lilli took Rosa's place in the line.

"She going to be okay?" Alesander asked.

Rosa shook her head. "Don't know."

They remained, the men tugging to leave, the women unable to do so. Lilli would not abandon her friend.

"How sick is she?" Alesander asked Rosa.

"Very," Rosa answered.

"We have to move," he said.

Voices came from ahead. Everyone froze. Even Anni sensed the change. Three men appeared, two in uniform. Two men supported the third.

"Danel?" Alesander exclaimed.

Danel and a border guard supported the other guard, who was unable to walk.

Attention moved to the new arrivals and problems they posed. Only Lilli kept her focus on Anni. Danel's presence muddied the picture. The border guards had problems. Rosa and Alesander had problems. Anni had problems. Everyone had problems.

Alesander met the three newcomers, the others staying back. Rosa stood between the two groups. Lilli knelt beside Anni. The border guards, Danel, and Alesander, were close enough for Rosa to hear. One of the guards slipped on loose rock, spraining his ankle. Danel saw it and offered help.

"Don't give a damn about them," the injured guard said. "Get me off the mountain."

Alesander agreed. No questions asked.

"Good," thought Rosa.

Anni saw men in uniform and became agitated. She screamed, "Polizei . . . polizei . . . polizei!"

Lilli's soothing talk was futile.

Anni stood, staring at the border guards, a crazed-feral look in her eyes. Rosa joined Lilli, each holding one of Anni's arms. She thrashed with the strength of a mad woman and broke free.

"Anni—no . . . " Lilli screamed.

It was too late. Anni ran wildly back the way they had come. Her gait was uneven—she listed from side to side. All eyes glued to her mad dash. Rosa and Lilli were slow to pursue.

Suddenly, Anni stopped and turned. Her face was a mask of anguished pain, saying "Enough!" She seemed to relax, her body slouched, then her face sagged. Lilli almost had hold of her arm when Anni screamed, "Nicht mehr! [No more]."

Her leap from the path was surprisingly strong. For an instant she seemed to hang in the air, arms and legs spread, like a child making an angel in the snow. Then she fell through air, out of sight.

Lilli's arms outstretched, reaching for her friend, to empty space. Rosa grabbed Lilli around the waist in the event she had a similar idea. The others watched in shocked disbelief.

Alesander came to Rosa's side. He grabbed Lilli's arm, pulling her from the brink.

"Tell her there's nothing she can do. She has to go with Danel. I made a deal: we help get the guard down, and they go with Danel."

Rosa was in shock, but she nodded her understanding.

Lilli cried, unable to comprehend that Anni had fully unwound, like a watch spring gone haywire.

Rosa embraced Lilli. "Go. Be strong," she whispered.

Then Lilli plodded down the mountain, one foot in front of the other.

———

Anni's placid face filled Rosa's inner screen. Frantic, lurching, grasping . . . then floating into the void, a feather, rocking back and forth, until her body splayed and broke unseen in the depths below.

Nightmares haunted Rosa for weeks. A bird, wings flapping, was tethered to the ground, unable to save Anni. Or there was the sensation of free fall, stomach in her mouth, blood rushing to her head: she was impotent, awaiting certain death, arms and legs pumping frantically to gain purchase in the air. Death awaited. Life after the mountain was impossible.

Rosa vowed to stay off the mountain until she left France. The dull, predictable life of Domaine Poussard sufficed for now. Between her winemaking apprenticeship, chores, and courier route, her plate was full. Much had happened in a year . . .

May yielded to the long, hot days of summer. Grapes ripened to plump juiciness. Lost in mindless tasks, Rosa often glanced toward the road. Sonny strolled nonchalantly toward her, and they embraced, her waiting over. The jagged edge of a barrel intruded, dashing her dream to harsh reality, like Anni, into the void. The not-knowing...

In August, a letter in Rosa's mother's hand arrived from Lisbon: "Havana, early September. Love . . . " Her parents had a future.

21

Sare, May 1943

Rosa traveled to Toulouse twice each month to collect and drop documents. Occasionally she made contact with anxious refugees arranging their departure. Traveling to the point of departure to meet Alesander—in Saint-Jean-Pied-de-Port, Ainhoa, or Bidarray—was the task of the refugee. Documents had to be completed. That meant more waiting and increasing anxiety for the refugees hiding in Toulouse or on farms or neighboring towns and villages, trying to elude arrest, internment, and deportation.

By the end of 1942, France was thoroughly under the Germans' callous thumb. The mountainous border was no longer a sieve; it had gradually tightened. The smuggling—more dangerous than ever—continued.

A sad, mentally unstable woman's inability to cope had led to tragedy on the mountain. They moved on. Danel, by helping the injured guard, had earned dividends that increased when Alesander brought him down the mountain. They exploited the opening. Essentially simple men with simple needs, the border guards had been as horrified as the others by Anni's leap. In exchange for turning their backs on a few refugees and providing information on patrols from time to time, the guards were able to line their pockets with extra cash. Thus two accomplices were gained.

Rosa's dislike for Meyer eased. He had treated her badly to test her resolve. Cold and analytic, occasionally charming, he was sincerely concerned about her safety. She never doubted his worth as a trusted ally or his commitment to the cause. For that alone she respected and eventually came to like him. Still, he could be a jerk.

"We're laying the groundwork for invasion," Meyer started.

"America's in the war—Brits aren't alone. Information on bases, troop levels, materials, and supplies must get to England. That means a trip to Paris."

"When?" Rosa was surprised. Her first thoughts were of Annette and Jean, not of a mission of her own.

"Soon. You'll need cover."

The thought had vaguely occurred to her.

"You have a lover—Celine's brother, André."

Rosa frowned. "I don't want a lover," she protested.

"You a modern French woman?" Meyer smiled enigmatically.

"Shut up!"

He laughed. "Only a cover. Don't go off on me."

"So tell me."

"You're a couple—he goes along. A man or woman alone is suspect, but a young couple . . . " He shrugged. "Andre's smart. Not a Jew, so it's easier for him to move around. His flat is nearby. From now on you stay there."

André Tournier was 30 years old, had graduated from university in Toulouse and served in the defeated army. He had taught history in a local high school before and after his service, but then he had quit, refusing to teach the lies demanded by Vichy. Now he scrounged a meager living.

"When do I meet him?"

"Dinner at 7:00—you, André, Celine, and me. Nice and cozy."

They sat at the back. Most of the tables would be empty until 8:00. Rosa liked André immediately, which she found disconcerting. He was the male version of Celine, though more attractive. Longish, curly blond hair fell over his ears. He smiled easily, his gaze warm and direct. She felt her face flush when he talked to her.

Needing equilibrium, she asked, "What do you expect from me?"

He leaned back, uncomfortable for the first time. Celine and Meyer looked on, amused.

He considered before answering: "Courtesy, cooperation, devotion to our cause."

Rosa pursed her lips, about to speak, but André continued.

"I know about your husband . . . my love life is already full." He smiled.

"Good." Rosa broke eye contact.

An amiable understanding was reached—they were to be lovers in public, friends in private.

Rosa, Meyer, and André met at the café after it closed. A candle flickered on the table, creating moving shadows. Meyer poured wine.

"It's bad in Paris," Meyer started without pleasantry. "Rumors of rafles [roundups] of Jews in July last year . . . worse, much worse than before. Jews registered with police then arrested, sent to prison."

"Another Kristallnacht," Rosa murmured.

"Listen to this." He read: "'Death to the Jews! Death to all that is false, ugly, dirty, repulsive, Negroid, crossbreed. The Jew is not a man but a stinking beast. We defend ourselves against evil, against death—and therefore the Jews!'" He looked up. "March '41 newspaper."

"What's new? I read that crap for years," Rosa sneered.

"What do you want?" André asked Meyer.

"Go to Paris. Meet a contact. He'll pass information—good stuff! Bring it back. We'll hand it off to someone sent through Lisbon. While you're there, find out what's going on."

"When?" Rosa asked.

"Tomorrow. You have to be there before the seventh." Meyer handed each an envelope. "Money for a ticket, hotel, and food. Memorize the instructions, then burn them. You're newlyweds, André and Rita Lucas, easy to remember. "

Rosa counted the money.

André folded the bills and put the small wad in his pocket. "Paris is a cesspool of Gestapo. Take no chances. Make contact and get out. Rosa, you know some people."

She nodded.

"If you can find them without delay, get information."

"Why us and not a larger resistance group?" André asked.

Meyer shrugged. "Don't know. Take it as an honor."

Excitement jousted with fear, both yielding to anticipation. Rosa told André about Paris, about Annette and Jean. After completing the mission, they would seek them out. Had Jean returned? Changes that had vexed her in the past now did not. Rosa had changed. In André, she saw an eager and enthusiastic partner, but he was green. She was a veteran . . .

"Why are you traveling to Paris?" the police asked.

"Our honeymoon!" André smiled broadly, raising Rosa's hand, showing off her wedding ring. On request, he produced a forged marriage license dated 3 May 1942. She smiled shyly. His ring came from a pawnshop near the station in Toulouse.

Hard eyes searched their faces as they passed. "I see Gestapo everywhere," Rosa muttered when they were safely beyond. They were tense and ill at ease, their conversation stilted and terse when they were alone. An hour into the trip, Rosa realized the problem.

"Sit close. We just got married—hold me," she whispered into his ear. Feeling his arm around her, she smiled. The tension lifted, at least in part.

"Cloak-and-dagger is new," André whispered back.

"You're doing just fine, darling."

André laughed, then hugged Rosa with both arms and kissed her forehead. How long had it been? Was Meyer right that she had forgotten? Guilt drenched her in a sudden downpour: "It's for the cause," she told herself.

Gare d'Austerlitz sat on the left bank in the 13th Arrondissement, neighboring the Latin Quarter, the 5th A. Marais lay directly across the Seine on the Right Bank. Signs in German directed them. They checked into Hotel Monge, a small inn on Rue Monge.

Their instructions were cryptic: "10 AM . . . 7 May, greet man wearing hat, briefcase in left hand on corner Rue Mouffetard—Rue Saint-Médard—'Bonjour Monsieur, is Pantheon a church or patriotic monument?' Miss connection, repeat next day; abort after two attempts, return immediately."

Rue Mouffetard's long sloping street of shops was familiar ground to Rosa. She had often pushed little René through Place du Pantheon, past bakeries and cafés. The area was unchanged but for German signage and uniforms.

The morning sun cast long shadows as they strolled to meet their quarry. They stopped on Rue Mouffetard for coffee and croissant. Back on the street, they stared into shop windows, stealing glances toward the rendezvous site.

"There, hat, briefcase in left hand," André whispered excitedly.

They walked to the man. "Bonjour, Monsieur," said André.

The hat jerked at the greeting. Nearly a head shorter than André, the man was thin, wore round wire glasses, his face pinched with worry. With good reason, should he be discovered he would be shot. He waited.

"Sir, is the Pantheon a church or a patriotic monument?"

His smile brittle, he looked from one to the other, cleared his throat and perhaps his nerves. "Interesting question. It was built as a church, but now . . . " He waved a hand. "Come . . . I will show you." He began to walk.

They followed him to the impressive entrance.

"You will see for yourselves that both of you are correct."

Inside was an enormous atrium surrounded by neoclassical columns and capped by a magnificent dome. The cool marble surfaces smelled of old stone and the long dead. Their voices carried—they must speak softly or be overheard.

"The Pantheon—Greek for 'Every God'—was built in the 17th century as a church dedicated to St. Genevieve. After the revolution," his voice took on a hard edge, "everything changed." He led them to an alcove, glanced around, making sure they were alone. "This is Voltaire's crypt." He hunched his shoulders and pulled an envelope from an inside pocket. André took the envelope, and it disappeared into his pocket. The exchange took seconds.

"So, you see the Pantheon is no longer a church but rather a mausoleum. Enjoy your time in Paris. Good day to you both."

Rosa's heart thumped, and a vein pounded in her temple, surely echoing within the vast rotunda. "Merci," she said softly to the stranger's back as he disappeared. Then to André, "Let's look around." Ten minutes later they were gone.

The late morning sun had warmed the air. Rosa walked quickly, then slowed for André to catch up. Her eyes scanned every face. A man on the corner smiled at Rosa. She grabbed André's hand and tightened her grip. The seconds ticked slowly by.

André hugged her. "Calm down. It's done."

"Too exciting for a simple girl." Rosa's head fell on his shoulder.

He kissed her neck. "Keeping up appearances."

"Don't get carried away," she giggled.

Taking a circuitous route to the hotel, they gawked like tourists while roiling inside. The walking calmed her. They chatted about nothing. Rosa stopped to stare into a shop window, examining the dresses on the mannequins. One displayed fancy undergarments.

"I need some of those."

Before André responded, she was inside. He shrugged and followed.

For 20 minutes, Rosa examined panties and bras. Frowning, she held one up for André. "Darling, what do you think?"

He puffed out his lips, uncertain, pretending to be interested. "Whatever you need, sweetheart."

She purchased one of each.

Back on the street, Rosa whispered, "Perfect husband . . . "

. . . André locked the hotel room door. Rosa threw the package on the bed.

"God—we did it!" Her eyes were wide with astonishment. "That was fun!"

"I thought you'd fly back. Model your panties for me."

"Dream on!" she answered sarcastically, then laughed.

"Let's see what the fuss was about," André unfolded three oversized pages of blueprints and one smaller sheet. He laid them side by side on the bed.

"My God!" Rosa burst out.

"Heinkel HE 177," André read from the top of the first page, then looked at the other two blueprints.

Rosa held the fourth page. "These are notes."

André looked up from the plans. "What do they say?"

"Technical problems . . . French production lagging . . . " She skimmed the page. "'February 1941—French production quota— 3,000 planes, 13,500 aero-engines. Problems with aluminum . . . coal shortage.' There are more numbers . . . "

"How the hell did he have access?"

"Who cares—it's fantastic!" Rosa's euphoria turned to anxiety. She glanced around the room. "Have to hide them . . . they make me nervous."

They folded the pages and returned them to the envelope.

"Where?" Rosa asked under her breath, continuing her survey of the bed, tiny table with lamp, small armoire, framed picture of the Eiffel Tower, tattered rug, and window opening onto an enclosed courtyard.

André followed her gaze.

"Not much to work with," Rosa observed.

"Carry it?"

"Too dangerous. There's got to be . . . " Her voice trailed as she paced and then opened the window. She leaned out, feeling along the sill. "Nothing."

"Have to think . . . only one more day," André urged.

Rosa removed the picture from the wall and turned it front to back. "If we can get this off . . . "

André manipulated the backing and soon had it apart.

Several minutes later they were staring again at the iconic image of the Eiffel Tower

22

Paris, May 1943

Agnes Capri's Cabaret sign was gone, and the windows were dark—a stark contrast to its neighbor, Le Petit Theatre.

Les Femmes Savantes (The Learned Ladies), a Moliere comedy, was playing. Posted on the wall next to the door, the playbill noted, "Annette Dufy in the part of Henriette." The curtain rose at 8 PM.

"We'll return after the performance," said André.

Then Rosa said, "Let's walk to the Marais. I want to see whether Jean . . . "

Holding hands, they strolled the Tuileries past the Louvre to the embankment. André browsed several bookstalls and purchased a book. They left the river to meet Rue de Rivoli, turning left, then right onto Rue du Roi de Sicile. Rosa had often walked that route with René and exchanged smiles and waves with the regulars. Not so today. Had she receded, long forgotten, like a toothache or last year's cold spell? The crowds seemed smaller than she recalled.

There were pigeons, heads bobbing, book dealers and artists selling on the embankment, obsequious collaborators plying German patrons—Marais's colorful people all chased crumbs. Rosa's beloved Louvre had closed, its treasures removed to undisclosed locations to prevent damage and looting. Partially reopened, it was skeletal, devoid of viscera. She refused to enter. An oppressive atmosphere permeated Paris; its people were under a microscope, constantly watched. The city had lost its magic.

In front of the butcher, where Jenny and Max had stood, Rosa now saw only empty space. Had Jenny found Max? Were they hiding in Paris? And Jean? Buffeted by memories, fond and bitter, she felt exhausted. She wanted to leave.

They stopped in the alley.

"You know what to do." André knew about the cop's late-night visit three years before that had sent them running to Annette. "I'll wait here."

Five minutes turned to ten. Rosa was jittery. Voices approached; she stiffened. Jean turned the corner. His smile lit the night. They hugged as André looked on.

They sat in the café, at the table where Jean and Rosa had drunk wine the night before he left Paris. André ordered wine and food.

"I couldn't . . . stay away. My life is here . . . nothing for me out there. I missed Paris." He pointed, absently. "I was a burden to them."

"I don't believe it."

"We argued. Catherine and Jacques sold the grocery. They're scared."

"Rightly so," André interjected. "After the rafles."

Jean's ashen face nodded. "I miss them all terribly."

"Where's Alain?"

"I don't know." Jean shook his head. "Missed him by two days. He left a note saying he couldn't face Germans occupying Paris." He paused. "Was I wrong to return?"

"Not for me to say," Rosa answered.

André, not so constrained, said, "Remains to be seen. Be wary—you and every Jew in Paris are at risk."

They were silent.

"Have you been hassled?" she asked.

"Not yet." He sounded tired. "They make mischief, spread lies."

"You have no reason to stay—*leave!*" Rosa implored.

Jean didn't answer. Instead he asked, "What's with you two?" He looked at André. "You're not Sonny."

"No," André agreed.

"Who are you? Why are you both here?"

"André's a friend, and Sonny's still missing. That's all I can say."

Jean frowned, dissatisfied with her answer. "Can you say when you're leaving?"

"Tomorrow or day after. I'll see Annette tonight after the play. Have you seen her?"

"No. What's she in?" He was just making conversation.

191

Rosa told him. Jean nodded but seemed uninterested.

"What have you heard from Catherine and Alain?"

"Catherine is in Marseille, homesick but . . . well, trying to leave France for . . . " He shrugged.

"South of France overflows with refugees . . . That didn't come out right."

"I saw for myself, and Catherine wrote as much. She wants me to come."

"Leave with us. Go to her," Rosa said, trying to keep the urgency from her tone. "Do you have a free-movement card?"

He nodded. "I needed one to return." Then he mumbled, "I don't know."

"Think about it. What about Alain?"

"His last letter was posted in Lyon. That was two weeks ago. He may have joined Catherine . . . " Jean massaged his forehead and closed his eyes, then sighed. "Alain will join the resistance. He didn't have to write it." He gave a weary shrug. "He's . . . angry."

"So are we," André offered.

"Be careful." Jean looked from one to the other, then slapped his palm on the table and forced a smile. "Enough about me—are you still in . . . ?"

She laughed. "Sare."

"A million years ago," Jean murmured.

"Seems so," she agreed. "My parents are in Lisbon, heading to Cuba. They went over the mountain into Spain, then to Portugal. It's possible for you and Catherine. Groups operate near the Mediterranean. Maybe Catherine and Jacques will find someone. Give me her address. I can help."

"You know about such things?" Jean asked.

Rosa placed a hand on his. "Tomorrow morning we'll talk more. Think about what I said." They left the café.

Cast members straggled out of the theater. Annette was not among them. Finally, she appeared with a woman. They talked for several minutes, then separated. Annette walked toward the Seine. They followed.

Annette turned on Avenue de Opera. Rosa caught up to her and spoke softly, "Annette!"

"Rosa!" she exclaimed, before seeing her.

They embraced.

"Call me Rita."

Confused, Annette nodded. "All right."

André waited nearby.

Annette eyes went from one to the other.

Rosa gestured with her head toward André. "André. I'll explain but not here. Can we go to your flat?"

"Of course. I moved into my parents' flat near Pont Mirabeau—why not? It's paid up, sitting empty."

. . . They sat in the kitchen at a table beside a window, overlooking the courtyard.

"Hungry?" Annette asked.

André nodded.

A loaf of bread, honey, marmalade, a pitcher of water, and bottle of wine appeared. "Not much—sorry."

"No matter. This is a lovely flat," Rosa said.

"Oui . . . oui . . ." Annette chirped. "I don't want to talk about the flat." She looked from one to the other: "Why?"

Rosa and André exchanged glances.

"Some kind of signal?" Annette asked sarcastically.

André laughed.

"Who is he?" She smiled at André. "Other than a good-looking man?"

Rosa didn't comment.

"What happened to Sonny?"

"Annette . . ." Rosa started, trying to be patient. "André is part of something that has nothing to do with Sonny."

"I don't understand."

"Sonny is still missing. André and I are . . . comrades, friends."

"Comrades," Annette repeated then her eyes narrowed with understanding.

Rosa told Annette about Rita Daurat and smuggling, including André. She said nothing about Domaine Poussard or her reason for being in Paris. "Jean's back. I offered help, getting him out of France."

"You can do that?"

Rosa shrugged. "I'll try."

"Poor Rita and her husband," said Annette. "Why are you here?"

"Can't say."

Annette's eyes sparkled with a mix of awe and envy. "At it again."

"Don't . . ."

"What . . . again?" André asked.

"Nothing," Rosa said. "Leave it . . . *Annette!*"

Feigning a pout, Annette moved close, put her arm around Rosa, and whispered, "Tell me why you're here?"

Rosa made no effort to break away. "To see you."

Annette laughed. "All that way for little me?"

"Can't tell you," André said.

"Why the hell not?" A sharp, brittle edge showed in her voice.

"It's secret. Please . . . let it be," Rosa begged.

Annette nodded a grudging acquiescence, but her pout was real.

"Where's Paul?" Rosa changed the subject.

"In Marseille, visiting his parents," Annette answered.

"To stay?"

Sadness flickered in her eyes like a firefly. "He's changed."

"War does that," André said.

"Did you see Alain?"

Annette nodded. "Paul, Alain, and I got together two, three times. Alain didn't stay long."

"Did he mention plans, where he was going?"

She shook her head. "Not to me. He might have told Paul."

"I was hoping . . . " Rosa frowned, then asked. "How are things for you?"

Annette's pliable face puckered. "There's little work. It took time for theaters to reopen after . . . "

"Humiliation of defeat," André supplied.

She nodded. "I finally found a small part, and that ended. Now I'm back at Le Petite Theater. Germans censor everything. Moliere passed the test."

"What about Paris in general?"

"Germans everywhere—all you need to know," said Annette.

"Tell us about the rafles," André said.

"Unspeakably sad. A stagehand's cousin was arrested—more than 10,000, according to rumor, were taken to the velodrome." She exhaled a long sigh. "Then he disappeared. That's all I know."

"Have you seen Jenny?" Rosa asked.

Annette shook her head. "Not since the club closed. I gave her your note."

"Maybe she got away," Rosa said softly, as an aside.

"Maybe," Annette agreed.

"What about Agnes?"

"Frankie said she telephoned from Bordeaux," Annette pursed her lips in concentration, "two, three weeks after you left . . . on her way to Algeria."

"The club's closed like a clam."

"There's talk of reopening."

They talked about theater, the club, and the future. Rosa kept the focus on Annette.

"Will I see you again?" Annette asked.

"Probably not . . . it was good to see you."

They embraced.

On the street, André said, "She's interesting, but we learned nothing."

"You didn't. Paul's in Marseille, and she saw Alain. Annette might be a useful contact in the future."

Rosa mourned the past. Nothing remained static. Her easy repartee with Annette had disappeared. Time and distance had tarnished their friendship—Annette had become someone she used to know. Necessity had sent each down a different path, creating a chasm.

Annette would persevere, but Jean? Rosa feared for his life. Their meeting had been serendipitous; his was a name plucked from many at the Jewish Agency. "Jewish Agency," she muttered. "Tomorrow."

. . . Early the next morning, along Rue de Rosier, Rosa fixed her attention on buildings not people.

"Here." She stopped. "Sign's gone. Let's go inside. It was up a floor."

André followed. Rosa tried a door. It was locked. She knocked, but there was no response. Disappointed, they stood on the pavement in front of the building. A woman scurried inside. Ten seconds later Rosa put a name to her face. Rosa followed her inside. The door was open.

"Hello," Rosa called out.

Madam Dreyfus appeared. "We're closed—shut down."

"So I feared," Rosa said. "Three years ago, out of the crowd at Gare du Nord, your warm smile welcomed us. 'Not that Dreyfus,' you said, and then your sent us here." Shea smiled wistfully.

"Saved a lot of questions." Her laugh was hollow as she searched Rosa's face. "Sorry, I don't recall. Didn't catch your name."

"Haven't said," Rosa hesitated and glanced at André. "We want information."

Her brow furrowed. "Everything was documented by a number of Jewish organizations, the Red Cross, and others."

André moved closer and spoke softly. "We're from the south for other . . . " he waved a hand in the air, searching for the word, " . . . business. We want information on the situation in Paris."

Madam Dreyfus wrung her hands. "Resistance?"

"Best not to know," André said.

Her question answered, she nodded solemnly. "All right . . . not here. Let me collect a few things."

They walked to a café and ordered coffee. Madam Dreyfus began: "Hideous German signs everywhere, their massive presence stamped indelibly. Army garrisons throughout the city. And Gestapo plotting the end of French Jewry."

"We heard about the rafles."

"Last July." She sighed, as if she was very tired. "Nazi propaganda about the Jews started before the dust had settled. Jews, Brits, and Freemasons are blamed for French defeat. Unfortunately, their films—*Le Péril Juif* [*The Jewish Peril*], *Les Corrupteurs* [*The Corruptors*], and *Forces Occultes* [*Occult Forces*]—have been very effective."

"You saw them?" Rosa asked.

She shrugged. "Forced myself. They were vile, full of lies. Then a huge exhibition, *The Jew and France*, was trumpeted as of great educational import." She grunted her distaste. "An enormous spider hung over the entrance—Jewry sucking the blood of France—pure trash." She opened her purse and fumbled inside. A cigarette appeared between her lips. Her hand shook slightly as she raised the fire to its tip. She took several drags, drank coffee, then continued.

"No public censure—many agreed, others were too afraid. Jews make handy targets. Most Parisians have never seen a Jew. We're clustered in Marais. Dissent is dealt with harshly. Privately, people are concerned, not just Jews."

"We read the filth in the newspapers," Rosa said.

"Many Parisians collaborate—police foremost. Greed brings them to the table. We're banned from swimming pools, can't teach, run a business, have telephones, sit anywhere but in the last car on the Métro—or *ride bicycles!*" Her head shook in sad disbelief. "Essentially, no participation in public life. Then the arrests." Smoke drifted into her eyes. She squinted at the cigarette, took a long final drag, and vigorously extinguished it. "We live in '*Greater* Germany.'"

"Why are you still here?" André asked.

She ignored the question. "Last October, synagogues were bombed. Homegrown anger at Jews, Boche called it." She scowled. "They did it. The rafles started in earnest early last year. All Jews, French, and foreigners were ordered to register with the police in September 1940. Many are underground. Our organization tried to help, but what could we do? Our doors were shuttered. We were powerless. In June '42 we were ordered to wear yellow stars, then French citizens were rounded up."

"I don't see a star," Rosa noted.

She shook her head. "I hide where I can. Today I had to get something—otherwise I'm invisible."

"Go south, into Spain. Don't stay."

Madam Dreyfus shook her head slowly. "I have no safe-conduct pass." Her resignation seeped like an open wound.

Rosa thanked her. Depressed and pessimistic, Rosa and André left for Jean's flat . . . Rosa waited in the alley.

André returned alone: "Jean said to come up. No need to hide in the alley."

Rosa hesitated, thinking it unwise to go up, but she went. They would not stay long. Jean looked shrunken in his chair, enclosed by bare walls. Rosa sat on the couch. André watched at the window.

"You should have stayed with Catherine . . . why?" Rosa broke the silence, her voice soft.

"I've thought about that since yesterday." His sigh of passive resignation was like that of Madam Dreyfus. "Everyone is gone, my art is gone, the flat feels lifeless. What the hell was I thinking?"

"The Jewish Center is closed, but Madam Dreyfus came. We talked," Rosa said.

Jean remembered, "Vivacious woman. Haven't seen her in ages."

"She told us about Paris, *things*."

"What things?"

"How Paris has changed," André explained. "She's hiding."

They talked for half an hour to no avail. Gentle prodding did not work. Jean had retreated into a shell. Had Rosa's arrival been a trigger? Paris had become his prison. She feared he had come home to die.

"Police car—go!" André exclaimed.

Ignoring caution had its costs. No time for fear—action took over. "Back door! Jean, now!"

André ran from the window toward the kitchen, urging both, "Go . . . go!"

Jean stared at her and remained seated. Rosa pulled his arm, but he resisted.

"André, help." Then to Jean, "Get up."

Finally, he got to his feet. They led him to the back door. Out the door, down the back stairs to the alley, they ran. André first, then Rosa, and Jean last. When they reached the bottom, Jean wasn't there. Rosa ran up a flight and found him on the floor. He must have tripped because he was clutching his right ankle.

"Try to stand. We'll help," Rosa said.

He tried but fell back. "I can't."

"We have to leave," André said with urgency.

Rosa wasn't listening. Her mind caromed, searching for a plan to save Jean from arrest, imprisonment, or worse.

"The mission," André hissed.

She looked at him and nodded. *Complete the mission at any cost.* She'd crossed that border long before. She had to get a grip.

"Rosa, you listening?"

She looked at him. "I won't leave Jean here." Then to Jean: "We'll get you outside, wrap it tight." Rosa was suddenly calm.

They carried Jean into the alley.

"Now what?" André asked.

Jean was silent.

"We'll go to the café around the corner and work this out."

Jean hopped on one leg, with André and Rosa supporting each shoulder. André ordered a carafe and three glasses.

"I'm an old fool," Jean muttered. "Look what I've done."

"Nonsense," Rosa retorted. "Who can help?"

Jean shook his head.

An air of despondency descended. Rosa thought of people she had met then remembered. "Marcel, your art-dealer friend . . . "

Jean hesitated, but Rosa prevailed. She used the café telephone and apologized for waking him, then explained the situation. He agreed to come and collect Jean.

"Go," Jean ordered. "I'll be all right."

"He's right." André put a hand on Rosa's shoulder.

Rosa hugged Jean. He was weeping. A tear fell onto her cheek.

"I love you," Rosa whispered and kissed both cheeks.

"Take care, my daughter." He smiled when she glanced back.

Fifteen minutes later, André fumbled with the frame, removed the envelope, put it back together and back on the wall. He jammed the envelope inside his waistband under his shirt.

They sat in a café on Rue des Écoles, in the shadow of the Pantheon. Rosa slouched with her head in her hands, speaking softly. "Stupid . . . and careless. Going in was wrong. I knew that." She would never forgive her lapse in judgment. Sonny would be cross. "Damn it!" She cursed under her breath. "If he hadn't tripped . . . "

"Rosa," André started, "Jean was at risk the moment he returned. He should have stayed away. Now, it's up to Marcel and to luck. Let's get the hell out of Paris."

"Complete the mission!" she murmured.

Part V

From the sublime to the ridiculous is but a step.
—*Napoleon Bonaparte*

23

England, June 1940

Sonny's enlistment was approved after two weeks of interviews, filling out forms, and waiting. He was assigned to an army base in Tunbridge Wells, West Kent, about 70 kilometers west of Dover and 50 southeast of London, for training.

"Operation Dynamo" had delivered Sonny and more than 330,000 allied soldiers, including 26,000 Frenchmen, to England from 26 May to 4 June. "The miracle of deliverance," Prime Minister Winston Churchill called it. Continental Europe was under Nazi control. Britain stood alone. Only the English Channel separated the warring nations. Sonny marveled at the changes: he had evolved from a kid scrounging in Berlin's Mitte to a member of the British Army.

Marching in formation, firing a rifle, taking orders, then learning the finer points of English cursing and slang consumed every hour. His muscles ached; his mind was numb from fatigue, the lack of sleep, awful food. No time to find friends—Jameson, MacTavish, and Shannon, or Otto and Mina.

Returning to France to find Rosa seemed possible though remote. Closing his eyes, he might see her silhouetted by the light of the window in the Pestalozzi flat, smiling when he arrived at the flat with chocolate. He held her close after Oranienburg, in the dress he had bought for her in Antwerp—or without it the night they married.

Then rumors circulated that the battalion was shipping out to North Africa. Australian troops had already landed in Palestine. Orders arrived. Plans for France evaporated. He was eager to fight Germany, but Africa was the wrong continent.

He waited in a barracks reserved for soldiers in transit. Someone shouted, "Churchill's on the wireless."

Within seconds the unmistakable growl—tough, understanding, grandfatherly—filled the room.

"The Battle of France is over . . . the Battle of Britain is about to begin." At the end Churchill said: "If the British Empire and its Commonwealth lasted a thousand years, men will say, this was their finest hour."

Sonny repeated, " . . . their finest hour." He would be part of that.

. . . Days before his unit was scheduled for deployment, Sonny was summoned to headquarters. Surprised, he saw Jameson smiling at him.

"Good to see you, Slick."

Perplexed, Sonny asked, "What you doing here?"

"That any way to greet an old chum? Shannon wants to see you. Follow me." Over his shoulder he said, "He got the 'Dick Shot Off.'"

"What?" Sonny laughed.

"D-S-O . . . Distinguished Service Order—for officers only. Blokes got their own name for it."

Shannon sat, his right arm in a sling, MacTavish at his side. Jameson moved next to him. Each wore corporal stripes.

Sonny saluted and stood at attention.

"At ease, Private . . . Slick," Shannon said.

They laughed.

"Thank you, Lieutenant . . . congratulations on your . . . " Smiling wryly, he looked at Jameson for help.

"Dick shot off—right Jameson?"

"Yes, sir!" They laughed again.

Shannon continued: "I made Captain—another reward for this." He raised the damaged arm then motioned with his chin to the bars on his shoulder. "Could have been worse."

"Congratulations on that too, sir."

"These two chaps got elevated as well—deservedly so."

Jameson winked at Sonny.

"I can't get rid of them. So . . . " he paused for effect, " . . . we're still together but not in the 44th. Sit down." He pointed to a chair, then dismissed Jameson and MacTavish.

MacTavish slapped Sonny on the back on his way out.

"How are you getting on?" Shannon asked.

"Fine . . . going to North Africa to fight Jerry."

Shannon nodded. "I know. I've been reassigned to army intelligence—getting information on the enemy, spying, that sort of thing."

"If that helps win war."

"I believe it can." Shannon leaned over the table, creating intimacy. "I have a proposition."

Sonny frowned, then understood and laughed. "Me, a spy?"

"Why is that funny?"

Sonny's hands rose in a gesture of disbelief. "Life is crazy."

For the next half hour Shannon gave Sonny the rundown on a new MI6 operation called Special Operations Executive—SOE. British intelligence agents would work with resistance groups in France and other occupied countries and with neutral countries, Portugal primarily, the continent's principal point of entry.

"What do you know about wolfram, also called tungsten?" Shannon asked.

Sonny shook his head. "Nothing."

"Wolfram is an essential element, for us and the enemy, for the manufacture of armor, armor-piercing shells, bearings, cutting tools . . . " his hand rotated in a small circle, " . . . critically important material for armaments. It's mined in central and northeastern Portugal. We need wolfram; Germany needs wolfram. Both need good relations with the dictator Salazar. His secret police force, PVDE, trained by the Gestapo, which makes us nervous, carries out surveillance and enforcement. Add the constant flow of refugees moving through Lisbon, some meddling in internal affairs, which adds to Salazar's nervousness. He fears political instability and intervention by Germany or by us—a delicate balancing act. Lisbon is our port of entry, our center of espionage activity—the hive where we find honey."

"So, I understand the need for wolfram and for intelligence, but why me?"

Shannon's brilliant green eyes held Sonny's gaze. "Good question." The fingertips of his two hands touched, as if he were holding a small, invisible ball.

"You speak German, you know Berlin, and you look like a German . . . " Three fingers wagged at Sonny.

"Accident of birth," Sonny interrupted.

"Exactly. We can use it to our advantage. I have a job for you."

"I have a job in His Majesty's army . . . in Britain's finest hour," Sonny said without irony.

Shannon chuckled. "Very good. I have something better."

"What's better than killing Nazis? I start in '38 . . . am good at it."

"You proved that."

Sonny nodded, then asked again, "What is better?"

"Work in Portugal with a new identity. We train you in necessary skills then drop you in Lisbon. Your cover will be as a German national, maybe not a Nazi, but . . . " he paused, " . . . say a businessman who lived in England for years, left when the war started. We'll think of something. We have a 'dead' file with real names. You'll get a proper ID, settle in Lisbon, work your way into the German community. Get to know fellows in the Abwehr. They're thick as thieves."

"Abwehr?" Sonny repeated the word. "I've heard of that before."

"German military intelligence."

"You want me to . . . ?"

"Infiltrate."

"Infiltrate," Sonny repeated, smiling. "I like that."

"Good." Shannon smiled. "Keep your eyes and ears open, report to a contact, collect stolen documents smuggled from France, whatever we need."

Sonny's smile turned mischievous. "Dangerous?"

"It is—I won't lie."

"Not bother me. I know danger." Tight spots, coming out the other end in one piece, were familiar territory. Danger was an intoxicant, tough to shake, like a narcotic. He knew that. The truth was, he liked it. And he'd be on the continent, closer to Rosa. "Do something for me, then I be your man in Lisbon."

"What?"

"Find people." Sonny told him about Otto, their smuggling operation in Berlin and what had happened to him. "Last saw him in Antwerp in May '39. He came here with girlfriend, Mina Dix. Her father was big shot in KPD—German Communist Party—he already here."

"A Bolshie?"

Sonny shrugged. "KPD was big in Germany . . . until Hitler. Better than Nazis . . . much better. But that not say much. My friends had false papers for Belgium. Dix, the old man, had papers for America. They may have flown the coop." He shrugged. "Find them or not, but try. If you do, I train . . . be spy."

"Deal." They shook on it, and Sonny provided the specifics on his friends.

The next day Sonny had orders for training as an operative at Wanborough Manor, a stately home in Guildford. The SOE—an espionage, sabotage, and reconnaissance operation—required stringent secrecy. The country houses, isolated from towns and prying eyes, were perfect sites. Wanborough Manor was one of many such facilities in England.

Major Ellingson, even at ease, remained ramrod straight, as if a pole went up his ass to his neck—as one of Sonny's fellow recruits noted. With his thin mustache and wire-rimmed glasses, the officer in charge of Wanborough was a caricature of a British officer. On the first day of Sonny's training, he opened with, "Look at each other." His tone invited rather than ordered.

Ellingson waited, too long, heightening tension. "Half of you will not survive, such are the hazards of war. Personal history is yours; keep it that way. I don't care if you like or hate each other . . . doesn't matter. But you're soldiers and will bond together while you're here. When we're finished, you will be assigned a dangerous mission. Remember," he paused for effect, "never trust anyone. I'll repeat, never . . . trust . . . anyone. Each of you is unique, special in a way that will help win the war but no better than any soldier. Take another look . . . you'll likely never meet again." The tone was set.

They were a motley crew: a Polish national, a Free Frenchman loyal to de Gaulle, several British officers—one tall, the other short—a charming and occasionally smug convicted Brit swindler, and a young woman from Holland. They shared one important trait: deep animus toward Germany stoked by grievous personal loss or injury to family or national pride.

The training was intense: armed and unarmed combat, calisthenics, espionage tradecraft, demolition ("A little pop in your day," quipped the instructor), Morse code, wireless, and other communication. Sonny and his mates kept busy from dawn into the evening—individually, in small and large groups, in classrooms and in the field. Total immersion was exhausting.

They took recreation when they could: cards, reading, walking on the grounds, tennis, and billiards. Sonny excelled at tennis to his surprise and delight. Trainers and military guards kept close watch over the incipient agents. No passes were given; no one left the manor.

Sonny talked to his mates, laughed at their jokes, told a few himself. But he kept the others at arm's length. He neither liked nor disliked them, with the exception of Eddie, the swindler. He was an outlier, sometimes ingratiating, never obsequious, and smart. Eddie, like Kid, was at times too talkative. Sonny also saw a flicker of himself in Eddie. He liked Eddie.

They were not trained to be killers, though that was not ruled out. They learned hand combat for defensive purposes—how to avoid a punch or the point to a knife. Kicks, strangles, bear hug, chair and match box attack were part of it. Sonny's favorite was smacking the ears—cupping one's hands and slapping an opponent's ears to break his eardrums or leave him concussed. Handguns were fired at targets, disassembled and cleaned. Drilling was repetitive, boring, occasionally bruising. Proficiency was expected. The trainees were often paired for learning and instilling camaraderie.

Agents required contacts, faceless couriers, men or women to meet in dark alleys and embassies, or to pick up anonymous drops in secret locations. They trainees learned Morse code. Sonny teamed with Eddie to operate, disassemble, and reassemble the wireless, and repair it, if necessary.

On the continent, authorities routinely opened mail. A letter dropped in the post might spell disaster, unless it was meant to spread disinformation. Steganography, the art of concealing messages, had enjoyed a long, honored history, back to the Greeks. Wax tablets, messages written on a courier's body, mixing multiple typefaces in the early days of the printing press, they learned, were ways of circumventing snoops through the ages. The favored technology of SOE was invisible ink. Made from a headache tablet—Pyramidon—it dissolved in white gin. A two-sided letter showed banal information on one side of the page, a message recorded in secret ink on the other. Upon the letter's receipt, the addition of a developer chemical might reveal its real message.

German spies used photographically produced microdots, a more advanced technology. Specks smaller than a pinhead were imbedded on paper, then covered by an adhesive. Reflective in the right light, they were often imbedded in the edge of a postcard or other thick paper. Sometimes simpler was better.

Every method had its risks. Radios were cumbersome, difficult to transport, and subject to eavesdropping. Secret messages might be discovered and read, a courier unmasked, a spy revealed. Discovery would prove fatal.

24

Lisbon, early November 1940

Wrinkles that he hadn't noticed before had crept into the corner of his eyes. Was it anxiety, or fatigue, or maybe he just looked older? He *was* older—and a little wiser maybe. Hell, 31 wasn't old! Then he noticed the slightly, wry turn of his lips—irony or disdain? He sighed as he adjusted his tie. Mirrors don't lie.

It had been a long, dark road—he had been a petty smuggler, part of a forged-document ring, a killer of the enemy . . . now he was a spy who had lost his wife along the way. He shook his head, then laughed, more grunt than mirth . . .

Sonny's landing in Portugal was another strange turn. Scared and starting with nothing, he began to help people and found nourishment in the danger of it. He made friends he'd never see again. He fell in love . . . he was lucky to be alive—lucky! "Huh," he grunted. His lover receded in the slow, cinematic fade-out of his mind, her tear-streaked face etched into memory. She vanished into the void. All they had wanted was to live in peace.

Sonny had become a killer; lifeless bodies littered the path behind him. He had no remorse—though his was a fitful sleep. His dreams were of what soldiers do; such was the imperative of war. Still, there were too many crazy turns—maybe the joke was on him.

Sonny shrugged into his coat. He had a job to do—how he would do it remained a mystery. Sighing, he opened the door, moved into the empty hallway and into the Lisbon evening. *Never trust anyone* . . .

Sonny had sailed into Lisbon in October—the first sight of it was impressive. *Satchel's Guide to Spain and Portugal* had it right. Wide as an inland sea, the busy Tagus River glistened in the sun like an emerald.

Set on seven hills, the houses—white, pink, ochre—piled one upon the other like children's building blocks. At the top, like a hat on Lisbon's head, stood guard the Castle of St. George—the old Moorish citadel, now Salazar's prison.

Lisbon had turned to rubble in 15 minutes by earthquake and to cinder by fire in 1755. Though it was rebuilt, a malaise burrowed deep in its bruised psyche. A poor city in a poor country, Lisbon suffered the decay of a long neglect nevertheless worn with charm and grace. Maybe the oldest city in Europe—going back to the Greeks, even the Phoenicians—Lisbon had been named Olissipo by Romans.

Run-down neighborhoods displayed the patina provided only by age. Plaster peeled from walls, ornate ceramic tiles cracked, accumulated dirt and grime—all were metaphors for a city long past its prime. Despite that, Lisbon shone in the late autumn sun. Green grass, blooming flowers, and fruit-filled markets, clanging streetcars, screeching tires, honking horns, and horse-drawn carts carrying produce, men hollering, and women balancing baskets on their heads provided a potpourri for the senses.

Hans, or "Hank," Baum, a German national, was Sonny's new identity. He had immigrated and found work in a London warehouse. Hard work and smarts had brought promotions, after four years to the position of assistant manager. Shannon's people left a paper trail.

When Britain declared war on Germany, the pseudo–Hank Baum was stuck in London. He feared internment. Luck and grit got him on a ship to Ireland in late '39, then on a freighter to Lisbon in October '40. The real Hans Baum had been arrested and interred days after war was declared. Documents—passport and visa—were in his possession, his photograph in place.

Hank Baum was an orphan of sorts, plucked from an untraceable, or nearly so, cast of characters. Someone who knew Baum or Sonny might crack the riddle—nothing was perfect. Adding his own embellishments, Hank became a shrewd opportunist, living on his wits tending bar at the Pink Slipper Club, a Berlin watering hole Sonny knew well. He had learned cursory English from expatriates at the club. An adventurer, he had emigrated in 1932, at age 23.

The assignment was simple but tricky. "Befriend Germans . . . they're thick as thieves. Socialize." Shannon had said. "They'll come

to you like bees to honey: Abwehr agents, Gestapo, and their contacts. A few are ours, but never mind." He waved that away, like
brushing a fly off his sleeve.

"Should I know the Brits?" Sonny had asked.

Shannon shook his head. "Too messy, might blow their cover.
Gather information as you go. Give it to your Lisbon contact at the
British Embassy—agent named Johnson. Not his real name,"
Shannon explained. "Ring the embassy, ask for Johnson in the press
department, say its Slick calling. That's your code name, as I like it so
well." Shannon smiled at the continuing joke. "In all communication
use it and no other. Understood?"

Sonny nodded.

Shannon handed Sonny a sheet of paper with the telephone
number and address of the embassy. "Memorize it."

Then Sonny called in his bargain. "What have you got on my
friends?"

"Sorry to say they flew the coop for America . . . from South-
ampton in June. Appears Herr Dix had enough clout to take his
family along. Your friend Otto and the Fraulein married."

"Stop with the German! They are enemies of the Third Reich."

"Sorry—old habits . . . "

Sonny didn't know London, so Shannon took him there for a
week. He stayed in a flat in Docklands, his last (assumed) address in
London. Jameson was from the East End and squired him around—
Buckingham Palace, Trafalgar Square, Big Ben, the Tower, London
Bridge, all the rest. Jameson drank with him in pubs and clubs.
Posters warned of spies: "Loose lips . . . sink ships" and "He's watch-
ing you!"

Early in September, while Sonny was still at Wanborough, the
aerial bombardment of London began and Churchill's Battle of
Britain was underway.

Then in October, Sonny departed for Dublin. His wardrobe—
suit, shirts, ties, coat, and shoes—fit a low-level manager barely
scraping by. He had saved some pound sterling—enough, not too
much—and he had a forged Portuguese visa.

Sonny spent his first week in a hotel in Bairro Alto, the high
neighborhood, up one of the hills, through narrow cobbled streets,
above and west of Alfama. Medieval Alfama was the only section of

the city that had not been destroyed in the great fire. He wandered there, observing and learning. A fork in the road went up or down, a lone tree rising from the junction. He stopped. Windows opened onto the narrow passage. A woman leaned out from one. Her eyes met his; then she turned away.

He walked down through a big park to the city center, which was crowded with lively, handsome people, numbering in the city in excess of 600,000, including refugees. Sonny felt Lisbon's strong pulse, and he liked it.

He stopped at a corner shop in Chiado, another neighborhood, below Bairro Alto, next to Baixa with Alfama to the east. *Deutschland* was printed in large script on one window, *Alemanha* on the other—it was the German propaganda office, proclaiming Hitler the "best defense against Bolshevism." People passed by; no one entered.

Rossio, graced by a lovely fountain and column of Pedro IV, was Lisbon's main square and anchor. Several hotels lay on its periphery, and people scurried across it to the main railway station. Up the hill to the west was the unrestored Carmo Convent and gothic church, a reminder of the earthquake. Adjacent Carmo Square was a quiet peaceful space honoring the detritus of Catholic excess.

Portugal had momentarily ruled the seas in the 16th century. Riches flowed but proved ephemeral. The Inquisition eliminated Jews from its population then. Thus in the 20th century, the Portuguese were generally ignorant of Jews, having few in their midst. Sonny read that many Spanish Jews had fled to Portugal for sanctuary during its infamous Inquisition. Others—Conversos or Marranos—converted to Catholicism. The victims numbered in the tens of thousands. The perpetrators were centuries dead, and Sonny harbored no ill will for the Portuguese. On the contrary, swelling numbers of Jewish refugees spoke well of them. Age-old hatreds lay elsewhere.

He walked past brothels, dive bars, and cheap hotels to the ship docks in Alcantra. After sunset, mist off the River Tagus created a dream world of fog and shadow. Hulking freighters, like aging pugilists, lined the river's edge. But the bars on the waterfront and in the tangled alleys of Alfama held him late into the night. He listened to mournful fado, sung mostly by women, about lost loves and marginalized lives. As he sat over whiskey, Lisbon's dark mood filled his head with visions of his lost love, a lover left behind—his story. Black-haired women, eyes like bits of coal, hovered, beckoning like Lorelei. Though tempted, he waved them away.

Waterfront cafés served mussels, piled high on the plate, and vinho verde—green wine. At night the dogs barked, and the occasional cock crowed. Lisbon's caldron teemed and bubbled with spies, overflowed with refugees desperate for escape and hustlers selling anything for money. Army deserters, fleeing the fight, found refuge. Lisbon was unlike any place he had imagined.

The politically neutral Portugal would not become involved in Europe's conflagration. That was Salazar's raison d'être, despite the ancient Anglo-Portuguese Treaty of 1373, still in force. But like it or not, Lisbon was in the thick of it—spies everywhere, fed by informants and protected by safe houses.

Sonny, with a contact's help, found a pleasant building on Travessa do Abarracamento de Peniche near Rua da Palmeira in Bairro Alto. At the corner stood a beautiful jade-tiled edifice that dazzled in the sun. His building, however, was more modest, a stone's throw from Jardín del Príncipe Real, a small park bordering a thoroughfare. Without Portuguese, he must get by on English and German, or in a pinch, his bit of French.

On his first day in the new building, Sonny toured the three stories, four flats per floor. His flat was on the first floor, west side, in the back. There was one flat above, one below. Built before the turn of the previous century, the bloom had come off the rose. The hallways were adorned with faded, flowered wallpaper curled at the corners—a nod to fin de siècle fashion—and worn but serviceable carpet.

Generally clean and moderately well kept, the place was affordable. His rooms had natural wood molding around the windows and doors, a nice touch. The flat was minimally furnished with table, several chairs, a soft divan, a softer bed, dresser, and a few pictures on the walls. The toilet flushed, hot water appeared on whim, and he fit in the bathtub. The kitchen had the rudiments. It was all he needed.

His building's front door opened onto Travessa Abarracamento do Peniche—a mouthful—and the rear door onto an alley with outlets at both ends. A fire escape was attached to the wall adjacent the rear door. Mailboxes in the small atrium inside the front door were numbered, with tenant names printed on each. The box for Sonny's flat, No. 8, read "Hank Baum." He would use Hank, not Hans, fit for an expatriate German forced to leave England at the outbreak of war—no hard feelings!

Several mailbox names seemed British and one German. He scribbled down names and flat numbers: Mr. John Mayhew, No. 2, ground, east side; Mr. and Mrs. Wallace Simpson, No. 12, directly above Hank's flat; and Herr Joachim Holtz, No. 5, front, south, same floor as Hank's. The others were Portuguese, maybe Spanish. He would wait patiently for chance encounters.

Before the end of the second day, Sonny faced a man in the hallway. Shorter, and perhaps a little older than Sonny, he seemed energetic and friendly, at least initially. He was John Mayhew.

"When did you move in?" Mayhew asked.

Sonny told him. He noticed a light narrowing of Mayhew's eyes— response to his accent, or did he imagine it? Like a stubborn rash, his accent was hard to lose.

"I left before Hitler came to power, have no interest in returning. Because of the war, I was forced to leave England." He shrugged, evidencing his powerlessness. "I wanted to stay, but I would have been arrested."

Mayhew nodded. "Nice to meet you." Then he turned and walked away.

Shannon had told Sonny, "Everyone has a reason for being in Lisbon. Figure out what that is." Who was Mayhew? Had he believed him?

Several days later, in the evening after dinner, Sonny saw an older couple at the front door. He introduced himself to Wallace and Margaret—"Peggy"—Simpson. Wallace's nose was red, his face pinched as if from too many lemons in his gin and tonic. He was several inches shorter than Sonny and she even shorter, with a pert nose and suspicious eyes. Both were 15 to 20 years older than Sonny.

They exchanged trivialities. Wallace did the talking, projecting false bonhomie, while Peggy eyed Sonny warily. No questions. Sonny was certain it was his German accent.

At the end of the week he saw a tall man, back to the hallway, locking the door to No. 5—Joachim Holtz. Sonny waited. The man turned. He was wiry, had thinning white hair, seemed very old, wore a dark suit. His small eyes, behind wire-rimmed glasses, widened in surprise, like the aperture on a camera lens, then quickly returned to normal.

Sonny smiled and bowed slightly. "Guten Abend. I am Hans Baum, your new neighbor."

"Ja, good evening to you," he replied in German. "Very pleasant to meet you. I have an appointment and cannot talk now. Perhaps later?"

. . . Three taverns and two small cafés were within easy walking distance. Sonny could wash down a plate of tapas with a half-liter of vinho verde and sit for hours. People wandered in and out. Sonny easily identified nervous refugees—their brows streaked with anxiety, eyes uneasily darting around the room.

A tavern on Rua da Palmeira, round the corner from the flat, became his favorite. With no name on the door, it had a dozen tables, a small bar to stand. He could look out the window.

"Hank . . . friend . . . sit," commanded Miguel, the innkeeper. He was short and rotund, with a thick black mustache in the Portuguese fashion. He offered decent food, warm greeting, and a bit of conversation in passable English. Miguel reminded him of Antwerp's Sammy.

"Why you in Lisbon?" Miguel asked on Hank's third visit—finally the critical question.

"A man must live somewhere, and Lisbon is a beautiful city," Sonny answered coyly.

"Lisbon is beautiful . . .the women too!" Miguel's smile broadened, his upper lip hidden beneath the brush under his nose. Then his eyes narrowed, and his lips pursed. "You have accent . . . German—no?"

Sonny laughed. "It is German—yes." Then he ordered.

Several days later, Sonny sat alone at a corner table, obscured in shadow, not exactly out there as bait. He had been in Lisbon for more than a month without a sniff. Was he doing it wrong?

Shannon had counseled patience. Let the enemy come to you. "You're a goat tied to a stake," he said.

His meal finished, Sonny worked on his half-liter and wrote in his notebook. He had aspired to be a writer but never quite managed it.

Now he had time to reverse the oversight. His English was not yet good enough, so he recorded his observations of Lisbon and its people in German.

Creaking door hinges sent his eyes to the vague outline of a woman followed by a man into the tavern. Miguel greeted them with his usual warmth and pointed to a table on the other side. Something in one of them led Sonny to take another look. He had known hundreds of men and women in Berlin, seen more on the road. The faces melted . . . If he let it, the riddle would be a sliver under his skin.

The woman was thin, with a youthful carriage—athletic, like a dancer. Her face was obscured, but he thought her dark—maybe Portuguese. She leaned over the table and spoke to her companion. Bearded and younger than Sonny, he seemed uneasy, worn and tattered, Semitic.

Sonny looked away, then back again. Miguel took their order. Something familiar poked at him, like déjà vu. Berlin, working the enterprise . . . Otto, Joseph, runners . . . Staring at them as if only the two of them existed, he filled in the gaps . . . a picture slowly formed, then became a movie as if projected on the opposite wall. Sonny, handing a forged passport and visa to . . . He snapped his fingers, impatiently, a game of trivia. He closed his eyes and relaxed.

Gazing at his notebook, he absently penned a line across the page, an oval, two eyes . . . poured wine and drank, stole another glance. Shave the beard . . . the face . . . eyes . . . Jacob—the trusted runner who had brought them clients! Sonny hadn't used him as much as Franz . . . didn't know him well, but there he was. Franz, Jacob, and Morris, the third runner—after Kristallnacht, all had gone.

Jacob scanned the room—by habit or precaution? Sonny averted his face, put a hand over his mouth, not wanting to be recognized in the tavern. Jacob and the woman talked. They ate. Sonny chewed his lip, waiting. Finally, plates empty, Jacob poured the last of the wine. Ten minutes later he paid the bill, and they left.

Sonny dropped several escudo notes on the table and waved to Miguel on his way out. Looking right, then left, he saw them walking down the hill toward Baixa, probably on their way to Alfama. Sonny followed through winding passages until they were alone.

"Jacob," he called, barely loud enough to be heard.

Jacob flinched but did not stop. His companion grabbed his arm.

Louder, Sonny repeated, "Jacob."

Jacob froze in midstride. The woman moved closer to him. Their faces were in shadow. Recognition was nearly impossible. Sonny had scared him. "I'm a friend," he said in German to calm him.

"Who?" came his reply.

"Sonny."

Jacob turned to face his pursuer. Still no recognition came.

"Sonny from Berlin."

The stink of fear emanated from Jacob.

Sonny moved closer. "Sonny from the Rucker Strasse warehouse."

Suddenly, Jacob melted in a smile of recognition. "Sonny! You scared the shit out of me."

"Sorry. Your beard threw me at first. I followed you from the tavern."

"Didn't see you," Jacob said, still unnerved.

His companion stepped out from behind him. "I'm Eva." Her smile was warm.

"Sonny," he extended his hand. "Nice to meet you."

"What . . . how?" Jacob started.

"You first," Sonny said. "But not on the street. Let's find a bar."

. . . They sat in a corner. Sonny ordered wine. "How did you get here?" Sonny asked.

Jacob had crossed from Belgium into France before the war started. He met Eva in Paris, in the Marais. From Poland, Eva had lived in Paris since 1933; she spoke Polish, German, and French. After war was declared, they were arrested and interred separately in Gurs, the big internment camp in southwestern France. When France unraveled, each had escaped and made it to Marseille. They reunited at the Jewish Center. A German couple took them over the mountain to Portbou, Spain, providing the appropriate documents.

"We finally have passage to Cuba—next week," Jacob said.

"Congratulations! I wish you the best," Sonny said. He told them his story, then described Rosa. "She goes by Rosa Sander, but she could be using a different name. She lived on Pestalozzi Strasse. I got a letter from Paris with an address: 32, Rue du Roi de Sicile. Do you know it? Did you see her . . . at Gurs, anywhere?"

They shook their heads.

Eva: "I didn't meet her in Gurs. It was big. She could have been there. I escaped with three other women—actually the guards let us go. We got to Biarritz, then took a bus to Marseille."

"I've heard nothing. I'm anxious for news, anything."

"Smugglers work the Spanish frontier, over the Pyrenees, from Banyuls to the Atlantic. Don't give up hope. She may appear," Eva said, placing a hand on Sonny's arm.

He nodded.

"How do you know each other?" Eva asked.

"Sonny was one of the guys in the smuggling ring in Berlin," Jacob told her.

Eva leaned across the table and kissed Sonny's cheek. "Sonny, I'm pleased to meet you."

Sonny smiled and lowered his voice. "Call me Hank. Forget we met. Have you seen Franz or Morris?"

"Lost track of both," he answered with a weary shake of his head.

"What's going on in Lisbon?" Sonny asked.

Jacob shrugged. "We don't speak Portuguese. Can't tell you much."

"We saw the big celebration—800 years a nation, 400 years of independence from Spain," Eva said. "Food was good, the mood festive, livened things up."

"We walked up and down Lisbon's hills, waiting to leave," Jacob added.

"Where you living?"

"In a cheap pension near the river. It's affordable, barely. With all the refugees, prices are inflated."

"Any trouble with the police or the Germans?

"Not us," Jacob said.

"Hear rumors," Eva started.

Jacob continued. "People on Nazi lists—Jews, anti-Nazis, liberals—disappear."

Sonny thanked them and paid for the wine. They hugged. "You need any money?" Sonny asked.

They looked at each other. Before they could answer, Sonny stuffed escudos into Jacob's hand. "Good luck . . . we never met."

A muffled "thank you" followed Sonny out of the bar.

25

Lisbon, Summer 1942

Don Pedro IV, languid and disinterested, baked on his marble pedestal. Towering 25 meters above Sonny's head, the old monarch gazed longingly at the water-spouting nymphs in the fountain at the other end. Searing afternoon heat sent pigeons and Lisboetas (residents of Lisbon) to cover. Sonny sat beneath an umbrella at Café Nicola, taking it all in. Week-old English and German newspapers, on bamboo sticks, were in heavy use.

"The foul smell of propaganda," Senhor Alameda said, eyeing the newspapers. A dapper man—charming, intelligent, a good conversationalist, retired teacher, and fluent in English—he was certainly a PVDE informant.

Sonny laughed. "Of course, but you do not strike me as a cynic."

His smile was wry, his eyes mischievous. "A cynic," he repeated. "A man who knows the price of everything, the value of nothing."

"Very good, Senhor Alameda." Sonny addressed him formally. He would never have used his given name, even had he known it.

"The infamous Englishman who said that—I cannot recall his name."

"Can't help you there." Sonny shrugged. "Its all the same to me—dictatorships have their cynics, democracies their hypocrites."

Alameda mulled that over, his brow furrowed, masked in concentration. Finally, he said, "Overbroad, I think. Each has his mixture of cynics and hypocrites."

"We both exaggerate, making our point. To Salazar's wisdom and credit, Portugal has remained neutral."

It was Alameda's turn to laugh—a barely audible titter. "Very diplomatic." Recognition flashed in his intelligent eyes. "Senhor

Wilde."

"Pardon?"

"Oscar Wilde—the Englishman I could not recall."

"Ah, yes, Oscar Wilde." Sonny's eyes alighted on a shimmering pool of water—a heat mirage—floating above the undulating waves of the Rossio's black and white cobblestones, "Roly Poly Square" to English sailors.

Sonny had read *Daily Standard* and *Die Woche* reports of the desert battle at a place called El Alamein, in Egypt. He was amused by the divergent coverage. German Panzers under the command of Field Marshal Rommel fought the Brits, refusing to give ground. Gen. Claude Auchinleck's Allied forces were close to pushing the enemy from Egypt. Clearly, neither side had gained advantage. The words *stalemate, impasse, deadlock, standstill,* were not used. Between the lines, Sonny gleaned that the Germans were too close to Suez for comfort. Speculation centered on whether the Americans would send troops now that the Japanese had forced them into the fray. Nothing else in either country's week old rags piqued his interest.

"Why do you stay in Lisbon, Herr Baum?"

Mildly surprised by Senhor Alameda's uncharacteristic inquiry, Sonny flashed into and out of mistrust, though he did not show it. He shrugged. "Lisbon provides a haven and it suits me. Portugal is beautiful and neutral—there is no war."

Trust no one.

"Yes, it is beautiful." Senhor Alameda's eyes narrowed, and he raised a bony forefinger, his laugh harsh. "Spies and deceit everywhere—a quiet war rages."

Smiling at the irony, Sonny leaned toward the older man. "I admit old loyalties are hard to break." He felt good feeding the old fellow a line. After all, it was his job.

Senhor Alameda nodded solemnly.

From the corner of his eye, Sonny caught sight of a portly man carrying an attaché. He passed the café. Sonny dropped a few coins onto the silver plate. "Pleasure talking to you, as usual, must be going . . . good day."

He followed Johnson past the neo-Manueline railway station toward Hotel Avenida Palace, a favorite of German diplomats, Gestapo, and other Third Reich bigwigs. Sonny glanced at the entrance and muttered, "Fuck Hitler."

Johnson got into a taxi parked at the queue. Sonny loitered for several minutes then hailed the next taxi in line: "Jardim da Estrela, por favor." Ten minutes later he watched Johnson stroll through the Botanical Garden, one of three regular drops. Sonny knew the drill and lingered, not crowding his contact. An explosion of color surrounded a huge cypress, the greenhouse just beyond.

Johnson left the park. Sonny dawdled five minutes, enjoying the solitude, then entered the greenhouse. Sweat dripped from under his arms in the stifling heat; the beautiful orchids seemed to smile. Reaching behind a big pot, he felt the envelope, then quickly stuffed it into his pocket. What did Johnson have in store for him?

Sonny made few decent contacts but not for want of effort. His rambles through the city yielded interaction with scores of men and women—mostly Portuguese and many Germans. The Brits were leery, as he expected. Surely, the German community of spies and their handlers knew of him.

He had few "business" contacts and no personal friends in Portugal. His only interactions were with bartenders, waiters, and strangers. Warned that his assignment would be a lonely one, he had not been prepared for the reality.

He missed a woman's companionship, one in particular. Three years had passed since he had been with his wife. Rosa could be hiding in France or even in Lisbon. Careful not to be overheard, he peppered every refugee he encountered with questions, hoping against hope he would hear about a woman, dark, exotic, and beautiful, in her late twenties.

He knew Rosa was alive. He felt it. Did she think the same of him? Or had she left him behind, taken up with another man? He couldn't blame her. Should he find a woman? Have a fling, nothing serious? Such thoughts had crossed his mind more frequently in recent days. Inaction and boredom did not help. He thought about Rebecca—young and alone. She had wanted him. Her death had saved him from a decision.

At a hotel bar, an attractive woman smiled at him from afar. She ambled to the bar, her legs slightly bowed, her bust heavy. She dropped her purse to the bar and asked him to buy her a drink. He did. Her heavily applied makeup drew attention to the lines at the corners of her mouth and eyes. He couldn't tell from her broken English whether her patron was Germany, England, or Salazar. He quickly realized he would gain nothing of interest from her, but she might from him. After one drink he bid her good night.

This was not Sonny's first contact with a woman, and it would not be his last. He hadn't gone to bed with any of them, though he could have. He wondered what he would he have done had Johnson ordered it. Yes, he would have followed orders. Deceit and lies were part of his job, adultery a minor indiscretion compared to the blood bath wrought by war. Mostly he did not think about it, though many beautiful, dark-eyed Portuguese women passed him on the street, sat at hotel bars, and listened to fado. They all reminded him of Rosa.

Mayhew remained cool and distant. He wasn't in the army, but he might be an agent—or Foreign Service. Thus far he remained a curiosity.

Certainly, the Simpsons had thawed. Several months after Sonny arrived, he ran into them at the little tavern just after they had finished a meal. Wallace waved to Sonny, inviting him to join them. She sipped strong coffee, and he nursed a glass of port. Gushing like a teenager, Mrs. Simpson told Sonny about the recent reception for Edward Windsor, the abdicated British King and his wife, Wallis Simpson. *Wallace* Simpson, her husband, had worked in the Foreign Service, Lisbon his last posting—hence the invitation.

Sonny bit his lip to keep from laughing at the irony of the ex-king's wife and the man at his table sharing a name. Mrs. Simpson, the exuberant little woman at his table, was as giddy as a debutante at her first dance. "Mrs. Windsor was absolutely gracious and charming. A shame she had been married."

"Twice," Wallace said icily.

Ignoring him, she continued, "Wallace had so hoped to be invited to a round of golf with the former king."

He exhaled heavily through his nose. "Given my former position, that would have been unwise."

"Nonsense!" She waved his objection away.

Sonny listened with amusement.

Finally Mr. Simpson asked Sonny, "What are you doing in Lisbon?"

Sonny shook his head forlornly. "Waiting for the war to end."

Mrs. Simpson nodded, but Wallace forged on. "Why Lisbon?"

Sonny told them. "I have great fondness for England but thought it wise to leave."

"At least you're not fighting for the Germans."

Sonny's face contorted as if his nose were pinched. "No—I fight for myself," he retorted.

The Simpson's bid Sonny good night, leaving him the table.

———

Sonny's circuit included colorful bars, taverns, and cafés. His neighborhood had them on nearly every corner and in between, but action was scant. Seedy bars near the docks, filled with dockworkers and sailors, and their women, were a different matter. Agents—men and women—plied sailors and dockworkers with liquor, pumping them for information. Sailors, more than the dockworkers, had information about shipping, news from other ports of call, and, for a little cash might agree to eavesdrop, or more.

What drew Sonny was not the sailors but the loitering German, English, French, Dutch, and East Europeans on the payroll of one side or the other. He talked with anyone willing talk with him.

Europe's refugees, mostly Jewish—German, French, Austrian, Czech, Slovak, Polish, Hungarian, whatever—loitered in cafés and bars, on the street, in the squares. They spoke in hushed tones, awaiting passage to wherever, desperate to exit the continent. Few were so fortunate as Jacob and Eva. They lived in every quarter of the city from Bairro Alto at the top, to Baixa at the bottom, to the oldest Alfama, the most prosperous Chiado, to outlying Belem and the resort of Estoril. Survival came at a heavy cost in money and emotion to many unhappy, anxious, frightened people.

Estoril lay on the coast, 15 kilometers west of Lisbon. It had become an international tourist destination of the wealthy. Sonny took the short train ride to the casino and hotel bars several times. Wealthy Portuguese, tourists, refugees, and spies mingled, while thousands of escudos rode on a single card or the random bounce of a little ball. Agents from every quarter grazed for juicy tidbits. But regular visits were beyond Sonny's means—he left Estoril to others; he would troll for his quarry elsewhere.

Sonny had fallen hard for fado. Uniquely Portuguese, it was most pure on the waterfront and Alfama, so that's where he went. Late at night, in dingy, smoky little bars, Sonny drank cheap red wine from barrels, listening to neighborhood women, and some men, sing of lost love and desperation. The songs he heard existed in the popular vernacular—or were contrived for the moment:

> Love, jealousy, ashes and flames, pain and sin;
> All this exists; all this is sad; this is fado.

Their voices conveyed to him a depth of feeling, a powerful message even without one's knowledge of the language.

After several visits to a little dive, Sonny met an old sailor. They sat at a table in the corner and talked. Sonny bought wine for his new friend. In turn, the sailor rewarded Sonny's generosity with animated talk of ports of call and fado. Long ago, having given up the sea, Filipe lived a quiet life alone, near the docks. A sturdy, spry man well into his seventies, he translated songs of melancholy and loneliness, learned over many years in British ports, into English. Was this sadness unique to Portugal?

"We call it *saudade*," Filipe said.

"What does it mean?

His wrinkled face frowned. Slowly, his head shook, as if he had a slight tremor. "No define . . . is national mood, more than sadness or . . . " He thought a moment.

"Melancholie," Sonny said the word in German, thinking it might be similar in English.

"Melancholy, yes," Filipe smiled. "Is good word for Portuguese people. Someone, I forget, he say it is Portuguese destiny, be sad."

––––––––

On a sultry evening in mid-August, Sonny sat amidst a lively crowd at Chave d'Ouro café on the Rossio.

"Desculpe, voce tem uma fósforos?" said a voice from the next table.

Sonny turned to a well-dressed man, smiling at him. Pointing to his ears, Sonny shook his head.

"Voce fala Alemao o Ingles?" He raised his hand so Sonny could see the cigarette. "A match?" He spoke in German. "I also speak English."

"Ah!" Sonny searched his pocket and fished out matches from Hotel Palacio.

"Thank you." He offered Sonny a cigarette.

"No, thanks."

The man lit his cigarette and looked at the matchbox, "Hotel Palacio" printed on the top. "A lovely hotel, nicer than the Parque, where I live. Don't you think?" He returned the matches. "This is a lovely café."

Sonny nodded but said nothing. Hotel Parque was the unofficial headquarters of the German legation in Lisbon. Hotel Palacio, truly magnificent, was England's turf. Of course, each side frequented the other's. After all, Portugal was neutral, and warfare was of the clandestine variety.

"Come here often?"

"Sounds like a come-on," Sonny smiled.

The man's grin seemed guileless. He waited.

Sonny looked around, back to his neighbor, then got to the question. "I spread myself around."

"Very democratic," the man said without irony. "Your accent is," his lips pursed in concentration, as if puckering for a kiss, "Berlin."

Sonny laughed and wondered whether the guy was trying to be funny. "Very good."

The superficial conversation, vague and evasive, as expected in a city of spies, revealed nothing of interest.

"This Saturday evening, the 15th," he dragged on his cigarette, "at Hotel Parque, we're throwing a fancy party for big-shots." His hand moved in a flourish, sending smoke in all directions. "Heavies from the German Legation, PVDE, and the Foreign Ministry will be in attendance." He took another drag. "See that man over there." He pointed discreetly toward a table in the corner where an older man in uniform sat with a much younger woman. "José Ernesto, senior PVDE."

Sonny glanced at a man talking earnestly, a woman staring in rapt attention. "Not his daughter."

He laughed. "Michael Gorman—I work at the embassy…hope to see you on Saturday." Then he extended his hand.

"Hans Baum." Sonny shook it . . .

. . . Sonny walked through a magnificent garden to the entrance of Hotel Parque. Though smaller than the Palacio, it was still expansive and opulent. Wrought-iron balconies, like big black combs, hung from the pale façade. Sonny faced a window overlooking the Atlantic, squinting from the glare off the water. German and Portuguese businessmen, government functionaries, spies, and hangers on mingled. Two big flags—Portuguese coat of arms upon red and green and swastika—hung languidly, side by side, evidencing the good relations between the two countries. The last time he had been at the Parque, he'd purchased drinks for an attractive Portuguese woman, surely an informant or spy. Gracious and polite, she probably would have been happy to spend the night with him. He learned nothing, but he enjoyed her company—that was all.

Sonny's eyes found Gorman's. Smiling, the man waved and came to Sonny's elbow. They shook hands.

"Hans, glad you came. Germans have to stand together."

"Agreed."

They talked about the weather, graduating to Europe's calm after the storm. Then Gorman asked, "Do you know anyone here?"

"No—should I?"

"That depends." He pointed to a portly man surrounded by several couples. "He's a big-shot in wolfram."

Sonny shrugged. "Don't need any of that."

Gorman laughed. "But Germany does."

Someone more important came into view, and Gorman waved. "I've got to talk to that man—have fun. Drop by anytime."

Drop by where? Sonny wondered, then shrugged. He loitered in the lobby then headed toward the bar for a drink before he left. Glass and chrome art deco chandeliers cast a dim light onto the bar and leather banquettes. Bartenders worked the long bar running along the far wall. Too crowded for comfort, Sonny stood near the door, surveying the room. The tables were full, and people hovered, hoping for an empty seat.

Standing two to three deep, the scrum at the bar seemed impenetrable. Still, he might push through or enter from the dining-room door at the opposite end. At that moment, several men in suits and uniforms and women in fancy gowns separated, creating a tunnel to the bar. If he was quick, he might run and order a drink.

Two or three men in uniform—PVDE or Gestapo, hard to tell—

leaned against the bar. One man brought a cigarette to his mouth. The light caught his golden hair. His lips sent a plume of smoke into the face of his listener. His arm moved up and down, as if gathering momentum for flight. His head turned toward Sonny, then away.

"Shit," Sonny hissed and froze. Quickly recovering, he turned from the doorway and left the hotel. He walked until he disappeared into Estoril's winding alleys. Albert Schwarz played through Sonny's mind in a continuous loop: gawky young man at the Berlin warehouse, cigarette dangling from the corner of his mouth, hands dancing in the air; in a group at a café, spilling coffee on his crotch, the victim of a crowd laughing at his expense; in a party of four Gestapo officers in a café; his photograph in possession of the dead man in Oranienburg; and the back of his head at the Belgian border, Sonny sneaking past. Then again . . .

What was Albert Schwarz doing in Lisbon—temporary or permanent assignment? What mischief was the Gestapo up to, beside its normal thuggery? No way Albert could know of Sonny's presence in Lisbon. Impossible! Paranoia toyed with reality. Sonny could not rid the thought of Albert dogging his life, again.

The next day Sonny dropped a note, requesting a meeting with Johnson. When they met, he told Johnson about Albert Schwarz, in turn learning that British intelligence had no record of a Gestapo officer of that name but that the Gestapo was involved in the smuggling of wolfram.

What was the connection between Albert Schwarz and wolfram? Gorman was an embassy attaché, maybe Abwehr? Recalling his conversation with Gorman, Sonny wondered how it all fit together. What he did know: Avoid Albert Schwarz or risk a confrontation that would blow his cover and destroy his mission.

"Keep a keen eye and hope for the best," Johnson advised.

Sonny continued his rounds. Hotel Parque was off limits; he would avoid Gorman. Everything else was on . . .

While the true Lisbon upper crust did not frequent bars, the city's tattered elite, in shiny suits and outdated gowns, gathered at chic, expensive hotel bars serving the finest port and cognac. Hotel Avenida Palace housed one of the prettiest bars in town. The long inlaid bar curved sensuously at both ends like a self-satisfied smile. Hitler's underlings and sycophants gathered there or at one of the ebony tables bathed in muted light.

Rumors painted every patron of the Avenida Palace Bar an informant or as receiving Nazi pay. Having a job to do, Sonny checked his pride at the door, figuratively held his nose, and plunged into Nazi excrement. From his position at the bar, Sonny pegged dour functionaries in wire rims and stiff collars. Menacing Gestapo sneered at everyone, even their own mirror images. Abwehr agents took unsuccessful pains to be invisible. Then there were, like Sonny, the miscellaneous. He would chat them up, let them talk, and learn.

"What can I get you, sir?" The bartender smiled enigmatically—serious, mocking, or ironic? He was tall and thin, in his early thirties, black hair combed back, perfect for his profession. The other bartender looked exactly like him. Alfonso and Alfredo were twins. Sonny never got them straight.

A man named Bitzler parked at the bar like a leaky ship at dry dock, always there. Sonny became a drinking companion, never a friend, though he pretended. They talked for several hours that first evening. Later, walking through the Rossio, Sonny had trouble recalling what Bitzler looked like. All he could describe was fair—fair complexion, fair brown hair, fair nondescript face, ordinary in every way, and forgettable—the perfect spy! Sonny might not be able to identify him on the street—and he had learned even less about who he was. Next time he would get down to business.

Sonny had taken a liking to the smokiness of single-malt Scotch in Wanborough. He ordered one on the rocks. Alfonso or Alfredo set it on the bar.

"What do you do?" Sonny asked, after exchanging greetings.

"Embassy attaché." Bitzler's answer was terse, as if the question were expected.

Sonny smiled. "Sitting in the embassy shuffling papers—riveting."

Bitzler laughed.

"Really, what do you do?" Sonny feigned amusement, as if he didn't care what the answer might be.

Bitzler's smile faded. "You're German?"

Sonny nodded in agreement.

"What are *you* doing here?"

"Sitting out the war, same as you."

Conversation fizzled. Next time, Sonny pledged again, he would plumb deeper. Soon spring took winter's place—but still there was nothing. He grew impatient. How long must he wait? Like a kid after his first kiss, he wanted more.

Bitzler drank too much—in that he was not ordinary. Morphing after several drinks from invisible man to boor, suddenly outgoing, laughing, talking, flirting with women. Like kindling, Bitzler might ignite a fire that Sonny could exploit.

On Sonny's fourth encounter with Bitzler, the man's eyes seemed unfocused. "Baum . . . good . . . see you."

Bitzler drained his glass, ordered another, and scooped a handful from the bowl of nuts. Talking nonsense, he projected his voice beyond the bar. "Hey, beautiful," he leered at a passing woman. Several single women sitting at a table nearby caught his attention. "Portuguese women are luscious."

Bitzler took a step, but Sonny pulled him to the other end of the bar: "Take it easy."

"Nah . . . " he gurgled like a baby, chewing too many nuts at once. He coughed uncontrollably.

"You'll offend 'Fritz' over there."

Bitzler craned his neck to look around, his eyes watering.

Sonny had glimpsed the man's reaction to Bitzler's antics. He had seen Fritz before, shaking his head with displeasure. Sonny nodded in his direction and smiled thinly, as if saying, "I'll do what I can."

Fritz returned the nod. Bitzler settled down but was too drunk to talk. Sonny left him at the bar.

Upon their next encounter, however, Bitzler seemed sober, at first. He said nothing about their previous run-in. Fritz was in his regular spot. Sonny changed tack and talked about why he left Berlin, his need for adventure and new horizons.

"Just got up and left?" Bitzler snapped his fingers, finished off his drink, and ordered another. "Impressive."

"I missed Berlin, but London's a great city . . . it blew up on me when Uncle Adolf invaded Poland."

"Shh!" Bitzler put a finger to his lips. "Attack dog nearby," he whispered, too loud.

Sonny shrugged and looked around. Fritz peered stonily at them from under his brow. "I'm still German . . . willing to help—if I can," Sonny said, winking at Bitzler, who stared back, as if he were a stranger.

Then Sonny felt a presence at his elbow. Fritz stood next to him—thick-chested but flabby, of average height, displaying a sanguine dueling scar on his puffy check. A monocle might complete the ensemble.

"Good evening," Sonny said.

The big head slowly turned and nodded. A broad nose dominated his unpleasant face. Unreadable, his hooded eyes floated above dark splotches, as if sleep were an interloper. "Same to you." His voice grated.

"Hans Baum." Sonny extended his hand, ignoring Bitzler.

"I am Heinrich Kepler."

They shook hands. Kepler scowled at Bitzler then turned his attention back to Sonny. "Join me." Kepler returned to his table.

"I've been summoned," Sonny said to Bitzler, who mumbled unintelligibly.

"Fool drinks too much," Kepler complained.

"He needs a hobby."

Kepler studied Sonny like a specimen under a microscope without comment.

Sonny smiled and shrugged. "Maybe he's simply misunderstood."

Kepler head moved slowly back and forth, making his jowls shake like curtains in a breeze. "Forget him. He's nothing. What exactly is it that you do?"

"You don't waste time. What happened to small talk? Get to know one another, then the personal stuff?"

Kepler's lips formed a grotesque smile. "Small talk," he snarled. "But if you insist—springtime is lovely, Portuguese are wonderful people, refugees flood the city like rats from a sinking ship." His scowl deepened with his sarcasm, his face a caricature from a Grosz cartoon.

Sonny grimaced at the sight of a man he would never trust. Kepler reminded him of a gargoyle on the cathedral's façade. "Refugees are a problem, though not for me."

"Stink of desperation!" Kepler's fist hit the table, spilling amber liquid.

Sonny grabbed his glass. "Fear does that."

Kepler breathed deeply through his nose, flaring his nostrils, emitting a thin whistle. Then he drank, flicked his tongue, like a lizard, snaring insects. "There is a new world order—Europe controlled by the Third Reich . . . "

Sonny interrupted, raising a finger. "Tell that to Salazar and Franco. Don't forget Sweden and the Brits, too."

Kepler's head nodded almost imperceptibly. "Portugal and Spain are sympathetic, their neutrality assured, so long as they remain neutral. Now tell me, what is it you do?"

Sonny projected his lower lip, giving the impression of thoughtfulness. "Survive."

Kepler's laughed, looked around cautiously, and retreated. He scratched his cheek and stared. Coal-black eyes revealed little about the man behind them. "Herr Baum . . . "

"Let's be informal. Call me Hank or Baum. We exchanged small talk . . . we're friends now. "

"Hank." Kepler's lips turned down with distaste, as if he had greeted the Führer as 'Adolf'—sacrilege.

"That wasn't so hard."

Kepler ignored that. "What the hell does *surviving* mean?"

"Self-explanatory, I would think." Sonny laughed. "I'm still alive in a world gone mad. Is that what you wanted to talk to me about?"

"All right. What do you do in Lisbon—*besides* survive?"

"Take in the sights: the beautiful castle at the top of the hill, though I wouldn't want permanent residence inside." Sonny shuddered. "The Cathedral, Pantheon Real, the churches, the lovely coastline to Estoril. You know, I saw men and oxen pulling a fishing boat from the water—very charming. Women walking with water jugs balanced on their heads. Quaint, very Old World, isn't it? And, of course, the taverns, cafés, bars, and incomparable fado. My guide-book says nothing about fado—a serious omission, don't you think? I could listen to its magic for hours."

Kepler was trolling. Sonny needed to talk, keep him interested. "Like Bitzler . . . I'm bored."

"Fado? I've heard of it. Maybe we will go to a café and listen."

"If that's an invitation, I know a little bar by the docks." Sonny leaned over, looked to either side conspiratorially, and whispered, "Rumor has it that spies pump sailors for information. Is that true?" He smiled disingenuously, as if he was in on the joke.

Sonny saw a crack in Kepler's façade—two halves of a picture patched, slightly off kilter.

"Why would I know that?" Kepler's feigned disinterest was unconvincing. "I understand you lived in England."

Finally we're getting somewhere, Sonny thought. "Congratulations on your sources," he said, acting surprised, hoping it showed on his face.

Kepler's shoulder's rose several millimeters in an apparent shrug. "It is my job to know what German nationals are doing in Portugal."

"What exactly is it that you do?" Sonny stole Kepler's words.

"Keep track of people."

"Uh, oh! Am I in trouble with Uncle Adolf?" Sonny kept his tone light.

"With Salazar's people, actually," Kepler answered.

Sonny knew it was a lie. "Ears everywhere." He raised his hands and waggled his fingers, unconcerned.

"Are you a British agent?" Kepler's gaze was piercing.

Sonny was ready, his laugh harsh but not overdone. "Why the hell would I work for them? I had to get my ass out of England or go to a camp, like some kind of . . . *refugee*."

"When did you leave Germany?"

"Read my dossier."

"Humor me."

Sonny sighed, then told the story.

"Work for us."

Sonny leaned back, surprised not at the offer but that it came so soon. No courtship or test of loyalty, at least not yet. "Doing what?"

Kepler stared too long at Sonny. Finally, he said, "You know people in England?"

"Of course."

"Give us some names—of people to work for us."

"You must be joking. I can't go back," Sonny protested.

"You misunderstand. Agents in England will contact them."

"This is crazy." Sonny was sincere. How could it work? But if he could worm his way in . . . leave the rest to Johnson?

"Think about it."

Finally, after 17 months, a hit . . . Sonny dropped a note for Johnson.

26

Lisbon, Summer 1942

Johnson's nose disappeared between the orchid petals. "Lady-of-the-Night, *Brassavola nodosa* . . . quite easy to grow, and a lovely fragrance. Magnificent! I could spend all day."

"Lovely," Sonny agreed without enthusiasm. "Let's get this over with."

Johnson straightened and looked at him in their first face-to-face meeting. His smile was brittle, perfunctory. "Of course. Were you followed?"

"No . . . don't think so. I took precautions."

"Patience has finally paid off."

Sonny had expected Johnson to rub his hands together like a cinema conspirator, but he did not. His note, written in secret ink on the back of a Portuguese handbill someone had handed to him on the street, outlined Kepler's proposal and briefly mentioned Bitzler. "What next?"

"Talk to Kepler. Tell him you thought about it and have several names." Johnson handed him a piece of paper. "Copy them. It must be in your handwriting. Then destroy my note. We'll arrest the agents and turn them or let them play." He shrugged. "Congratulations, you are now a player. Kepler will trust you."

"Who is Kepler?"

"Abwehr, mid-level, maybe higher, we think."

"And Bitzler?"

"Nobody—forget him."

Sonny put the paper in his pocket. The meeting had taken less than two minutes. Johnson's nose was in another orchid when Sonny left the greenhouse . . .

That evening, Sonny held Kepler's gaze. "How much is this worth?"

"Tsk . . . tsk!" Kepler shook his head sadly. "I thought you were doing this for love of country."

Sonny smiled. "Sure, as much as the next guy, but I have expenses. I'm not working. You have to pay for names."

Kepler was playing him, and Sonny went along. They haggled until they struck a deal. When it was over, Kepler said, "You negotiate like a Jew."

"Thanks," Sonny said with an exaggerated grimace.

They both laughed. Sonny silently cursed him.

"I'll have your money tomorrow."

"And you'll have the names."

The following day at Avenida Palace, Sonny counted his money while Kepler unfolded the paper with the names Sonny had copied.

"Hilda Hawkins, Lexham Gardens, Earls Court; Bobby Grim, Mellish Street, Docklands. Both London," Kepler read.

"I can't recall the numbers, but your boys can find them if they're still there," Sonny said, stashing the money in his pocket.

"We will find them." Kepler folded the paper and held it between his fingers. Waving it like a fan, he asked, "Why should they help us?"

Sonny shrugged. "I know them. Money means more than country, unless they have had a sudden injection of patriotism."

Kepler laughed.

———

In late summer, a welcome respite from Lisbon's stifling heat lay just around the bend. Sonny had heard nothing about the operation from Johnson or Kepler—best not to know, he figured. Neither were there further sightings of Albert Schwarz. Nevertheless, Sonny feared an inopportune meeting at the Avenida Palace bar and so suggested a new place for rendezvous with Kepler: "Walls of the Avenida Palace Bar can't be trusted." He didn't add that a thin, twitchy, blond Gestapo officer might turn up.

Kepler bought it. They would meet on the 1st and 15th of every month at 7 PM, in a small café several streets behind the Avenida Palace. Quiet and anonymous, it was perfect.

Tonight, Sonny headed to his favorite little bar in Alfama, looking forward to an evening of fado. Along the river, the fog was opaque as a curtain, making it a perfect setting for intrigue. Questionable women trolled. Dangerous men—Gestapo or PVDE—might lie in wait, hidden in dark corners, leaving an occasional corpse strewn in the gutter. Or so he imagined. Since he had made his deal with the devil, he trusted no one. Walking cobbled streets, he listened and watched for tails.

Crowded and hot, he leaned against a wall. If Filipe was there, Sonny couldn't see him. A big woman in a tight dress, eyes closed, hands clutched to her bosom, warbled her slow ballad of hurt and pain accompanied by a lone guitar. So palpable and sincere was her longing, her "saudade" touched the core of his separation from Rosa.

She finished her song, and someone took her place. Sonny pushed to the bar for a glass of wine. Returning to his spot, he noticed a sad young woman for the first time. A man had stood between them. Now another man sang, but he failed to move Sonny. The young woman was crying—not an uncommon occurrence at fado. He doubted she was Portuguese.

He moved closer. "Fado is very sad," he said in English.

Surprised, she shook her head. Her big eyes were flecked with red. "German or English?"

Her body tensed as if she would flee, but she stayed.

"Which is it?"

"German, a little English," she mumbled.

He gave her his wine. "Drink—are you hungry?"

She drank then wiped her mouth on her sleeve. "I haven't eaten since . . . "

Sonny gently took her arm and led her to a café several doors away. They sat on a bench at a small table. Sonny ordered bread, tomato salad, grilled sardines, and wine. "You'll feel better."

"Who are you?" she asked.

"Your guardian angel—for tonight." He smiled.

Cocking her head, she looked at him suspiciously. "What do you want?"

He shrugged. "Just to talk."

When the bread arrived, she wolfed it down.

Sonny watched her eat. "Where are you from?" he asked.

"Berlin, but I was born in Dessau."

"Moses Mendelssohn was born there."

"How did you know that?" she said.

"My uncle told me a story." Sonny smiled at the memory of his beloved, misanthropic uncle. "When Mendelssohn arrived in Berlin, it was written in a log: 'Today passed six oxen, seven swine, and a Jew.'"

She smiled for the first time. "I never heard that."

"Learn something new every day . . . " Sonny voice trailed.

"Who are you?" she asked again.

"A friend."

"German?"

Sonny shrugged. "I'm a man, living in Lisbon."

The rest of the food arrived. They ate in silence.

"What's your name?" Sonny asked when they were finished.

"Jenny . . . " she hesitated.

"Both names?"

"Jenny . . . Wolf."

"Jenny Wolf, call me Hank. Are you alone?"

Tears welled in her eyes. She nodded. "My brother was arrested in Paris. I don't know where he is."

"I'm sorry. When did you get here?" Sonny asked.

"Eons ago—October 1940. I'm stuck here."

"That's when I arrived. Where are you staying?"

"Mouraria—its cheap."

"Is it safe?" Sonny knew the slum's reputation as a rat hole—it was between the castle and Rossio.

"They leave me alone."

"How do you support yourself?"

She dropped her gaze, out of embarrassment, guilt, shame, or all three. She did not answer.

Regretting the question, he said, "Sorry . . . " Rumors circulated of desperate women taken to prostitution. He would leave that part of her past undisturbed.

"How did you get here?"

"Started in Paris. A woman saw me on the street with my brother, then later when I was alone. She was with a young child, not hers . . . we talked. She offered help . . . got me a job."

"Doing what?"

"Dancing in a club. She left Paris with the club's owner. Her friend, an actress, delivered a note. On it was the name of a winery in a place called Sare, in Aquitaine. Her friend said I should go there."

"Where is that?"

"Near Spain. But instead, I was arrested and sent to Gurs, a camp near Sare, but out of reach. We had no news, then one day the gates opened, guards disappeared. We heard the French lost, the war ended. I got to Marseille—there were rumors of visas. Maybe find Max . . . I didn't know what else to do . . . " She looked away, her jaw clenched as if never to open again.

"Did you find visas?"

She shook her head as if exorcising a bad dream. "Waiting . . . waiting. . . . waiting." Her words were a mantra of frustration. "Like Lisbon but worse. I remembered my friend's invitation, but you needed a permit to travel. I didn't have one. What did I have to lose?" Her questioning eyes challenged Sonny, but he didn't answer. "I learned how cheap my life was."

"You made it to this place . . . Sare?"

She shook her head, again. "No. I heard about a couple taking refugees over the mountain into Spain from Banyuls-sur-Mer on the Mediterranean. She's German, a Jew, and she took me and others. I gave the border guard cigarettes, can you believe? Safe passage for a packet of cigarettes . . . "

Jacob had mentioned a couple. "Were they married, the couple?" Sonny asked.

Jenny looked bewildered by his question. "Maybe. I don't know."

"What's her name?" Sonny had to ask.

"I can't. I promised. She's in big trouble if it gets out."

"I understand. Then tell shat she looks like—old, young, light, dark?"

"A little older than you, light brown hair, pleasant looking."

"Okay. What about the friend in Paris? Did you see her again?"

"No."

"What's her name?"

Jenny stiffened. "So many questions. You're nice to feed me, but I don't know you . . . I don't trust . . . anyone."

"Smart policy," Sonny agreed.

"You're German."

"Accident of birth. I'm a Jew like you."

"Why should I believe you? You don't look it."

"I'm from Mitte. Why would I lie? Let's go outside and talk. Too many ears in here."

A big ship was docked at the pier. Cargo dropped slowly into its hold from a crane, like a huge flightless bird feeding its young. Bright lights shone, casting long shadows on the water. Men and some women passed. The bars were busy. Fishermen would soon dock with their catch.

Still warm near midnight, they walked past the ship toward the Rossio. He glanced over his shoulder and saw a man. Had he seen him near the café? Sonny stopped near a church. "Let's meet later." Not wanting to frighten Jenny, he said, "I want to tell you a story but not now." He took escudos from his pocket and put them in her hand. "Take these."

She pushed back but not hard. He closed her hand around the bills. "Tomorrow, the botanical garden at 2 PM in the orchid house. You know where it is?"

She nodded. "What's happening?"

"I'll explain later. Go . . . be safe."

When Jenny was out of sight, Sonny walked around a corner, then stopped and scanned the street. Several people loitered; a few walked past. Who was shadowing him—Kepler, PVDE, Gestapo? He shuddered. Maybe Johnson was keeping an eye on him? He started toward Bairro Alto, then stopped.

"Screw 'em all," he muttered, then turned into an alley and hid in a doorway. He waited five minutes then slowly returned to the street he had vacated. Ahead, a man moved slowly, his head turning, clearly looking for someone.

Sonny's pursuer's face was obscured. Moving quietly through shadows, Sonny stalked the pursuer. Heartbeat accelerating, focused, he silently slipped into a doorway. Suddenly he itched for confrontation, wanting to put his intensive training to use, but he held back. He began to relax, even cracked a devious smile: the mouse had turned the table on the cat. His pursuer shrugged, hands on hips, head turning from side to side—the birds had eaten Hansel's breadcrumbs.

The profile of the man seemed familiar. Sonny discarded one face after another until one remained. Standing in the hallway, leaving the building . . . a man opening his mailbox . . . Now he knew.

Abandoning his perch, Sonny quickly covered the distance until only a few meters separated them. "Pleasant evening," he said in English.

The man jumped and wheeled toward Sonny—his mouth a gaping hole, his eyes full moons.

Sonny laughed. "Mayhew! What's with the game of blind man's bluff?"

"What's so goddamn funny? You nearly gave me a heart attack." Mayhew sucked air as if he had run up the hill.

Sonny chuckled. "You're a bigger amateur than me. We on the same side?"

"King and country, old chap." Mayhew smiled, composure regained.

"Then why follow me?"

"Let's find a more secluded place to talk." Mayhew led Sonny down the alley where he had first eluded him. They stopped in a dark doorway. "I was ordered to keep an eye on you from day one."

"Why not just tell me, and we ignore each other? Then I don't get spooked when I see a shadow and think its Adolf's boys."

"Point taken. Who was the woman?"

Sonny shrugged. "I met her at the bar, listening to fado. She was hungry. I fed her."

"Mister Nice Guy. Listen, you've just wormed your way into the honey pot—don't muck it up over a skirt."

Sonny refrained from telling him to piss off. Instead he asked, "Any bites on the home front?"

"Meaning?"

"Did we get a nibble on the names I passed to Kepler?"

"It's ongoing. Best they don't tell you—or me, for that matter."

"You going to keep being obvious?"

Mayhew laughed. "I'll do better next time."

"Are we friends now?"

"Hell, no, you German piece of shit!"

———

Jenny moved gracefully, reminding Sonny of the young Portuguese women balancing baskets on their heads. Her dark, sad eyes were like those of fado singers or women who sold themselves in Alfama. She had skimmed along the bottom and survived. But Sonny wouldn't talk about that.

"Orchids are gorgeous things," Sonny observed as they strolled through the orchid house.

She had yet to speak.

"You made it home all right?"

"I'm here." Her first words had bite. "What did you want to tell me?"

"A story."

"Men usually want more than that."

"I want information."

She stared hard, as if looking inside his head. "Thanks for the money."

"You're welcome."

"I don't know anything worthwhile."

"I'm looking for someone."

"Go to the police." Her tone was sarcastic.

Sonny laughed. "She's not here, at least I don't think so. Last time I saw her, she was headed to France. I never made it. That was over three years ago."

Jenny, still staring at Sonny, nodded. "Sorry. I do know how that feels."

"You've had it as bad, probably worse. We're survivors. We'll make it." He held her gaze. Nothing else to say about that. Common experience, pain, and privation brought some understanding, at least for him.

"Who is she?"

"My wife."

A gardener sprayed the orchids with a fine mist, then turned his head to greet them.

Jenny answered in Portuguese.

When they had passed, Sonny asked. "You speak Portuguese?"

She nodded. "I'm good with languages."

"You met a woman in Paris, maybe others, maybe my wife."

"It's a big city."

"32, Rue du Roi de Sicile," he repeated by rote.

"What's that?"

"Her last address in Paris."

"I don't know it. What's her name?"

"Rosa . . . Rosa Sander. She might have used Fischer."

Jenny backed away as if she had been pushed. Her eyes widened as if she had seen a ghost.

Fearing danger, Sonny looked around. No one was there—just the gardener. "What?"

"Rosa?"

"That's her name."

"Rosa is the name of the woman who wrote the note and got me the job."

Sonny's mind raced, but he forced an outward calm. "Describe her—please."

"Quite beautiful . . . dark hair, eyes. A little older than me." She shrugged.

Sonny hands grabbed Jenny's arms. His eyes bored in on her, drilling for riches beneath the surface. "Where did she come from? Was she married?"

"From Berlin. But her husband's name was Sonny . . . "

He hugged Jenny and began to cry—it wasn't Jenny he was holding. Jenny kept still. When he finally let go, his smile was blinding.

"Do I call you Hans or Sonny?"

"That's a long story."

"Unfortunately, I have time." Jenny smiled.

"First, tell me all you can about your time in Paris."

She did. "The cabaret closed after Agnes Capri left. Rosa's friend Annette let me stay at her flat in Montparnasse. She acted at the theater next to the club. They were all good to me. Annette passed the note from Rosa with the name of the winery. It's called . . . " She placed a finger to her lip. "It'll come to me."

"You stayed in Paris—after Rosa left?"

"Hoping Max would show . . . " Her despondency returned.

"He still might. Don't lose hope."

Her eyes said otherwise.

"You made it here. Why can't Max?"

She bent to smell an orchid.

"I want to help you. I'll get you a flat near mine."

"You can do that?" She looked perplexed.

He looked around the greenhouse, pondering the question as if the orchids held the answer. It was quiet except for the gardener's faint humming. Then he said, "In the meantime . . . "

"Domaine Poussard," she interrupted, barely audible.

"What?"

"The winery in Sare. I remembered."

Domaine Poussard," he repeated. "Now, all I need is a plan." He had to get to France. There had to be a way.

Jenny was his only connection to Rosa, and Sonny pumped her for everything she knew. She told him about Agnes, Annette, and Jean. "She was very fond of Jean, talked about him often. Her got her an identity card and made her part of his family. I never met him."

"He must be a good man," Sonny said. Then he told his story— though not all of it.

Afterwards, with a little help, he found a cheap, clean flat in a decent building near his. Jenny moved in. Then he worked on Johnson to issue a Portuguese visa for Jenny and to find a job using her impressive language skills. After several weeks of finagling, Jenny was offered a translator job. She could pay her own way and do her bit for the war effort.

Jenny and Sonny, lonely and in search of loved ones, soon became friends. Going to fado clubs, having late dinners, strolling Jardim Botânico and the river, taking walks to Belem and along Alfama's narrow, winding cobblestones, they had long talks, good for both of them.

In October, the shorter and cooler days made the summer heat a welcome memory. Sonny suggested they take the train to Estoril. Never having been there, Jenny readily agreed. Her newfound economic security allowed room for a bit of enjoyment—she was no longer the hungry, young woman crying at fado.

They passed the massive Jerónimos Monastery in Belem, then followed the coastline. Sonny knew the opulent casino and fancy hotels, thick with spies and Albert Schwarz.

"Not bad," Jenny mused, watching the meandering coastline. "If the world weren't crumbling, I might like it here." Jenny's fluency plus her dark hair grown long, her dark eyes and complexion, let her pass easily as Portuguese. She had put on weight, and she looked healthier, though she was still slight. A sardonic, cynical sense of humor, the product of her experience, emerged.

For Sonny, Jenny was as link to Rosa. He took partial credit for Jenny's transformation and assumed the role of protector. Best of all, he now had a true friend. That afternoon the two of them strolled the lanes of Estoril, window-shopped, and perused the minor works of art adorning walls and windows in the area's ubiquitous churches. Slowly the day drained into evening.

Beneath the awning of a charming café, one of several overlooking the ocean, they ate grilled sardines and drank wine. Business was slow. Few sailboats floated in and out. A few people walked the beach. It was warm, but the water was too chilly for swimming. The panorama of beach and harbor, sky and ocean of endless blue, gave them hope. Nothing in his fractured world could disturb the quiet of the peaceful Estoril night, Sonny mused.

The sun's declining rays reflected off the water in a fiery light. The two friends finished their glasses of port. Soon they would return to Lisbon. They agreed: no talk of work or war.

"Anywhere in the world, where would you go?" Sonny asked.

"Anywhere?" A fingertip touched her lips.

Sonny nodded.

"Not here, though it's beautiful. Europe is infected with a terrible virus. One place," she mused. "New York." She pointed, "Far across the ocean. America's promise of endless possibility for reinvention, so they say."

"They?" Sonny laughed.

She nodded. "Cognoscenti. They tell us what's what and make a mess of everything."

"Pretty smart and cynical for a kid."

She laughed. "Don't know about the smart part. When I was a kid, I looked at pictures of New York in magazines . . . bustling, exciting, interesting, new."

"I know the feeling. Photographs stimulate the imagination. Travel the world, paging through magazines. I dreamed of being a journalist." He told Jenny of his two published reviews. He sighed. "But that faded and died."

"All our dreams faded. Where will you go?"

"When I find Rosa, we'll leave Europe for . . . " He shrugged. "Probably England, maybe America, but who knows?"

A group of approaching men distracted him. Ten men, some in uniform, brought with them the whiff of unpleasantness; PVDE, Gestapo, or both, and government functionaries out for a bit of pleasure. Jenny and Sonny stopped talking and watched—nothing to fear, yet.

One of the men in uniform held a cigarette in his hand. Sonny watched it move to his mouth, then away, a plume of smoke obscuring his face. The lowering sun reflected off his hatless, golden head, creating a halo above a sharp-edged face.

"Not again!" Sonny stiffened. Closing his eyes, he opened them, willing the image gone. But the man was still in the frame, talking, laughing. Still, there was no indication the group would stop . . . "Shit!"

Jenny's eyes went from Sonny to the group, confused then concerned. "What . . . who is it?"

"Someone I used to know in Berlin . . . Gestapo. I saw him at the Parque six months ago," Sonny whispered, turning away, showing the back of his head to the street. "He'll walk in front of us, maybe stop here."

"Which one?"

"Blond, with the cigarette."

She scanned them. "I see him."

"Stay where you are. I'm going to the men's. Keep an eye on him. When I'm done I'll wait by the door. You give me the 'all clear.' If he stops here, leave and meet me at the station." He put money on the table and left.

Sonny walked past the waiter to the back of the darkened, empty restaurant, past the kitchen, toward the door. He glanced back to the patio—nothing. The barely functioning loo was in the alley. Upon returning, he heard men's voices, a mix of Portuguese and German. He saw Jenny's head. She kept her gaze toward the sea.

Voices approached from the patio. Stuck inside, Sonny looked among the tables then to the kitchen for a hiding place. The kitchen was too small. In a corner near the front was a small bar with several stools. He dashed behind the bar and waited. Bottles of whiskey and port lined a shelf above him.

Footsteps passed him and disappeared. This started a parade of what seemed like 15 minutes. Sonny tried to climb into a cabinet, but there wasn't enough room. The waiter took orders. Footsteps came around the bar. Sonny looked up at the shocked face of a middle-aged man with a ready smile and bright, intelligent eyes. Smile fading, he stared. Then he nodded, as if agreeing with what his eyes saw, but he kept staring. He said nothing.

Sonny smiled wearily, shrugged, and put a finger to his lips. He immediately went to the universal language. Pulling a wad of escudos from his pocket, he thrust them at the waiter, and mouthed "okay," another universal.

The waiter looked toward the patio, then down at Sonny. The cash disappeared into his pocket. Nodding at Sonny, he reached for the bottles, put them on a tray, and took them outside.

What if the waiter betrayed him, told someone he was hiding behind the bar? His legs hurt from crouching. He was hemmed in, unable to move, vulnerable.

Then the bar moved, and something rapped the surface. Someone was leaning against it. A gruff voice called, "Garçon, whiskey." A hand tapped impatiently. Seconds passed in what seemed like minutes, hours. Sonny feared the man would come around, take the bottle, and see him.

"Sim, Sim, Senhor." The waiter moved behind the bar. A knee hit Sonny in the back. He reached for a bottle and was about to set it on the bar, but a hand snatched it from him. Not a thank-you, nothing spoken. His footsteps receded. Sonny heard a Portuguese-accented voice: "Scotch whiskey." Then muted voices from outside.

The waiter stood still for a few seconds, then grabbed Sonny's sleeve and pulled. Sonny moved quickly behind him into the kitchen, then into the alley. He waved, but the waiter was already inside.

Jenny was pacing in front of the station when Sonny arrived.

"You scared the hell out me—what happened?"

He told her, then asked, "What about you?"

"They wanted me to drink Scotch whiskey with them. One came on to me." She grimaced. "I said my mother was waiting for me in church. Another one said, 'Go child.' And I did."

"Quick thinking. You'll make a good operative. But that was too close."

27

Lisbon, Early June 1943

Saturday evening a breeze from a furnace blew onto his face as Sonny walked from his apartment. He gasped, then felt limp like a noodle. Perspiration beaded on his upper lip and dripped from under his arms. A clear sky bedeviled the chance for a cooling rain.

Albert had receded from Sonny's thoughts before that second sighting in October. He was shaken. Jenny had been at risk. When Sonny told Johnson, he responded, "Stay out of Estoril." *He* was a great help.

Sonny was looking forward to another evening of fado. He heard footsteps keeping pace from behind. Annoyed, he did not bother to look, but soon a shadow was abreast of him: Poster boy for the New Reich, young and blond, but with sweat beading his brow and such limp hair, only a shabby image of Übermensch.

"Herr Baum . . . " the voice pitched on the high side, almost feminine.

"It's too damn hot!" Sonny snapped. He had never seen the man.

The young Parsifal stammered, "Ah . . . ah . . . "

"What the hell do you want?" Sonny was impatient though he knew.

"Herr Kepler waits . . . "

Sonny stopped, hands on his hips, eyes raking over the man. "Listen, messenger boy . . . "

"My name is Klaus."

"You're new . . . Klaus. Berlin just send you?"

"Yes, sir."

Sonny sighed. "All right., I'll go—alone. Don't need a chaperone."

"I am to accompany you."

"Were you lying in wait?" Sonny accused, his night of fado, drinking, conversation, mulling about his future, about Rosa, fading from view. Facing Kepler was a low priority tonight. It was the first time he'd summoned. What did he want?

Klaus nodded sheepishly.

Sonny sighed. "Follow me!"

When they reached the café, Klaus melted away.

"Here as requested, Herr Kepler." Sonny clicked his heels.

"Sit down, Baum," Kepler said, already annoyed.

Sonny sat. "What's so important it couldn't wait?"

Kepler stared, unblinking. "Berlin is very pleased."

Sonny's lips drew back in genuine surprise. "I merited attention?"

"Your contacts have proven productive." Kepler produced an envelope from an inside pocket and handed it to Sonny. "A bonus."

"Thank you." Sonny stuffed it in his pocket without looking inside. "Is that all? I have a night of fado ahead."

"Fado, fado—that's all I hear from you."

Sonny's laughter further annoyed Kepler. "No! That's not all."

Spittle flew from Kepler's bulbous lips, landing harmlessly on the table. Kepler was always out of sorts, probably had an ulcer. Sonny waited.

"I have a job. I need an inside man to help with a shipment of wolfram."

"Smuggling?"

"Don't be crass. What do you know about wolfram?" Kepler asked.

Sonny reeled in Shannon's wolfram lesson and dusted it off. "Not much . . . I read something, somewhere . . . " tapping his index finger on his lip, " . . . it's mined in Portugal . . . hardens metals . . . for tanks, shells, bearings, cutting tools." Sonny's hands came up, indicating that was all he knew. "Oh! We need it. England needs it."

"Essentially that is correct. Of course, it is more complicated. England purchases more Portuguese wolfram than we. Have you heard of the SS *Corte Real*?"

Sonny frowned. "No . . . a ship?"

Kepler's big head nodded slightly. "A Portuguese ship, carrying contraband—wolfram—to the enemy, sunk in October '41 by us.

Not the act of a neutral nation. The crew was ordered to abandon ship, then we sunk it, with no loss of life."

"Hmm," Sonny hummed. "Salazar probably didn't like that."

"Decidedly not—money lifted from his pocket. He is a tough negotiator. England pays him more, and an export duty on every ton brings yet more pound sterling to his coffers. We have made inroads but never enough for Reichsminister Speer, our Berlin overlord. Thus we use *extraordinary* methods."

"Extraordinary," Sonny repeated. "So it is smuggling."

"Perhaps as you describe. I am not involved in that aspect."

"What do you need me for?"

"There is an operation run by the Gestapo." His mouth angled into a sneer and stayed there, allowing his fleshy face to catch up. It was grotesque. "They requested a local man, one of ours, to help." His heavy shoulders shrugged. "I need someone—someone I trust—an inside man—to watch and report."

"Nice to know I'm trusted."

Kepler took a cigar from an inside pocket and rubbed it between his thumb and forefinger. "Do not get carried away." The corner of his lips fought gravity toward what was technically a smile . . .

"Gestapo?" Sonny questioned. Albert Schwarz's presence in Lisbon was beginning to make some sense.

"It is the Gestapo I do not trust. They are too meddlesome and brutal for my taste." He flicked his wrist dismissively, light flashing from his gold ring. "Report to Bragança on the Spanish border on Tuesday, 8 June, to a Gestapo officer."

"Three days from now!"

"Your command of arithmetic is commendable." Kepler's lips parted in a radiant smile. "And do remember that we pay you to do something . . . once in a while."

Ignoring the jibe, Sonny asked, "Where the hell is it?"

Kepler's heavy shoulders lifted in a slow shrug. "In the envelope, along with cash, map, and directions."

"How do I get there?"

Kepler sighed in what might have been exasperation. "Train . . . then hire a driver."

"The officer's name?"

Kepler's cigar levitated until he clenched it between yellowed teeth. Red, yellow, orange, a hint of blue, flared at the tip of a match. Flame met tobacco. Puffing like a steam engine, Kepler, without moving, disappeared into the fog. An exhalation extinguished the match's bright orange glow, dissipating the cloud.

Sonny feigned a cough and waited like a loyal soldier.

"Sturmbannführer Herbert Goren."

Shrugging, Sonny said, "Don't know the name."

"Of course not. Why would you? He is mid-level Gestapo who so far as I know has never been to Portugal. Follow instructions. You will drive in a truck convoy through Spain to France. I admit it is a daring gambit." He frowned, looking thoroughly disgusted.

"You don't approve?"

His head moved slowly from side to side, frown fixed. "Risky for 20,000 tons of wolfram. If we are caught . . . "

"Then we won't be caught."

"Make sure of it." Crimson glowed as Kepler inhaled, then exhaled a billowy blue-gray cloud from the side of his mouth. "Upon your return to Lisbon, report immediately to me. Keep your eyes and ears open."

Sonny digested his mission, wheels spinning: A truck convoy through Spain to France—*France!* The thought of Rosa there shoved Kepler aside. Finally: entry into France, finding Rosa, whisking her away! Images of Rosa floated through his mind—the first time he laid eyes on her . . . Oranienburg . . . their wedding day . . . in bed together . . . Mons . . . In the blink of an eye, everything had changed. He nearly snapped his fingers.

Kepler stared at him. "Damn it, Baum—stay with me!"

"Right . . . sorry." He scratched his forehead. "You said France?"

"Where else?" Kepler was impatient.

Sonny struggled back into the game. "How many men involved?"

"Goren might be alone or have someone with him . . . on the quiet. I have not been fully briefed. The Gestapo . . . " he scowled, a short journey for his mouth, "does not keep me informed. Others will be Portuguese or Spanish, and, of course, you. Insinuate yourself fully into the operation. Goren expects you."

In one sulfurous flash, the time and circumstance of Sonny's life seemed to be falling into a closer harmony. Once upon a time, long ago, he'd had control of his life, or thought he did—a conceit.

Perhaps it was a dream. He'd come from petty smuggler to secret operative—through time and circumstance—serendipity. Life was a bouncing ball on a giant roulette wheel . . . Then the thought of Albert intruded. Might he be the other man?

Sonny nodded. "All right."

"Do not disappoint me," Kepler grumbled.

Exactly what Sonny intended. Handed a chance, he would snatch it. Laughing at the absurdity, he walked to the Rossio and faced Don Pedro IV. His only thoughts were of sabotaging the shipment and finding Rosa—two themes competing for primacy. He had to work them together. But first he must contact Mayhew or Johnson. Mayhew offered his best chance . . .

. . . Sonny ran from the taxi, entered his building, and knocked on Mayhew's door. Footsteps! The door opened a crack.

"Who . . . "

Not waiting for an invitation, Sonny pushed the door open and slipped inside.

"What the hell?"

"I have a new assignment." Sonny gave him a quick outline, then read the cryptic note aloud: "Train to Bragança, hire car. Drive south through Samil. Stay south past fork on road. Turn left—first track to a farmhouse—row of cypress trees along track leading to the house. Goren will be waiting."

Mayhew went to the telephone and dialed, waited, then said, "Mayhew . . . we need to discuss the new book." He listened. "*Now.*"

Hanging up, he said to Sonny, "Meet at the back of the national archive. Leave. I'll follow in five minutes."

. . . They sat in an automobile parked off Marginal Road, halfway to Estoril. Mayhew's cigarette glowed, then dimmed, in monotonous rhythm. The car's engine ticked and knocked until quiet.

Sonny handed the instructions to Johnson. "I have to report to a Gestapo Sturmbannführer. We can't let them have the wolfram." His priorities were muddled. Overhead, a thin sliver of moon hung precariously.

Johnson and Mayhew exchanged glances.

"Too late to assemble a commando team. Difficult in the best of circumstances and Portugal, being neutral . . . " Johnson let that hang.

"Only our man Baum knows." Mayhew tilted his head toward Sonny. "We have men at the embassy . . . take several to the spot . . . then 'Bob's your uncle,' the wolfram's ours."

"Steal it from them?" Johnson murmured.

"Precisely," Sonny agreed.

"If the Gestapo or Kepler get wind of it?"

"How?" Sonny asked.

"I agree—not likely. He trusts you, gave you a bonus, probably pocketed some of it. It's the PVDE I worry about. If Salazar discovers our chicanery . . . he might explode, throw us out of the country," Johnson mused.

"Our chicanery? Germans are stealing it in the first place." Mayhew said, incredulous. "Salazar's juggling act plays both sides."

"A pox on both," Sonny said.

Sonny surveyed the train car—no familiar faces. Mayhew and a young Pole named Karpov had left for Bragança the day before. Sonny's contact, Senhor de Souza, a Portuguese operative working for MI6, would meet him at the railway station.

It was morning, 8 June, the day of his expected arrival. He had taken the night train, transferring in Coimbra and again in Vila Real. Bragança was as far from Lisbon as he could go without leaving Portugal—about 500 kilometers away. According to *Satchel's* short entry, Bragança was a stronghold of yore for a family of that name. Apparently worth visiting, it was on a tough road, passable only in good weather. Sonny imagined a castle on a hill with a river.

Jenny knew something was afoot and pumped Sonny for information. He told her he was leaving Lisbon and would be gone for a while.

"How long?" she asked. Not getting an answer, she became annoyed. Sonny did nothing to dispel her mood.

The tiny station held the usual loiterers—cop, old lady, several old men, several children, a janitor leaning on a broom, talking, and a young woman talking to the fedora. He smiled under his bushy mustache, a valise dangling from an arm. Nonchalantly, de Souza turned toward Sonny, then back to the young woman. He kissed her on both cheeks and walked from the station.

Sonny followed him through the medieval town, acting like a

tourist. He checked for tails, making sure he was not followed. After 20 minutes, de Souza disappeared through a doorway. Sonny entered and closed the door.

"Senhor Baum, I am Senhor de Souza."

"Olá," Sonny greeted him. The room was dark and smelled of cooked food. He waited 15 seconds for his eyes to adjust. Mayhew and Karpov stepped from the shadows. More movement—and Jenny stepped out.

"What the hell?" Sonny exclaimed.

Mayhew shrugged. "She snuck onto the train. We had no idea . . . must admit she's pretty good."

"Now what?" Sonny asked. He looked at her. "Why? This is dangerous."

"You mean no place for a woman."

"Yes!"

"Forget it. She's here. We're wasting time," Mayhew said.

Scowling, Sonny turned to Mayhew. "What have you learned?"

"De Souza told us about a wolfram mine called Ribeira, 15 kilometers south of here. The farmhouse, if you want to call it that, is on the same road, so it corresponds to your instructions. He told me that Goren, if it's him, and another man arrived yesterday by automobile. A young woman was with them."

"She German or Portuguese?" Sonny asked.

"Don't know."

Sonny scrutinized de Souza's pleasant face. Fastidious in a tie and coat, he might be a clerk or bureaucrat. "How does he know?"

"*I know!*" de Souza exclaimed in English.

Sonny's palms patted the air. "Take it easy. I want to be sure."

"We're all nervous." Mayhew said.

"My cousin . . . he is police captain. His town, he know what happens. And I have friends in mine. Germans pay to steal wolfram."

"Over the past week more lorries than usual drove through Samil, then turned toward the mine." Mayhew pointed to a table. "I need some light."

They stared at a map. De Souza held a kerosene lamp.

"Turn it up," Mayhew ordered. "Good." He pointed to an X on the map south of Bragança. "The house is here . . . " then his finger traced a line from town, " . . . road goes to Samil and south along this side road a short distance to the house." He tapped his finger. "The second X is the mine, about five kilometers farther. Gestapo stole the wolfram or made a deal with the owner."

"What's the route out of there?" Sonny asked.

"Dead end—backtrack to Samil road, then south and east to a town called Miranda do Douro, and cross into Spain. They won't go back to Bragança," he shook his head. "Too obvious, too likely to be seen."

Sonny opened his mouth to speak, but Jenny got there first.

"If Senhor de Souza's cousin is a big-time policeman, why doesn't he arrest them?"

"Good question," Sonny said.

"Now you glad I came?" she asked, sarcastically.

"No." Sonny smiled reluctantly.

"And steal our thunder or rather our wolfram." Mayhew turned to De Souza. "What do you have to say?"

The man rubbed thumb on fingertips. "My cousin, he getting . . ." They understood.

"No help from the cops if we 'cock' it up," Mayhew observed.

"You pay him, he help," De Souza offered.

"Hmm . . . something to think about," Mayhew said.

"Describe the man with Goren," Sonny asked De Souza.

"Assistant—big man . . . dark hair." He shrugged. "That all I know."

Sonny relaxed. No confrontation with Albert, yet. He turned to Mayhew. "Our arsenal?"

A thin, mirthless smile creased Karpov's face. He spoke for the first time in heavily accented English. "Vee have guns—one Enfield, two Vebleys . . . and for you, Valther PPK . . ."

He reached into a bag on the floor and brought out the Walther. He handed it to Sonny. "Best you have German gun." He placed a box of ammunition on the table. "Also, six grenades . . . three knives—enough for job."

Sonny examined the Walther. "Excellent! Please put it all on the table."

Their little arsenal grew.

Hard-edged at 27, Roman Karpov had seen death and caused it, leading to his unwavering hatred of all things German. Dark, penetrating eyes hid a troubled soul. He rarely smiled. Experience had taught him that trust was a scarce commodity. His family, of Polish heritage, had lived in Kiev for generations. The Germans had overrun Ukraine in June '41 on their way to Moscow. Now few remained.

Karpov had joined the partisans, but they were disorganized and lacked weaponry. Fearing a lost cause, he fled through the Balkans, abandoning family and friends. English army, Polish army in exile, Free French, the Soviets—it made no difference so long as he got revenge on the Germans. Landing in North Africa, he had made it to Lisbon and offered his services to His Majesty.

"We'll get back to you," someone at the British embassy had told him. Months later Mayhew found him in a cheap boardinghouse on the waterfront. His English rough but passable, Karpov claimed to have killed his share of, but not enough, Germans. Mayhew took him to a remote spot northeast of Lisbon for a few physical tests and target shooting.

"You might prove useful," Mayhew had said with British understatement. "Report to the embassy tomorrow. Give them your name. You'll be taken care of."

Karpov worked for Mayhew, his duties as needed. Thus far he had done a few mop-ups, dealing with Portuguese informants hassled by German operatives, nothing big. He hadn't killed any Germans—yet.

"I want to make sure we all know what to do—it's my ass on the line," Sonny said, then nodded to Mayhew.

"All our asses are on the line," Mayhew corrected. "We'll each carry a pistol, ammo, and two grenades." He grabbed a knife. "And one of these—you never know. De Souza says the drivers will not be a problem." He looked at the Portuguese man.

He nodded. "They poor farmers, some miners . . . they take side that pay."

"Good. Still, Goren may have paid some of them to shoot if necessary. Be careful! We want the drivers alive." He looked at Sonny. "Baum—you're Baum until this is over, and maybe after, depending . . . "

"On what?"

"We'll talk later." Mayhew held his hand up, a traffic cop stopping the line of inquiry. "De Souza takes you in his truck to the house, drops you, then leaves. You walk in. Assume sentries watching the road, maybe even in Samil. The house sits on a hill with an undisturbed view in both directions. It's rustic, made of granite, one story, set high with steps up to the door. Looks like there's a cellar with two outside doors. Front right is a small porch with another door, one window on each end, and two windows on the front and back. A man with a high-powered rifle could knock off anyone on the road—though Goren should have no reason to think treachery is afoot."

"He's Gestapo. He lives by treachery," Sonny shot back.

"Baum . . . right!" Karpov surprised them with his outburst.

Mayhew did not react. "You're alone until after dark. Karpov and I will be dropped at a turn in the road, out of sight of the house. We walk in and hide."

"I have rope . . . tape to tie sentries if needed," Karpov added.

"Careful with grenades. I want to stay in one piece." Sonny said.

"Maybe a few to stir things up." Mayhew rubbed his hands together, savoring the notion.

"I want information. Give me time. Don't come in like American gangsters, with guns blazing.'"

Karpov looked confused.

"I'll explain later," Sonny said.

"We think there are only two Germans, and the woman, maybe a local man." Mayhew explained, "No prisoners—understood?"

Karpov grinned.

Sonny nodded. "Understood."

"Got my feet wet in Belgium . . . been waiting to punch Jerry in the snout ever since," Mayhew said. And to De Souza: "You ready?"

He nodded.

"What about me?" Jenny had been silently watching, listening.

"Forgot about you," Mayhew said.

"Go to hell," she said.

"You weren't invited to the party," Mayhew said calmly.

"How hard is it to pull a trigger?"

They ignored her question.

"Got something to eat?" Sonny asked.

In half an hour they were ready. Jenny was gone.

28

Near Samil, Portugal, June 1943

Not knowing the men they would kill made it . . . well, it was better not to think about it, but Sonny did. In the end, better them than him. He had a plan, but he had said nothing. Would Mayhew cause trouble? He would deal with that later.

A rutted road wound through inhospitable land. The hills were dotted with boulders but few trees. It was no good for farming and barely adequate for livestock, but maybe there were mines? They rode in silence. Sonny wedged his arms against the dashboard as the small truck bounced and jerked.

"We here." De Souza stopped after driving about 10 minutes.

Sonny checked the chamber of the Walther for the fourth time, then felt his pocket for the ammunition and knife. He was sweating in the cool air. He leaned into the truck. "Thanks. You won't see me again unless something goes wrong." He grabbed his satchel with the change of clothes and toiletries. De Souza disappeared around the bend making dust.

Sonny caught some movement in the corner of his eye. He pointed the gun at—standing in the road five meters away—Jenny.

"Hi, Sonny." Her tone was almost cheerful.

"Ah, shit!" He cursed through clenched jaw. He dragged her behind the lone tree on the side of the road. "It's *Baum*. You want to get us killed?"

She displayed the Webley uncomfortably. "I took it."

He hadn't noticed it was missing. "Ever fired a pistol?"

"Teach me."

He sighed in resignation, then spent several minutes providing the rudiments of small firearms. "It's heavy and it kicks . . . hold it steady with both hands . . . squeeze the trigger, don't pull . . . and don't shoot yourself in the foot—or me anywhere. Got it?"

"Looks easy."

"Until you have to shoot someone. Hide until Mayhew and Karpov get here. Make sure they know it's you so they don't shoot you by mistake."

She nodded.

"Say it."

"I will . . . promise."

"Now get lost!"

Sonny reached the foot of the hill beneath the house. It was 5 PM, the sun was still fairly high, clouds sharing the blue with several birds. Despite the desolation, he liked northern Portugal. Maybe he'd return with Rosa, raise a family in Bragança, mine wolfram. He still wore a smile as he climbed the track to the house.

"Hello," he shouted to avoid surprise. "It's Baum."

The door opened. A man walked out. His legs were slightly spread, his hands on his hips. He wore gray pants and a white shirt, like a banker on holiday. "Come . . . been expecting you." His deep voice spoke German.

"Sturmbannführer Herbert Goren." He extended a hand. About Sonny's height, Goren was thicker in the torso, graying at the temples. Small blood vessels traversed his nose, slightly purple at the tip. Despite the flaws, his regular features rendered him blandly handsome. Bright blue eyes like beacons were his only memorable feature.

They shook hands. "Henry Baum. Everyone calls me Hank."

"I shall call you Baum." Something in Goren's blue eyes told Sonny he was being toyed with. "Obersturmbannführer Schwarz tells me that you have been very helpful to our *friends* in the Abwehr."

Sonny felt color rise in his cheeks. Momentarily nonplussed, he gave round one to Goren. Had Goren noticed? Albert Schwarz knew about Baum but not about Sonny. He was formless and colorless, not yet unmasked. He willed his paranoia back to darkness.

Sonny needn't have worried. Goren had launched into a diatribe against the Abwehr. Suspicion and jealousy were the guiding principles behind the relationship between Abwehr and the Geheime Staatspolizei, Gestapo—an open secret. Kepler's distrust was Sonny's reason for being there. The lines between intelligence and security were fuzzy and constantly breached. Each side accused the other of crossing into its turf.

"I have done my duty, Sturmbannführer Goren," Sonny said calmly.

Goren's head tilted back and a pleasant laugh emerged, reminding Sonny of the late, lyrical Gestapo lieutenant cremated in Oranienburg. He wanted to kill him now but refrained.

"Ja, call me Sturmbannführer—military discipline." Goren's mouth twisted to a spiteful smirk. He leveled a raptor's stare at Sonny, then suddenly shouted, "Scharführer Schmidt!"

Sonny's head jerked. The door opened. An unsmiling platter of a face set upon a big pedestal with legs and arms filled the space. "Jawohl, Sturmbannführer," emerged in a harsh whisper, its humanity wrung out like a sponge squeezed dry.

"Schmidt, meet the Abwehr's Baum. He will help with our little job. Where's Maria?"

"In the kitchen, Sturmbannführer."

Sturmbannführer . . . Sturmbannführer . . . Sonny was already sick of the annoying mouthful. Tracing the outline of the Walther in his pocket, he took a breath, and said, "Hello, Schmidt."

Schmidt nodded but said nothing.

To hell with niceties, Sonny thought, turning to Goren: "Sturmbannführer, what is your plan?"

"Leave at dawn from the Ribeira Mine. All you need to know."

"How many times have you made the trip, Sturmbannführer?"

"Twice." He held two fingers aloft. "Why you are here is a mystery. Well . . . to spy on us, I suppose." His smile was insincere. "My orders are to be cordial."

Sonny ignored the bait and changed subject. "What documents will I use?"

"Sturmbannführer . . . "

Sonny blanched but managed to say, "Sturmbannführer, what documents will I use?"

"Questions . . . questions . . . too many damn questions! Tomorrow all will be clear. Ten trucks in a convoy cross the border into Spain, on to Irun and into France." His tone was impatient, as if he were talking to a dull child. "Enough! Schmidt!"

Schmidt appeared again. "Jawohl, Sturmbannführer."

"Bring food and send Maria."

Heels clicked, hammer on steel. Goren's factotum disappeared.

Within minutes, Schmidt reappeared with a plate of sausages, cheese, peppers, tomatoes, and bread. "You're lucky to be in Portugal, Baum. Plentiful food—not rationed like in Berlin." He pierced a sausage by a knife. It disappeared into the Sturmbann-führer's maw. Chewing loudly, he poured vodka into two glasses. "Dammit—Maria!" His mouth full of sausage, he screamed, *"Maria!"* Bits sprayed from his mouth, like bullets. Then to Sonny: "Eat, drink!"

Wary, Sonny raised his glass, watching Goren. He'd learn what he could while Sturmbannführer Goren drank himself into a stupor.

"Ach . . . there you are. Baum, meet the lovely Maria."

Sonny turned to a woman, dark and beautiful, no older than 18. "Hello," he said and smiled.

Maria's eyes went from Goren to Sonny and back to Goren as if seeking approval before accepting the greeting.

"Say hello to our guest."

"Hello," she said dully.

"English, Deutsch?" Sonny asked.

She shook her head. Something was wrong.

To Goren: "Do you speak Portuguese?"

"Why? We understand one another, don't we, Maria?" His smile dripped with false empathy.

"Where did you find her?"

"On loan from a friend in Lisbon."

Sonny nodded, feigning approval, hating Goren more.

He flicked his wrist. "Later," he said, summarily dismissing Maria.

Fear creased Maria's face, and her shoulders sagged, as if she wanted to disappear. She left the room.

"Sturmbannführer, where were you before Portugal?" Sonny overcame his distaste.

"Unlike you, some have had it hard." Goren's lips parted in a gro-tesque smile. Bits of sausage stuck between his teeth. Raising his glass, he toasted, "The Führer!" Draining the glass, he fixed his eyes on Sonny's. "You have an interesting dossier."

"A man has to try."

Goren's laugh seemed genuine.

"Have I been thoroughly vetted?"

Goren poured more vodka then drank. His blue eyes pierced Sonny like daggers. Sonny felt the corners of his mouth tighten.

"Why bother?" Shrugging, he lifted his gaze from Sonny. "Your bosses in Berlin ejaculated over the information from their London agents." He leaned forward and grabbed a hunk of cheese. "Too good to be true—Baum?" The cheese went into his mouth.

"No idea. I made the connection. Kepler never shared his information."

"Very diplomatic. You should have been a politician—lie, cheat, equivocate . . . like my boss." His eyes widened in mock despair as if he were disclosing too much. "*Shit!*" His eyes glassy, like translucent marbles. "I *hate* politicians." His knife sliced through the air, impaling phantom politicians.

Sonny shook his head. "Never liked politics." That was true.

"What's England like?"

Caught off balance again, Sonny righted, gathered his thoughts, and slung bullshit. "Most Brits are all right. I made some money, but the war proved inconvenient."

"My apologies on behalf of the Führer. We had them trapped in France. . . . " Goren made a fist: "Fucking army . . . Dunkirk."

"Too much success, too quickly, too easily. Generals got nervous," Sonny offered.

"Their excuse . . . they shit their pants!" Goren shook his fist, then opened it, his fingers splayed. "Had them by the balls, then let go."

"I agree." Sonny wouldn't argue, and it was probably true. "Sturmbannführer, where have you served in your illustrious career?"

Goren leaned back and drained his vodka, the food on the table forgotten. "Unfortunately, I missed the French escapade."

"A shame," Sonny commiserated.

"I was needed in Berlin . . . to catch underground assholes."

Sonny leaned forward, interested. "Successful?"

Goren smirked. "Got a few. Takes time to root them out." The hand that had the Brits by the balls made a slow, shoveling motion.

"Like who?" Sonny fished.

"Some church group had a mole in the Abwehr, your paymaster— gave information to the Soviets. Traitors!" He slurred the word.

"Gave your exalted organization a black mark." A shaky finger danced toward Sonny.

Karl and Polly, Emil and Joseph—old friends—flitted in then out of Sonny's thoughts. He mustn't dwell on them or be distracted. "Did you come here from Berlin?"

Goren nodded. "First, I spent time with the SS on the Eastern Front . . . before it went to hell. *God!* Stalingrad was a disaster. Can't think about it." He poured vodka into his glass and topped Sonny's. "Goddam Jews! Europe's curse." His voice was plaintive.

Sonny anticipated the tirade to follow. "What do you mean?"

"I hate them as much as the next man, probably more than you, Baum." He could have been talking about influenza or winter.

Sonny kept his hands on his knees—away from the Walther.

Goren closed his eyes and grimaced, looking stricken. "Einsatz-gruppen was hard work."

"What's that?" Sonny's voice turned hard. He was afraid to know.

Goren buried his face in his hands, not noticing Sonny's change in tone. His words were muffled. "Mobile killing units—we followed the invasion in '41, dealing with Jews along the way—Einsatz-gruppen C, starting in Krakow, then Ukraine." He shook his head. "Got shot in the leg." He pulled his pant leg, pointed to a scar on his right calf.

Sonny made an exaggerated show of looking. Self-inflicted, he thought.

"Got the hell out. I've beaten the shit out of dissidents, shot a few, but shooting old men, women, children? Made good men crazy! So they started gassing them." A terrible cackle rose from deep inside, laughter—no, demonic possession. Goren repeatedly tight-ened and relaxed his fists.

"What are you talking about?" Blood drained from Sonny's head. He felt dizzy. He gripped his thighs for balance. If anyone deserved death . . . Goren's voice intervened.

"Like an abattoir—there won't be any left . . . "

The rumors were swirling. The London *Daily Telegraph* reported 100,000 Jews killed in concentration camps like Sachsenhausen, where Rosa's father had been held. Now Einsatzgruppen! No rumor. Refugees had told Sonny about the roundup of thousands of Jews in Paris at the Vel d'Hiv velodrome, where men raced bicycles. Were they dead? It was far worse than he had imagined on his darkest day.

Suddenly Sonny saw the blank faces of men, women, and children, grandfathers and grandmothers rounded up and murdered by the likes of Goren. Sick with anguish from generations of pogroms . . . He was filled with blind, unfettered hatred. The color drained from the room, leaving a black-and-white world—it was Goren or him.

Sharing food and vodka with the Einsatzgruppen nauseated Sonny. He raised his glass, gulped air, until his head was back in the room. He was not normal—he never could be. Sonny needed information on the smuggling operation—or he'd kill the freak now.

"It's over," Goren said. "Damn war . . . leadership won't admit, can't . . . "

"I don't get it." Sonny was confused. Goren was proving more complicated than he had thought.

"Soviets move west . . . we lost an army in Stalingrad . . . America will invade, then . . . "

"Why bother with the wolfram?"

"I have orders," he sighed, "regardless of the futility. And there is money to be made when the war's over." He waved one hand and drank with the other. "Forget what I said. Drink . . . eat . . . " gesturing, "and Maria . . . " His sad, bloodshot eyes drifted toward the kitchen.

Goren had to be watched—wounded animals are dangerous.

"Steal what you want. It's not my concern." Sonny lied. "What other mines are there?"

He waved both hands in the air. "Beira . . . and up here . . . secret mines . . . sell it illegally. We buy . . . English buy." Goren fixated on something across the room that only he could see. "That little shit Salazar has no idea."

"How long have you been in the wolfram business?"

"Not long—we rotate, so we can't steal too much. That's the domain of Schwarz and his cronies." Goren sneered. "Deals with small operators, makes a profit."

"Work the spread?" Sonny asked.

"Clever boy. Have to be sly." Goren winked, distorting one side of his face. "When we," he pointed at Sonny, "return from France, I report to Obersturmbannführer Schwarz. I've reported to him since Krakow." He shrugged. "Routine."

"In Berlin?"

"*No!*"

Sonny recoiled, feeling the weight of the Walther.

"Here . . . Lisbon."

Sonny calmed and leaned over the table. "Sturmbannführer," he glanced toward the door, expecting Schmidt to crash through, then back at Goren, " is there extra money for us?"

Goren exhaled between closed lips, making them vibrate, sending bits of spittle into the air. His face turned dark, ugly. "Trying to cut in, Baum?"

Too far into the game to back down, Sonny smirked. "Why not? It's there for the taking?"

Goren stared without answering as the expanse between them widened. Suddenly he shouted, "Share with you?"

"Just a thought." Had he gone too far? His implication set the hook.

Suddenly Goren was waving a pistol in the air, then pointing it at Sonny. He laughed and set the gun on the table.

"Get my attaché . . . it's on the cabinet."

The errand boy did as instructed, keeping a wary eye on Goren.

Goren clumsily separated some papers, then handed Sonny a map of Portugal. The northern half was dotted with red circles like rose petals on a white field.

"Mines."

Sonny counted at least 25, and there were more.

Swaying, Goren poured vodka then fell back into his chair.

"You have a family?" Sonny turned to an innocuous subject.

"What?"

"Family in Berlin?"

Goren nodded. "Parents dead . . . mother died in a bombing raid."

"Sorry."

"Wife . . . two children lived with her. Children were in school . . . wife working." Drunken melancholy filled the room like a malodorous wind. Suddenly Goren straightened as if he were jolted by electricity. His face contorted, and he shouted, "Maria!" She did not come, so he yelled her name again. Still nothing. He grabbed the revolver and fired at the ceiling.

Scared, Sonny jumped to his feet, reaching for his Walther.

"Where the hell are you?" Goren bellowed, shaking with anger.

Finally, the door opened slowly, and Maria walked into the room.

"When I call, you come!" Goren yelled.

She cowered by the door. Schmidt stood behind her.

"Get out here, Schmidt."

He did not move. "Don't hurt her," he said softly.

Goren's eyes bulged with anger. "Shut up!" He raised the pistol toward the young woman or Schmidt. Maria raised her hands in surrender. Her mouth opened as the fear in her eyes became terror.

"Goren!" Sonny screamed, pointing the Walther, its safety off.

Goren turned toward Sonny. A shot rang out, and Goren fell off his perch onto the floor. Sonny had not fired.

Schmidt stood over Goren, a pistol in his hand. "Crazy asshole!" he screamed at the body.

"What the hell?" Sonny asked of no one, perplexed.

Now Schmidt pointed the pistol at Sonny. "Sturmbannführer Goren," his words were slow and contemptuous, "nasty, greedy, thief . . . stole money from wolfram deals, would not share. Worst of all, he was mad."

Sonny stared at the pistol being pointed at him. His right arm held the Walther, useless, limp at his side. "Einsatzgruppen?"

"Too many good men ruined. The obsession with Jews made us monsters, turning men like Goren into freaks. You saw him. He would have killed her." His head tilted toward Maria, his eyes still glued to Sonny.

"And you, Schmidt?"

"I was always Gestapo, never SS."

"What now?" Sonny was buying time, waiting for Mayhew and Karpov.

Schmidt shrugged. "I've got wolfram to deliver."

"Without Goren, how does that work?"

"I've been at it for two years, before Goren . . . can do it with my eyes closed. What do you want, Baum?"

"To stay alive, see another sunrise."

Schmidt laughed. "Very good."

"And money?"

"You looking for a new partner?" Sonny asked, trying to sound hopeful.

"New partner?" He chuckled. "That's a good one. Goren's partner was the devil. The problem is . . . " He gestured toward the dead body on the floor.

"Hard to explain," Sonny agreed.

"Not really," he mused.

"And Maria?"

"She's a kid."

"Gestapo with a conscience. How quaint!" Sonny said with mock sincerity.

"I'm still a man—not like him." He kicked the corpse.

"A man with a dilemma," Sonny offered, adding, "two witnesses to self-defense."

"In an ideal world, where laws govern," Schmidt countered with sarcasm. "Goren was an officer. I'm not."

"What are you going to do?"

A dog barked in the distance—the outside world did exist. Their heads turned toward the intrusion on their melodrama. Mayhew and Karpov must have heard the shot. What was taking so long?

Sonny raised the Walther but not quickly enough. Schmidt must have anticipated his movement and fired. The bullet passed through empty space into a wall. Rolling to his left onto the floor, Sonny pulled the trigger an instant after Schmidt. He couldn't see whether his shot had connected.

That's when Mayhew crashed through the door, Karpov close behind. Another shot was fired. Schmidt lay still.

29

Near Samil, Portugal, June 1943

Shaking his head didn't stop the ringing in his ears—it only made Sonny dizzy. His nostrils rebelled to the stench of cordite. His head ached. Two were dead. He was still holding the Walther, one shot fired. Had his bullet killed Schmidt? It didn't matter. Goren was the one he wanted.

There was the feeling of having been here before . . . then it came to him—Aachen, five years earlier. This time only the bad guys were dead. After several minutes, Sonny's headache receded and he could begin to think straight. But the noxious odor remained. Maria was in shock. Jenny comforted her. Mayhew reported no sentries outside.

"First we get the bodies sorted, then fill us in," Mayhew said to Sonny.

Finally, they found a shovel and covered the two bodies with dirt.

"Rot in hell!" Sonny muttered.

"Maybe we should have dug it deeper. Damn barking dog might dig up the bodies," Mayhew observed.

"Vee be far away," Karpov shrugged.

"You're right." Mayhew nodded then turned to Sonny. "What did you learn?"

Sonny told him about the mines, about Schwarz and Goren and their operation. "Goren was Einsatzgruppen, on the east front."

"What's that?" Mayhew asked.

He told him. "Murdering Jews. He was drowning his massive guilt in vodka."

"Good riddance!"

"Schmidt denied me that joy. He called Goren a greedy bastard, thief, and raving maniac. No argument here. Goren walked the edge

267

—then flipped over." Sonny made a circular motion with his hand.

"Was he going to shoot Maria or Schmidt?" Mayhew asked.

"Wouldn't have surprised me."

Sonny retrieved the map, then emptied Goren's attaché, spilling documents and money onto the table: A bill of lading for the sale of 200 tons of wolfram from the Ribeira Mine; passports, Spanish letters of transit, French visas with Nazi stamps for Goren, Schmidt, Baum, and Maria Louro; 200,000 escudos wrapped with twine; correspondence between Goren and Obersturmbannführer Schwarz, and Goren's personal letters.

Karpov silently moved next to Jenny.

"What did Maria say?" Sonny asked her, noticing Karpov.

"She was afraid . . . Schmidt felt sorry for her. The language barrier was hard."

"I doubt Goren was interested in conversation," Mayhew said.

Maria sat, head cradled in her hands, no longer whimpering.

"She was a present to Goren from a crazed Nazi in Lisbon." Jenny's mouth curled with anger.

"That's what he told me," Sonny confirmed.

"She's afraid to go back."

"Was it Obersturmbannführer Schwarz? Ask her," Sonny directed.

After a short back and forth, Jenny said it was Schwarz.

"Tell her to describe him."

"Why?" Mayhew asked.

"He's the Gestapo I saw twice in Estoril. I knew him in Berlin."

More back and forth between Jenny and Maria.

"Thin, golden hair, nervous hands flying, talking all the time, smoking . . . "

"That's him—the only German in Portugal who knows me."

"Maria's scared. She knows too much," Jenny said.

Hearing her name, Maria stood, chewing on her lip, eyes darting to the door.

"No one will harm her—tell her."

Jenny did as she was told.

"De Souza can handle her," Mayhew said. "I'll give him some money. There's a Mercedes out back. Schmidt must have driven them here." Switching to Portuguese, he asked Maria, "Did you come from Lisbon in the car out back?"

She nodded.

"Anyone else with you?"

"No." She shook her head.

"Good! We leave at dawn for the mine."

Sonny noticed Jenny and Karpov talking, heads close…

———

Sunlight peeked over the hills, turning the rugged, empty landscape into stark beauty. Softer shades of brown and green would color the land as the day emerged.

Karpov drove with Mayhew in the front seat—Sonny, Jenny, and Maria in the back. Unsure of what their reception would be at the mine, they kept their weapons ready. Rough road made the five-kilometer trip slow going. But in less than a quarter of an hour, trucks, machinery, and a lone structure came into view.

Mayhew told Karpov to stop in front of the small building. The three men exited the car. The door to the building opened, and a short, stout man walked out. He frowned. "Who are you?"

"Your new partners," Mayhew said in Portuguese.

"Goren, that you?" came a voice from inside the building.

Mayhew uttered, "Trouble?"

Mayhew pointed to each side of the door. Sonny and Karpov glided into position, pistols ready. Mayhew kept the squat Portuguese between him and the door. Within seconds, a man appeared. Unshaven, stocky, taller than the Portuguese man, dressed in work clothes, he looked German. He saw Mayhew and stopped. Pistol barrels dug into his ribs.

The man groaned. "What?"

"English, Deutsch, Portuguese?" Mayhew asked.

"Take your pick," he answered in English, then looked from Karpov to Sonny. "Do they have to do that?"

"Answer my questions. Who are you?"

"Rolf Peterson."

"From . . . ?"

"Originally, Sweden. I have lived in Portugal for years. I am a geologist."

"Why here . . . why Goren?"

"Can I smoke? Guns make me nervous."

Mayhew nodded. Peterson reached into his pocket. Karpov

quickly stuck the end of the barrel under his chin: "Slow."

"Easy! I have no weapon, only cigarettes." Slowly, he removed a pack, put a cigarette between his lips, and lit it. He offered one to Karpov, who took it.

"He paid me. Where is he?"

"He's . . . " Mayhew shrugged, " . . . busy."

Karpov laughed softly.

Peterson's eyes went from the guns back to Mayhew. As he squinted, understanding came into his eyes. "You English?"

"God save the king!" Sonny said in his German-accented English.

This time Mayhew laughed.

"I have no horse in this race," Peterson started. "They paid me. Now you pay me. I happily change employers. God save your king!"

Mayhew considered for several seconds, then said. "My only other option would be to kill you."

Peterson grimaced. "No. That is a bad idea. I can help."

"Problem is, can I trust you?"

"Pay me enough. I know the mines. You need wolfram. I will help."

They bargained for several minutes and agreed on a number.

"All right, settled." Mayhew and Peterson shook hands.

To Karpov, Mayhew said, "Watch him."

Mayhew dealt with the mine manager, explaining the new arrangement. His name was Pinho. Guns scared him. Money eased his fears.

Sonny leaned into the car window. To Jenny: "Problems solved."

Then to Mayhew: "That was too easy."

"Cash—the great persuader." Mayhew turned toward the trucks. "I have to set up the convoy."

"Mayhew!" Sonny called.

Mayhew turned. "What?"

"I cannot return to Lisbon, the only survivor and with no wolfram. Kepler will know, and Schwarz will find me."

Sonny and Mayhew stood five meters apart. Neither spoke for a moment.

"Instead of killing Peterson, I'll kill you," said Mayhew.

Sonny stiffened.

Mayhew smiled. "Relax, I mean metaphorically. We'll find a

body—there's always a body."

"So I'll be, sort of dead, then like a cat . . . live again?"

They laughed.

Sonny frowned and shook his head. "Don't like it. Kepler will want to see me on the slab. Better I disappear. It's safer."

Mayhew moved closer, a conspiracy in the making. "You have a plan?"

"Drive a truck to France."

Mayhew laughed. "Very funny! Really . . . what's the plan?"

"I just told you."

"We killed two men, almost a third, to prevent that from happening."

"I have to get to France, somewhere called Sare . . . in the Pyrenees, near the Atlantic. According to Jenny, my wife is there . . . or was."

"Huh?" Mayhew responded, his eyes narrowing. "Your plan all along?"

Sonny smiled.

"I take that as a yes."

"Goren's documents will get me there." Sonny shrugged.

"And a bill of lading for 200 tons of wolfram in one truck carrying 20 tons. Explain that to a Spanish border guard in German or English . . . you don't speak Spanish. Or do you? And how's your French?"

"Minor details," Sonny paused before continuing. "All right, bad plan. How's this: I ditch the truck over the border, take a train to Irun. Then 'Bob's your uncle,' I'm in France."

Mayhew's laughter died. "Better, but we need all the wolfram."

"Don't make me steal the truck at gun point. I'll make sure the wolfram never gets delivered."

Mayhew rubbed his chin, thinking. "Can't let you do that . . . " Then his eyes sparkled mischievously. "Got a better idea—take the car, go in style. It's too hot; we need to get rid of it anyhow. Gestapo will look for it." Pausing, he hummed, "Hmm, Yes! This is good. Drive across the border, abandon the car somewhere in Spain . . . take a train."

"Finding it will complicate matters," Sonny responded.

"Burn the goddamn car!"

Jenny had moved beside them, hearing the conversation. "I want to come. You need someone who can actually communicate."

They looked at her.

"Too dangerous," Karpov said.

"I'll be all right, Roman." She touched his arm. There was intimacy in her touch and voice.

Sonny wondered what they were doing outside the house.

"Then I go, too," Karpov offered.

"Christ!" Mayhew moaned then cupped his face in his hands. "Invade France? Hell, no. I need you! If Jenny wants to go, that's up to her, but I think she's crazy—it's all crazy." He nodded and mumbled something. "And how about this: If Jenny goes, she uses the papers your wife needs to get here. Then what?" He shook his head in frustration then walked away.

"Just crazy enough to work," Sonny said to Mayhew's back.

Karpov moped, but he would do as ordered.

"Since when?" Sonny whispered to Jenny, gesturing toward Karpov.

She shrugged. "Why not? He's nice . . . we're like two halves of a whole."

Sonny nodded. "You two can romance when we get back from France."

They culled the documents, pulling visas and passports. Jenny was dark like Maria, but everything else—hair, facial features, eyes—was different. No time to change photographs. Sonny culled the correspondence between Goren in Lisbon and Schwarz in Berlin—letters starting in June 1942 and ending in May 1943 upon Schwarz's arrival in Lisbon. Nothing in the letters incriminated either man in the scam, but Goren had implicated Schwarz.

"I've got some money, but we need to hit Mayhew for more—expenses and bribes. Then we go."

Sonny had so many questions for Rosa: What had happened to the past four years? Why southwest France? How did she get there? Was she with her parents? Then Mayhew's voice played in his head: "Jenny goes. So do the papers your wife needs."

Think it through. Traveling on a German passport and valid visa—would provide excellent protection. He wouldn't be expected to speak Portuguese or Spanish. There would be no trouble until the

Gestapo figured out that the wolfram had never left Portugal for France. They would search for Goren, Schmidt, and Baum, a man who did not exist. So far it looked good.

Rosa needed documents. Sonny might need Jenny, but he needed documents more. Go alone. Jenny and Roman could get acquainted. But at the edge of Sonny's thoughts stood Albert—smug, fidgeting, smoking, scheming Albert, poking a finger in his eye, waiting for Sonny's return . . .

. . . Emil taught Sonny to drive a truck though he rarely drove himself and never operated a car until Wanborough, where they drove the grounds, spun the tires, fishtailed. It was great fun.

"Be safe. I look forward to meeting Frau Baum."

They shook hands.

"Remember to check the petrol!"

Sonny waved and drove away—alone. Jenny had taken his decision with equanimity, maybe even relief. She had two good reasons to stay in Portugal—her work and a new lover. Both might get her to England.

Sonny backtracked on the Samil road, then go south and east to the border town of Miranda do Douro, then across the border to Villadepera, Spain—500 kilometers from France. Entering Spain was easy. He exchanged escudos for Spanish pesetas at a bank. His German documents were perfect because they were* real. Hard questions, harder to answer, would face him at the French border— Purpose of travel? Coming from where? Why no safe-conduct pass? He'd have plenty of time of think.

. . . Cutting between picturesque green hills terraced with vineyards, the Duoro River meandered 50 kilometers to Zamora. At midday, the sky bleached to pale blue. The sun was hot. Wind-blown dust from fields and hills clung to Sonny's skin. His shirt clung to his back. Grapes hung in clusters on the slopes; there was grain of some kind on the flats; cows grazed there. Trees he didn't know the name of, the kind that dropped colorful leaves in the autumn, stood in clusters on the hillsides like islands. The arid land, home to ancient Iberian civilizations of which he knew little provided an empty canvas for his imagination to color with characters and plots. Long before, Sonny had read Cervantes's story of the chivalrous Quixote and his trusted cohort following him on an ass—a romantic, ridiculous escapade. Was his own search for "Dulcinea" just tilting at windmills—more idiotic than quixotic? He laughed.

Zamora's medieval town hung above the river, its craggy outline visible against the empty sky. He crossed an arched bridge into the city and found the railroad station, then left to scout for a spot to ditch the Mercedes. On an empty stretch of road between two hills, he passed an abandoned house. He parked behind the house, out of sight.

"Remove the license plates, discard them somewhere not to be found, stick a handkerchief or piece of paper into the petrol filler . . . light it and run like hell!" Mayhew had advised.

Using the toolkit from the boot, Sonny removed the plates. A newspaper from Villadepera rolled into a cylinder protruded from the gas filler, a lone candle on a birthday cake. On first try, the match died, but the second met with sweet success. He watched from behind a corner of the house. The paper burned slowly, then a red-orange flame shot from the rear of the automobile.

The explosion was loud but not excessively so. Sonny jogged away toward the town, in five minutes turning to watch a column of black smoke rise from the fire. By the time he reached the edge of town, he was breathing hard and sweating. Now just a tourist with satchel slung over his shoulder, he looked for a café . . .

After a nice meal, with most of the town on siesta, he walked empty streets to the railway station . . .

. . . At 7 AM on the following day, Sonny's train arrived in Irun, at the mouth of the Bidassoa River, which emptied into a big delta called Txingudi Bay. Spanish authorities glanced at his documents and stamped them.

The guidebook map told Sonny that Irun was a terminus for other locales in Spain and at the heart of the Basque country extending into southwestern France. That included Sare and Domaine Poussard. The Pyrenees mountains formed the border from Mediterranean Sea to Atlantic Ocean. According to Mayhew Basques had carried goods back and forth for centuries over smuggling routes. Franco's enemies had retreated over the mountains into France, and most recently, refugees had fled the opposite way.

Goren's guilt-ridden and ghastly confession of Einsatzgruppen sent Sonny's thoughts cowering into dark corners. The horror of

Kristallnacht paled to mass murder on that scale—it was incomprehensible. His anger gave way to sadness, then to despondency. The thought of Rosa cheered him, but his cheer was tempered by the fear that she might have been snared in the Paris Vel d'Hiv roundup. What fate awaited them?

Sonny had assumed his documents would suffice. Now in France's shadow, he felt unsure. Should he find a Basque to smuggle him across the Pyrenees? Or hire a boat? Neither option seemed reasonable. Locating a smuggler, then penetrating the well-guarded ports, seemed undoable. Even if he succeeded, his passport would lack an occupied France stamp and safe-conduct pass.

Using his passport held risks. Hans Baum's saga—Berlin to London to Ireland to Lisbon—was unique at best, a lie at worst. Still, Kepler had bought it. Berlin had bought it. Hell, he got a bonus! Maybe he could drop Kepler's name and the Abwehr connection.

Staring out the window, ignoring the landscape, Sonny struggled to concoct a credible cover, distracted by worry that the passport and visa meant for Rosa and hidden in his satchel would somehow disappear. Was his trip for naught? A faint flicker of doubt . . . Rosa was gone, with a new lover or worse. Round and round it went. No answers came.

Finally, mentally exhausted, Sonny muttered, "No." He would use his documents. Imagining a bored officer behind a desk in a cramped office, papers stacked high.

"I'm on holiday!" Sonny would say, then shrug and wink at the guy. "My Abwehr contact in Lisbon gave me a bonus, a holiday in France. I've never seen Paris." Run a bluff . . . be bold, believable. Drop Kepler's name. Lay money on the table if necessary.

"Cash—the great persuader," Mayhew had said.

Sonny stared out the dirty window. The image of man laughing, slightly crazed eyes, reflected back. Who? He stopped laughing. He glanced around the rail car. Nobody seemed to have noticed. He sobered. What would he do?

It was too soon for Schwarz or Kepler to know what had happened at the house off the Samil road. Kepler's instructions had been to contact him in Lisbon upon his return. Goren's convoy was working its way slowly to France—Kepler and Abwehr, Schwarz and Gestapo, would not think otherwise.

Part VI

Astound me! I'll wait for you to astound me.
—*Sergei Pavlovich Daighilev*

30

Hendaye, France, border crossing, 10 June 1943

Sonny watched as spies, agents, military men out of uniform, and a smattering of businessmen left the train. There were also several couples on holiday. He heard French, Spanish, and some German, but no English spoken. He had shaved and washed before Irun; he looked presentable despite his wrinkled jacket and pants. He stepped onto the platform, clutching his small satchel.

After 30 minutes, Sonny stood at the black line on the floor. A dour Frenchman in uniform waved him forward.

"Bonjour Monsieur—passeporte, visa, s'il vous plaît."

"Bonjour," Sonny replied, producing the papers as requested.

The questioning began.

Sonny shook his head. "Je ne parle pas Français."

Without looking up the clerk asked, "Deutsch?"

"Jawohl," Sonny nodded.

The clerk quickly thumbed through the passport and visa. "State the purpose of your trip to France," he said in slightly accented but perfect German.

"Holiday—I have never been to Paris."

"Where do you live?"

"Lisbon."

"For how long?"

"Since November 1940."

"Before that?"

"England—it's stamped in my passport. Surely you saw it." Sonny affected impatience, pointing at the passport in the man's hand.

He met Sonny's eyes and stared, waiting for a response.

Sonny gave none.

"Wait here!" He disappeared through a door.

Within a minute, the door opened. An officer in the uniform of the customs service said, "Herr Baum, please come in." The officer was tall and thin—he looked like a schoolteacher.

The room was windowless and claustrophobic. A desk, a file cabinet, and two chairs took all the available space. His interrogator moved the chair, closed the door, and returned the chair to its original location, then motioned for Sonny to sit. The man sat, pushed his glasses up his nose, and stared with big eyes. He said nothing.

Sonny waited. Was he supposed to break down and confess? His thoughts were interrupted.

"Herr Baum, I am Captain Lefevre, Customs Service, Occupied France. Your passport is . . . interesting." He scratched a bushy eyebrow.

"Thank you." Sonny hoped his forced smile wasn't obvious.

"You have traveled from Portugal. Why do you carry only a small satchel?"

Expecting the question, his answer came easily. "The result of a hasty decision. I took only what fit into my satchel. I plan to buy new clothes in Paris."

Lefevre frowned. "You are German, and you lived in London. As a student, I wanted to go to London, but . . . " he shrugged, " . . . I could not. Why did you go?"

"Adventure . . . to make a living—the usual."

"The problem is, Herr Baum, that we are at war with England." His stare returned.

"So I heard," Sonny said, deadpan.

Lefevre put a hand over his mouth to stifle a laugh that nevertheless came forth.

"I'm sorry. That's frivolous. I left Germany in '32. I was 23 years old. Then I fled to Lisbon when the war started."

Lefevre composed himself. "Where did you get the French visa?"

Another question that Sonny had anticipated. "Through normal channels," he answered confidently. "I have *important* contacts at the German Embassy in Lisbon." He crossed his arms over his chest and waited. His Abwehr connection was his ace in the hole if need be.

Lefevre's face registered nothing. He nodded. "May I look inside your satchel?"

Sonny shrugged, then set it on the desk. Lefevre made a cursory inspection, then said, "Herr Baum, have a pleasant stay in France." He stamped the passport and handed Sonny a safe-conduct pass for a month's stay.

"Thank you," Sonny said, as he perused the pass. "I won't be here that long. Have to return to Lisbon."

They shook hands, and Sonny left the office, troubled. That was too easy. He flipped through the possibilities: Checking Sonny's story would take days. Or had Lefevre, a cautious bureaucrat, feared the truth and let him pass? Or was it something else?

An enormous photograph of Hitler's meeting with Franco, Spain's dictator, in 1940, adorned an entire wall of Hendaye's rail station. Sonny learned there was no train service to Sare, but a bus left every two hours for Marseille. Sare was only 25 kilometers into its journey.

With time to kill, Sonny walked to the bay Hendaye shared with Irun. Hungry, he ordered grilled fish and white wine at a little café. The ease of his entry at the border consumed his thoughts. He felt uneasy and ate quickly, then returned to the station. Would he be followed? He felt exposed.

It was nearly 2 PM when Sonny found a seat in the back of the bus. He opened a window. Diesel exhaust fouled the air. His restless eyes scanned street, doorways, and windows, seeing everything and nothing. Something sharp jabbed him when he leaned against the side of the bus. Patting his pocket, he felt the outline of the screwdriver he had used to remove the license from Goren's Mercedes. He had forgotten to toss it.

Travelers and street vendors filled the streets and sidewalks around the station. Nothing seemed out of the ordinary, except for him. Taxis queued, waiting for passengers. Then Sonny's gaze landed on a black sedan parked opposite him, its engine running. A man's arm rested on the open window, a cigarette stuck in his fist. The fist moved to mouth and back to the window. A fleecy cloud drifted from the car. Shadow obscured his face. "Gestapo" could have been printed in huge letters on the door.

It was hot and hotter on the bus. Sonny felt the sweat on his brow and lip. Should he leave the bus and disappear? He had returned to Germany with a French accent. He glanced around looking for escape. Then the bus lurched, leaving the station.

Sonny watched the sedan until it was out of sight. When the bus passed the outskirts of town, he leaned back in his seat . . . The comfort was fleeting. In the corner of his eye, Sonny saw a black object overtake the bus. A hand waved the bus over from the passenger window of the black sedan. The driver slowed to a stop.

The bus door opened, and a man in suit and tie entered. Sweat glistened on his brow. Sonny couldn't hear what he said to the driver. He walked between the seats, then stopped next to Sonny. Stocky, with light brown hair and a mole on his right cheek, the man leaned forward, his right hand on the back of the seat in front of Sonny. His coat fell open, revealing a shoulder holster. He spoke quietly so others would not hear, commanding, in German, "Come with me."

"What . . . why?" Sonny asked, buying time. He felt the screwdriver and his eyes rested on the butt of the revolver, within easy reach. If he were taken in, stripped and searched, it would be over.

The man's face registered mock disappointment, as if he had been let down. "Because I said so."

Sonny looked into his eyes and nodded. When the man relaxed, Sonny slammed one fist into his groin and with the other hand grabbed his tie. The man's muffled scream reverberated through the bus as he doubled over, gasping in pain. Sonny grabbed the pistol from his holster and pulled his tie. When the Gestapo came forward, Sonny hit him on the side of the head with the butt of the pistol. Unconscious, the man fell onto the floor, wedged between the seats, next to Sonny.

Breathing heavily, Sonny stepped over him and walked down the aisle, satchel hanging from his shoulder, pistol in hand. The passengers were scared silent. The driver stared wide-eyed and put his hands in the air. Sonny jerked his thumb over his shoulder toward the back of the bus and said in English, "Gestapo asshole."

Contemplating his next step, he looked down at the waiting car. Cigarette smoke drifted from the driver's side. The driver was waiting, probably bored—advantage Sonny.

"Thanks for the lift," Sonny muttered as he left the bus. He held the pistol shielded by his body and approached the passenger side of the car. The driver faced forward, a cigarette moving slowly to his mouth.

When Sonny was even with the rear of the car, the driver turned in his seat. "Erich!" he shouted.

Silence. A door of the sedan opened, and a Gestapo stood in the street, pistol in hand. He looked at Sonny, then at the bus. "What the . . ." Confusion turned to understanding, and he raised his hand.

Sonny shot him once in the chest.

As the Gestapo fell onto the road, his pistol fired wildly. Sonny ran to the driver and kicked the pistol away. The Gestapo lay still, probably dead. Sonny threw his satchel in the car, jumped in, put the car in gear, and drove away. The episode had taken less than two minutes. He had an hour before every cop and Gestapo agent would be scouring the area . . .

. . . The bus was maybe two kilometers from Hendaye when it was stopped. He bought a ticket for Sare, so they would be waiting for him here. Where should he go instead? The jagged peaks of the Pyrenees were on his right, to the south a winding road. He figured to go north, so he drove toward Sare, looking for another road, and then saw the words "Saint-Jean-de-Luz" accompanied by an arrow pointing to the left. Within 15 minutes, houses dotted the hillsides again the backdrop of the blue Atlantic.

He had to get rid of the car. He retraced his route until he found a rough dirt track, turned and drove to a grove of tree, then stopped. His hands had clutched the steering wheel so tight, they ached. He tried to focus his thoughts but couldn't. Calm down! He took several deep breaths and wriggled his fingers.

Suddenly, Sonny realized how silent it was. He shook his head and laughed. Until this moment he hadn't fully appreciated the enormity of his problem. He had killed one Gestapo agent and injured another. Enjoy the peace, he thought—it might be his last.

He spoke no French. He needed help. His only thought was find the Underground—but how? The exhilaration born of his sudden, violent confrontation was dissipating, a sinking helplessness replacing it. No! Don't succumb to fear, or desperation will be next. He stuffed his fear back inside its hole. Digging his fingernails into his palms to help focus his thoughts, he set off toward town.

Within 20 minutes Sonny was in another pretty, seaside resort with sailboats in the harbor, people about, Gestapo everywhere. Under his jacket, the heft of the pistol jammed into his waistband. It was better than a screwdriver, so he'd decided to keep it. He had to get off the street, find refuge. Hungry and thirsty, he looked for a tavern—the shabbier and more out of the way, the better. At harbor's edge, on the other side of the tracks, away from the center of town, he found one.

In the late afternoon, the tavern was nearly empty. Sonny ate warily, eyes on the door. He figured to lay low until dark, then return to the tavern and see who showed up.

He walked along the quay, the working part of the harbor. Weather-beaten men labored on small boats. A German navy boat was prominently moored there, an armed guard stationed at the dock. Laborers tended to be socialist, maybe even Communist, not likely collaborators, though there might be infiltrators. He felt more secure among the laborers. This felt right. He had to trust someone. He had nothing else.

It was nearly midnight when Sonny returned to the tavern. Five of the ten tables were occupied. A few men stood at the bar. None seemed to have been there upon his first visit. Maybe they had cleaned up, though they didn't look fresh. His antennae up, all Sonny heard was French. What had he expected? Then something familiar, music to his ears: "Boche!"

"Shh!" One guy hushed the other, then said something under his breath. They argued.

Sonny waited an hour for them to leave, then followed from a safe distance along the harbor's edge to a row of shabby, warehouse-like buildings. They stopped at a door and talked. One lit a cigarette.

Sonny made his move. "Bonsoir."

Heads turned. One nodded, and the other returned his greeting.

"English?" Sonny gambled, fingering the pistol.

Frowning and clearly suspicious, the one smoking a cigarette put a forefinger near his thumb, and said, "Little."

"I need help."

The rigging of boats bobbing on the water jingled the only sound beyond their voices. Sonny heard them speaking in French before the guy with some English motioned with his free hand. "Come."

The other guy looked hard at Sonny, then left. Better to have only one of them. He followed the smoker into a dark, open space. The shapes of what might be boats teased his vision. Sonny heard a scraping sound, then light illuminated the corner, revealing a workbench, tools, motor, and several boats.

The guy was broad through the shoulders and chest, about Sonny's height. The dim light cast harsh shadows on his face. Hands on hips, legs spread apart, he said, "Who . . . you?"

Sonny wondered that himself. "I am English and in trouble. Boche will look for me. I need the Underground, the Resistance. Can you help?"

"Where you come? You not sound English. This," he searched for the word, "piège . . . " He looked away, squinting, then nodded, " . . . trap?"

"No. I left Germany." Sonny pointed to his chest. "Jew. I trained in England to fight Boche." He held up his fists in a boxing pose. "I came from Portugal to find my wife. She is hiding. Gestapo tried to arrest me," he hesitated, "I ran." Sonny waited, unsure of what the man understood.

He stared at Sonny before answering. "Before war I take boat to England in Le Havre . . . " he pointed, probably north. "Boche end work. Now fix . . . Boche boats . . . navy." His nose wrinkled as if his words had unleashed a noxious odor. He sneered, "They can go hell!"

"Good." Sonny said, almost cheerfully. "Can you help?"

"Name? I . . . "

"No!" Sonny interrupted, wagging a finger. "Not safe, better I not know."

Humming like an idling motor, he nodded. "Bon."

Sonny waited.

"Okay." The man waved for Sonny to follow, then led him up a stairway at the back of the warehouse. At the next floor, they passed through a small room to the opposite corner, where a ladder led to a trap door. He pointed up.

Sonny climbed the ladder into the attic. He could stand there, barely. An inadequate light bulb glowed from the middle of the room. Boxes, dust, and other debris littered the floor. A small window opened at each end, but there was none on either side.

"Sleep. In morning bring food."

"Merci." Sonny took the man's hand and shook it.

After an uncomfortable night of fitful sleep, Sonny awoke as dawn broke through the window. He waited. Finally, he heard movement. The trap door opened.

His friend held a big cup and a baguette. After handing them to Sonny, he said, "Boche look for English spy . . . kill one Gestapo, hurt other one." He pointed at Sonny. "You?"

Sonny nodded.

"Where this happen?"

"Two kilometers from Hendaye. Gestapo stopped the bus." Sonny told him the rest.

The man smiled, then patted Sonny's cheek. "Bon! Can no stay. Boche angry. When dark, I take you to Basque friend . . . he help."

31

Southern France, June 1943

Sonny's new friend had an old Renault truck with an open bed. His plan was to hide Sonny under a tarp behind several boxes, where he would feel every bump, dip, and turn.

"Five-teen kilometers to farm." He flashed the fingers and thumb of his right hand three times.

"Roadblocks?" Sonny asked. "And a cop looks under the tarp."

They considered that, then the fellow grunted. "Walk."

"Where?"

"Small village—Ahetze—pilgrim road to Compostela, very old church." He nudged Sonny in the ribs. "You go, be good Catholic." He laughed.

Sonny chuckled. "And you . . . good Communist?"

He placed a finger to his lips. "Shh . . . "

Around 11:00 they walked through the quiet town to the northeast corner. Minor acts—placing broadsheets against the occupiers or listening to Brits on the wireless—drew Gestapo attention, but Sonny's dustup meant big-time wrath. According to his friend, the rumor was that an English spy was on a killing spree. The Gestapo was a vicious pack of dogs after a fox. From the town, they walked through fields beneath a dim beacon of half-moon, dangling from a partly cloudy sky.

"If trouble, you run," Sonny told his friend. "I do not want you involved. I have a pistol."

The man whistled softly. "Where you get?"

"Took it from the Gestapo." Sonny tried to be calm, but he was scared.

They walked up a hill to a point overlooking the main road north to Biarritz. "We watch." The man pointed to his eyes, then the road.

Within 10 minutes an army truck drove slowly north, a spotlight beam moving in an arc from side to side. It disappeared past a curve.

"Wait," Sonny's companion ordered.

In five minutes the same truck, or one like it, came from the opposite direction.

"No go . . . until safe."

Sonny pointed to his watch. "Time the trucks."

His friend nodded. "Run when big hole."

In half an hour they felt safe enough to make a move, seconds after the truck passed. Ten minutes to the road, then they waited for the truck to pass again, before crossing it into a field. Through more fields, up and down hills, past darkened farmhouses with barking dogs, they trekked for more than an hour, then stopped for a 10-minute rest.

"You sure we aren't lost?" Sonny was worried.

"We good," he answered cheerfully.

They started again and within an hour Sonny's rescuer stopped and pointed. The outline of a church steeple rose above the trees. Sonny squinted, then nodded, "I see."

They steered around the town. Pale clouds skittered past the moon. Shadowy trees rose in clusters at the edges of the fields. Soon a farmhouse surrounded by a stand of trees was visible. A light shone in the window.

Sonny's friend pointed: "You stay." He walked to the house, a vague outline against the dark. A rectangle of light appeared then quickly disappeared—the door opened, then closed. Minutes ticked by. Sonny tried to stay moored in the present, not to think about the future.

Finally, his friend returned. "Come."

When they were in the house, his friend slapped him on the back, and said, "Good luck!" He was gone before Sonny could thank him.

Sonny looked at the farm couple. The man was thin and wiry, with strong hands. The woman was round, with a pleasant face. She smiled at him. Both were probably around 40 years old. There was no sign of children, though maybe they were grown and on their own. A simple crucifix, a token of devotion, hung on the wall.

"Merci. English . . . Deutsch?" Sonny asked.

They shook their heads and smiled in return.

"Eau, s'il vous plaît," Sonny requested water.

A glass appeared, and he drank.

The man lit a lantern and beckoned to Sonny, then led him to a shed. Pointing to a space on the floor, he closed his eyes and rested his head against his hands, simulating sleep. "Le matin," he said. Then he pointed two fingers downward and moved them to suggest walking. In the morning Sonny would walk.

Straw scattered on the floor of the shed provided a makeshift bed. Exhausted, Sonny lay down, and the next thing he knew, he heard the creaking of the door. Then a long shaft of light hit his eyes, and two hands clapped him awake. He was on his feet and into the house within minutes. After a cup of hot coffee and some bread, he thanked the woman. The man handed Sonny a beret and led him from the house.

They walked up and down hills, through cultivated fields and forests, avoiding roads and people. Sonny ignored his aching feet and the midday heat. Twice they stopped at a farm for water and a little food. Sonny stayed back, averting his eyes, letting his new friend take the lead. If a collaborator saw them they would not know about it until too late. Finally they reached the outskirts of another town. Sonny's friend pointed and said, "Ustaritz." But they went around the town.

Sonny was handed off twice more in the same manner, ultimately arriving at Saint-Jean-Pied-de-Port at sunset. For the first time since fleeing Saint-Jean-de-Luz, he entered a town—one with the same saint in its name. They crossed a river, then climbed a hill through a warren of narrow streets. Just before the town ended, the man stopped at a doorway and knocked.

They went inside. A tall, angular man with a hawk nose confronted Sonny. His eyes were sharp and penetrating. He stared silently. Sonny's guide departed, leaving him alone with man. Finally, he moved Sonny to a table with a bottle of wine, two glasses, cheese, and bread. He said something in French.

Sonny shook his head. "No Francaise."

The man's right eyebrow rose as if Sonny's response was provocative. Then, in English, he ordered, "Eat."

Sonny ate while the man drank wine and watched. His face

disclosed little.

"We go to much trouble, bring you here. Who are you?" He asked after too much silence, his English reasonably good.

"Thank you. I am in a spot of trouble."

The man laughed heartily. "Your accent German but understatement English. Your name?"

"That is complicated. My papers say Hans Baum, but I am Sonny Sander or Landauer from Berlin."

"Too many names," he said dryly. "What I call you: Hans or Sonny?"

"Sonny. And you are?"

"Frank. Why you running?"

"I think you know."

"Tell me . . . Sonny." He had all day and night.

"I beat a Gestapo agent with his pistol, then shot his partner . . . near Hendaye." Sonny laid the weapon on the table.

Frank stared at the pistol and nodded. "Very good."

Sonny shrugged. "He would have shot me."

The man's thin lips were in a pout as if he was considering what to say. "You speak no French. Why you in France?" His tone was incredulous, the question a good one. "I hope England and America have better plan for liberation of France. An army of non speakers, yes, but . . . " He raised his hands in frustration.

Sonny laughed.

Frank's eyes widened with surprise. "Not mean to be funny."

"It sounds foolish . . . let me explain." Sonny took a deep breath, then started: "I arrived in Lisbon in November 1940."

"And before Lisbon?"

Sonny told him about Antwerp, Mons, Lieutenant Shannon, Kid, Rebecca, Dunkirk, and Wanborough Manor. "Shannon thought I'd be better in counter-espionage."

"Spy?" The man's face moved from confusion to interest.

"Making contacts with Germans, getting information. Not really a spy."

"Spy! You Communist in Germany?"

"No politics. I smuggled Jews out, then ran from Hitler with my wife."

Tapping his nose with a forefinger, the man smirked. "Not look like Jew."

Sonny shrugged. "The hand I was dealt…kept me in one piece." He explained Hans Baum's backstory, his mission, the wolfram episode, and coming to France to find his wife.

Shaking his head thoughtfully, Frank said, "Your . . . mission make problem for us. Gestapo not take revenge on French people, yet. They look for British spy, not Frenchman. Maybe French people hide you, or you cross Pyrenees to Spain."

Sonny nodded. "Sorry. My plan fell apart. I thought my papers would get me to Sare. What will you do with me?"

Combing fingers through his hair, Frank shook his head from side to side. "Not know, must think."

"Help me find my wife and get us out?"

The laugh was harsh, completely devoid of mirth. The man lit a cigarette and offered one to Sonny.

Sonny shook his head and stared at Frank expectantly, unsure of his position.

"We Resistance, not private detectives looking for lost wives."

"I know where . . . " Sonny started.

"I cannot help," Frank interrupted. "We have a war to fight."

"How do you fight?" Sonny asked, wanting to keep Frank engaged, maybe to change his mind.

"I start in Armee Juive—Jewish Army—get Jews out of France. Damn Boche make it hard to cross Pyrenees. Last year Boche invade Vichy, take over." He snapped his fingers. "Like that—done!" He slapped his hands twice. "Vichy done. You know of Vel d'Hiv in Paris last July?"

Sonny nodded. "I heard, and I bring more bad news." Sonny told him about Einsatzgruppen, about Goren, and what he said about Germany being finished.

"How you know this?"

Sonny explained.

Frank was silent for several moments, then said, "Germany not finished in France. Comrades arrested every day . . . informers everywhere. What you say is very bad. Makes what I do more important. I want Resistance bigger. I come from Toulouse. British airplane drop small guns," he pointed to the pistol, "bullets, radios. We print newspaper, denounce criminal occupiers. Now is time to attack railway, gun storage, power lines, food supply. Lyon, Toulouse, Marseille, all of France starves—Boche steal everything."

"When Germany invade USSR, Stalin order Communists attack Germans here." Frank jabbed his index finger on the table several times. "Strategy is make Boche send more soldiers to France. Communists think that help USSR." He shook his head. "German officer shot dead in Paris Métro. Boche take revenge on Frenchmen. Many innocent die. Then Communists stop." He lit another cigarette. "We secret army . . . better organized. But have far to go. Boche help us with hated STO, Service du Travail Obligatoire [Service for Obligatory Labor]. You know it?"

"No.

"Like you say, it go bad for Boche in Russia . . . Boche need workers so . . . . " he shrugged.

"Ah!" Sonny understood. "Frenchmen forced to work in Germany."

He nodded. "But . . . " holding up a forefinger, " . . . many men go underground. *Maquis*, Corsican word—wild brush country—first Resistance happen. They make army. In Pyrenees they hide."

"You came looking for men?"

He nodded. "Prepare for invasion. Now we bother, like mosquito, stay ahead of enemy. Me—Jew and Resistance fighter; double problem." He took a long drag on his cigarette. A plume of grey smoke hung in the air. "Follow rules: Use false papers. When police barricade, I no turn back. Walk on side of road with cars coming to me. See better what come from behind. Always break messages into little pieces, burn them. No nightclubs, black market cafés, first-class carriages—they raided. Rules?" He shrugged. "Men, women, follow rules, still arrested. Others not follow rules and not arrested. Still, better to follow rules."

"I can help." Sonny needed Frank. A memory twirled in his head like a wobbly, spinning top. Sitting in a Wanborough classroom, listening to a uniform, preaching from the *Partisan Leader's Handbook*—the "bible," he called it. It was used for sabotage training in firearms, communication, disarming an adversary, and so forth. Somewhere in the dark, dusty recesses of his memory lay explosive detonation, train derailment, three years ago. "I trained on radios, explosives, some combat. You know I can shoot."

They stared at the pistol.

"British drop bombs on rails . . . gun storage . . . other places." Frank took a long drag from his cigarette, shook his head, and exhaled, nearly disappearing in the smoke. "Not so much . . . in south."

"I scratch your back. You scratch mine." Sonny smiled. He'd bargain like in the old days at the warehouse. Never pay retail—his father's mantra was good advice.

"What . . . scratch back?'"

"I help you . . . you help me." Smiling, Sonny pointed to Frank, then to himself.

"How?" Frank smirked, unmoved by Sonny's offer.

"Prove my value to you."

He sighed. "You . . . as British say . . . albatross on my neck." Then he sat silent, apparently thinking over Sonny's offer.

Sonny poured wine, waiting for an answer.

"First we leave, go other place. Stay too long, dangerous."

He gave Sonny detailed directions to a farmhouse in a village named Irouléguy.

"I go . . . you follow 10 minutes." He shook Sonny's hand. "Welcome to Resistance life."

Halfway there it began to rain, softly at first, then harder. Rain was good. Cops are lazy, like to stay dry . . . The dark stretches of road under heavy, black clouds complicated Sonny's search. He had to get on top of every sign to read it. Finally, he saw the sign for Domaine Irouléguy, and the outline of the big oak tree, at the head of the track. Between neat rows of grapes, he passed dark structures on the way to a small outbuilding. A light shone in the window. Sonny knocked three times and was admitted.

Frank was there with another man. Short, stocky, strong, and sporting a broken nose, he looked tough, probably was. There was no introduction, only a nod.

To Sonny, Frank said, "I think . . . you go with him . . . loosen rail tracks. Something you learn at fancy manor." A map lay on a small table. "Here," he pointed to a spot between Saint-Jean-Pied-de-Port and Saint-Martin-d'Arrossa. "Six kilometers." He motioned with his head to the broken nose: "He take you. Maybe explosion later . . . if goes good."

"Then you help find my wife?" Sonny asked.

Frank shrugged.

For the next week, every night, away from the towns and villages, Bernat, the broken nose, and Hank—no longer the object of a pointed finger—derailed trains. They operated within a radius of 20 kilometers of Irouléguy, loosening the rails. Frank liked this technique, calling it as effective but less destructive than bombing and saying it prevented unnecessary deaths. They could destroy an entire train on a mountain curve.

They unscrewed bolts on connector plates with a wrench, then pulled the track out of line with a crowbar and ran like hell. When the train passed over the loose track, one wheel, then another, came free of the track. Brakes slowed the train, but the trip was over. The train wobbled and threatened to derail, or actually derailed and toppled over. When a tremendous screech echoed through the night, they had succeeded.

Sonny stayed at Domaine Irouléguy, sleeping on an army cot. Bernat worked at the winery. During the day Sonny stayed inside and daydreamed. A fly landed on the table, then zipped away. "How many times per second did its wings flap?" His esoteric Uncle Simon might taunt, poking a finger in Sonny's chest: "Well?"

As a youngster, Sonny had laughed and shook his head.

"Two hundred times per second," Simon would snap. "Everyone should know that."

When the waiting became intolerable, Sonny sneaked into the fields and woods behind the farm and walked in circles. Someone had to know he was there, but apparently no one who cared. So close to Rosa . . .

After Sonny had five successful derailments, Frank appeared with a new assignment. Sonny hadn't mentioned Rosa or Domaine Poussard by name. Now he'd call in his credits and ask for help.

"Soon I help . . . plan change."

"When?" asked Sonny

"This more important. You blow up bridge." He made a sound: "Boom!" His eyes were wide with excitement, like a child at the circus.

"What?"

"Train from Hendaye to Dax, north . . . from Spain . . . carry cargo. Come over bridge, Irun to Hendaye, on Bidassoa River at border."

"I came over that bridge—you want me to blow it up?" Sonny was incredulous.

The man's smile was sly and sarcastic. "Like Brits say: 'Brilliant.'"

"Frank, I can derail a train with a small bomb—but a bridge?"

"Our man help."

"I killed a Gestapo near Hendaye—remember?"

"No problem, our secret." He placed a finger to his lips. "Boche not know."

Sonny's laugh was hollow. "Only my life on the line!"

Frank shrugged as he unfolded a map. "Seventy-five kilometers . . . you go alone . . . meet man with much dynamite. He take you to place near bridge. He have plan."

"How do I get there?"

"He," pointing to Bernat, "deliver wine to Hendaye. You go . . . he drop you in Basque village, Biriatou, very beautiful, near small mountain called Xoldokogaina. Your contact in village."

"He speak English?"

Frank shrugged. "I think. Man code-name 'Chien' [cat] at house with blue door in Biriatou. Bernat know it. Chien has more men and what you need for job."

"When?" Sonny asked.

"Sunrise."

———

Sonny bounced for nearly two hours, wedged between barrels of wine covered by a tarpaulin. The truck stopped, and the driver's door opened, then closed. There was a stream of light through an opening in the tarp, then Bernat slapped his hand on the side of the truck. Sonny slithered onto the road and was gone.

After 15 heart-pounding minutes of wrong turns, he found the blue door. He knocked twice, waited, then knocked twice more. The door opened a crack. Young eyes peered out, then blinked.

"Chien?"

"Oui."

Sonny's contact was a boy no more than 17 years old.

"English?" Chien asked.

"Yes . . . you?"

He nodded. "Learn in school."

"You my contact?" Sonny hesitated.

The boy nodded. "Father work, mother in next village visit mother."

"Will they return?"

"Father gone all week . . . mother two days."

"They know what you do?"

He shrugged. "Boche kill brother in Belgium . . . *hate* Boche!"

Sonny recognized the anger. "Should you be in school?"

Chien shook his head. "This more important."

"Where are the others?"

"He come when dark."

"Only one?'

"Enough."

"Where is the dynamite?"

"By river."

"Show me."

The boy led Sonny through the village to a small warehouse that led to a dock. A boat was moored there, *Emilie* painted on its stern. Sonny followed him inside to a room at the back. Chien moved a box, revealing a trap door. Sonny took several breaths and climbed down. Chien moved the beam of a small torch around the musty, low space. The beam rested on a stack of wooden boxes, at least 10 of them. The top was been pried off of one. Inside were sticks of dynamite.

"Where are the detonators?"

"There." The beam moved past cobwebs to a box in the opposite corner. Inside were "T-heads," spools of wire, tape, and batteries. Sonny had played with that stuff at Wanborough, blowing things up.

"British military supply?"

"Oui. Airplane drop . . . we hide."

"Let's go," Sonny said, anxious to leave the cellar. He was counter-intelligence, not a saboteur, and he had forgotten most of the training. Pacing the small house, he remembered only bits of it. He smiled at the image of Eddie setting the fuse and running like hell, then tripping over a cat.

Closing his eyes, Sonny recalled bits of his instructor's discourse on T-head detonators: "Electric current . . . filament red hot . . .

burns . . . ignites detonator. Join T-heads together . . . clean wire . . . never touch anything . . . attach remaining bare ends to battery . . . "

"Huh," he grunted in satisfaction. He hoped that was enough.

They ate and drank wine, taking the edge off. Chien left saying he would return with a man. The sun disappeared. An hour later, a warning knock came at the door. Chien entered with a tall, thin, dark man, exotically handsome, like some Spaniards Sonny had seen. He offered Sonny a strong, calloused hand. They shook.

He smiled and said in English, "Hello, I . . . "

"No names," Sonny protested.

The man shrugged and said something to Chien.

"If goes bad, he crosses to Spain. Boche never find him."

Sonny laughed. "Good for him, but what about me?" Then a name from Wanborough popped into his head. "You are Eddie. I am Otto." He smiled, thinking of his friend, somewhere.

Chien translated. The guy he named Eddie shrugged. "Okay . . . Otto."

"Tell me the plan." Sonny demanded.

"Night, we take boat, fill dinghy with dynamite, explode under bridge."

Sonny winced at the boldness. "How? What about river patrols?"

Twenty minutes of tedious translation later, he had the specifics. A Boche patrol boat passed under the bridge every 15 minutes, up and down the river. Spotlights on shore made routine sweeps of the bridge from water to deck but at no set time. An old man, part of the group, had a small fishing boat. Sonny had seen it tied to the dock. Boche knew the harmless old man and the boat. Nothing would be suspicious in its going to sea early and returning late. A small lifeboat on deck would be the chaos delivery system—dynamite, armed with detonators.

At dawn, Eddie and Sonny—not the old man and a crewman—would take the fishing boat downriver, under the bridge into the ocean. Chien would stay behind. They would spend the day "fishing." Eddie knew how to fish and might actually catch something. Sonny would fix the fuses and the wire. Just talking about a day on the water was enough to make him queasy.

The patrol shift changed at 11 PM. Fresh guards replaced the men on the patrol boat and those on shore. That—plus the element of surprise—was Sonny and Eddie's advantage. At this point, life on the fishing boat would get interesting and tricky: pass under the bridge, drop the lifeboat into the water, tie it to a bolt on the bridge, continue upriver, unspool the wire, attach to detonator—boom!

"Sounds good . . . in theory. Is there enough time to tie the lifeboat?" Sonny asked, making sure he understood.

"Oui," Chien said.

"Crazy," Sonny muttered as he rubbed his forehead. "What about the spotlight?"

Chien smiled. "We have plan. How you say . . . " he put a finger to his lips, " . . . ah . . . distract."

"What?"

"Friends make electricity go off by bridge and Biriatou."

Sonny was impressed. "How?"

He made a cutting motion with two fingers. "Friends cut wires same time bomb goes boom!'"

"Very good."

"No see under bridge . . . anywhere." Chien grinned.

"Ees good!" Eddie said, smiling broadly.

Their smiles were infectious, though Sonny was less enthusiastic.

"Me and friends watch river . . . if you in water—okay?"

"Okay," Sonny answered uneasily.

"Bon!" Eddie said.

They were quiet, lost in thought. Sonny broke the silence. "What else have you done?" Then added, "Don't tell me where you live—best not to know."

Through Chien, Sonny learned that Eddie and others had guided refugees over the Pyrenees. That dried up by mid-1941, when the Germans started patrolling mountain passes—too dangerous. That's when Eddie began irritating Boche with minor stuff—railroad derailments and electrical sabotage. He wanted to hit hard, but allies had to invade before they could take up arms. This would be Eddie's first big hit.

"What the hell! We're all amateurs!" Sonny noted.

"And you?" Eddie asked, through Chien.

Sonny told them about northern France, Dunkirk, England, Lisbon, the wolfram. Then about coming to France, looking for his wife, the problem on the bus, the Gestapo. "You help find my wife," he paused, "when we're done with this . . . caper," nearly adding, "if we survive."

"Caper?" Chien frowned.

Smiling, Sonny said, "Job, when the job's finished."

Sonny put the pistol on the table. The documents in the satchel—he wanted them on his body. He asked for something to keep them dry. Chien found a piece of oilcloth.

They stared at the gun. Eddie held it, aimed at the door and smiled. He nodded at Sonny and said something.

"You have done much," Chien translated.

Sonny nodded. "More to do."

Then down to business. He calculated the amount of dynamite needed to blow up the bridge, the length of wire needed to avoid sinking the boat, the best time to activate the detonator and not draw Boche attention while they were under the bridge. How would they do all that and survive? Maybe they should pray. He smiled and muttered, "What the hell."

32

Biriatou, June 1943

Sonny lay on the unforgiving floor, unable to find physical or psychic relief or sleep. Was this a suicide mission? He was stuck on the possibilities, ending with the boat exploding and the bridge undamaged–his body riddled with bullets . . .

If the bridge was so damned important, why hadn't someone up the Resistance chain convinced the Brits or the Americans to drop a bomb? Easy—turn the bridge into rubble. Boche protected the bridge around the clock, even during shift changes.

He was stuck, with no place to go, no one to help him. He couldn't walk away. He couldn't even chat up the locals. He couldn't go to Sare—the Gestapo was surely watching. He was being used. Frank didn't even have to threaten him, but the message was clear: Help us or Boche will get you! And they still might. He was stuck. Goddamn Frank!

Finally, it was time. He felt like he'd boxed 10 rounds with Max Schmeling, and a bone in his butt hurt. Stretching loosened his limbs but did little for his anxiety. No one spoke. They ate a small breakfast and packed food for the day, synchronized their watches. In 10 minutes they were on the dock. Others had stowed boxes of dynamite, fuses, and other paraphernalia on the boat. Sonny checked to make sure.

Villagers had to have seen him. Would they inform, or were they all in on it? Could be the old bit about operating in plain sight, like using the old man's boat.

Sonny knew boats floated, were prone to sinking, never stopped moving—all annoying traits. This one was about 10 meters from front to back; it had an open area with a box at the rear, and a small forward cabin.

Chien told Sonny that the boat's owner was sick and didn't care what happened to it. And his crewman had gone underground.

The night before, Chien had asked, "Otto, if you from Germany, why you fight Boche?"

"I escaped Germany. I am a Jew."

He nodded but seemed confused.

Sonny saw the unsolved puzzle on his face and said, "Nazis attacked Jews, so I left. You fight because your brother died."

"Georges go to war, die for . . . nothing." Bitterness, acid on stone, etched the simple phrase: "Boche take everything, leave us nothing."

The foredawn sky was opaque and gray. Sky lightened by sun hidden beyond the hills when the boat's motor coughed phlegm, like an old man. They pushed off and chugged along, spewing a fury trail of exhaust.

Three and a half kilometers to Txingudi Bay—a pretty horseshoe ringed with golden sand—then out to sea. They passed the Nazi gunboat. Eddie pointed to the spotlights—two of them, one on each side of the bridge. The river widened, then suddenly narrowed at the outlet to the bay.

Numerous fishing poles, line, and several nets were lashed on deck. The day's catch would be stored in the box at the back of the boat. Eddie turned north and chugged parallel to the coast for about 15 minutes, cut the engine, and dropped anchor, preparing to catch fish. The day was spectacular—sunny and warm, with a slight breeze. Sonny watched Eddie set a line and cast. He proved a proficient fisherman.

"Thon [tuna]," he called the fish.

Sonny retreated under cover of the cabin, leaving Eddie to his thon. Sonny figured about 50 pounds of dynamite would do the job. (The Brits used pounds, not kilograms). If memory served, 50 pounds of dynamite buried 3 feet under a railroad track lifted a locomotive 10 feet, more than 3 meters, into the air. Impressive, a nice round number, and what he'd use with 5 "T-head" detonators.

He laid the detonators side by side, cleaned the wires with a knife blade. He connected the wires of the detonators into a series, securing them with tape, leaving one wire exposed at each end. Then he reviewed his handiwork: Five happy children in a line holding hands, one empty hand at each end. He checked his work again.

He tied each 10-pound bundle of dynamite with rope, then carried them all to the lifeboat, secured them in a row to the bottom of the lifeboat with rope. He wiped sweat from his upper lip then dried his hand on his pants. His hand shook slightly as he inserted the first detonator into a bundle. Flexing his hand several times, he continued until all five detonators were inserted. He double-checked to be sure the wires remained connected. Two remaining wires protruded at opposite ends. They would be connected to long wires, then to the battery—later.

Wire was wrapped around a spool marked "100 yards," just short of 100 meters. Sonny estimated that 30 meters from the bridge was far enough away to avoid being blown up with the bridge. Connecting the wires to the battery completed the circuit. For safety, he set the battery well off to the side. He figured 35 meters, allowing for the width of the bridge, would be about right. He cut two lengths of wire and attached each to the wires protruding from the dynamite. It was educated guesswork. Bridge demolition hadn't come up in his training. For all he knew, the explosive concussion would swamp the fishing boat and sink it.

An hour later, Sonny went on deck and sat. Watching Eddie fish relaxed him. Staring out to sea, he almost forgot about the mission. He felt Rosa next him, "quite beautiful . . . dark hair, eyes," as Jenny had described her. Sitting on the bench, he turned as if she were there, but a sudden shout startled him. He stood, head swiveling, searching for danger. Then he relaxed. Eddie had landed a huge tuna, at least a meter long. The silvery fish jumped and wiggled until Eddie plunked it on the head with a mallet, stunning it. He muscled it into the box already holding its smaller relatives.

Sonny absently massaged his head. He watched Eddie move confidently around the boat. He admired his courage and Chien's— two compatriots. Would they survive? He was scared, but that wasn't all bad. Fear kept him focused.

Emil, his old friend, fighter, steady hand, and guide, had taught him well. They had run the gauntlet together. Would he be surprised to know Sonny had landed in British intelligence and was derailing trains, blowing up bridges for the French Resistance? Or would he consider Sonny's return to France a fool's errand? Was he a fool? He left the questions unanswered. Life played strange tricks on one.

Being hunted by the Gestapo might become a bad habit. It had his name, an alias, and a description for the wanted poster, and it must be watching Sare. He was accustomed to risk but not to pursuit. In a few hours, if he was lucky, he'd be on the run again. But still no Rosa. So close to be blown into a million pieces, strewn like confetti across the Pyrenees, now. Rosa might raise her eyes heavenward to see bits of him fly overhead. Would he rain down upon her in his final act?

Nazi patrol boats moved along the coast, ignoring the small fishing boat. Credit the old man for that. The afternoon passed as the sun became an enormous bright ball balanced on a tightrope. Unfailingly predictable, the sun faded, its signature red and orange smeared across the horizon. Total darkness enveloped the boat within 15 minutes. Other boats had headed to dock . . . Suddenly it was 10 PM, just one more hour before *Emilie* would return to the bridge.

Eddie raised the anchor and steered her toward the harbor "slowly as she goes." Lights strung like pearls before them, a comforting sight. Nearly half an hour to kill and just 20 minutes to the bridge— Sonny's pulse quickened. They slowed through the harbor, finally entered the river.

Sonny glanced at his watch, 10:52. He held it for Eddie to see.

"O . . . kay . . . Otto. Vive la France!"

They crept barely above idling speed under the bigger, automobile bridge. Ahead he could see the arches of the railway bridge above the water. His heart pounded recklessly. They floated. Sonny had unrolled the wire from the lifeboat and set the two coils on the deck. His watch said 10:59. The dark outline of an arch appeared on the left. Port or starboard, he wondered which. Eddie cut the engine, put it in reverse, then in neutral.

"Now," he whispered.

The lifeboat went into the water, Eddie jumped in, grabbed a ring attached to the arch, threaded a rope, and tied it. He was back in the boat. Less than a minute passed before he engaged the forward gear. The *Emilie* slowly moved from under the bridge. No shots . . . no blinding searchlight, complete darkness. Chien's friend had done his job. Luck was with them so far.

Sonny was too excited to be scared, too focused to notice anything else but the wire. Sweat dripped from his underarms and upper lip, his hands were moist, which made it harder for him to grasp the wire. Still he fed more wire. One end was already attached to the battery. The wire tightened—now! Contact . . . eardrum-splitting boom . . . massive sunburst of red, orange, yellow hanging across their horizon . . . a familiar stench.

The concussion knocked Sonny onto the deck. The *Emilie* rocked back and forth but stayed afloat. Eddie goosed the throttle, and Sonny felt the boat lurch forward. A sudden downpour of bridge bits rained onto the river. A big chunk fell harmlessly between the two men, smaller pieces onto their heads.

"Bananas," Sonny muttered. It smelled like bananas.

Suddenly it was quiet. Then shouts from shore punctuated the stillness. Eyes searched for the enemy. Random shots fired into the river. The sliver of moon in a cloudless sky probably outlined the boat. Some bullets landed there, sending splinters everywhere.

"Ah!" Sonny's left thigh felt hot. It was wet—blood. Severed artery? He thought of Shannon's shattered arm, Willy's shot in the shoulder before he died. This is not that bad, he thought, willing it to be. His jaw clenched—it hurt like hell.

The boat's motor roared—Eddie opened the throttle to full, but its fastest pace was barely a trot. Lights were out along the north side of the river. The headlamps of cars and trucks shone from the darkness. Vehicles bounced into action, sending shafts of light into the air every which way and onto the river. Driving quickly along the river, they disappeared as the road veered away.

A faint buzz came from behind the *Emilie*. The patrol boat was downriver.

"Eddie! Boche!" Sonny screamed, trying to get onto his knees. He couldn't. Again, he yelled, "Eddie!" Crawling, he pulled on Eddie's pant leg.

Eddie looked back, sized up the situation, then tied the wheel with a rope set out for that purpose. He grabbed Sonny around the waist, lifted him up, and they fell into the water. The *Emilie* continued her steady course, upstream, engine droning. Submerging into the cold water's embrace, Sonny prayed that "resistance baptism" would not be his last mortal thought. After an eternity of mere seconds, he popped to the surface, struggling for air, saved. His left leg was useless. Eddie's arm pulled at his throat. His head barely above water, Sonny jammed a hand under Eddie's arm to keep from strangling.

Dragged onto shore, Sonny lay breathing hard, spitting water. He tried to stand. Eddie grabbed his arm, got him up on one leg. The *Emilie's* engine grew faint—was the patrol in its pursuit? A light flashed—a movement on the river at the edge of his field of vision. Eddie fell to the ground, pulling Sonny with him. They ate dirt as the gunboat's spotlight swept the shoreline. Small bushes and grass obscured the light beam.

"Niemand [nobody]," a voice said.

The patrol continued upstream. Eddie lifted Sonny onto his good leg, and they walked. After several hundred meters a man appeared out the darkness, like an apparition. Sonny stiffened.

"Allons-y [let's go]," said the apparition.

Eddie said something. Someone's hand went under Sonny's other arm. They stopped to check his wound. They talked. Something tight went around his leg. They talked more, then lifted him again to his good leg. Weak from blood loss, disoriented, and probably in shock, he could have been anywhere. Voices came in and out, but he did not understand.

"Otto . . . Otto."

Someone shook his shoulder.

"Otto."

"Huh?"

"It Chien."

"Chien? Chien . . . "

"Oui. Hurt bad. Take you place safe." Chien was a vague, faceless outline.

"Where?"

"No worry—sleep."

"Bridge?"

"Kaboom!" Chien laughed. *"Fin!"*

Sonny smiled and passed out.

Raining? He wasn't wet. Small stones fell from the sky. Bullets musically whistled past, faint overture of something familiar—what? Bulletproof, impenetrable, immortal. He lay on a bed of straw, his face washed. "Where am I?" A warm compress lay on his brow, a woman's soothing voice. "Rosa!"

No answer. When his eyes next opened, the light pressed against a curtained window. He lay on a small bed in a dark room. Two figures, unaware he was awake, talked nearby.

"Chien . . . Eddie . . . " Sonny called, weakly. Chien appeared at the side of the bed with another man. Not Eddie—but the man who had helped him on shore.

"Where am I?

"Biriatou."

Sonny groaned. He still didn't know where he was.

"You move . . . soon . . . other house."

33

Rosa, Domaine Poussard, June 1943

Paris taught Rosa to be more cognizant of risk. It had been a year without a whisper from Jean. She had posted letters to Jean and Catherine shortly after her return. She needed something, anything. Not knowing sent her into dark corners. Thoughts of Jean locked away in a terrible camp tormented her.

"Maybe he had moved?" she calmed herself. Where? Maybe Marcel, the art dealer on Place de Vosges, had him safely hidden. She had no last name or address. What if Jean had received her letter but decided not to answer because of the risk? Just like him, she thought.

Days after her return to Sare, the Paris police force had turned to devil, arresting thousands of Jews and imprisoning them at the Vel' d'Hiv. Surely Jean was not among them. No stranger to cruel loss, Rosa felt new despair creep into the secret vault reserved for Sonny, Kristallnacht . . . now Jean.

She had written Annette, asking for help. Finally, a response came. She knew nothing of Jean or Alain, and Paul had not returned. Annette was alone but acting. Rosa resigned herself to whatever was Jean's fate, yet hoped . . .

On her first trip to Toulouse after Paris, Rosa pressed Meyer for another mission to Paris. He had nothing to offer, and even if he had, she would not be chosen. After Vel' d'Hiv, it was too dangerous for her and for the network. He was firm. She did not argue.

Denied Paris, Rosa resumed delivering documents and messages to Toulouse, Lyon, and elsewhere. She volunteered for more, worked harder—penance for her perceived blunder with Jean. Rest would come when the war ended. On each trip, feeling the train gently sway, she stared out the window, which brought Mons uncomfortably back. Mons was always her entry point for thoughts of Sonny, of their leaving Belgium for a new life. Berlin equaled pain—she finally overcame the simple arithmetic, but the pain of their separation lingered.

She refused to wallow in self-pity. Too many others were suffering greater loss. What else was there? She had work to do.

Rosa was successful at her job—she made her deliveries, and she hadn't been caught. Heart pounding, palms coated with sweat like a thin layer of early winter ice, she was scared and exhilarated every time. Get to the station, avoid notice on the train, deliver the documents, then return home. Same routine, again and again.

"Reason for travel?" Visiting a friend in Toulouse or Lyon. "Name?" She had a list of names with addresses. Faces became familiar along the route. Some smiled. Others stared. She looked authority in the eye and never flinched. Being frightened was different from showing it.

After each successful mission, Rosa felt relief and excitement. Yet her ragged nerves were hard to calm. Could she take up arms? Could she kill again? When she thought of Oranienburg, she did so dispassionately. The pain was gone. Had Emil been right? Would she wish she had killed more? Open rebellion was not yet feasible. Reality tempered her small contribution.

Rosa's world was a dichotomy: the languid peace of the winery versus the thrill of resistance. Fooling the enemy kept her spirit alive and strong as she toiled at the winery. Returning from a mission amounted to a sort of psychic deceleration, screeching to a halt at cliff's edge before tumbling into the abyss. She was thankful for Domaine Poussard's safe refuge. The mundane chores of life calmed her.

She was troubled by a recurring, haunting dream: Missing her train, she stood nervously on the platform in her wedding dress and work boots. She waited in vain for the next one. German soldiers smiled obsequiously or leered dangerously but never spoke or noticed her strange attire. She was always alone, her anxiety deepening to despair.

Her husband and lover was missing, maybe dead. She used a dead woman's identity. She had fled Germany only to live in another country under its occupation. Still, compared with the lives of thousands of others, hers was good. She had learned to make wine. She had purpose in the Resistance, a good friend in Javi, trusted compatriots in Meyer, Celine, André, and Alesander—and Dominic and Irene treated her like family.

Rosa felt thoroughly French. Her German accent was probably lost to French-speaking Germans and most of the French. Irene encouraged Rosa to read from the small library in the house— Proust, Zola, the English writers Dickens and Shakespeare, the Americans Poe and Twain. Her fluency and vocabulary vastly improved through opportunity born of war and alienation.

After Paris, Rosa discarded Lucas and reverted to Rita Daurat, her nom de guerre. There were no assignments with André, though she saw him several times in Toulouse. When Rita's name was called, she answered without hesitation. Still, she would never feel completely comfortable inside Rita.

Wine making was more fulfilling than any other work at the domain. The process, though difficult, time consuming, and a study in contrasts, held her interest. Growing grapes, like the Resistance, was messy and unpredictable. Sun, temperature, and water determined the pace. Soil—minerals and acidity—assisted by human husbandry determined quality. Wine making was orderly, requiring technique and patience, what many in the Resistance lacked. She learned about when it was time to harvest. She learned the varietals—txakoli for dry, white wine; cabernet franc; cabernet sauvignon; and tannat, the traditional grape, for red. She crushed grapes into must—juice, skin, seeds, and stems—then removed the solids at the proper time, fermented twice.

"Nature cannot be hurried," Dominic often said.

The work was strenuous but satisfying. Her hands grew calloused, her back and body stronger. Summer sun darkened her skin to a light bronze, and her hair grew long. She wore pants, not a skirt, and sturdy boots, more comfortable and protecting than her usual attire. For travel, she wore the dress her mother had sewn. Whatever she needed—blouses, pants, shoes, sundries—Irene bought for her. She gave little thought to her appearance. Good hygiene and clean clothes were enough.

What never changed were the vague traces of her Semitic heritage—dark hair and eyes, full lips, and olive skin. Southern

France was home to many swarthy people, more so than the north, far more than Germany. Sare was off limits—too many Germans made it too dangerous for a woman with a false identity—except for a mission. Tense brushes with officialdom were rare. When her identity card was requested, she usually received a polite response, "Merci, Mademoiselle."

Shortly after Dominic learned of Rita Daurat and her involvement with Meyer, he asked whether she was serious about her new identity. Rosa frowned in response, confused by the question's obviousness.

"Then come to church with us . . . keep up appearances and control rumors. Let them know you're Catholic—it's important to some people." He smiled and added, "Don't worry. We don't go every Sunday."

She laughed uneasily and made a hasty conversion. Something so simple and obvious had never occurred to her. Irene provided the rosary, and Javi gave her a primer in ritual. Rosa became an indifferent Catholic, but she did attend church with the family. She even accepted bread and wine, though she drew the line at confession. Javi told her that the priest's brother was a Maquis.

Domaine Poussard was self-sufficient, more than a vineyard and winery. Its residents ate well from the big vegetable garden—potatoes, beans, carrots, onions, cabbage, broccoli, asparagus, garlic, and fragrant herbs in dizzying amounts. Abundant sweet strawberries and raspberries grew there all summer. Several goats were penned for milk and chickens cooped for eggs and the pot. Ducks and geese roamed at will. Leon patrolled the farm, keeping other dogs away, providing good company, and signaling arrivals. Two cats—Winston and Franklin, who made war on the mice population—and a third cat—Emil, a loving companion—lived with her.

All the remaining land was planted with grapes, no room for grazing cattle. Dominic had bartered barrels of wine for beef, satisfying for both parties. But that practice died due to the occupier's greed.

"Boche rapes France of resources and produce, including my wine!" Dominic railed. "What those thieves pay for a barrel of wine barely covers my costs. They strip away our livelihood and dignity!" He growled. Dominic's anger turned to sympathy and then support for the Resistance. He was not alone. Its numbers grew.

One night, Rosa lay awake in bed. Emil was curled at her feet, a warm breeze rustling the curtain. She recalled someone saying, "Life is the sum of a person's biography." A successful life meant the sum of its quality, after subtracting the rest. She thought that made sense and considered her biography, one that would never be written: Resisting, killing a man, learning a new language, making wine, laughing, crying . . . Hers was a life better lived than she had thought possible. Yet the darkness, like the occupiers, rarely lifted. Such was her state of mind at Domaine Poussard, Sare, Aquitaine, France. in June 1943.

———

Meyer had sent for Rosa. She met him at the café, as usual. He was in an expansive mood, also usual.

After nodding curtly, he began, "Most French keep their heads down and work. Many are willing accomplices—to their everlasting shame. Many passively support the Resistance, but we need more." He drank wine then sucked on his cigarette. "Our numbers spiked after Service du Travail Obligatoire. Ironically, or maybe not, STO is our greatest recruiter. Vichy is dead, German occupiers now control all of France. Word is that the Allies bomb Sicily and Italy. That foretells of an invasion of Europe's underbelly—Italy. Then the coast of France, the next battleground."

He raised his glass: "To the Allies—our only hope."

Rosa and Celine exchanged glances, smiled, and joined the toast.

Celine whispered, "He's insufferable—constantly lecturing."

"I heard that!" Meyer bellowed.

They laughed, but both agreed.

"What is my assignment?" Rosa asked.

"A message," Meyer answered. Her message to Alesander was to meet a man in Saint-Jean-Pied-de-Port to receive further orders. She knew better than to press Meyer for the specifics.

Alesander's commitment had grown steadily. Ferrying refugees over the Pyrenees—except for emergencies—had come to an end. It was too dangerous. Fighting awaited Allied invasion, so he bided his time derailing trains, cutting electrical and telegraph wires, soiling the German army's water supplies, disseminating broadsheets, and the like—important work but not fully satisfying.

After three days, Alesander returned in the middle of the night with a man. Early the next morning, he found Rosa among the barrels. "Someone wants to see you . . . in the shack."

Startled, she asked, "Who?"

He shrugged. "Go see."

The little shack was used exclusively for secret visitors. She walked beyond the vineyards, past the stand of trees at the rear of the farm. Leon loped ahead, his nose to the ground, stopping at every other tree. Rosa knocked on the door. When it opened, her jaw dropped.

"Alain!"

He wrapped his long arms around her.

Several days' growth of beard and a mustache added years to Alain's youthful face but did not diminish his warm smile and bright eyes.

"Wonderful seeing you, Rosa."

"How . . . how did you find me?" Her smile was wistful.

"You told me, but I forgot. When I returned to Paris, Father was gone, but there was a note. This place was on it." He tapped a forefinger on his temple. "Now it's engraved inside."

Still in a mild state of shock, she said, "You survived."

"Of course." His smile was engaging, like Jean's. "And so did you."

"One must . . . " she faltered then told him everything that had happened after he left for the front in January 1940: Work at the club, Annette, Jenny, Jean, Catherine, the family's departure, and fleeing with Agnes and Tony; smuggling her parents, refugees, and soldiers over the Pyrenees, being a courier, returning to Paris. "In May, I saw Jean. Police came, like before. We ran, but he twisted his ankle. He called Marcel for help. I hope . . . " Her eyes clouded as she fought tears.

"Like before?" Alain asked, confused.

Rosa barely regained her composure. "Days before the invasion, returning from the club late, I saw police leave the building. They were looking for me. We ran to Annette, but first Jean took his art to Marcel."

"Marcel told me, but I thought it was later."

"No. In May I returned to Paris on a mission. We were at the flat, and my partner saw cops enter the building. We had to get out in a hurry. They could have been after someone else," she sighed, wanting to believe it, "but I don't think so. I ignored a bad feeling and went to the flat. I never . . . "

"How could you know?" Alain asked softly.

Rosa held Alain's gaze, despite the pain. "No. I failed . . . " Rosa wept for the first time in more than a year.

Alain held her and stroked her hair. "Father loves you."

"I love him," Rosa responded. "He saved me—literally."

"You became his companion, someone to talk to. I love him, but he's a hard man to know. He talked to you, not to Catherine and me. He holds things in."

"Funny, how that works," Rosa mused. "I still had to pry it out. He told me how he met your mother."

"That much I know."

"He said I reminded him of her." Her head shook. "Not physically with but a similar attitude toward life—'je ne sais quoi.' But she was artistic, bohemian. That's not me."

"I was too young when she died. He rarely talked about her . . . as a kid I didn't ask. Maybe you fulfilled an image of her. Mother was pretty—so are you." He shrugged. "He raised us alone, did a good job, at least with Catherine."

They laughed. In Paris, they had become close after only a week. Now together again, they stood silently, thinking.

"I don't think he cared any more. He wasn't the same."

"Surrender must have been a terrible blow. But why go back to Paris?" Alain asked.

"He missed Paris, felt a burden to Catherine. I think . . . maybe he couldn't live anywhere but Paris. I just . . . " A tear rolled down her check.

"Don't carry that burden. Father made his choice. I already pieced some of it together."

Confused, she shook her head. "How?"

"My contact in Saint-Jean-Pied-de-Port told me I could find refuge at Domaine Poussard. The name clicked. He told me about your mission and the old man you left behind. It had to be Father."

"Frank?" Her face screwed into a question mark.

He nodded.

"Sometimes, I can't believe any of this actually happened—Sonny gone, the war, Paris. It's all too fantastic. Now *you're* here after learning about your father from some guy in the Resistance you never saw before."

"Laughably absurd if it wasn't real."

"Too real. Have you seen Catherine?"

"In Marseille a year ago, but I haven't been back. Jacques joined the Maquis." Alain paused, then continued, "Maybe Marcel hid Father, and she's heard from him."

"I hope," Rosa murmured.

"And you?"

"I found a home." Her gaze was distant, disoriented; then she turned. "I look at you and see Jean."

He smiled. "Where are your parents?"

"Mother wrote from Lisbon. They were headed to Cuba. And still no word from Sonny." She paused. "Call me Rita, Rita Daurat. Who are you?"

"Henri Roulette."

"Like the game?"

He nodded. "Poor fellow died at the front in May 1940 . . . from Lyon. Gave me the ultimate gift, existence. Like you, freed me of my Jewish ancestry. So far . . . " He shrugged.

"Any word from Paul or Annette."

He shook his head. "Not since Paris."

"Sorry, I haven't asked how you are."

"Hungry." He smiled.

"Of course. I'll get food."

"Not yet. Let's talk. I can't stay long." He told her about the terrible fighting, about Dunkirk, his crossing the channel, then returning. "We landed in Dordogne on 21 June, but there was no fight left. My unit disbanded. I returned to Paris, saw Annette and Paul, then drifted south. I eventually got to Frank."

"What were you doing before you got here?"

"Annoying the Germans."

Rosa laughed, then her smile faded. "Were there civilians in Dunkirk?"

"Hard to say. We didn't linger. None were on our boat, the *Hebe* —Greek goddess of youth. I kept a diary when I could. I'll write a history of the war when it's over—if I survive."

"I hate talk like that."

"I'm a realist. Father used to say, 'Don't confuse longevity with virtue.' Quality. not quantity. Fact is, I might die tomorrow, but, " he smiled, "I won't. Why didn't you leave when you had the chance?"

"Couldn't . . . Sonny . . . " She stopped, overcome by those taken from her and the reunion with Alain.

He took her hand and kissed it. She wiped the tears away.

"You're sweet like your father. I'll get food."

Alain ate. They talked for several hours, then he left . . .

Days later, Rosa opened the spigot on an oak barrel, releasing a trickle and tasting the red wine blend. Grimacing from the bitter tannins, which the second fermentation would smooth out, she spit the mouthful into a bowl and moved to the next barrel.

Seeing Alain took her back to the flat on Rue du Roi de Sicile, then to the little café the night before Jean left Paris. He drank most of a carafe while she encouraged him to leave. Two years later, he returned a broken man. Germans had sullied his Paris. She tasted the bitter residue.

On 20 June 1943, in parching, relentless sun, visitors arrived at the domain—two Germans, probably Gestapo, and a French interpreter. One wore a crimson bruise on the side of his head. They asked about the wine—red or white, what vintage—but tasted none. Dominic gave them several bottles. Then they turned to the real reason for their visit. As they took turns asking questions, the interpreter barely kept up. Had there been any recent arrivals? Were they harboring a British terrorist? Did they support the Resistance? Everyone was summoned, identification reviewed, each closely observed. More questions.

Rosa was summoned while she was moving barrels. Too exhausted to be frightened, she stared at the sanguine spot decorating the burly man's skull as he studied her identification, then her. Had he noticed her staring? He returned her card. Rita Daurat passed the test. Accustomed to police and Gestapo scrutiny on the move, Rosa sensed something different this time. This was her home, her safe refuge. Those thugs could have dragged her away. That reminded her of Paris. A cold shiver ran through her.

Someone dangerous must be on the loose, she thought. It was a good thing Domaine Poussard had no visitors. There had only been two since Alain. Something had happened to warrant Gestapo interest. She recalled the ugly bruise adorning the brutish man's skull.

Several weeks later Rosa looked for Alesander. Javi told her he'd be gone for several days. That meant a mission. Two days later, in the afternoon heat, Javi and Alesander stood together. She joined them.

Alesander's mouth tightened.

"What?"

No answer.

"I'm part of this operation." Rosa showed her anger at their lack of response.

"Better you don't know," Javi said.

"You don't have to tell me. Someone's coming. And after the Gestapo . . . "

"Can't be helped."

———————

Sonny had moved from town to village to farmhouse, in and out of consciousness, over three days. His comrades stanched his bleeding, as best they could, bandaged his wound, and gave him water. Hidden and safe from arrest but weak, he needed rest. Somewhere along the route, a man, maybe a doctor, expertly cleaned his wound, put on a proper dressing, and disappeared.

Willy Ehlers, confederate in the Thiemann Strasse burglary, Neukölln, Berlin, in 1938, came to him in a dream, whispering, "Don't die like me." Then Shannon, his arm in a sling, green eyes glistening in the sun, pointed his finger, admonishing, "What the hell you doing in France chasing after your wife? You've got work in Lisbon."

Jameson and MacTavish stood in the background, making faces, laughing, and mouthing "Slick . . . Slick . . . " Kid and Rebecca talked, ignoring him. Rosa appeared in the distance. He yelled, but nobody heard. Was he dead? He woke with a start. His lips were shards of broken pottery. His throat felt the same. He hadn't eaten, had swallowed just drips of water; he was stork thin. His leg hurt like hell, and he was dirty, but he was alive.

"How you feel?" A man, maybe familiar, but Sonny couldn't remember, asked in English.

Sonny flicked his tongue over parched lips and croaked, "Water." He drank. Water spilled onto his chest; he drank more. "Where . . ?" He grimaced. It hurt to talk.

"You safe."

Sonny tried to rise but fell back. He took several breaths and managed, "How long?"

"Three days." The man held up three fingers.

He drank more water. Fog partially cleared, but it was like running a hand through a cobweb.

"Who Rosa . . . Kid . . . Rebecca? You talk in sleep."

Sonny shook his head. "Where is the guy I was with?"

"Later . . . he come . . . Gestapo looking." He pointed at Sonny and smiled. "Do good on bridge—boom!" He spread his arms wide.

Sonny's memory was a chalkboard wiped nearly clean. Raining bits of bridge . . . catching a bullet . . . into the water . . . darkness. Sonny shook his head in frustration.

Later, the guy he had named Eddie came with another guy.

"Take you where work . . . you be strong . . . go back to . . . ?" He shrugged.

"Portugal . . . first . . . find . . . wife." He almost said her name.

"Where she?"

"Near Sare."

They carried him to the back of a truck and covered him with hay. Hours later, after bouncing over the rutted, dirt tracks, conveying pain to his leg with every jolt, the truck finally stopped. Two men carried him a long way to a little house and put him a bed. He felt a wet tongue lick his face—a dog? Then he slept. Eddie brought him food and water. Another, shorter, stocky man came later

Eddie smiled and made a fist. "Okay . . . good," as far as his English took him.

Sonny cackled and tried to smile, then fell asleep.

The sound of the truck and Leon's bark awakened Rosa—it must be the visitor. They would take him to the old shack in the valley. She went back to sleep and forgot about him. She had barrels to sort, grapes to inspect, cleaning to do, helping Irene in the garden.

"I heard Leon," Rosa said to Irene, as she pulled weeds. "Was it wise, after the Gestapo . . . ?"

Irene knelt, swept hair from her forehead, and shook her head. "Javi and Alesander are in too deep to turn back, and they have Dominic's blessings. Pray the Gestapo doesn't return."

Later Rosa saw Javi near the house. "Who?"

"Guy injured on a mission four days ago."

"The one the Gestapo . . . " Her voice trailed away.

"Think so, but for something else."

"Busy guy—what else did he do?"

"Blew up a bridge."

Rosa whistled. "How injured?"

"Shot in the leg. Alesander got him away. Then friends took over, got him here. His wound has to be cleaned every day. There's medicine, bandages. He's weak. We have to move him and soon."

Rose returned to work, but the thought of the man in the little shack stayed with her. After dinner, she congratulated Alesander. "Too bad about . . . him."

He nodded. "He will live. I will take him his dinner."

Suddenly curious, Rosa asked, "What's he like?"

"Not one of us."

Rosa frowned. "How?"

"No French, only English. He told the boy he was German and the Gestapo was after him."

Now curious, she said, "I'll take his dinner." Could Alain have returned? No—he wasn't German. Carrying food and water in a basket, she walked between the rows of grapes in the lowering sun. Glancing at the towering mountains of the southern horizon, she felt insulated from the evil of the world . . . if only life were so simple.

Alesander had forgotten to tell her that the man was looking for his wife.

Sonny was bored. His needlelike pain and weakness made the admonishment not to leave the cabin a joke. He could barely limp outside to relieve himself. If he could walk, he would pace the cabin. There was a pitcher of water to clean his wound, though not enough to bathe. He did have clean clothes. A bottle of white powder and bandages sat on the table. His wound was cleaned and his dressing changed daily. Dinner would break the monotony.

The days meant nothing to him but light and dark. No one told him where he was—best not to know. He was done with Frank, his mission complete. The Gestapo was looking for two guys. Sonny smiled. As soon as he was stronger, he would look for Rosa.

He unfolded the oilcloth, examined the passports and visas. They were undamaged. Maria Louro's documents would work at the border. Fingering his passport, he frowned. Hans Baum would be known at every checkpoint along the French-Spanish frontier, maybe all over France. He had to go over the mountain into Spain.

He glanced at the pistol. Though it tied him to the Gestapo killing, he might need it. If they caught him, he was a dead man, so he might as well kill a few more. Eyelids heavy, leg aching, and tired from the day's exertion, he fell asleep . . .

Rosa knocked lightly on the door. No answer. Quietly opening the door, she entered. Small curtained windows kept the cabin dark. She saw a man's outline on the bed, his back to her. Setting the basket on the table, she removed the food and water. Passports, visas, and a pistol sat on the little table next to the bed.

She sat in the chair and waited.

The man groaned. His body stirred.

"Bonsoir," she said.

"What?" the voice croaked.

She stood and walked toward the bed. The man groaned and turned his body toward the voice. Groggy, pained eyes met hers. As if from photographic paper dipped into a chemical emulsion, a faint image emerged—grays turned black and white, defined space, something familiar?

"Dreaming," Sonny muttered in English

Rosa straightened . . .

34

Domaine Poussard, June 1943

Candles flickered in the gentle breeze. Time stretched, detonator-wire taut. Recognition flared. Ticking time resumed.

Sonny saw Leon standing next to Rosa. Then Leon walked to the bed, sat beside Sonny, and waited. It was very quiet. She was a mirage, a shimmering puddle on a hot day. His eyes played tricks on him. Dreams came often—this was another illusion, though it seemed real enough. Breaking eye contact with the comely apparition, he looked at the dog. He stroked its soft fur. He heard its tail thump on the floor. The dog was real.

Rosa moved closer, pulled by magnetism. She bent forward, brushed hair from her eye, moved her lips soundlessly, unable to speak. The man had a scruffy beard like dirt on his face but eyes vaguely familiar. She dismissed the idea as fanciful. Then she remembered Alesander's words: "German . . . spoke no French."

"Sonny?" She muttered, her voice small, hesitant—had she even spoken? She moved closer.

The man in the bed stirred. Their eyes met and held a second time. He blinked.

"Rosa?" he asked tentatively.

"Oh, my God!" She covered her mouth with her hands, stanching further sound. Dark eyes widened. She fell to her knees, her hand to his chest, to his face, feeling hot skin, making sure he was real.

"Rosa." His voice was nearly inaudible.

"Yes."

"I'm dreaming."

"No!" She grabbed his hand and squeezed. "I'm real."

"How . . ?" he muttered.

"Life." Rosa shook her head in wonderment, then kissed his forehead. A tear fell onto his cheek. "World upside down again," she muttered, caressing his cheeks with her hands. Then the tips of their noses touched. Sparks flew. The old shack smoldered but did not ignite. The world was righting itself. She laughed.

Questions too many to answer piled one atop the other. They talked at once, stopped, and began again. They laughed.

"You first," Sonny said after a long beat.

The years they had been apart, from their time on the train in Mons to that in Sare, blurred, then began to sort themselves out. A fragmentary and incomplete picture formed, their insatiable longing satisfied in the blink of an eye. Each step took them deeper into a disorienting reality. They coupled in a surreal dance. Their craving had been so great, they were unprepared for the moment of reunion.

"Inevitable?" Sonny asked.

"An explanation as good as any other," Rosa agreed, a smile on her lips. "Jenny was the key."

Sonny squeezed Rosa's hand. "Then only time and logistics…"

"Only?"

"Several hurdles," he admitted. "Gestapo everywhere, can't swing a cat by the tail without hitting one."

She laughed. "Careful, I have a cat—Emil."

Sonny smiled. "I must meet this creature." He nibbled her neck. After several moments, he said, "I couldn't let the Gestapo take me in. It went sour. I got lucky, found a friend…then Frank. Said if I helped him, he'd help me find you."

"Frank?" Rosa asked, curious. "Describe him."

"Tall, thin Jew. Quite the manipulator…kept sending me on missions." Sonny sighed. "Had no choice, no place to go."

"Meyer."

"You know him?" Sonny was surprised.

She told him about Daniel Meyer.

"Incredible. What do you do?"

She told him.

"Very impressive. If I'd only said your name…"

"Alesander, yes. Frank would have denied knowing me. In his world, only missions are important. He's difficult but committed. Resistance is hard work; many are caught. But you know that."

"I'm not complaining. I'll thank Frank if I see him again." Sonny winced.

"Does it hurt?"

"Less now."

Rosa's smile brightened the shack. "I'll be your nurse."

Sonny gestured toward the table. "Sprinkle on the white powder after washing the wound. Then bandage it." He yawned. "First, brandy for the pain. I think there was morphine, but it's finished."

"Sleep. I have exhausted you. I'll return when darkness falls."

Before closing the door, she glanced back at Sonny. He was real, not a ghost. Walking back, her mind reeled at the sudden turn her life had taken. Her naïve dream had turned into reality. Her faith had been rewarded. How had he done it? Jenny, British Intelligence, wolfram, the Resistance—nothing could explain it. His story seemed incredible, too much to digest. Yet there he was.

Rosa returned under cover of darkness and spent the night. Consumed by details of their lives, they talked until Sonny tired. Then they laid together, bodies close for the first time in four years. She longed to lie naked next to Sonny and feel his skin next to hers. But they were together. That was enough for now.

In the morning Rosa cleaned the mess of tangled flesh on Sonny's leg, another new experience. Sonny drank brandy and clamped his teeth on a folded towel. She hated the pain she caused him.

After several days, Sonny could walk with help. Rosa led him to her cottage in the dark. He shaved, bathed, put on clean clothes, and became a new man. Emil mewed when Sonny stroked his soft fur. They shared Rosa's bed that night. Exhausted, Sonny slept, intoxicated by the scent of lavender on Rosa's hair and body. The years melted away. She hadn't used lavender since Antwerp.

Rosa had changed, but how? Sonny recalled scant joy in Berlin in November and December 1938. Rosa's defiance and bravery in Oranienburg had come at a great cost—nearly her undoing. Antwerp had brought them the freedom to marry. But still she had suffered. Remarkably, that earlier woman had vanished, somewhere between Antwerp and Sare. No longer haunted, she had flourished, had become a strong, independent woman.

He knew she had help along the way or she could not have survived. In Paris, Jean had been her mentor, father figure, and friend… And the others—the nightclub owner and singer Agnes, the actress Annette, and Catherine. Rosa's friends all, but names without faces to him. They had supported and shaped her. Then the Poussards had sheltered her. The Resistance had taken Rita Daurat into the heart of German occupation. She was brave. He was proud of her accomplishments. Her loyalty to him was humbling.

He hesitated, wondering in his weakened state just how loyal she was. Did Rosa love him or had she outgrown him? She had found a new home in Sare and sustenance in the Resistance. Was there someone else in Toulouse or Lyon? Clouds of doubt swirled around him. She no longer needed him.

A disconcerting insecurity he had not felt since the invasion shook his confidence. Alone for hours at a stretch, he felt vulnerable…Gestapo everywhere…isolated, unable to run. *Trust no one.* Agitated, paranoid, scared, Sonny reached for the pistol…his hand stopped in midair. He held his breath. Rosa had betrayed no trust, given no truth to his fears. It was in him, not in her.

Rosa came through the door—as beautiful as on the night he first set eyes upon her. In that she had not changed, and he was reassured. She was leaner and stronger, her hands calloused, her skin darkened to light bronze, her hair longer, her smile radiant when she smiled at all. He planned to know all aspects of this confident woman.

Sonny had changed, too, but he gave little thought as to how. Smart enough to evaluate his life, he chose not to. He moved forward, rarely dwelling on the past. What good would come of introspection? He willingly accepted the demands of war and had no regrets about the men he had killed. They would have killed him, and they had killed Kid, Rebecca, Rebecca's father, and the others. Their deaths would be with him forever, but introspection was a peacetime luxury.

Rosa stared at Sonny while he slept. Four years was a long time. Who was he? Not a stranger, but different from the man she had slept with in Antwerp. He looked older. His eyes creased at the corners, though the pain from his leg might be causing that. Perhaps wiser, he was certainly bold and brave enough to have made it to Sare nearly intact. Probably he was a good judge of character, cautious about others, lucky to have found help along the way. All were good survival traits. Was he still ready with a quip to lighten his burden or to cover his insecurity and fear, to keep others at bay?

That first night he had magically appeared at her door on Kristallnacht, a ghost rising from the mist. Again in Oranienburg, where she had stood with the dead Gestapo at her feet, thinking he had lost her…and now, when she had feared him forever lost. She marveled at his ability simply to show up. How had he done it?

Thinking back over four years of turmoil, dislocation, and death, Rosa noted that it seemed even longer—so much had happened in their short lives. Oranienburg and Berlin were dirty spots on a map. Fate had taken her from Antwerp to Paris after that terrible detour in Mons. Then there was Jean, lovable Jean…the bomb-riddled road to Biarritz…and becoming Rita Daurat. Then coming to Sare to serve in the Resistance. Broken lines and ruptured lives had led to this spot, light years from where they had started…

Sonny's long shadow had followed Rosa from Mons to Paris to Sare. Did she believe in guardian angels? It was tempting to put her fate in the hands of others. Her father had plucked Jean's name, just one among many others, from that board…fate? Were Alain, Paul, Annette, Catherine, and Agnes—all the friends she had made—also fate? She had done it without Sonny. With help, she had navigated the streets of Paris and escaped ahead of the Germans. She was not the woman Sonny had last seen in 1939.

Now she was French—she spoke French, read French, and felt French. He did not know that person. And how well could she know him? Self-absorbed, angry, and scared, she had treated him dreadfully that first, terrible night. Yet he had returned. She had needed him or someone like him. He had kept up her spirits as her mother's had declined and her father languished. For hours they had talked of everything and nothing. He had been hopeful and supportive in the bleakest of times.

When he dropped the bomb of his smuggling Jews from Germany, she hadn't believed it. What? At that moment, the person she most needed had appeared. Was it fate?

Rosa had used Sonny for what he could do for her. She had been vulnerable—that was her excuse. He would smuggle her from Germany, where she felt strangled. Sonny could deliver. Should she feel guilt or shame? No. Sonny knew. She had told him. And he had wanted something from her—companionship, love, and family. A bargain of sorts.

Trauma had bookended Rosa's nine months with Sonny. The first month was an endless string of horrors until the relief of Antwerp was lost again in Mons. She resisted returning to every scene of the drama. Instead, she recalled Annette running through the Montparnasse warehouse with the other actors. Rosa had been bewildered and amused, found a bit of happiness. She had confided in pert Annette and become her hero. A half-smile came to her lips, then faded. And Alain and Paul, and dear Jean—where were they now?

In Paris Rosa's pain had receded, abetted by time and distance. The nightmares of Oranienburg had faded... Anger toward the perpetrators had filled the hole inside her to the point that she wanted revenge. Now she'd kill that creep and feel nothing.

Sonny had made her feel good during that bleak time. She had learned to love and be loved. Then on that damn train to Paris... How well did she know Sonny? How had he coped with death and fear, the currencies of a war in which everyone lost?

He must be a good spy, with that special gift of blending, appearing to be German, not Jewish. He could mingle with the enemy. His clandestine meetings in Lisbon's bars and cafés and on the street seemed to have been like those for her in Paris with André—romantic in a heroic, adventurous, mysterious way. He had come close to but eluded death. Rosa sighed. They were not so different. But he was a fugitive.

She had remained faithful. Had he?

———

Rosa had honored her vow to remain in France until he arrived. The joy and anguish of Paris and Jean's place were etched in her memory. The Resistance had filled the hole in her heart. She had finished what she started and become a whole person. Then Domaine Poussard had become her home . . . She would remember it all.

Now it was too dangerous. Portugal . . . with Sonny . . . beckoned. She could not do it alone.

When Sonny stirred, she said, "You were crazy to come."

"What?" he murmured.

"Are you crazy? I need to know."

He yawned, then rephrased her question, "Why am I crazy?"

"For coming to France."

He smiled. "Crazy about you."

"Don't be flippant."

He sat up in bed. "It's true. The thought of finding you kept me alive. I never looked at another woman."

"Not even looked?"

He smiled. "Well, it's hard not to look, but that's all. Then I found Jenny. She told me about Sare." He shrugged. "Then opportunity knocked." He was quiet for so long Rosa thought he had finished, but he continued: "I fell in love with you the instant I saw you."

"I remember." Her gaze traveled beyond the little cottage. "You fell for what you saw, not for what you knew. And I needed you. We barely know each other now."

"We spent so much time together on Pestalozzi Strasse."

"Little more than a month."

"A violent month but in many ways intimate. You suffered. I felt responsible. A strong bond formed, at least for me."

"Along the way I fell in love with you. You pulled me through, but don't feel responsible. That Nazi got what he deserved." Her voice turned icy cold. "Oranienburg is a distant memory."

Sonny nodded. "Then Mons . . ."

"And war," she interjected.

"We would have been together in Paris."

"I was cheated. The pain was terrible. My parents left. I was alone. Jean let me stay . . . no, more than that, he saved me. Helped me become an independent woman. Gave me a family. Annette was a great friend. Agnes gave me a job, then an exit. I found Jenny, someone I could help. I learned to take care of myself. Then this wonderful family saved me. I was lucky."

"You still are. We're going to Lisbon, then to London."

"Join my parents in Cuba or . . ." she shrugged.

They were quiet a moment, then Rosa said, "We have scars . . ."

He gently placed a fingertip to her lips. "We're safe and together. That trumps everything."

"You don't seem troubled by any of this?"

"Can't let it, not anymore. I watched them execute a mother and daughter and two old men." Sonny closed his eyes and cringed, reliving the experience. "I hit bottom, swore I'd kill the guy who ordered their deaths." He shook his head. "But the Germans got him, along with Kid, Rebecca's father. We buried them and ran." He sighed. "Kid and Rebecca never saw England."

"I'm sorry." Rosa's voice was barely a whisper.

"Nine months, Kid and I were together every day. We were close. I knew Rebecca for a couple days. I felt responsible for her. She didn't have anyone."

"You were with Kid as long as we were together." Rosa thought that was important.

"Yes," Sonny acknowledged. "Funny, tragic world, isn't it?"

"You're a good man."

"You think so?" Sonny had yearned to hear those words from Rosa.

She smiled. "I do. And you were right about danger being intoxicating."

"We have that in common."

"We do."

"Why didn't you leave?" Sonny asked.

"And miss nursing you back to health?"

"Now *you're* being flippant."

They laughed.

The first day, Rosa handed Maria Louro's passport to Sonny. "Look at her picture. She's very pretty, but I don't look like her: eyes smaller, nose is different, cheeks, everything."

"Ask Javi to fix it."

She nodded.

"Though it may not matter," Sonny went on." I can't go through a border check. Hans Baum is a dead man. We have to go over the mountain."

"It's dangerous."

"What isn't? Once we're in Spain, we'll be okay. Still, talk to Javi."

In a week, Sonny was able to walk—with a painful limp. Javi delivered a passport with Rosa's photograph. There was no farewell dinner, no party— just hugs and a tearful good-bye.

On the first of July, eight days after Sonny's arrival at Domaine Poussard, Rosa with Javi and Sonny with Alesander met on a dirt track outside Ainhoa. This lesser-used route was closer to Sare. Which passes to take and when to take them was a game of roulette.

Alesander's French border guards could be of no help—Boche now patrolled the border. But a smuggler friend had compiled a rough schedule of patrols based on his observations over months. Guarding every mountain pass all the time was impossible, though the randomness of the guards remained a concern. Another factor in their favor was the Boche success: the smuggling had declined, necessitating fewer patrols and so providing opportunity. If Alesander's friend had it right—Ainhoa was the route to take.

Alesander would guide them to the summit. After the journey with Anni, Rosa had vowed not to make the trip up the mountain until she left with Sonny. Sonny's leg slowed him but did not prevent his travel. He had money, cigarettes, and his pistol. Rosa had packed two dresses, Sonny's finally washed handkerchief, several other garments, and the Kertész and wedding party photographs.

A partially cloudy sky covered a half-moon. Visibility was good. A million stars winked at them from behind the treeless, jagged mountaintop. Their ears twitched, eyes constantly on the lookout.

Four hours into their trek, Hans Baum and Maria Louro entered Dantxarinea at the Spanish border. Language problems were sorted out and documents presented. The guard frowned as he pointed to the passport page where the French exit stamp should be.

Cigarettes and cash changed hands—problem solved. They boarded the bus to Pamplona, caught the train to Irun, then traveled south through Burgos, Valladolid, and Salamanco, switching trains to Ciudad Rodrigo and Fuentes de Oñoro at the Portuguese border. Their German documents gave them a free pass through Spain. Now they were beyond Gestapo reach.

Swaying to the motion of the railcar as the Spanish countryside flashed by, Sonny and Rosa found the intimacy they had craved. They left their compartment only to eat and use the facilities.

"I have two stories, short ones, to tell you," Sonny started. "The first in Aachen, December '38. When I left several days behind you, four were dead. You were too fragile then. Three Gestapos—and Günter—died. Two had their necks broken by Emil. I shot the German officer, and his bullet hit Günter."

"Günter had met us at the train." Her voice trailed.

"Emil made it back to Berlin. Katrina—Günter's wife—intended to cross into Belgium and go to Fritz. Before I left Germany, a lovely

328

old lady gave me refuge. Crossing the border, I slid past Albert Schwarz." Sonny sighed. "My war started early."

"What an ordeal. And the second story?" She waited.

"Goren told me what might have been his confession. Einsatzgruppen mobile killing units roamed the eastern front, murdering Jews—men, women, and children. He reported to Albert Schwarz, his commanding officer, in Krakow. Goren was raving mad, though there may have been a glimmer of humanity somewhere inside. He died shortly afterward, shot by his sergeant protecting Maria Louro."

"Ugh," Rosa groaned. "Hug me."

They embraced in silence . . .

Late on the following day, 2 July 1943, they reached the Portuguese border.

"I have to telephone a friend before we cross." Sonny told Rosa.

"Who?"

"My partner in crime." Sonny winked. He limped to a telephone box in the train station.

"Does it hurt?"

"Only when I walk," he smiled. The language problem was overcome. The telephone rang five times.

Mayhew's voice said, "Hello."

Sonny heard noise in the background. "It's Hans Baum." Silence. "Hello . . . Mayhew?"

"Sorry . . . you took me by surprise. Where are you?"

"At the border, Fuentes de Oñoro. Any instructions?"

"Call back in 15 minutes." He hung up.

Sonny told Rosa. They waited . . .

Finally, Mayhew: "Go to Hotel Madrid. Wait until I come or send someone using my name. Don't leave." He disconnected.

"We're spending the night. He's coming."

Hotel Madrid, the only one, was in the center of town. They checked into a room on the second floor, overlooking the pretty square. They slept late the next morning, ate breakfast, then strolled the neighborhood. In 1811, Gen. (Arthur Wellesley, Duke of) Wellington had defeated the French Gen. André Masséna, providing the backwater town its moment in history. There was little to see, not even a monument, but they enjoyed the walk.

Mayhew waited for them in the small lobby of the hotel. They shook hands. Sonny introduced Rosa.

"Bonjour." Rosa smiled at Mayhew.

"Plaisir de vous rencontrer." He returned the greeting, then grabbed Sonny's arm. "To your room."

Sonny locked the door.

"Glad you made it back safely and found the lovely . . . " Mayhew hesitated, " . . . Rosa."

"We need new documents," she said in French.

"Oui, bien sûr." Then to Sonny in English, "Any problems?"

"A few." Sonny's harsh laugh came out in a snort. He told Mayhew everything. "Activities on the train are classified." He winked.

Mayhew smiled. "A very busy man. How's the wound?"

"Healing. What were the reactions to the wolfram caper?"

"All hell broke loose." Mayhew laughed. "Two days later your old pal Obersturmbannführer Schwarz went to the mine with his cronies and got an earful. My source says they also went to the house. We left it in a bit of a mess, probably blood on the floor. Don't know if they found the bodies."

"What can they do?"

He shrugged. "They know we hijacked the wolfram and probably killed Goren and his factotum. Schwarz raised bloody hell with his PVDE contacts. Word traveled up the chain, and apparently Salazar isn't happy. We've been trying to get him to embargo wolfram sales to Germany, but he refuses. He's a grand master at playing both sides."

"How do you know this?"

"Lisbon is still a teeming cesspool of intrigue. Some things never change."

Sonny laughed, then told Rosa the story in German. Pointing at Mayhew, he asked, "They know you stole the wolfram?"

"Me . . . personally?" He shook his head. "Don't think so. That would make it too hot for me in Lisbon. So far no problem—they know it's gone and that we took it. As for you?" He shrugged.

Sonny thought about that. "Do they think I'm dead, or did word get back here about Baum in France?"

"Don't know."

"Any retaliation?"

He shook his head. "Not yet. First, I nursemaid you both to Lisbon, then to Jolly England." He pointed at Sonny. "Your cover is blown sky-high. When you're back in Lisbon, a cobbler will get you both new shoes."

Part VII

If when saying goodbye to life,
All the birds in the sky
Gave me while leaving

Your last look,
This look of your own
Love that was the first

What a perfect heart
In my chest would die
My love in your hand
In those hands
Where my heart beat perfectly
—*Fado lyrics*

35

Lisbon, July 1943

Stumbling, the sailor hurled a string of obvious obscenity at the prostitute. His companions caught him and laughed uproariously. Hands on her ample hips, shoulders back, she struck a pose through their laughter. Sonny put an arm around Rosa and guided her around the scrum. Safely past the raucous group, they held hands and continued their stroll. The strains of a lone guitar and a fadista's voice floated from a tavern's open door. Sonny stopped suddenly, jerking Rosa back.

"Let's go in," he said, and before she could answer they were inside the crowded space. At the far end of the small bar a man strummed his guitar, and a young woman, eyes closed, hands clasped to her bosom, sang as if her days were numbered.

Sonny ordered wine. They stood at the bar, pressed between other patrons, Rosa leaning against him. He pulled her closer. They swayed to the simple melody of the guitar and voice that filled the room. An anonymous voice occasionally joined in. Nobody seemed to mind. Thunderous applause and whoops of approval rewarded each song. After her fourth song, the singer bowed and disappeared into the crowd. Sonny and Rosa left before another singer took her place.

Outside, Rosa said, "Such depth of feeling in her expression! I didn't need to understand the words. It's majestic and very romantic. I understand why you love it so much."

Sonny leaned against a building and pulled Rosa close. They kissed. "Very romantic," he said breathlessly several minutes later. "You don't need to know Portuguese to love it. Really good fadistas convey sensual stirring and overpowering saudade."

"What's that?"

He explained. "The lyrics might be banal and uninspiring, but they are always heartfelt."

Sonny's enthusiasm for fado charmed Rosa. For the first time since Antwerp, she felt happiness—or at least what she thought it must be. It had been so long. Germany and the war seemed far away. Warm memories of Paris and Sare lingered. Though Antwerp had proved ephemeral, would Lisbon be different? She had learned that nothing lasts . . . but she held it tight.

They strolled to their flat in an agency safe house near the dock in Alcantra. Hidden in a row of decaying buildings with peeling window frames, gouged doors, and sagging roofs, it was the perfect front. Inside, the flat was comfortable and relatively clean, its furniture minimal but serviceable. Rosa hung the Kertész and set the wedding photograph on the little dresser. Sonny's handkerchief, her totem during his absence, remained unused in a corner of a drawer.

Sonny grew his beard, wore a hat, dungarees, sweater, and short jacket. Black-rimmed eyeglasses from the agency's disguise bin completed the disguise. Surrounded by sailors, refugees, petty criminals, prostitutes, spies, and the destitute, they blended in. Rosa felt safe in the hot Lisbon air of neutral Portugal.

Late in the evening, two days after arriving in Lisbon, Mayhew visited them. "Not sure when you'll get back to mother. Damn war and all. Sadly, you're rather low on the list. Be patient, have fun, but be careful. No visitors," he ordered. "People coming and going is a signal. Make sure you're not followed. Meet Jenny, or anyone, in a bar, tavern, café, or park. Avoid cafés on the Rossio and," he smirked, "Hotel Avenida Palace."

After his French adventure, Sonny considered such minor restrictions inconsequential. His leg healed without infection or damage to the bone. Walking strengthened his mangled muscles, and the embassy doctor predicted his slight limp would eventually disappear. Johnson kept him on the payroll, and the crown paid for the safe house. With money in his pocket, he could resume his life. The bars, taverns, and cafés in Alcantra and Alfama beckoned.

Rosa had only one friend in Lisbon, though her connection to Sonny and MI6 required caution. Their safety could be illusory—she followed the rules. Her reunion with Jenny was another of life's strange twists. Jenny had moved into Karpov's anonymous Alcantra flat, not far from the safe house. She and Karpov had become a couple.

"You move . . . my small flat in Alcantra," Jenny imitated Karpov's heavily accented English.

They talked and laughed and occasionally shed a tear. Tough times had followed Jenny to Lisbon. "Then I met Sonny, and everything changed."

"It's quite extraordinary. And you've changed." Rosa saw a poised and self-assured young woman.

"Thanks to Sonny I had a place to live and a job at the embassy."

Rosa hesitated, then said, "I'm sorry for abandoning you in Paris."

"Nonsense." Jenny took Rosa's hand. "You got me off the street and into the club. Thank you."

"It must have been awful in the camp."

"Not as bad as you might think. They let us go. It got scary with Germans on the move. Then I made it to Portugal."

"And Max?" Rosa inquired, striking a nerve.

Jenny's face sagged. "It hurts. I fear he's lost."

Several days later, Rosa met Roman Karpov at a little waterfront café. The young, intense, nearly humorless Ukrainian of Polish heritage initially put her off. He was another injured soul with a compelling story. Alone, like Jenny. A sadness flowed from him like water from a ruptured pipe. He reserved his rare smile for Jenny. He was kind to and solicitous of her, and that won Rosa over.

Any meeting of the four friends became a veritable Tower of Babel. No single language accommodated all of them. Karpov spoke no German, refused to learn, or so he claimed; his English did improve. Rosa spoke little English and, determined to learn, had enrolled in a class. Only Jenny spoke fluent Portuguese, though Karpov got by on the street. Rosa and Jenny spoke French and German. Jenny and Sonny spoke English. For Rosa and Sonny, German remained an unavoidable necessity. An outsider listening to the rapid-fire, time-consuming conversation, reprised in German and English, would be amused.

Lisbon sweltered in the heat. People with means exited the city for Sintra, 30 kilometers to the north. For centuries, the aristocracy had taken refuge in its hills. A palate of pink, orange, yellow, and red stucco turrets, towers, and crenelated walls set into green verdant hills created Sintra's considerable charm. Fifteenth-century palaces and estates—some even older—shared tight, undulating spaces with newer, equally extravagant buildings. Pretty parks with tree-lined promenades led to splendid fountains of water-spewing sea serpents.

The cool late-September days were no deterrent to visiting Sintra. From the rail station it was a 10-minute walk to town. Sonny and Rosa linked arms and strolled through winding, narrow streets of fairy-tale architecture. Since Lisbon's streets were filled with many a black Mercedes, Sonny paid little heed to one passing him in Sintra.

From Sintra, a road meandered through forest to the pretty seaside village of Azenhas do Mar. White stucco houses topped with red roofs perched high on a cliff over the Atlantic. The bus was nearly empty, and only one car passed. Sonny casually noted its license plate. In 15 minutes they leaned against the railing on the cliff's edge promenade. The tide was out, and sand extended beyond a small pool. Several people frolicked in the water. Two boats bobbed languidly, like dogs curled before a fire, bodies rising and falling with each breath.

"Hungry?" Sonny asked.

Rosa shrugged. "A little."

"How does a pitcher of vinho verde and a plate of seafood sound?"

She smiled. "Now I am hungry."

They held hands as they walked up the winding path to Restaurant Piscinas. When they reached the top, Sonny stopped. The black Mercedes, same plate number he had memorized, was parked at the end of the road, nowhere for it to go but over the cliff. Its occupants were out of sight. Government officials and the rich drove Mercedes, as did Gestapo and German Embassy officials. Sonny felt uneasy.

"That car," he pointed, "keeps turning up. Let's catch the bus back and eat in Sintra."

"Who?"

He shook his head. "I'm supposed to lie low. Too isolated here, and I don't want any questions." They moved into an alley, then heard voices.

"German?" Rosa whispered.

Two men walked toward the café from the direction of the village.

Sonny stiffened.

"What is it?"

"Albert Schwarz," he said through clenched jaw.

"That creep from Berlin?" Rosa shivered.

Sonny nodded. Rosa knew all about Schwarz and his involvement in the wolfram episode. "Who is he with?"

The two men stopped at the restaurant's door and talked. Neither wore a uniform. Albert's blond hair was short. His hands constantly moved in an endless pattern of nervous energy, a cigarette in one of them, like a prop. The other man listened, nodded then said something. They laughed, and Albert put a hand on the other man's back, guiding him inside.

Sonny and Rosa returned to Sintra and lunched in a small café. "So, he's still here."

"Still?"

"I saw him at Hotel Parque last year. He didn't see me." Sonny held Rosa's gaze, gathering his thoughts. Finally, he nodded and said, "Would he have recognized me?" His eyebrows lifted. "You've heard the story." He felt the need to repeat it. "Eyes gave me away . . . October '37 . . . across the square in Aachen. Smuggling with Emil, Gestapo Albert mingling with the Wehrmacht. Scared the hell out of me. Sent me underground."

Rosa put her hand on Sonny's.

"We had last spoken," Sonny continued, tapping his forefinger on his lips, "sometime in '32. Then I saw him in '35 at a Berlin café with his Gestapo buddies. He saw me, but," Sonny shook his head slowly from side to side, "ignored me. Would he recognize me with a beard? Don't want to take the chance."

"Of course not. Why would you?"

———

Summer turned to autumn, which gave way to winter, then to spring 1944. The war raged on. Mussolini had been deposed and arrested in July 1943. Allies swarmed Italian beaches several months later, gaining a foothold. For Italy, the war was lost, but Germany fought on as the Allies moved north, up the boot. By January 1944, German losses on the eastern front had brought the Red Army to the old 1939 Polish-USSR border. Increased pressure on Germany from the West was sorely needed to give Russia relief and to liberate France.

Rumors spread of an Allied landing somewhere on the French coast between Dunkirk and Cherbourg.

Sonny itched to get back to the fight. He loved tavern hopping and enjoying fado with Rosa, but otherwise he had nothing to do. He was bored. Knowing Rosa's position, he kept that to himself. The strength in his leg returned, and his limp disappeared. The only residues of his injury were the memory and a nasty scar. His cover blown, there was no way to get back into espionage, and anyway, he was far from the front.

Rosa and Sonny spent days walking in Alfama and along the riverfront. They took dinner in one of the little neighborhood cafés or cooked at the flat. Then it was off to one of several taverns for fado—or not, for a quiet evening of reading. The war made making any decisions about their future premature, though Rosa occasionally broached the topic. They would have a life after the war ended and a future to plan. She sensed Sonny's restlessness and knew he missed the action. She was restless too but for a different reason. War had worn her out, and she wanted a new life.

Jenny's work had become clerical—document collection and translating—though from time to time Mayhew sent her into the field to contact women known to fraternize with Germans. What came from those efforts was beyond Sonny's reach or interest. Karpov roamed the docks, sniffing out information from sailors and longshoremen about the German smuggling of looted property and the turning of German agents.

On 6 June 1944, everything changed. The Allies invaded France at the Normandy beachhead. Fighting was fierce. Liberation was at hand, the end of the war near. Rosa cheered while Sonny stewed at being out of the action. Rosa's assurance that he had done his bit only partially soothed him. Stuck in a cage, he paced warily. He might have gone mad if not for fado, the charm of Alfama, and Rosa.

Rosa's classes improved her English, and soon she could converse with Sonny in her new language. Soon they would go to England, she hoped . . . but Sonny had nothing to do. He was a marked man and needed to stay out of sight. His options were limited. There were days they spent strolling Alfama, making an occasional visit to a museum, taking the trolley to Belem. They were in love. Their intimacy came naturally . . . except that Sonny put talk of their future on hold.

Portugal experienced small interruptions, minor inconveniences paling in comparison to massive invasion and confrontation. In May, Salazar's opposition staged labor strikes resulting in mass arrests—to harm his regime. Communists were blamed for the strikes.

By 1944, however, some privation reached Lisbon. Bread, a staple, was rationed. Cafés, groceries, and bakeries, full earlier while the rest of Europe suffered, were now depleted. Dissatisfaction and disillusionment spread. A week after the invasion, Salazar opened a new national soccer stadium near the marginal coast. Mayhew called it a "tone-deaf move for a shrewd operator like Salazar."

According to Mayhew, the allies had become less concerned about Salazar's assistance. In 1943, America and Britain obtained base rights in the Azores, a crucial strategic position in the Atlantic. The new focus was on Salazar's profits from the sale of war supplies, particularly wolfram. A July 1943 BBC broadcast warned Portugal that gold bullion bearing German insignias would be considered stolen, eligible for confiscation. Panic flowed through Lisbon's numerous gold dealers.

"Dealers ask the Bank of Portugal for new gold, like old shoes needing new soles. They deserve to lose it all," Mayhew chuckled. "There's so damn much gold in Portugal, it might sink into the Atlantic." Leaning in, creating an aura of confidentially, he said, "A big shipment of gold, originating in Germany, arrived through Switzerland. Traced it to a Buick dealership on Avenida de Liberdade."

Sonny laughed. "Guy selling cars fronting for the Germans?"

"You heard right. Safety deposit boxes all over Lisbon are stuffed. Our guy at Portela Airport watches arrivals. Flights leave Berlin with no passengers but full of gold. Bank of Portugal and custom's officials clam up, act stupid. Damn it! We want that gold."

They were quiet, thinking. Then Sonny asked, "Who of Hitler's finest are skimming, ready to take off?"

"Hard to say," Mayhew said.

"What are you doing about it?" Sonny asked.

"Watching Gestapo and embassy big shots . . . it's hard without men on the inside, and we don't have enough manpower."

"Sorry, I can't help. Can you turn the ones who know the end is near? Guys with wet fingers in the air?"

"Who would that be?"

"A guy like Goren," Sonny offered.

"That Nazi piece of shit. Most of them are more subtle."

"Schwarz?"

Mayhew shrugged. "Ask him when you see him again." Mayhew knew about Sonny's near confrontation at Azenhas do Mar. Nothing had come of it.

Sonny's laughter died as he recalled the man with Schwarz. "He was going into the restaurant with someone, but I didn't get a good look."

"I like to know my enemies. Could you ID him from photos?"

Sonny shook his head and frowned. "No, but Rosa might."

The next day Johnson escorted Sonny and Rosa to a small, windowless, basement room in the British Embassy. Several files lay on a metal table with two chairs waiting. Churchill stared at them from the wall.

"Have at it," Johnson said. "Find Schwarz's friend, then find me."

For the next hour they opened files and viewed photographs. Rosa stopped and stared at one in her hand. "Sonny . . . " Staring back at her in black and white was a pleasant face, clean-shaven, ordinary, half smiling, eyes friendly, maybe 35 years old. "I vaguely recall thinking he looked nice for a Nazi," Rosa mused.

"Don't let that fool you," Sonny responded as he studied the photo.

Rosa turned the picture over. Written on the back were the words "Herman Becker; mid-level Foreign Service? Transferred to Lisbon from Berlin. Doing what? Hair color—brown. Height approx. 5 ft, 10 in. Weight approx. 12 stone."

Pointing to the description, she asked, "What's a stone?"

"Brits do things different." He explained feet and inches and did some calculating. "He's about a meter, 78 centimeters, tall, and he weighs 76 kilos."

Rosa leaned on her elbows, cupping her chin in her hands, studying the picture. "Hmm," she hummed, "think it's him . . . " She shrugged.

They found Johnson and explained. He thanked them and said they would hear from Mayhew.

Two days later, Rosa and Sonny returned from dinner to find Mayhew waiting outside the flat. Grinning broadly, he said to Rosa, "Congratulations, Rosa. We confirmed that the guy in Sintra with Schwarz is Herman Becker." Then to Sonny, "We put a tail on him. He went straight to Schwarz. Remember the gold I told you about?"

Sonny nodded.

"We hear things. Can't be sure, but think they're planning something. Schwarz was pissed about losing his share of the wolfram swag. The great patriot!" Mayhew said, sarcastically.

"Not the motherland's loss he's sorry for?"

"A cynical pragmatist," Mayhew offered.

"What?" Rosa asked, impatiently. She understood most of what they had said; Sonny explained the rest.

"Then find out what they are up to. No problem for a big-time operative like you." Rosa laughed, then said to Sonny, "You cannot. Schwarz knows you." She gave an exaggerated Gallic shrug.

Mayhew nodded. "Yes, of course."

They were quiet, thinking how to infiltrate.

"Both are under surveillance," Mayhew mumbled, "could be nothing."

Mayhew returned the next day. "There's big news: Abwehr sources say an attempt on Hitler's life failed."

"How?" Sonny asked.

"Don't know. Hundreds, maybe thousands have been arrested."

"Will it reach to Lisbon?"

Mayhew shrugged. "Radio transmissions from Berlin have spiked. War goes badly . . . matter of months until Adolf's thousand-year Reich crumbles like fairy dust. Deteriorating morale in the Wehrmacht officer corps and Abwehr leadership. Our two krauts know all this. The twins, Schwarz and Becker, probably aren't rabid Nazis. Either could be called back to Berlin to face the music or sent to fight the Bolshies. If they plan to run with the gold, now's the time."

Again, Rosa got most of it.

"Do you have a plan?" Sonny asked Mayhew.

His hand rose, like a traffic cop. "In a minute. Pressure on weak links here has yielded information of value. No one wants to be on the losing side; allegiances shift. We're finally getting information from customs and the Bank of Portugal. Remember the Buick dealer?" He didn't wait for an answer. "We found another. This one's in your old watering hole."

Sonny frowned. "Avenida Palace . . . Kepler?"

Mayhew nodded.

"He's involved with our twins?"

He shrugged. "No surprise that the twins would hang around Avenida. And it's Kepler's unofficial headquarters. Within the last 24 hours we traced a shipment from the airport to the hotel. If we're right, it's gold from Switzerland. Orders from London are to get it. Either the twins . . . "

"Or triplets," Sonny interrupted.

"Okay, all three. I doubt they're keeping it safe for Adolf."

"If I can help, I will."

Nodding, Mayhew said, "You, Karpov, another guy you'll meet tomorrow, and me. Got to act tout suite or the gold's a memory."

"What's the plan?"

Rosa sat silently, listening, catching words here and there. Something was brewing. That scared her. "What's going on? I thought you were done fighting."

"I haven't heard the plan yet. They might not be able to use me."

"Don't have to hear it to not like it. You get hurt . . . I'll break your neck!" Her tight smile was hard, mirthless.

Sonny laughed nervously.

36

Lisbon, 4 August 1944

The next day Sonny went to an empty Alfama flat, two flights up, in an old building. A single light bulb hung from the ceiling, and a sheet covered the window. Portuguese operatives working for MI6 lived in the other flats. Five rickety chairs were arrayed in a circle, four filled—Karpov, Mayhew, Sonny, and a new guy, Andrew Danielson. Thirty minutes later Jenny arrived. They would be undisturbed.

To Jenny, Mayhew said, "Thought I'd bring you in at the outset." He smiled with resignation. "You'd turn up anyhow."

"Good—you're trainable," Jenny responded.

He introduced them to Capt. Andrew Danielson, army commando, newly arrived from London. A big, barrel-chested man, he stood nearly two meters high, had a brush-cut hair and mustache. After shaking hands, he said, "Good to be part of the team. Your last job was a corker. This one's more dicey, being in Lisbon." Pausing, he made eye contact with each of them before continuing. "No problem—we'll pull it off."

"You know the plan?" Sonny asked.

"Helped draw it up." Danielson's smile was disarming.

Mayhew cleared his throat, getting their attention. "Let's get this show on the road. We've got a plant in the hotel, keeping an eye out." He looked at Sonny. "You willing to call on Kepler in his den? Feed him a story . . . "

"Wouldn't Kepler know about Baum in France?" Sonny interrupted.

"Not necessarily. You didn't mention him or Abwehr at the border. Everything is filtered through Berlin. The lines of communications are fraying, what with Yanks and us pushing back and

Soviets breathing down their necks. The story we've cooked for you has a credible thread," Danielson said, pointing for emphasis.

"A thread? I don't like the sound of that," Sonny objected. "All right, what do I tell him that doesn't get me shot?"

Danielson laughed. "A good cover story."

"Can hardly wait to hear," Sonny deadpanned.

"We," Danielson flicked a thumb in Mayhew's direction, "took you hostage, forced you at gun point to the mine. When our backs were turned, you took a runner—stole Goren's car."

"What happened to Goren and his sidekick?"

"Mostly the truth," Mayhew offered. "British agents rushed the house, shot Goren and his man, and sent the girl home. The hostage bit covers you if someone saw you at the mine."

"I held a gun on the guy at the mine . . . remember?"

"He's with us," Mayhew answered.

Sonny frowned. He didn't like it, but let it go. "Is Maria a problem?"

"She's with family north of Porto, well hidden."

"Where have I been hiding for the past year, should anyone ask?" Sonny asked, sarcastically.

"Spain."

"Really?" Sonny laughed. "Might as well toss my bullet-ridden body in a grave with 'dumbest man in Europe' on my headstone."

Karpov thought that very funny, Jenny not so much. She delivered her elbow into his ribs. He stopped laughing.

"You drove Goren's car to Spain. You had the documents and some money. You know the story—tell it. No lies." Danielson looked at Mayhew. "What's the town?"

"Zamora, where you burned the Merc. You stayed at a little place name of Pensione Zamora. It exists. One of our guys will take care of inquiries."

"For a whole year?"

"You were afraid to come back. Now, with the allies touring France, it's bleak for Adolf . . . " Mayhew smirked cruelly, as if squashing a cockroach.

"What do I want from Kepler?"

"Money! You need cash to get to Argentina, Cuba, anywhere."

"Assuming Kepler buys this load of shit," Sonny started, "what then? Ask him where the gold is buried?"

Karpov laughed, and this time so did Jenny.

"Sort of . . . " A thin smile crept onto Mayhew's lips.

Sonny was incredulous. "Goebbels' 'bigger the lie' crap?"

"Precisely," Mayhew agreed. "Too fantastic to conjure—he'll believe it."

"After a few hours, it won't make a difference—Bob's your uncle, we'll have the gold," Danielson added.

"If it's there," Sonny said.

"It is," Mayhew answered with assurance. "Don't know exactly where, but it is. Can't invade the hotel and poke around."

"Why not? If it's done right, no one would know," Sonny offered.

"Too risky," Mayhew answered. "You'll do it for us."

"And not risky for me?"

"Well . . . " Mayhew started.

"And what about the twins?" Sonny interrupted.

Mayhew smiled, pleased to get back on track. "Becker lives at the Avenida Palace, shows up at the bar every evening. Schwarz attends infrequently. He lives in Bairro Alto. We want the gold, but if we can get our hands on one or both of the twins and turn them?" Mayhew extended his hands palms up, offering another piece of the plan.

Danielson leaned forward, spoke to Sonny: "That gold was stolen from Jews and every country in Europe. That motivation enough?"

Over several hours they reviewed the plan, fleshing out Sonny's backstory. Jenny would be planted at the bar, her eyes and ears open and a pistol in her purse, drinking with any man willing to buy her one, She would stay until Sonny left. Mayhew, Karpov, and Danielson would be outside, nearby.

"Not close enough," Sonny said.

"Unavoidable," Mayhew answered.

———

Sonny told Rosa that an operation was planned, but he provided no specifics.

"Tell me."

"Can't."

"I thought you were done with this undercover work."

Sonny shrugged. "Guess not."

"It's your neck on the line, not Mayhew's. You're the honeypot setting a trap. I don't like it. He'll always come back for another mission, like Frank."

Sonny listened calmly, then said, "It's my job. I'm a soldier, no better than others."

"You're a spy whose cover is blown," she responded angrily.

"Okay, a spy. This operation takes advantage of my former position. That's all I can say."

"You've done your duty! Why risk it?"

Sonny shook his head. "We're still at war. Men and women do the impossible every minute of every day. You did. I've seen too much death to let this scare me. It will work."

"How many times did you cheat death? Three, four, probably more?" Her dark eyes bore holes in him, refusing to budge. "Years of separation and yearning . . . flushed away by misadventure?" She flicked her wrist dismissively.

Sonny lowered his head. "I have to go. I'm still part of the team."

"No. You volunteered. I heard you." She locked onto his eyes, refusing to let go. "To lose you now . . . " The tears slid down her cheek.

They stood separated by an impenetrable wall of silence.

"What do you want?" Rosa asked, breaking the silence. "The war will end soon. We have a future to plan."

Sonny nodded but said nothing.

"Look at me," Rosa said softly but firmly. "You risked so much for me, helping in ways I can never repay. I first fell in love with Sonny the smuggler, then with you. You were my first real love."

"Mine too."

"That kept my spirit and will strong, kept me in France when my parents left. Something changed when I found the Resistance, or it found me. It started in Paris, then flowered in Sare. I gained strength and confidence. For all the turmoil, I felt safe. I had trustworthy comrades, but I stood on my own, independent, no man to lean on. I became more like you: taking risks, liking it, and being alone. I had no complaints other than wanting you." She shrugged and her lips curled into a thin smile. "We're not that different now. But it's glaring at us."

The same question she had pondered in the little cabin in southern France poked through: How well did they know each other?

They had been separated longer than they were together—more than three and a half years. Could Kristallnacht, Oranienburg, and forged documents sustain them? She knew why Sonny had fallen for her and wasn't troubled by it. Back then she had used her femininity as a lure. That was part of her game. But no longer. They had moved quickly beyond infatuation to exploration to romance and, finally to commitment—too quickly? The usual thrust-and-parry had yielded to the exigencies of the moment.

Their courtship had been abbreviated by their lack of time. Coming together as one was love. Deep affection, caring, and longing—not just sexual attraction—were love. In Berlin, Sonny had pulled her through terrible times. That was love. But how deep was it?

"What's glaring at us?"

"We couldn't foresee the hardship or the success—how we would grow—separately. Can we forge a new life, move on with different needs and desires?" She hesitated. "I want a normal life, part of what I had in Sare. I miss it. I want the mundane chores that come with that kind of life—cooking, cleaning, washing, working. I want the scent of spring flowers, the noise of children playing. I want a family. Is that too much to ask?"

Sonny considered her question. Rosa had shed the fragility she showed in Antwerp. Her independence might lead to a different path—one without him? She had flourished. Were they being pulled in opposite directions?

"Are you asking too much?" Sonny repeated her question. "No."

His terse response troubled her, but she ignored it and asked, "What do you want?"

Sonny leaned forward, taking her hands in his. "I don't know what I want. I went through a lot, never gave up hope of finding you."

"You found me—now what?" She instantly regretted the flippancy of her response. "I'm sorry."

A thin smile crossed his lips. "That's okay. I ask that too. Remember when I told you about the high I got from smuggling?"

"I know exactly what you meant."

He nodded. "Of course, you do. On the run to Lisbon, back to France, finding you was my obsession. That kept me going—the work was secondary. Along the way, I got pretty good at it." He absently rubbed the scar on his leg, thought about the blown bridge, eluding capture, being shot. "People died. I was scared, but I kind of liked it and," he paused, "I like the excitement . . . danger . . . don't know if I can live without it."

"Doing what?" Frustration framed her question. "Another war when this one's over?"

He shrugged. "I don't know."

"I learned to garden, work in a winery, became an apprentice winemaker, though I have much to learn. Pretty good for a city girl." Her shrug was self-deprecating.

"Very commendable . . . for a city girl," Sonny teased.

"I said it because there's more to life than war. Thousands of soldiers will do it."

"More to life," he repeated, unconvinced.

"If you want to." She nodded. "Do your 'little of this, a little of that' until you find your footing. We'll cross the Atlantic . . . far away. I haven't seen my parents in four years. I need to know they're safe and secure. I want them to know I'm alive, that we're alive." She paused and nodded, as if struck by a sudden idea. "There's something else—an unease, a restlessness. Is it me or you?"

"It's me," Sonny shot back, "I'm bored. I've gone from intense work to nothing in a matter of days. My body has stopped, but my mind is still racing. I should be helping win the war. Injured soldiers return to action when they're healthy. Why shouldn't I?"

Rosa had no answer other than, "I don't want you to."

Sonny face sagged. "I know, but I can't turn my back on Mayhew. And I can't get the past five years out of my head." He whispered, "Don't know if I want to."

Rosa and death, alienation and war, had been his life, reduced to a blur—a dream from which he'd wake in a sweat—condensed to a list of headings: Kristallnacht and Rosa, death in Oranienburg, more death in Aachen, Antwerp and marriage and Sammy, Mons and losing Rosa, Wortel then Marquain, Kid and Victor, captain's greed, death march and long road to Dunkirk, Kid dead, saving Shannon, Rebecca dead hours before salvation, England and MI6, Lisbon and Wolfram, France and Rosa, now Lisbon and gold.

"You don't have to," Rosa agreed. "You can't pretend those years never existed. But I stopped being afraid and wiped Oranienburg off the slate. My fear is gone. I made amends, and it receded. Other things—Paris and Jean—stay with me, will never go away." She aimed her index finger at him. "Our measure is what we do next— you and me."

"You know what you want. I don't. I'm . . . " He stopped.

"What?"

"I don't know—hell! Pulled by my past."

"It should pull," she pointed toward some distant, unseen horizon, "but not enslave you. Since that horrible night you knocked on my door, we've known despair and flight, war, and survival. Our only period of calm was Antwerp—eight short months in 1939. You were my anchor. It shattered, and we were lost to each other for four long years. Hope kept us alive. Now here we are."

Sonny leaned in and kissed Rosa's forehead. "I lost a good friend and companion in Kid. I only knew Rebecca for a few days . . . seemed like I'd known her forever. We buried her father and Kid. Then I buried her. She was alone like me. You lost Jean and your friends in Sare. I lost you. Loss is all we knew."

"That's why it's important to plant new roots." Rosa felt dissatisfied and at loose ends. Now was the time to patch their lives together, but instead, the threads were unraveling. She needed finality, at least movement toward that new horizon. Sonny was trapped in another mission, yearning for his former life . . . something. Could he move on? Would he?

"My thoughts drift to Berlin," Sonny said.

Rosa grimaced but said nothing.

"Joseph and Emil were my family before you. And Karl and Polly...Johnny? I think about them . . . "

"Say you find them when the war ends—what could possibly be there for you and me? What? I wish your friends well, but that's over." Her voice was hard. She shook her head. "I can't go there."

"What about Jean, his son and daughter?"

"Hardly a day goes by that I don't think of him."

"Do you want to know?"

"Sometimes, but," she took Sonny's hand in hers and squeezed, "I can't go back. Thinking of it makes me anxious . . . afraid." She shivered. "It wouldn't, couldn't, be the same." Her frown made her nearly unrecognizable.

"My life was stolen from me," she went on. "I was 20 in '33. I can't and won't live among such people. Two years ago, Paris was soiled by the occupation, and that will always be so for me. Things can never be what they were—in Paris or Berlin or Lisbon. I carry Jean's fate on my shoulders. Maybe Alain and Catherine, Jacques and René, are alive." A faint smile came to her lips. "Annette will probably become a famous film star. No. I'm done with Paris and Berlin, same with Lisbon. I look forward, not back. What's lost can never be reclaimed."

"That's a little harsh. What about us?"

"Not us. I'm talking about . . . " What had she meant? She flushed.

"What?"

"I want us to be together, united as one. Germany and Europe are lost to me and should be for you, too."

Sonny nodded. "I understand."

"Do you?" She searched his face for an answer. "What's tugging at you? What's pulling you in a different direction?"

Sonny looked away.

"Am I right?" She persisted.

He looked at her and said, "I don't know. Everything is different. Change, change, change . . . We'll talk more after the operation."

"Then, let me help," she demanded with such vehemence it surprised her.

Sonny blinked. "What? After everything you said, you want in?"

She wasn't sure why she had said it and shrugged. "Don't you trust me?"

"Of course, I do, but we just . . . " He shook his head perplexed. "It's not my operation."

"Then ask Mayhew."

Without answering, he kissed her forehead. "I've got to go."

Her offer to help Sonny confused her as well. Where had it come from? She didn't know what to think. One thing was certain—she would not play the dutiful wife, sit still and wait, like a dog, tail wagging, begging for a bone. Her anger grew, but she needed to rein it in. She needed information . . . Jenny!

Five minutes later, Rosa left the flat. Walking gave her time to calm down and think. Her mind was moving, but she didn't like where it was taking her. Jenny and Roman worked for Mayhew. Like

Sonny, they accepted the risk. She was through with that life. Was she selfish? Damn right she was! Her safety and security were threatened. Goddamn war!

"One more mission, just one more, always one more," she repeated angrily under her breath. Damn Mayhew—just like Meyer! She stopped when Jenny's building came into sight and watched the door. A man exited: not Roman. Several minutes later, it opened again. This time it was Roman. She waited until he was gone.

She knocked twice, waited, then once—their signal. Footsteps . . . the door opened, a crack, then all the way.

"Rosa. What are you doing here?"

"Let me in!"

"I've got to go."

"What the hell's going on? I'm not leaving until you tell me."

Jenny sighed and let her in. "I can't."

Rosa stared at Jenny. She would have laughed if she weren't so angry. "You look like a . . . call girl." In a sleek red dress, Jenny had made up her eyes and face; her short hair was artfully waved. She was very attractive in a feral sort of way.

"At least a high-class one," she responded dryly.

"What's Mayhew got you doing?"

"Can't say—let it go, Rosa."

"Then I'll follow you . . . don't try to stop me."

"Oh, God," Jenny moaned. "If I tell you just enough, will you leave?"

"Maybe . . . "

Jenny shook her head. "Yes or no?"

"All right . . . all right—yes!"

"We're playing a game on Kepler at the Avenida Palace. I'm sitting at the bar while Sonny meets with him. That's all."

Rosa's eyes narrowed, her tongue traced the outline of her lips, thinking. "That can't be all."

"We've got the place covered—Roman, Mayhew, and another guy. It'll work. Go home and wait for Sonny."

"I don't like it."

Jenny shrugged. "Can't help that, but this is important. Don't interfere. You could get hurt."

37

Sonny strolled into the Avenida Palace at 8 PM, a short-barreled, semi-automatic Beretta pistol in a shoulder holster under his suit coat, just in case.

"Honeypot . . . walking into a trap . . . we have a future to plan," Rosa's words of foreboding swirled in his head. Not now, he muttered. Opening-night jitters, nerves raw . . . he had to focus and be in control. Then that familiar feeling coursed through his veins, his regular fix—an old friend come to visit.

Sonny walked past Jenny to the end of the bar for a good view. She looked fetching in her red dress. Their eyes met for a brief second. Someone, his back to Sonny, was giving her his full attention. Kepler hadn't arrived and Bitzler, his old drinking companion, was nowhere in sight. Alfonso—or was it Alfredo?—greeted Sonny like a long-absent friend.

Silently, Sonny reviewed his come-on to Kepler. Several minutes later, the man waddled into the bar. A scowl creased his face into two uneven halves, like a Picasso abstract. He sat down hard, which made his jowls shake. He was thoroughly unpleasant. Hasn't changed a bit, Sonny thought.

Sonny waited several minutes, drained his drink, then made his move. He stood without speaking. The surprise in Kepler's eyes was priceless, gave Sonny hope that he had a chance. Kepler looked older, more haggard. Losing a war and quarreling with the Gestapo does that.

Kepler's eyes widened to golf ball size. "Baum!" His voice was hoarse, hard for Sonny to gauge.

"That any way to greet an old friend?" Sonny feigned insouciance.

Kepler scowled, still not indicating on which side the coin would land. "Sit. Tell me about it."

Sonny took his time, telling the story as they had rehearsed.

Kepler kept on his poker face. "What the hell did you do in that piss hole for over a year?"

"Women were pretty," he shrugged, " . . . well, some were . . . and willing."

Kepler laughed without mirth.

"Food and wine cheap." Then Sonny's easy demeanor darkened. "And it beat facing those damn Brits again . . . don't like shooting, makes me nervous. They killed Goren and Schmidt. I was next.

"We anticipated the worst, but no bodies were found."

"Really?" That answered one question. Sonny leaned over the table for the punch line. "I picked my spot. When they looked the other way, I grabbed Goren's car and drove . . . to Spain."

Kepler stared for several beats. Sonny saw the gears of his brain engage. Then his lips moved. "Smart move . . . then you burned the car." His tone showed a tinge of respect.

"You knew about that?"

His head moved slightly in an apparent nod.

"Couldn't leave a trail."

He stared at Sonny, impassively, and drank. His pink tongue licked bulbous lips. "I don't know what to think, Baum. You disappeared . . . the thought occurred that you betrayed Goren to the English."

"The thought occurred," Sonny mimicked, "that my disappearing act could be interpreted that way," He looked away, then back, and smirked, "if you didn't think I was dead. After the Brits unloaded on Goren and Schmidt. I wasn't going to stick around." He held Kepler's steady gaze.

"You can understand my suspicions . . . " His heavy shoulders lifted several millimeters.

"Came back, didn't I?" Sonny countered, trying not to overact.

Kepler ignored that and said, "Goren's Gestapo friends were very angry when two of their men disappeared, presumed dead." His lips pursed into a thick oval, like a car tire. "Schwarz made a big stink with me and the PVDE." The corners of his mouth turned up slightly into what might have been a smile. "Angering the Gestapo isn't a healthy habit, but I found it refreshing—so, all was not in vain." A low rumble escaped Kepler's mouth. His jowls shook, eyes narrowing to slits, his face wrinkled to a prune—laughter?

"I told the Gestapo that if Goren and his man were presumed dead, so were you."

"Very noble of you."

Kepler's head tilted slightly forward in an abbreviated bow. "The ruckus died. Nothing splashed back onto the Abwehr resulting from their . . . fiasco. So . . . why come back now?"

"Handwriting's on the wall! Germany's an accordion squeezed from both ends—Soviets from the east, Americans in France. How much time, six months?" Sonny shook his head sadly. "Can't live in Spain. I need a safe haven—before," his face soured, "the Brits catch up to me. Salazar might not be so accommodating after Hitler."

Their talk turned to France and losses on the eastern front. Kepler was decidedly gloomy. "I will forge on—ever the good soldier! I have an agency to run and can't afford defeatist talk." He raised his glass and said sourly, "To the Führer." Then he came to the meat. "What do you want?"

Sonny rubbed the tips of his thumb and forefinger. "Money to finance my trip to the New World."

More rumbling from deep inside Kepler.

"Is that funny?"

"Why would I bankroll your flight?"

"For old times," Sonny smiled.

"Bah!" Kepler waved his hand dismissively.

"Money's gone, spent everything in Spain." Sonny leaned close. "Word on the street is that big bird carries gold to Lisbon." He paused. "And it's sitting in your favorite hotel." He rested the point of his index finger on the table, pointing down, to hell.

Kepler's eyes remained flat, until the word *gold* hit his ears. His eyes flickered just a millisecond. "Pay no attention—rumors."

"Did you know that Goren, besides being off his nut, was a thief, his boss a thief?" Sonny snorted a cynical laugh.

"Thieves?"

"Funny, when you think about it—Goren skimming from wolfram sales, only to have the Brits snatch it from him. Goren was screwed, really *screwed!*"

"How do you know?" Kepler asked.

"You didn't know?"

"One never knows for sure."

"Goren said they made deals with small miners. Unfortunately, we never got around to how it worked, but I can guess: Buy low, sell high, age-old axiom. Isn't that right?"

"Brilliant observation," Kepler said. "You know more than I."

"Do you know Goren's story?"

"Never met the man."

"More's the shame. He could have enlightened you on Einsatzgruppen. Ever heard of it?

Kepler's mouth tightened. He shook his head as if he didn't want to know. Sonny enjoyed watching Kepler squirm.

"A man in your position should have." Sonny shrugged. "A hellish, demented organization—Nazi killing spree." Suddenly feeling dirty, Sonny seethed. "I didn't sign on for that shit!" He barely controlled his anger.

"Neither did I."

"Didn't know or didn't sign on?"

"Both."

"You're army intelligence. You had to know. The army turned its back."

"Rumors, rumors, rumors! Einsatzgruppen was rumor. Our Abwehr chief, Canaris, is sympathetic to the British, another black rumor—backstabbing by Himmler."

"Whatever," Sonny said, coldly. "I want a piece to help me get over the guilt. Then I'll leave this pile of shit behind."

"What do you mean?

Sonny's laugh was harsh. "Don't play dumb—money, some gold bricks."

Kepler didn't answer. His eyes strayed across the room.

Sonny turned and looked at the nice-looking face Rosa had identified from the picture. "An ally? Ask him about Schwarz and the gold."

"Not one of mine—don't bring it up," Kepler said with finality, then lowered his voice. "Schwarz is his friend. I don't trust either."

Sonny tsk-tsked. "Traitors in your midst?"

Kepler did not respond.

"Are you in on it with those degenerates?" Sonny asked.

"No."

"You want to bust their little ring?"

"How can I do that and give you a piece?"

Sonny shrugged. "You're a smart man."

"With the Gestapo in on . . . " Kepler started.

"Schwarz, not the Gestapo," Sonny interrupted. "Himmler would cut off his balls, put them in his mouth, then shoot him—or worse, the Russian front."

Kepler shrugged. "Himmler's in Berlin. I have to deal with Schwarz. I want to live to the end of the war."

"A principled stand. And maybe near at hand."

Kepler ignored his quips.

"Does that mean the gold is going to disappear?"

Kepler's eyes moved over Sonny's shoulder. He turned to look. Height and weight were right—pleasant but ordinary, half-smiling face, about 35 . . .

"Heinrich, good evening," Becker said by way of greeting. His high-voltage smile lit up the corner of the bar, then rested on Sonny.

Kepler nodded. "Herman Becker meet Hans Baum."

The smile faded. "*The* Hans Baum?"

Sonny raised his palms heavenward. "I surrender—in the flesh."

Becker's mouth opened slightly as if he were to speak, but he didn't.

"Are you going to join us?" Kepler asked.

"No, thank you, I have to meet Albert in an hour." He nodded to Sonny. "Nice meeting you, Baum. I look forward to hearing your story."

They watched him leave.

"What's Becker doing in Lisbon?"

"Foreign ministry sent him from Berlin six months ago."

"What does he do, besides plot with Schwarz?"

"Snoops," Kepler answered, distracted.

"It would be a feather in your cap."

"What?"

"Safeguarding the gold for the Reich," Sonny said.

Kepler's silence ending the conversation, Sonny got to his feet and leaned over the table. "I set up a good intelligence chain for you, now

I want a stake in my future . . . Kepler? You hear me?"

He raised his eyes to meet Sonny's. "Come back tomorrow night." Kepler finished his drank and waved to Alfonso—or Alfredo—for another.

Sonny walked past the National Theater toward the Rossio. Within minutes Mayhew was abreast of him.

"Follow me." He led Sonny to a quiet alley. "Well?"

"Kepler seemed to buy it, but he could be stringing me along. He denied knowing about any wolfram pilfering. When I mentioned gold, he reacted—it was slight, but he didn't bite. Becker made a brief appearance then left to meet Schwarz." Sonny shook his head and frowned. "I don't know where the gold is."

"Tell me everything."

Sonny talked for 10 minutes.

"Damnit! The gold is at the Avenida Palace," Mayhew exclaimed. "Go to the room . . . wait for me with the others. I have to talk to my inside man."

It was near midnight when everyone assembled. Each reported, Danielson first: "A sentry in civilian clothes was posted outside, near the rear door. He walked back and forth, looking around, occasionally slipping inside."

"We handle him . . . no problem," Karpov said.

Sonny reported on his meeting with Kepler.

Jenny had let a blond embassy underling named Fritz buy her a drink. She nursed it, while he downed three and became talkative. "I asked how well he knew this wonderful hotel. He took it as a come-on. He had never been in a room, but he said he would gladly book one."

"I keel him," Karpov grumbled.

Danielson chuckled. "You'll get your chance."

"Settle down. Nothing happened," Jenny said. "I got him headed him in the right direction and asked about the rest of the hotel— banquet rooms, charming little nooks, the cellar, that sort of thing. He said it has a pretty lobby, otherwise nothing special. Then I struck . . . gold." She smiled. "A couple days ago, three of them moved heavy boxes of files into the cellar—'Nothing charming about that,' he laughed.

"I steered the conversation to Fritz's scintillating work at the embassy. Did you know that he actually shook hands with the head of the PVDE?" She groaned. "It took me 10 minutes to pry myself loose after Sonny left."

"Excellent!" Danielson exclaimed.

Everyone turned to Mayhew.

"Our game of hide-and-seek bears fruit." Mayhew rubbed his hand together, grinning. "My contact said one of dishwashers was in the cellar when boxes were carried in. Storage rooms are down there, but he didn't know which one. We found the gold. Jenny confirmed it."

"Fritz never said what was in them and how many," Jenny offered. "Didn't want to raise suspicion, so I didn't ask."

"They aren't files," Mayhew concluded.

"Super-secret stuff," Sonny said.

Mayhew waved that idea away. "Secrets are kept at the embassy."

"It's gold," Danielson agreed.

After talking all sides of the question, they agreed.

Mayhew pointed at Sonny. "Tomorrow night, demand gold and cash from Kepler. Tell him you think you know where it's hidden. We want to lure him into the cellar. Jenny will watch. If and when, she'll come and get us."

"If he refuses?" Sonny asked.

"Threaten to blow the whistle, to say he's in it with the twins."

" . . . Could get hurt," Rosa repeated as Jenny walked away.

Back at the flat, Rosa contemplated her next move. On a tourist map of Lisbon she traced three points of a triangle: Avenida Palace, Restauradores Square, the National Theater. She could watch the hotel from behind the big obelisk on the square or in the shadow of the theater and wait. She owed Sonny.

She arrived at the Rossio around 8:15 and walked to a spot in the alley behind the National Theater. Nobody familiar walked past or into the hotel. Around 9:00 Mayhew walked past the hotel and the station, then crossed the street to the Rossio. The sun had set; the twilight played with color. Soon it would be dark.

A man with a familiar gait strode from the hotel. Rosa sighed with relief. Sonny walked in the direction Mayhew had taken. When he was gone, she left for the flat.

Sonny did not arrive at the flat until last past midnight. He had taken precautions to avoid being followed. He was not.

Feigning sleep, Rosa asked groggily, "How did it go?"

"Fine."

"Done?"

"Tomorrow." He sounded fatigued. He kissed her and fell asleep.

38

Hotel Avenida Palace, Lisbon, the next evening

Kepler's table was unoccupied. Sonny took his place at the bar and ordered a drink. It was a few minutes after 8:00. Jenny was engaged in conversation—perhaps with Fritz? Kepler was a man of routine, but by 8:30 he had not appeared. Something had interfered with his nightly session in the bar. Another 15 minutes passed—but still no Kepler.

A well-dressed young man strode to the bar—blond, bland, obviously German. Sonny thought he was the same man who had interrupted his evening of fado the year before. He handed an envelope to Alfonso or Alfredo and gestured with his chin toward Sonny, said something, and left. Sonny held the sealed, unaddressed envelope, felt its heft, then ripped one end. Inside were Portuguese escudos, at least a thousand—not a fortune but a start. He smiled, his interest piqued.

There was also a handwritten note in German on plain white paper, presumably in Kepler's hand, that said, "Come down to the cellar—end of corridor. Now!"

Placing the envelope and its contents in the inside pocket of his suit coat, Sonny found Jenny's curious eyes. A faint flicker of undefined urgency passed between them. Jenny's face momentarily morphed into a question mark. Sonny shrugged, vexed. He picked up his glass, his thoughts firing like pistons in a throttled engine. No choice but to do as Kepler instructed. At least he knew where the gold was stashed. But had Kepler just admitted his misdeed, or was Sonny being lured into a trap? Bland, blond delivery boy lying in wait?

. . . Sonny sighed. Rosa may have been right. Fear swirled in his

362

head until he grabbed it by the throat and squeezed. He felt as if he were in a dark alley near the docks. Somehow that was comforting.

Had someone else—Becker, Schwarz, or both—written the note? Cash led to Kepler, though that did not eliminate Becker or Schwarz. Any of the three, or all or them, might still stumble onto the scene. Sighing, Sonny chewed one nut, then another, and stared into his glass. He should have listened to Rosa. He'd done his duty, finished with clandestine service, nearly died, and beat the odds . . . Always another mission. Would he die now in a stinking Nazi hotel cellar?

He was in too deep. Have another drink, calm down. No, he needed to run on all cylinders to meet whoever awaited him. Sonny felt the Beretta's weight and relaxed a little. Raising his eyes to find Jenny, he found her gone. Jolted, he tasted bile and alcohol and grimaced. He drained his glass. Jenny was smart. She must be in the loo . . . or she had left for him to find her . . .

He scanned the lobby. There, by the elevator, a splash of red—Jenny waited. The man at the front desk looked up and smiled, then returned to what he was doing. An older couple, well dressed, sat in two armchairs—the man dozed, and the woman read a newspaper. No one else in sight. Quiet.

Sonny walked to the elevator and stood facing the closed door. Carved cherubs on the molding smiled at him. Jenny ignored him.

"A note from Kepler. Meet him in the cellar, end of the corridor—now," he whispered and walked away. He glanced toward the grand staircase with swooping balustrade leading to the mezzanine, opposite the entrance. Leather club chairs hunched, arms thick like wrestlers, in intimate groups, empty but for the old couple. He walked toward the dining room, his steps muted by rich, red oriental rugs. Light twinkled from ornate crystal chandeliers. A seductive rainbow of cut flowers sat atop a round table in the middle of the lobby. He paid no attention to either.

The kitchen was at the rear, where he would find the steps to the cellar. He thought about the sentry. Nazis were so damn paranoid. He glanced into the dining room, half full of German embassy staff, Gestapo, and Abwehr spies. He came to two dark wooden doors. Suddenly one opened, as if on cue. Sonny jumped in surprise. A man dressed like a waiter emerged carrying a tray with food and drink. He walked to the elevator and pushed the call button.

Sonny's hand was on the knob of the door that the waiter had exited. He looked back. The front-desk clerk's head was down, the elderly couple was lost in the fog of old age, a red dress floated toward the exit. Rugs, chandeliers, cherubs, and colors faded. He focused on his mission.

Sonny took a deep breath, then opened the door and slipped into a hallway. Voices, clanging pots, and laughter could be heard but not seen. Two doors opened onto the hall—on the right was a small office. The other was to a pantry with a door at the other end.

At the end of the hall, he peered around the corner. A double door led outside and opposite a big opening—the kitchen. In between, shelves filled the walls. The clatter was loud. Beyond stood another opening—stairway to the cellar? Was the sentry waiting in the cellar, or had Kepler muzzled his hound?

Sonny moved to the head of staircase. No sentry in sight. Light from the hall illuminated the steps, casting his shadow. Another light, at the bottom, seeped up toward him—easier to see and to be seen. He turned the switch, preferring darkness, and silently descended. Ambient light barely illuminated a big, open room. Dust motes danced on the floor. He saw vague outlines of cans, boxes, and kitchen miscellany—nothing of interest. The light from a single bulb at the far end of a corridor running the length of the hotel beckoned.

Moving farther into the dead end, Sonny felt uneasy. The sounds from the kitchen grew faint. Had he acted impulsively? Should he have found Mayhew or Danielson? Kepler might not be alone. Jenny knew! Reassured a little, he sighed with resignation.

Opposing doors stood at attention like good soldiers about every three meters down the hall. Turning every knob slowly, he found most of them unlocked. He looked inside, staring into darkness. About halfway down the corridor—voices! He froze, unable to decipher words. Moving closer, he heard a man speaking German.

Momentarily staggered by a jolt of fear, Sonny kept going, his solitary comfort the Beretta. Silently he moved until he stood at edge of the doorway.

"Where the hell is he?" It was Kepler.

"I saw the envelope in his hands." Another voice—the bland underling.

Sonny took several breaths, clenched his fists, and entered the room. Squinting from the harsh light, he said, "Sorry it took me so long." Smiling, appearing calm, he glanced around the sparse room, about four meters wide and five meters deep. Boxes were neatly piled against the back wall; he quickly counted 20. A spread eagle and swastika were stamped on every box.

Kepler turned to his underling. "Leave us." Then: "You got your money."

Sonny nodded. "A nice start."

Kepler emitted a low, rumbling laugh, devoid of humor. "What's your game, Baum, if that's who you are?"

"Who I am?" His surprise was only half-feigned. "Hans Baum, the guy that got you good intelligence. Did you forget?" Sonny's laugh was cynical. "I need money. You've got some." What game was Kepler playing?

"Nobody except at the highest levels knows about the gold. What's your access? You working for that prick Schwarz?"

Sonny's dumbfounded expression was utterly sincere. He was losing ground, had to catch up. "Schwarz? Hook up with the Gestapo? You think I'm crazy?"

"How then?"

"Rumors abound—you said so yourself. Gold has been coming through Portela for a couple years. Big shots like you don't lift and deliver. People watch, listen . . . add two and two." Sonny shrugged.

Kepler stared, his lips puffing in and out, like fish he had seen at the Berlin aquarium. "Baum, you gave us moles in England—then nothing. Berlin had a wet dream, then nothing but shit."

"Not my fault."

"I started to wonder . . . well?"

"Berlin was happy, gave me a bonus."

"Everything about your story is too convenient. Living in England, disappearing after Goren and his man were shot. And a year in Spain—bah!"

Sonny laughed as if to say the notion was ridiculous. "Believe what you will, but I want out!" Sonny gestured toward the boxes. One was open. "How about I fill my pockets?" Sonny took a step.

"Go to hell!" Kepler pulled a pistol from his pocket.

Sonny stared at the round black eye of a Luger.

"Whoa!" Sonny raised his hands. "Easy, Kepler. Let's call it even.

I don't want to die over this."

"Give me the envelope," Kepler demanded. "You're a small man, playing with the big boys, Baum—way over your head. You think you can make demands, then walk away?"

Sonny reached into his coat as if for the envelope. He tried to think of a response as he fingered the Beretta's grip. The sound of footsteps in the hall grew louder. No effort was being made to hide the approach. Couldn't be Mayhew and company.

His pistol still pointed at Sonny, Kepler shifted his gaze to the door and the soft, steady rhythm of the footfalls. Sensing opportunity, Sonny chopped Kepler's wrist with the edge of his hand. Fat and slow, Kepler dropped the pistol. It clattered to the floor,

Groaning, he muttered, "Asshole."

Standing in the doorway, hands on hips—not Mayhew or Danielson but Becker. His gaze drifted from Kepler to Sonny, then found the pistol. "What drama unfolds?"

"None of your fucking business," Kepler growled, rubbing his wrist.

"Heinrich, I'm afraid it is." Then, turning to Sonny: "And you?"

Sonny stared at Becker, trying to make sense of the confrontation. His mind raced round the track, trying to figure who was stealing the gold. The deal with Kepler was off. Becker faced off with Kepler. All bets were off.

"We . . . we had a deal," Sonny stammered.

Kepler laughed derisively.

Sonny explained: "Kepler said to meet him in the bar. He wasn't there. I got an envelope with money and a note summoning me here." He waved his head toward Kepler. "He pulled the Luger. We heard you coming. I knocked it out of his hand."

No one moved, the pistol, like a lost glove, lay were it had fallen.

"What deal, Heinrich?" Becker asked. He took a package of cigarettes from his pocket and lit one without offering one to the others. He exhaled; the smoke drifted to the ceiling.

"Baum's lying. He told me about the gold. Nobody else knew. He got the information from someone—English or one of ours, a traitor. He wants gold."

Becker looked from Kepler to Sonny, dragged deep, exhaled, and asked, "How did you know about the gold?"

"Rumors of gold, lots of it, coming through Switzerland from Germany. People at the airport see, and they talk." Sonny rubbed his forefinger and thumb together. "A shipment came to the hotel. It added up."

"Clever fellow . . . " Becker started

"Or British plant," Kepler finished.

Sonny shook his head. "Its not hard to figure. War's lost. Berlin's a pile of rubble. Gold is all that's left of value."

Becker shook his head and said to Kepler, "If Baum's right, what are you doing down here?"

"Making sure the gold's safe from people like you," Kepler snarled, distaste curling his thick lips.

"Questions but no answers. Gentlemen, we're going in a circle taking us nowhere." Becker leaned on the doorframe, sucking smoke. He pointed to the boxes. "When did that shipment arrive?"

"Don't play dumb, Becker," Kepler sneered. Then, pointing a finger at Becker, he said, "You're stealing the gold."

Becker laughed.

"One of you is," Sonny agreed.

"What's your story, Baum?" Becker turned on Sonny. "First, you're part of the wolfram operation. Then Brits steal the wolfram. Three men, including you, disappear, presumed dead. But here you are in a cellar full of gold. Makes for a good story but not one that would endear you to Berlin."

"I told Kepler what happened with the wolfram. Brits killed Goren and Schmidt, took me hostage. I got away in Goren's car, drove to Spain, and stayed there. Bad luck on the wolfram deal, but I survived. I admit asking Kepler for money," he shrugged, "maybe a few bars of gold. I got a future to think of." Sonny needed to talk, give his guys time to get there.

"Hmm," Becker hummed, his head, moving slowly side to side, his gaze never leaving Sonny's face, considering. "May be the truth, but Kepler *is* a thief. I was sent by Berlin to monitor the gold—too much pilfering, enough to rouse suspicion. Kepler's the man. We have proof."

"Bah!" Kepler bellowed. "You have nothing. You're an errand boy for a middling Wilhelmstrasse bureaucrat. Get out of here, both of you!"

Becker laughed. Kepler's eyes bulged with anger, and his arms pumped as if he were running in place. A vein in his temple engorged with blood. He stammered and stuttered, but no words came. His paroxysm sent him dangerously close to the edge. His heart might explode.

Then, moving remarkably fast for a fat and sedentary, middle-aged man, Kepler fell to the floor. Grabbing the pistol before either of the other men could respond, he fired with a terrible blast. Sonny cringed. The bullet ricocheted around the room. The stench of cordite filled his nostrils. He hadn't been hit—no one was. Still, they were all surprised.

 Kepler sat on the floor, his breath labored, pistol pointed at Becker's chest.

Sonny's hand remained on the Beretta, his arms crossed over his chest. Had anyone heard the gunshot? He glanced at Becker, who was smiling with unnerving calm, as if he were in charge. Then Sonny saw his pistol, pointed at Kepler. He could have made it a trio, but he didn't know where to point.

Sonny nearly laughed at the surreal sight. Kepler might fail to see the humor, take it as another insult, and shoot him—an unsatisfactory outcome. When the ringing in his ears receded, he asked dryly, "Now what, gentlemen?"

"Drop the gun, Kepler," Becker said with conviction but little authority.

"So you can shoot me?"

"There has to be a solution," Sonny said hopefully. Maybe Mayhew, Danielson, or Karpov—or all three—were in the corridor ready to spring. The longer the stalemate lasted, the greater peril he was in, though either might shoot at any time. Keep talking.

"This Mexican standoff gets us nowhere," Sonny said.

"What the hell's that?" Kepler asked.

"This!" Sonny gestured with one hand toward both men.

"Baum's right," Becker said, as he scratched his cheek. "Heinrich, let's agree to disagree about your stealing Reich gold." He shrugged. "Neither of us wants to die. Do you want to die, Baum?"

"Not today!"

"And you, Heinrich?"

Kepler did not answer.

"Then we should drop our pistols. I'll back out with Baum and leave you in the cellar. A gunfight solves nothing."

"I want safe passage to South America," Kepler demanded. "Can you do that?"

Becker seemed to consider Kepler's request. It was quiet—the only sound Kepler's heavy breathing and the throbbing vein in Sonny's temple, boom, boom.

In the corner of his eye, Sonny saw a figure fill the doorway. Help had arrived—Mayhew? Another pistol shot rang out. Kepler crumpled into a heap. Into the room stepped Obersturmbannführer Albert Schwarz.

39

In the cellar, Hotel Avenida Palace, Lisbon, later that evening

Sonny held his breath, waiting for another shot. None came, but the ringing in his ears was intense. He exhaled slowly and looked down at the heap on the floor. Kepler wasn't moving.

"Didn't want to kill him . . . " Schwarz stopped abruptly, his words cannonballing rat-tat-tat: didn't-want-to-kill-him. No remorse, more like regret at having to do it himself. He holstered his pistol under his suit jacket and lit a cigarette, offering one to Becker. Within seconds, a fog off the Tagus River filled the room.

Sonny's ears pricked to Schwarz's reedy, alto-clarinet voice, deeper than he remembered, probably because of the smoking. He had last heard it at the Belgian border, more than five years earlier. The Gestapo was on the prowl for the killer of three of their cohorts, for *him*. Walking head down, collar up, Sonny had not seen his face that day, but the voice, gestures, and dancing cigarette were his. Hearing it now, not entirely unexpectedly, was jarring.

Then a second image came to mind: Being trapped in another claustrophobic, dingy cellar, months before the Belgian border incident—the boxes of stolen Jewish property stashed on Thiemann Strasse, Berlin. The gold bullion in Lisbon stunk of the same rancid game.

"Standoff. No choice. What took you so long?" Becker said.

"Loose ends . . . " waving a hand, Schwarz created a jagged stream of smoke.

"What about the body?" Becker asked anxiously.

"One of my men will . . . " Schwarz said, his words dripping with distaste, ". . . deal with him. Let's secure the room . . . get the hell out of here."

"Oh!" Becker's eyes widened. He had forgotten Sonny. He spoke, almost as an afterthought, "Albert, this is Baum." He pocketed his pistol; Kepler's Luger remained on the floor forgotten, as was the dead man.

Years of fear and rage clogged Sonny's throat. He nearly gagged. Primal instinct told him, "Kill or be killed." His arms still crossed his chest, his right hand near the Beretta. He met the eyes of his former friend and nemesis. Heart churning, *chug, chug,* like a locomotive, he managed, "Hello, Albert, long time no see." He sounded far too casual for a man walking in a lion's den.

Albert Schwarz's big, unblinking eyes, stared without comprehension. His face was a mask of perplexity, lips silently moving. His hands suspended in midair, the cigarette a half-meter from his mouth, an airplane stalled in flight.

"What?" Becker looked from one to the other.

"We knew each other in Berlin—before Adolf," Sonny said.

Albert Schwarz nodded, nonplussed. His discomfiture allowed Sonny to relax slightly, though he stayed on guard, fingering the Beretta. The puddle of blood grew at his feet. He waited, less than sanguine about his options.

Red ember glowed from Albert's cigarette. Life returned, and his lips pursed as a plume of blue-grey smoke drifted toward Sonny. He seemed contemplative rather than dismissive.

"It's great you two are having a reunion, but we've got a corpse at our feet," Becker said with some irritation. "Albert?" He snapped his fingers several times.

Albert Schwarz's eyes went from Sonny to Becker. "I said my men would deal with it." His annoyance flared, a sudden squall threatening to engulf them.

"All right, all right! Then let's get out of here."

"What the hell?" Albert said to Sonny. "This is nonsense." His eyes widened, his mouth a perfect circle, like another of those fish at the Berlin aquarium. "Unless . . . "

"Sell to the highest bidder. You're not the only ambitious guy in the world," Sonny shot back.

Albert sucked hard on the cigarette, exhaling lazily. "They let you go at the mine. You were on the inside. Baum?" His high cackle was like a demented chicken. "Hell!" His ejaculation startled Sonny.

To Becker, Albert said, "His name is Sonny . . . a Jew from Berlin's Mitte . . . can't remember his real name—no matter."

Neither man moved. Becker might as well have been a store mannequin.

"Now what?" Sonny asked.

"It's up to you." Albert shrugged. "And good to see you too, Sonny." Insincerity tinged with menace. Then he sighed, tired of the confrontation.

Mixed message received. Now it was Sonny's hand to deal. "Too bad about Goren. He was a real *prince*." Sonny spread the sarcasm. "Told me all about Einsatzgruppen." To Becker, "You know about those mobile killing units out east—slaughtering women, children, old people, and men? Kepler pretended not to know."

"Shut up," Albert said without conviction.

Sonny ignored him. "Were you following the Wehrmacht out east, stoking fires of annihilation? If I had to guess, killing innocents for the glory of the Reich pushed Goren over the edge." Sonny snarled the last words as his anger grew. He took a deep breath, calmed somewhat, and continued. "You know who killed Goren?"

"What is this—20 questions? The fucking British killed him!"

Sonny laughed, then abruptly cut it off. "Wrong! Schmidt killed Goren, protecting the girl. Goren was a raving lunatic, waving his pistol, firing it in the house, terrorizing the girl. If he hadn't I would have."

"You're a real gentleman." Albert smirked. "Goren had his . . . problems, but he was a good man. Why should I believe you?"

Sonny shrugged. "True enough." His eyes swept the room. "Your word is gold."

Albert's laugh was mocking. "Very good!"

Becker's eyes moved from one to the other. His mouth opened, but he was interrupted.

Another figure filled the doorway—Kepler's bland, blond assistant, who had delivered the note to Sonny, had returned. "When do . . . " he started, then stopped, surprised by the crowd. He looked from one man to the other, then to his boss on the floor. Stepping back, he suddenly had a pistol in hand. "Who . . . ?" His voice, hard as the concrete floor, reverberated in the small space.

"Who?"

"Good for you, loyal to your boss," Sonny said, followed with an audible sigh. He might have inserted, your "crooked" boss, but he refrained. "Obersturmbannführer Schwarz shot him."

"No, Klaus, don't believe Baum or whatever his name is. Kepler was going to shoot me," Becker pleaded. "The Obersturmbannführer saved my life."

Klaus looked at Schwarz with cold contempt. "You Gestapo bastard!"

Rosa, dressed in black, melted into the night, or so she imagined. Praça Dom Pedro IV, the street circling the Rossio, was well lit, but she hid in the shadows. It was 8:30 on a lovely evening, warm in the twilight. Couples strolled past, a reminder of what she and Sonny might be doing. Shrugging away disappointment, she glanced around the corner toward Pedro IV, frozen above the swirling, vertigo-inducing surface of the square. A fine mist blew from the fountain.

She wanted a weapon, settled for a small paring knife, having demonstrated her proficiency with one six years earlier. It was in a skirt pocket, not stuck on a tabletop. She smiled wickedly. Sonny carried a pistol, and she figured the others all had one too. She took what was at hand. Her gaze returned to the hotel entrance. Sonny and Jenny were inside.

No one she recognized went in or out of Avenida Palace. She might have seen Mayhew at the edge of the square, walking quickly toward the river. But he disappeared amidst the strollers, before she could be sure.

A splash of crimson against a sandy coastline caught her eye. Jenny, in a dancer's perfect posture, was at the hotel entrance, looking right, then left and back. She was too far away to read her expression, but she was looking for someone—Mayhew? Rosa resisted the urge to call out.

Jenny walked toward the Rossio. Why would she leave the hotel? Had something happened? Or was it part of the plan? She threaded her way quickly between people. When the cluster parted—there was no Jenny. Rosa ran toward the spot and turned in a circle. She had disappeared like a puff of smoke. Now what?

She could watch from the outside, stay hidden, or stroll the Rossio and look for Mayhew and Jenny. Where was Roman? Forget the new guy—he could be standing next to her. She had to act. But what good was she outside? Something important might happen, might be happening now—inside.

She could walk into the bar . . . take a quick look . . . back out. She would be French if anyone talked to her. Her eyes fixed on the door. She felt the lure and liked that idea—poke around, learn something. She hesitated. If Sonny or Mayhew saw her, she'd be sent home. She might wreck the operation.

She was conflicted. She had wanted Sonny to quit. Getting a cold shoulder didn't sit well. She wanted a piece of the action, part of the risk. Memories of Paris, of echoing footfalls in the cavernous Pantheon, of stolen documents passed by a stranger before it turned dark, of fleeing ahead of the police, of Jean unable to escape. Her eyes stung. She closed them tight. Not here, not now. She pulled her lower lip until it hurt, focusing on her task, determined.

"Go!"

She was inside the hotel, energized but wary. Her eyes quickly raked over the lobby's opulence and found the bar. From the doorway she glanced from table to table then across the long bar. It was half full, with more men than women. Several men had their backs to her . . . but no Sonny. The bartender smiled at her. She smiled back, shook her head, and shrugged as if her companion had not yet arrived, then returned to the lobby to wait. Her eyes were drawn to the crystal chandelier, glistening like a thousand little suns, as she considered her next move.

A movement diverted her attention. A young, fair-haired man approached her. Averting her eyes, she pretended to study the enormous flower arrangement on the table beneath the chandelier.

As he passed her, he said, "Boa noite [good evening], senhorita."

"Boa noite," she repeated softly. Turning, she watched him disappear behind a door, one of several.

Sonny hadn't come out the front door; perhaps he had gone before she arrived? That might account for Jenny's behavior. Or he might have used the rear door, leaving alone or with someone. She rejected both options. He must be in the hotel, in a guest room or behind the door the young man had opened. Feeling silly for being suggestible, but . . . Needing to think, she headed for a comfortable leather chair beckoning from the corner.

————

"What now?" Sonny asked Klaus. He needed to keep him talking, give his friends time.

Albert looked from Sonny to the young man. "You going to shoot me? Shoot Becker? Then," he gestured toward Sonny, "Baum . . . Sonny, whatever he calls himself? Your boss was stealing gold—he was a crook for Christ's safe. Don't be a fool. Put down the pistol."

"Who the hell are you to lecture me?" Spittle sprayed from Klaus's lip, and he lunged, nearly hitting Schwarz with the barrel. "Skimming off wolfram. Goren was just your last partner. Baum barely got away—he's no better, slithering back, hands out." His lips curled in disgust as he turned on Becker, pointing the pistol, menacingly. Becker flinched.

"And you sanctimonious piece of shit. A mole sent by Berlin," his laugh was harsh, "to *investigate*. You're stealing gold with him." He cocked his head toward Schwarz.

Sonny was confused. He thought Kepler the culprit, now Schwarz and Becker. Was everyone stealing gold? Time was running out, and there were too many guns in the room. Where the hell was Mayhew?

"Mind if I smoke?" Albert asked and reached inside his jacket.

Klaus jerked and thrust the pistol at Albert's head.

"Easy, boy," Albert cautioned.

"Don't call me boy." Klaus's nostrils flared at the perceived insult.

Albert slowly opened his coat, just enough to show the top of a cigarette packet but not his holstered pistol.

"Remember he's got a pistol," Sonny said.

"That's right," Klaus mumbled. "Put it on the floor, slowly . . . And yours," he motioned to Becker.

"What about his?" Schwarz gestured toward Sonny.

Klaus waved the pistol. "Well?"

Sonny shrugged, then placed the Beretta carefully on the floor, safety off.

Three pistols lay at their feet. Klaus couldn't kill them all with one shot. Who would be first?

Becker spoke. "Someone will call the police. Then what?"

"You and Schwarz hang for my uncle's murder." That caught everyone's attention.

"Uncle?" Sonny murmured. "Way to go, Albert," he goaded, his words reverberating like an earthquake.

Albert took a drag from his cigarette. His lower lip dropped into a sneer, then retreated to accommodate a perfect smoke ring. "You knew what he was doing—you're his accomplice." His eyebrows lifted, creating deep pleats in his brow—question answered before it was asked.

Rosa stared at the door the young man had opened and closed. Kneading her hands, she realized how much in the dark she was about the operation. Her sudden appearance could upend the cart. For an instant, she contemplated returning to the flat—to acting the dutiful wife.

Maybe the guy who went through the door worked for the hotel. She recalled his greeting, his accent—Portuguese or hint of hard Teutonic German? Could have been German. What was the worst that could happen? Act flustered at opening a door she shouldn't have, stammer in French. Wouldn't be the end of the world. After all, Lisbon wasn't occupied Paris.

Looking over her shoulder, Rosa saw the front desk clerk busy doing something. The old couple was out of sight. Several guests had taken the elevator. The dining room was busy, people coming and going. Turning the doorknob, she pushed the door and quickly entered the hallway, falling against the closed door. She was nervous, her breath shallow. The faint sound of activity must be from the kitchen. Ignoring the doors in the hallway, she walked toward the sound to investigate, then stopped and retreated. Check the doors—nothing.

Another hallway led to the rear door and an opening, no two openings. A man! Rosa slid back into the darkness and peered around the corner. A suit had come from outside and disappeared into the nearest opening. He was bigger than the one in the lobby and not kitchen staff. Security guard? Cop? The guy returned, chewing on something. His head turned, and she heard, "Obrigado [thank you], tchau." She clearly heard his German accent. His arm rose in a backwards wave, and he was out the door, gone.

Sensing opportunity, Rosa walked toward the kitchen, stopped short, looked inside. The Lisboetas ate a late dinner, so the kitchen was busy, no one just standing around. Sonny wasn't washing dishes. She smiled at that absurdity, then walked quickly to the second opening. No one called out to her—she must not have been seen.

She stood at the top of a stairway. Below was the dark cellar. She turned the light switch on the wall next to her. A bulb flared to life, illuminating the area at the bottom. Chewing on her lip, she considered her next move. Was someone down there? Then her feet moved down the steps to the bottom. Nobody was there.

Rosa saw boxes of produce and kitchen paraphernalia. Standing among bowls, plates, large pans, pots, she was in her father's shop near Alexanderplatz, Berlin, 1935. A funny feeling in her chest turned to anger. Her father, forced out of business, had lost everything. She silently cursed. Then her ears twitched to the sound of a voice. Her head swiveled, but no one was in the room. Opposite the stairs, a long corridor led to a light. It seemed far away. Instinctively, like a moth, she moved toward the light. Then she heard another voice, muted, unintelligible. A foggy haze spilled from a room at the far end of the corridor. Walls, floor, ceiling, and doors appeared as vague outlines along the long hallway. She was looking toward the object of Sonny's mission—had to be. She needed to hear what they were saying. That meant moving closer. Cautiously she entered the hallway. She moved silently, stopping, slowly turning doorknobs, then stepped inside an open one, and waited. Repeating the process, she worked her way quietly down the hall, light on her feet. Her breath was shallow, her senses on high alert. She lost track of time. Then she was 5 meters from the light spilling out of the last room.

She hadn't considered what to do when she got close. A little knife for a weapon and in too deep to turn around. Had she seen those work tools in one of the rooms? Which one? Tiptoeing back, she opened one, then a second door . . . the outline of a bulb. She pulled a string: a blast to the eyes of white, colored around the edge. Then she saw a bench displaying screwdrivers, pliers, hammer, wooden mallet, and pry bar. The hammer and mallet were unwieldy. She lifted the steel pry bar, swung it, and liked its heft. Softly tapping her new weapon against an open palm, she pondered her next move.

Klaus ignored Albert's accusation, giving credence to his charge. Crow's feet crept around the corners of his eyes and his mouth formed a hard circle. Rivulets of perspiration trickling onto his brow, he seemed to be losing his impulse control.

Annoyed, Albert pushed and jabbed. Sudden movement—an insult, a fly landing on his forehead—might cause him to pull the trigger. Sonny had to lower the temperature. He stood on the periphery—but for how long?

Klaus's hand, holding the pistol, trembled. His mouth opened as if he were about to speak.

"Run out of lies?" Albert prodded the injured animal with a stick.

"Damnit . . . end this!" said Becker, another forgotten man.

"He's right," Sonny agreed. "We leave the room . . . all live to see another day." He was improvising.

Albert's cackle was derisive. "Nice try, Jew boy!"

Klaus turned on Sonny.

Sonny shrugged. "It's a little chilly in here. Pay no attention to Albert. He's trying to distract you. You got bigger things to worry about." He gestured toward the boxes.

"That true, Baum?" Klaus asked.

"How does your demented Nazi ideology resolve this petty squabble? Got your copy of *Mein Kampf* handy? Or handle it like Goren's Einsatzgruppen? Schwarz was part of that—right, Albert? Probably poisoned cats and dogs for fun when you were a kid."

"Shut up!" Albert snapped.

"I don't give a shit . . . " Klaus's eyes flickered, " . . . you're a Jew, you work for the Brits . . . a fucking spy. Fooled us once, not again." He set his jaw and nodded, as if that answered a question.

"Of course, he's a Jew," Albert answered, amused by the turn of events. "He sold . . . what did you call it, Sonny?" He snapped his fingers. "A little of this, a little of that." His tone was mocking. "From a warehouse full of Jews. Right Sonny?"

Klaus's gaze flitted from Sonny to Albert, back and forth in a manic dance, his fuse shortening. Becker twitched, scared. Albert's amused smirk spoke his indifference to death. Sonny represented their only point of agreement.

––––––––––

Womblike darkness enveloped Rosa as she pulled the cord. She found the doorknob and pulled on it slowly. Through the crack, she saw an empty corridor with the same hazy light seeping at the end.

She silently moved on tiptoe, two doors farther. She turned the knob, opening the door soundlessly. She heard a man's—not Sonny's—voice. Quickly inside, she left the door slightly ajar, her ear against the jam, eavesdropping as she had on her parents as a child.

First voice: " . . . sanctimonious piece of shit. A mole sent by Berlin," then laughter, "to *investigate*. You're stealing gold with him."

Silence for several beats, then another voice, "Mind if I smoke?" and the same voice again, "Easy boy."

First voice, again: "Don't call me boy."

A third voice said, "Let's come to an agreement. We can't stand here forever. Someone will call the police. Then what?"

"You and Schwarz hang for my uncle's murder." The first voice again. That one sounded familiar—the voice in the lobby.

The words were muffled, hard to understand, but *murder* and *uncle* came through clearly. Whose uncle—in that little room?

The second voice: "Obviously, you knew what he was doing—that makes you an accomplice."

She closed and leaned against the door. Someone was dead…not Sonny. He was bulletproof, but he was in there. Fear crept in under the door and surrounded her in the dark—like in that warehouse in Oranienburg, the dead Gestapo. Sweat gathered on her brow, dripped from under her arms onto her sides. She shivered. Her thoughts caromed, collided. Several deep breaths calmed the traffic in her head. Finally, it slowed to a crawl. "Good," she whispered.

Then a plan, of sorts, came to her. "No retreat. Get closer." Where were Mayhew, Roman, and the other guy?

She tightened her grip on the pry bar, feeling more in control. Nazis killing each other was good—they should all die! She smiled bitterly. Her hand shook as she slowly pulled the door open. She slid silently to the next to last door across from *the* room. Momentarily frozen by shadows on the floor, she grabbed the knob. That the door might be locked hadn't occurred to her. It opened with a creak—a barking dog in the silent night. Cringing, she squeezed inside.

Slowly closing the door brought a mournful wheeze. Her senses sharpened by fear and exhilaration, she pressed her ear to the door. No sound penetrated it. She would wait, for what she was unsure.

40

In the cellar, Hotel Avenida Palace, later yet

Sonny needed to take the focus from himself. A faint groan came from the corridor.

"What's that?" Klaus rasped.

Albert shrugged. "Take a look." He lit another cigarette.

"Kitchen worker at the other end," Becker offered.

Albert flicked his wrist impatiently, launching smoke in a haphazard pattern. "Go look!" he shouted, breaking an uneasy silence. His eyes narrowed.

Sonny jerked involuntarily. Klaus flinched and chewed his lip. Gestapo training in action, Sonny figured.

"Jumpy . . . hearing things?" Albert asked, disdainfully. Taking his time, he took another drag then exhaled an extravagant smoke ring. "If anyone's out there, he's one of my men. Be careful, Klaus."

Becker unbuttoned his collar. Klaus gulped and waved his pistol. Albert smirked. All were scared but Albert, which scared Sonny even more. Kepler's bloated body, unsubtle reminder of mortality, was temporarily forgotten. Was Kepler the template for what lay in store for him?

Klaus's eyes darted to the doorway then back to Schwarz, his jaw tense, his hand flexing on the pistol's grip. He shuffled to the doorway and quickly looked into the corridor.

"Well?" Schwarz asked.

Klaus shook his head.

"British agents coming to save me," Sonny offered.

Schwarz sniggered. "Charge of the Light Brigade?"

Sonny wondered, hoped, the same. Where were they? Jenny must have passed the information on.

"Let's get the hell out of here!" Becker's face reddened, and sweat soaked the front of his shirt. The stink of fear clung to him like tar.

"Get a grip, Herman. Klaus is in charge of this operation." Albert stared at Klaus. "Isn't that right? So . . . " he took a long drag on his cigarette, " . . . we staying down here until the war ends? Won't be long. What do you think, Sonny—four, six months, maximum? Americans in France, Bolshies moving across Poland . . . should be in Germany soon—unless Adolf's got something up his sleeve . . . " Albert looked pained. "What am I thinking? No food, water . . . one of us will have to take a leak. Actually, I do."

His unctuous smile revealed tobacco-stained teeth. He shook his head, then leaned forward conspiratorially. "Let's leave . . . figure this out later. Be a good boy, Klaus."

"Fuck you! Call me boy again and . . . " His hand tensed and the pistol fired. The bullet pinged off one wall, then a second.

In a quick motion, Albert grabbed his pistol. Sonny had the Beretta in his hand.

"Shit!" Becker screamed and fell to the floor, clutching his leg. "Hit me, asshole." Blood seeped onto his pants.

Klaus made no effort to cover his faux pas, if it was one. "Next time I won't miss." Then he saw the pistols.

"Keeping hostages is difficult, creates tension . . . miscalculation." Albert had a cigarette in his mouth, his silver lighter poised to ignite in one hand, pistol in the other. "That still leaves two of us," he looked from Sonny to Becker, "well . . . two and a half." Then he saw Sonny's Beretta. He laughed. "This is too much."

Klaus waved the pistol dangerously from Sonny to Albert. Thin red lines flowed from dilated pupils, tiny roads on a map leading nowhere, as his eyes widened.

"An idea?" Albert ridiculed.

"We get out of here."

"Ach! Klaus has a plan." Albert oozed sarcasm.

"Pick up your friend." Klaus jabbed with the pistol.

Sonny and Albert exchanged glances. Albert's held disdain, Sonny's disgust.

Albert closed his eyes, sighed, and shook his head as if dealing with a mental deficient. "Then what?"

"We lock the room and . . . " Klaus's eyes darted from his dead uncle to Becker to the gold.

"And, and . . . ?" Albert prodded and poked.

Becker moaned, clutching his injured leg. A sanguine stain had seeped onto the floor. "Lean me against the wall . . . give me a nail."

Albert put a cigarette in Becker's mouth, his pistol aimed at the young man. Becker's pale face glowed orange as flame met cigarette. A furry tail of smoke streamed from Becker.

"Carry him upstairs. Your men take him to the hospital . . . secure the gold . . . you answer for my uncle's murder." He made a chopping, guillotine-like motion with his free hand.

"Don't think I like that last part." Albert grimaced and shook his head. "Besides, you're not holding all the cards." Then he glanced at Sonny and asked, "What do you think?"

Sonny shrugged. "No difference to me as long as I'm not involved."

"Pick him up and move." Klaus spoke through clenched jaw, his voice cold, calculating.

"I could shoot you," Schwarz said calmly.

"Then I shoot you," Klaus quickly added.

"Not a good result, Klaus," Sonny cautioned.

"I have nothing to lose."

Something crawled on her leg. She swiped at it, fell against the wall then laughed, nervously. Five, ten, thirty minutes had passed in the dark, musty room when finally her ears pricked to the muffled pop—gunshot. Panic hit hard. Sonny!

"Not him. It's not Sonny," she said softly. It couldn't be. Convinced of that, she a managed to wiggle from panic's grip.

She turned the knob and slowly pulled the door open. It merely moaned. Through the narrow opening she saw an empty corridor. Within seconds, two men filled the doorway. One was blond and held a pistol and supported an injured man. She saw the stain on his pants—blood? She recognized Becker from Azenhas do Mar. The blond guy was Albert Schwarz.

She clutched the pry bar so tight her hand ached. Quietly, she shut the door.

Muted conversation came from the corridor. She pulled the door open a sliver. Shadows moved on the floor. Two more men emerged from the room. Each held a pistol. One was Sonny. The other was the man who had greeted her in the lobby. He locked the door.

Rosa held her breath and closed the door.

First Schwarz backed out, awkwardly supporting Becker with one arm, pistol at the end of other, eyes darting from Sonny to Klaus. Then Sonny came into the corridor, followed by Klaus. A triangle of pistols moved back and forth, each watching the others. No instructions were required.

Klaus was trigger-happy and playing over his head. Schwarz hid behind Becker, looking for an opening. Sonny doubted they would make it to the stairs.

Memories intrude at the strangest of times…You never know what triggers a distant, forgotten event. One popped now from the vault in Sonny's head—it was a photo from a dead man's wallet. Excellent timing, Sonny thought.

The scrum moved slowly, attracted by the light at the end of the corridor.

"Albert, what happened to your friend, Lt. Franz Walter?"

Schwarz stared at Sonny, and his lips disappeared into a straight line. He stopped. His eyes fluttered several times. Sonny was pleased to have confounded him and laughed, a further provocation.

"Hear he disappeared weeks after Kristallnacht," Sonny taunted. "He carried a picture of you and him with a couple other Gestapo chums."

Still no response, just an uncomprehending stare.

"We killed him . . . *dead* . . . my wife and I . . . Well, she wasn't my wife at the time. Walter planned to rape her. She stabbed him. I hit him with a brick—crunch, ouch." Sonny cringed for effect. "How many women did he rape in that cold, empty warehouse? You part of that?"

"Liar!"

"You disappoint me." Sonny feigned offense. "That fire in Oranienburg, his cremation, up in smoke—poof! Pretty good idea, wasn't it?"

Schwarz's face reddened with anger.

Klaus's eyes darted from one to the other, back and forth. Patience and reason dangled at the end of a frayed string. "Enough," he shouted, and his arm jerked. His pistol discharged.

Becker slumped from the bullet in his chest. Schwarz was slow to react, but he returned the fire. Klaus fell to the floor.

Sonny pulled the trigger. Schwarz yelped. Then Sonny fired twice more. He was unsure of what he had hit.

———

Sonny and Klaus had shuffled past Rosa's door. Her ear was pressed to the crack.

"Liar!" Someone exclaimed.

She heard Sonny's voice, but only "Oranienburg" came through. One gunshot—then several more in quick succession.

She pulled the door open and stared at Schwarz's profile in front of her. Her gaze ran from his cruel mouth to the pistol in his hand. Automatically she lunged, slamming the pry bar onto Schwarz's wrist. His pistol discharged. In her fury, she struck a second blow. His skull creased, and he collapsed. Mere seconds had elapsed.

She turned and looked toward Sonny, anticipating the look on his face. He wasn't there. Her gaze fell to the floor. He lay motionless on his back, next to the other man. She ran to next to him. A red blossom covered his shirt. She held his head in her arm.

Seconds or minutes passed. Someone ran past her. A man knelt next to her—Mayhew.

"Where are you hit?" he asked Sonny, his voice shrill.

Sonny gurgled. His face was pale.

"Shit!" Mayhew cursed.

"Do something . . . do something!" Rosa screamed.

Danielson had Sonny's shoulders and Mayhew his legs. They carried him up the stairs and outside. Around the corner a car waited. Mayhew had not asked Rosa what she was doing there.

Sonny was wedged in the back seat between Mayhew and Danielson. Rosa sat in the front. Mayhew shouted instructions at the driver, who drove through the Rossio to Praça do Comércio, then turned toward Belem.

"Where we going?" Rosa asked in French.

"Private hospital," Mayhew answered.

Sonny was unconscious. No further words were spoken.

The car turned right, then into an alley, where it stopped. The driver ran inside a building. Mayhew and Danielson lifted Sonny from the car. Two men dressed in white met them. They placed Sonny on a stretcher and went inside. Rosa followed.

Inside the building was the odor of disinfectant. Sonny and the two men had disappeared. Rosa, Mayhew, and Danielson remained in a room with white walls and bright overhead lights. An empty desk set against one wall, several chairs on the one opposite. Corridors ran in both directions.

"We have to leave. I'll return," Mayhew said. "They'll take care of him."

41

Hospital, Belem, early 7 August 1944

Exhausted at well past midnight, Mayhew and Danielson walked into the Alfama flat.

"How . . . will he?" Jenny asked. Her distress dropped a pall on the operation's success.

"Too early," Mayhew answered, then sighed. "Two dead—Kepler and Schwarz—the other two Krauts wounded, one critical."

Karpov arrived and asked about Sonny. Mayhew told him.

"What was Rosa doing in the cellar?" Mayhew asked.

Jenny told him about Rosa confronting her. "She saw me in costume. I told her we were pulling a scam on Kepler at the Palace. I'd be in the bar when Sonny met with him. I told her to go home and wait, that she could get hurt."

Mayhew chewed on that, then said, "She killed Schwarz, but his pistol fired."

"Gutsy lady," Danielson said.

"I'll talk to her later at the hospital. I need to know," Mayhew said. "Sonny couldn't tell me anything, not yet."

Maybe half an hour passed. Rose tried weaving the facts into coherency. Her thoughts were muddled . . . Hit his wrist . . . bullet ricocheted . . . Oh my God! Should have struck a split second earlier . . . Did Sonny stop shooting? Why? Where were Mayhew and the others? . . .

Tears dried on her cheeks. A knot tightened in her chest, ached. Breathing seemed difficult. She sat down, concentrated on inhaling, then exhaling. Unable to sit still, she paced. Worry gnawed at her. Sonny was fighting for his life. Then her fear bled to anger and

386

grew—anger at Sonny for volunteering, at Mayhew for asking, at herself, at . . . everything that breathed and walked.

"Don't die. Not now," she muttered, wanted to scream it. They had a life to plan. They had agreed to talk after the mission. That's what they should be doing now. Not being here, in this empty hospital. She chewed on her lip. Had she been unfair, too hard on Sonny? She knew what she wanted and expected Sonny to know as well. No. She had been honest.

Had four years of war, work for the Resistance, fear, made them strangers in the dark? Could they not recognize one another upon the sunrise? They had spent a mere nine months together— November '38 to August '39. How could they know each other?

She had lived without Sonny for four years—in Paris, fleeing to Sare, working, and joining the Resistance. Without him, she would not have survived Berlin and left Germany or made it to Antwerp. A fleeting thought of Berlin brought the memory of her father's abduction. She felt a jolt of fear, then more anger. Vicious men had sought to destroy her family, and they nearly did. Thousands had their lives destroyed.

Sonny had returned day after day of anxiety, days of fear, and death for some. She had been scared. He was her comfort and support. She had suffered for killing that Gestapo monster in Oranienburg. Killing another Gestapo asshole now meant nothing. Sonny's mentor Emil had said, "She'll wish she had killed more by the time this is over." She wished she knew Emil. She owed Sonny so much, but . . .

"I love Sonny," she said aloud. She had to say it, because she had doubted. There were reasons—long separation, future plans. They had become different people. Was she wrong to doubt? Life was filled with doubt. How can anyone be sure? They had been apart so long, it was only natural. She would tell him when he awoke. Guilt had crept in, making her uneasy.

Rosa was frightened more then she had ever been. More than when she was in Oranienburg, during the time of her father's arrest, or when the cop stopped her in Paris. Sonny might . . . die. Don't think it, she told herself, but she did. Wanting something so badly and getting it, then losing it again . . . too painful to contemplate. He was all she had. She wanted Sonny at her side, on equal terms.

Being alone no longer frightened her. Jean, poor Jean, had helped her become independent. Rosa had found courage in Sare. Why was she so scared now? Time and separation were their enemies. Time distorted everything. Time tested her. She had been trapped in Berlin with her father imprisoned, but she had started to heal in Antwerp. After Mons, she had run the gauntlet and passed the test. She survived, independent and confident. Now, time stood still while she waited for news of her husband's fate.

She trusted Sonny. He loved her. They needed time—that was all. But why was it taking so damn long? Was Sonny dying as she waited? Doubt! Damn doubt.

Alone, tired, fearing the worst, she heard something like a siren inside her head. She winced and covered her ears with her hands. The pain was intense, and then it stopped. She gasped. Her head ached. Was she going mad? Do something!

Rosa walked the length of both corridors, past closed doors, listening for voices. Nothing. What kind of hospital was this? At the end of the second corridor was a door with a window. She saw stairs. She climbed to the next floor.

Faint voices came from the end of a corridor. She walked to an open door. An older man in a white smock, dotted with red, leaned on the wall. His eyes were red from fatigue. A younger man smoked a cigarette. A big table dominated the center of the room. Smaller tables were littered with medical paraphernalia. Rosa walked in.

Surprised, the man in the white smock asked, "Who are you?"

Rosa stared at the blood-spattered man and murmured, "No."

42

Hospital, Belem, 7 August 1944

The other man left the room. Rosa waited 15 . . . 20 . . . 30 minutes. Finally, a short, plump man appeared.

"Where's Sonny?" she demanded, without introduction.

"You must be Rosa," he said in unaccented French. "My name is Johnson."

Rosa had heard the name before. She glanced at the man in the blood-dotted smock, then at Johnson. "I want to see him."

"That is impossible just now. He's been shot . . . "

"Damn it! I was there . . . tried to prevent it." Rosa's anger flared.

"Calm down. I know how you must feel."

"Tell me how I feel," she spat the words. "Don't patronize me."

"I'm sorry." Johnson colored slightly, then pursed his lips. "You can't see Sonny because he's getting a transfusion. The doctor removed the bullet. It punctured a lung, was close to his heart."

"Then take me to his room. I'll wait for him," Rosa demanded.

Johnson nodded . . .

. . . Rosa paced away the hours before Sonny was wheeled into the room and onto the bed. He was immersed in white: bandages, sheets, walls, curtain over the window. His face was alabaster pale, but he seemed at peace. A bottle filled with liquid was tethered to his arm by a tube. She supposed it was the morphine.

His eyes were closed, his mouth slightly open. His chest rose and fell in continuous rhythm, a good sign. Rosa sat in a chair by his bed, dozed intermittently . . .

Sunlight pressed against the curtain. She walked around the bed, stretching her limbs. Sonny moaned. She leaned over him.

"Sonny, it's Rosa."

"Rosa," he muttered. His eyes, unfocused, moved over her face. She leaned closer. "Yes."

"How . . . ?"

"Shot by Schwarz . . . " Her throat clogged with emotion and she stopped.

He mumbled unintelligibly.

Rosa bent forward, waiting for Sonny to say more. Focused on his mouth, her mind was wiped clean. No words came. His eyes closed. She felt another presence and stiffened. The doctor had entered the room. She told him that Sonny had spoken. He spoke a little French.

"Will he live?" she asked.

He scratched his chin, then pursed his lips, the ritual of buying time before answering a hard question. He moved his head slowly from side to side. "All I can say is that he is not good."

"I need to know," she said in French.

"I'm sorry."

Mayhew appeared later that morning. He greeted Rosa with a tight smile. "I talked to the doctor. He has nothing new to report." Several moments of uncomfortable silence passed until he said, "We need to talk."

"Then talk."

"Tell me what you saw and did."

She told him. "I had experience in the Resistance." Then, through clenched jaw: "I resented being excluded."

Mayhew looked at Sonny, lying peacefully, then back at Rosa. "I concede your anger. You're not employed by His Majesty. We aren't taking volunteers."

"I don't need your permission," she snapped.

"No. I'm angry too."

"For the same reasons?"

Mayhew pursed his lips and did not answer.

"Where were you? What took you so long?" she asked.

"By the time we got in the cellar, it was too dangerous to move."

Rosa thought about that and shook her head. "Never mind." A veil of silent resentment descended over her.

"He's my comrade and friend. I fear . . . "

"I don't really care about *your* fears," she snapped.

Mayhew removed an envelope from his pocket. "This was in

Sonny's jacket." He handed it to Rosa.

She stared at the envelope in her hand. An uncomfortable silence filled the white room. They were done talking. Mayhew left. She threw the envelope on the floor.

Danielson arrived shortly after Mayhew had gone. Rose met him formally for the first time, but conversation was impossible due to the language barrier—for which Rosa was grateful. He saluted Sonny, wished Rosa well, and was gone.

Jenny and Karpov came in the afternoon. Rosa and Jenny embraced. Karpov hugged Rosa, then stood, uncomfortable, watching.

Rosa told them what Sonny had uttered.

"It's something," Jenny said hopefully.

Karpov left after half an hour. He had work to do. Jenny stayed.

"Tell me everything," Rosa asked. "Please."

Jenny described her vantage point in the bar, then talked about meeting Sonny at the elevator and leaving the hotel to warn Mayhew about Kepler's note to Sonny: "It was all about the gold. London wanted it. We had information that the gold was delivered to the cellar, and Kepler's note confirmed it. He was stealing it, and we think Schwarz and Becker wanted in. Mayhew talked about turning one of the three men. We had a good plan until they blundered onto the scene and . . . well, you know. Kepler's body was in the room where the gold was stored, shot by Schwarz or Becker. We think it was Schwarz, and he's dead now, too."

"Good!" Rosa looked at Sonny's still body. "Jenny, what did I do?"

"What any good operative would."

"Didn't work out so well."

"You did all you could."

"If only I'd hit him a second earlier."

Neither spoke for a long moment. Jenny broke through the curtain of silence, "Don't carry that burden. You're not to blame."

"No?"

"No! Schwarz pulled the trigger. That the bullet ricocheted . . . "

Rosa tensed as she interrupted, "I know all the words. He shot Sonny, but I was part of it." She sighed and looked away. "I'm taking it out on you." Her voice trailed off.

"Don't worry about me."

"The pain," Rosa faltered, placing a hand on Jenny's arm for support. "What if he doesn't survive?"

"You mourn, then go on living. Twice I was down, and two people helped when no one else would—you and Sonny. I lost Max, then found Roman. You find the strength to live. I know you have it."

Jenny saw the envelope on the floor and picked it up. She opened it. "Where did this money come from?"

"Money? Mayhew . . . "

"Where did he get it?"

Rosa shook her head.

Jenny put the envelope on the chair, then left the room . . .

So it went for the next two days. Sonny regained consciousness for brief periods, then lapsed into unconsciousness.

The two of them had argued. She hadn't wanted him to go. She had lost. But then she had wanted in on the operation. What was that about?

On the third day, Jenny came again. She stood next to Rosa. They stared at Sonny, his face pale and immobile. His breathing was labored. His pulse had weakened from the loss of blood and the havoc played inside his chest cavity by the careening bullet. Only the irregular movement of his chest and an occasional eye twitch gave evidence of life within.

Jenny took Rosa's hand and held it.

"What's going on?" Rosa asked, more to make conversation than anything else.

"The gold is on its way to London. We left Kepler and Schwarz in the room where the gold was stashed—too many curious eyes to remove them without being seen. And where would we dump them? They'll be found soon enough, maybe have been already. Let the Gestapo and Abwehr ponder the demise of their darlings."

"And the other two?"

"Klaus is already on the street, and we dropped Becker at a local hospital for treatment. They'll point fingers . . . until both are hung as traitors. One of our Portuguese operatives paid off the kitchen staff. There was too much commotion for someone not to have heard the shots or seen the men coming and going. When the word finally leaks, the PVDE will investigate. By then our trail will be as cold as the bodies in the cellar."

"Stolen from under their noses," Rosa mused. "Sonny would be pleased to know how it turned out."

"He'll know," Jenny said.

A doctor entered the room. He went through the motions, feeling Sonny's pulse, and listening to his lungs and heart. He looked at Sonny, hand on his chin, his clouded face telling all. He spoke to Rosa in French. She heard little.

Sonny was fading away, his shadow dimming. She could feel it.

43

Hospital, Belem, 10 August 1944

According to the calendar on the wall behind the nurse's desk, it was Thursday. It might be midmorning—Rosa wasn't sure. She stood in Sonny's room, at the window overlooking the alley where the car carrying him had stopped. How many days ago?

She focused on the building across the narrow open space. A long crack in its stucco façade caught her eye. She traced its snaking journey between windows to the roofline. Broken, in need of repair. How long had it been like that? Would it ever be fixed? Who would mend it?

A sound from behind made her turn toward Sonny. A nurse checked the tube in his arm. She smiled at Rosa. Rosa may have smiled back. Alone with Sonny again, she sat next to the bed and took his hand in hers. It felt cool.

"Why?" she asked, silence greeting her question for the hundredth time. "Say my name, or ask another question, anything," she begged. "That would be enough."

Sonny's grasp tightened slightly. Rosa straightened. "What?"

No answer, but something had happened. She stared as if she were another person, watching her watch Sonny. A strange feeling washed over her. Her mouth slackened. She heard a faint gurgling sound, followed by a silence so complete it might have been a scream. She was unable to move. She knew. Sonny was dead.

Rosa held his hand until the nurse entered the room. Five minutes, 30, or 60 passed. Her eyes stung with tears.

Sonny lay dead.

Rosa resisted a recounting of events, but they came unbidden. Berlin—filled with sadness, fear, and trepidation, yet comfort in their companionship. Antwerp—contentment, a sort of happiness. She closed her eyes. They walked through Old Town, holding hands, marrying at the courthouse on 3 April 1939, Mina and Otto, and her parents their witnesses, a celebration at Sammy's Café. Their first night . . .

Then painful separation, not a single anniversary together until Lisbon. Hoping Sonny would find her—amazed when he did. They would start anew. At least she wanted to. They would have talked it out. "After the mission," he had promised. Always the damn mission! They would have worked it out. They would be together. Her doubts evaporated.

"Fighters and survivors—damn you Sonny!"

Her meandering mind conjured two London MI6 bureaucrats conferring in headquarters after the gold was secured, congratulating themselves. One said, "Remember that German Jew who saved Shannon's life?"

The other man played with his monocle and frowned. "Vaguely."

"He didn't make it."

"Dead?"

The other man nodded.

"Unfortunate. Must have been a good lad—still, a successful operation. Give his wife a medal, something shiny. Time to move on."

One little pawn . . .

Hope had kept her going—from Mons to Paris to Sare, then to the Resistance. But now it failed her. She would go on, as Jenny said. But she was a boat turning in circles in a pond—without a rudder.

She was a 31-year-old widow, born 30 December 1913—a date on a calendar. She remembered one wonderful childhood birthday . . . Her father held her little hand at the zoo as she shrieked with joy at the lion's den. All subsequent birthday celebrations paled by comparison. Then Hitler had come, and there was little to celebrate.

Birthdays, holidays, and anniversaries were just numbers on a calendar. Their first wedding anniversary *together*, on 3 April 1944, was their fifth in years. They had celebrated with dinner and fado then back to the flat, and . . . But the numbers were etched into memory: 9 November 1938, 1 September 1939, 10 May 1940, and, now, 10 August 1944.

Two days later, Sonny was buried under a gray sky threatening rain at the British Cemetery in Lisbon, adjacent to St. George's Church on Rua São Jorge. Henry Fielding, the famous British author, was Sonny's graveside neighbor. Rosa, Jenny, Karpov, Mayhew, Danielson, and Johnson attended the short service. Johnson praised Sonny's loyalty and bravery. Mayhew told them how Sonny had unmasked him on the street. Laughter broke through their somber mood. Jenny recited the "Mourner's Kaddish." Each mourner threw a shovelful of dirt onto the casket in the grave. They hugged Rosa, muttered condolences, then dispersed like birds.

Alone, Rosa returned to Alfama by tram, to walk the meandering lanes Sonny loved so much. She needed to be alone, but she stopped at the door of his favorite fado and was pulled inside. With a glass of wine, she sat in corner absorbing the saudade.

In the flat, she sat alone in darkness pressing Sonny's handkerchief to her face. Her parents returned from the periphery. She wished they were with her. They had comforted her when she cried after skinning her elbow, when her best friends left for America. Suddenly she missed them. They were all she had. She would tell them everything.

Rosa sat on the floor in the corner, her legs pulled tight against her chest, swaying side to side, comforted by the rhythm...She awoke with a start. Light shone against the curtained window. Another day . . .

Her appetite waned, and it showed. Her facial bones gained prominence, cheeks hollowed, and shoulder blades sharpened. Her clothes hung loose on her narrowing frame. She washed her face and brushed her teeth, stared at the stranger in the mirror. Then she left the flat to walk the ancient narrow winding paths she and Sonny had frequented.

Lisbon sweltered in the summer heat, but Rosa seemed not to notice. From Alfama she walked along the river to Praça do Comércio, to the Rossio, then up to Bairro Alto, slowly down the steep incline of the funicular to Avenida da Liberdade and back to the Rossio. Avenida Palace, like a bad dream, intruded . . . She turned into the alley behind the National Theater, where she had hidden.

Walking relieved her pain and cleared the demons—questioning voices and disturbing thoughts, unwelcome squatters in her head.

Summoning a future still lay beyond her grasp.

She spent most evenings in Sonny's favorite fado bars, listening to songs she did not understand but that moved her to tears. Nothing seemed important but the moment, and the moment was sad beyond her imagination.

Jenny sat with Rosa in the flat, often in silence. Her mere presence was comforting.

One evening, as they walked, arms linked, from a club toward the flat, Rosa started talking. "My body aches. Other times I'm numb. I feel empty, as if there's nothing inside me."

"You're not eating. Should you see a doctor?" Jenny suggested.

She shrugged. "I'm not hungry. He'll just tell me to eat."

"You have to eat."

Rosa nodded, more in acknowledgment than agreement, and was quiet for a long moment. Then she said, "We had a shared history. Not in any normal sense, but a shared longing and separation. We never doubted we'd reunite."

"It's a beautiful love story," Jenny said.

"A tragic love story." Rosa corrected. She felt the need to recite their history, but Jenny had heard it before . . . "Sometimes, I wish my special someone, Sonny, had been the man next door, or that we had met in a coffee shop or on the street. Not the way we did. That we would have had a long courtship."

"The elusive normal," Jenny muttered.

Rosa nodded. "It's good to talk. Thank you for listening."

Weeks disappeared with monotonous and painful continuity. But near the end of September, something changed. Rosa experienced stomach cramps and her breasts felt heavy. She had not menstruated for several months.

"I think I'm pregnant," she told Jenny and began to cry. "Why?"

44

London, October 1944

Rosa sailed to London with Jenny and Karpov. She was housed in the officer's quarters on an army base near London. Jenny and Karpov lived down the hall in the same building.

Two months had passed since Sonny's death. Rosa's appetite had returned. She had gained weight and felt healthier, at least physically. Still her anger, guilt, and sorrow sometimes seemed unbearable. Each vied for primacy, recklessly whiplashing her. She dreamed of drifting at sea, shipwrecked, stomach huge with child, flailing in salty water, struggling to breathe, and sinking into the abyss. Awaking breathlessly, she paced the room, unable to sleep.

For a time, Rosa considered her pregnancy as life's cruel joke—revenge for her misdeeds. Fists clenched, she railed at the perceived injustice of her pregnancy. Sonny had been taken from her, leaving a child for her to bear and to care for alone.

You can't have Sonny. You must have his child. Finally, she had enough and muttered, "stop." Accept that Sonny is dead and you are pregnant. Accept it and look to the future. Our child must not be unwanted. It is Sonny's legacy—a lover's gift. Slowly her thoughts percolated into an attitude fully formed. Regardless of how contrived or melodramatic, that would be her touchstone. Step one in confronting the pain of Sonny's death and her current condition. Shed self-pity. To do otherwise would be self-indulgent wallowing.

Rosa needed work to occupy her time and, she hoped, her mind. Jenny and Karpov continued to work for MI6, though for them the war was over. Jenny translated German documents and Karpov guarded MI6 headquarters at St. Ermin's Hotel, London. Jenny introduced Rosa to her supervisor. Word spread, and within days she had a job. Rosa sniffed Johnson's hand in the process, but she had no proof. Rosa sat at a desk next to Jenny reading German and French documents. Part of her job required attending an English course on base.

She could find peace only by reconciling the past and her part in Sonny's death. That was imperative. She forgave John Mayhew. Her anger had been misplaced. Mayhew was a cog in a massive machine in which Sonny had become entwined. Sonny's sense of duty and insatiable appetite for danger would not allow him to turn his back on the mission. It would been like failing to breathe . . . John Mayhew and Sonny had become friends as much as spies could, so she made things right with Mayhew on the eve of her departure. She thought they had parted as friends.

She endlessly reviewed those two fateful days in August—from the time Sonny told her of the secret mission until the fatal shot. She hoped to understand and come to terms with Sonny's death. She might then shed her guilt.

What could she have done differently? If Sonny had fired three shots, why hadn't a single one found its target in Schwarz? Why hadn't he kept on shooting? Did he think he had hit Schwarz already? Was Sonny a lousy shot? Would Schwarz have killed him in any scenario? Could Sonny have lived? What had taken Mayhew so long?

Rosa's hypothetical scenarios changed nothing. Schwarz had killed her husband. She repeated the refrain until it became her mantra. Sonny's death was not the fault of Mayhew, of Sonny, or of her. Schwarz and the Nazis were to blame—it was simple and obvious. She had done all she could. Still . . .

"We knew the risks—Roman, Sonny, me," Jenny argued. "You were in the Resistance. You knew the risks and accepted them." She paused, then added, "Death was always a possibility. Sonny volunteered for a more dangerous role than ours. He accepted that. His life turned on risk and danger."

"I know what the words mean." She tapped a finger on her chest. "It's in here that I struggle to understand and accept."

And so it went.

On a chilly, rainy evening, several weeks after her arrival, Rosa answered a knock on the door of her little room on base. She faced a man in uniform with flaming red hair.

"Hello, Mr. Shannon," she said.

His smile exaggerated his brilliant, jade-green eyes. "Glad to finally make your acquaintance, Mrs. Sander."

"Call me Rosa."

"Rosa. And I am Michael." He extended a hand. "Your accent is more French than German." His hand was warm.

"I am glad. I feel French."

Michael spoke in French. "Sonny was a good man. He saved my life."

"Speak English, please. I learn. He saved me. I miss him very much."

Sitting on the bed, she motioned him to the only chair. He looked around the room. Had he come to share memories of Sonny? Hers came in random bursts: Standing in the doorway and in the empty warehouse, embracing in the train to Portugal, watching him stride from that awful hotel, the cellar debacle. Or had he come to talk about the war that was nearly won, Germany squeezed from both ends? Or was it something else?

Finally, she asked, "Did you know I was pregnant?"

"Yes, I did." He sighed. "Sad yet joyful—congratulations."

She nodded. "Yes, both. How did you know?"

"I am a spy."

Rosa smiled. "Of course. You know all about me."

"Sonny spoke of you often and how beautiful you are. He was right. Pregnancy agrees with you."

Rosa felt her face flush. She was at a loss. She hadn't felt this in years. Before Sonny, she had lived for such words, but now . . . she had rejected any man's gaze but her husband's for years. She was not ready, not yet, maybe never.

She felt her head shake then stopped. "I am sorry. Thank you."

"No, I'm sorry. I made you uncomfortable. I meant it as a compliment. I came because I had to meet you, and I have something for you."

"What do you have for me?" Rosa's composure returned with her curiosity. She looked beyond Michael's red hair and green eyes to a boyish face that would age well. She recalled childhood books picturing boys who looked like Michael. She smiled, then remembered he had been shot in the arm. "How is your arm?"

"Mending. I live with it." He rolled his right shoulder, reached into his pocket, and removed a small box. "There is small consolation, but . . . "

Rosa's gaze rested on the little box. "What?" But she knew.

He handed the box to her. "The George Cross."

Rosa laughed.

Michael blinked, perplexed.

"I am sorry. I must explain. After," she waved a hand, "I was very," she hesitated, then said, "cynique."

"Cynical," Shannon supplied.

"Cynical," she repeated the English word. "I was cynical and angry. I have awake dream your MI6 would give me medal. I forgot until now."

He smiled. "You imagined."

"What?"

"You said *awake dream.* I think you meant *imagined.*"

"Ah, yes, *imagined.* Thank you. "

His smile still in place, he nodded and turned serious. "There is no cynicism. England is thankful to men like Sonny."

"Tell me about this George Cross."

"It is named for the king, started to 1941 to honor civilians performing acts of gallantry. I nominated Sonny for saving my life on the battlefield when he was a civilian. His work in Lisbon, then in France, was icing on the cake."

"Icing on the cake," Rosa repeated, holding the blue ribbon attached to the silver cross with St. George and the dragon. Etched on the back was, "Sonny Sander—10 August 1944." She stared at the shiny object in her hand. A comfortable silence ensued.

Finally, Rosa broke through. "Is *gallantry* more than *bravery?*"

He tilted his head, considering her question. "It's an old word, but it means the same. The Crown likes to use old words, especially for the battlefield."

Rosa nodded. "How many have been given?"

Shannon shook his head. "Couldn't say . . . but not many."

She returned the medal to the box. "It would be too sad if this was all I had to remember of Sonny, but there is more . . . " She patted her belly.

"You also have memories."

"Yes, of course." She looked into Shannon's eyes. "They are the greenest I have ever seen."

He smiled broadly. "Sonny said we had a brief encounter in northern France during the invasion. He remembered my eyes."

"He told me."

"I have other news. You are entitled to survivor benefits and a stipend for your child. I will see to it."

"What is that?"

"A monthly payment from the government for your loss and assistance for the child, whose father died in battle."

"Another memory?" Rosa asked with an edge in her voice.

Michael looked around the room, then into Rosa's eyes. He did not respond.

"Again, I am sorry. Sometimes my bitterness comes out. I try to be better than that."

"I can only imagine what you are going through."

"That word again."

"Nothing can replace Sonny. Money will help you live. If there is anything I can do . . . " He handed her a card. "Please contact me any time." On the card were his name and a couple of telephone numbers. "Either number will reach me, eventually." He was reassuring.

"Did you get me the job?" she blurted. "I thought it was Johnson, but now . . . "

"You needed work."

"Thank you."

"Remember to call should you require anything."

"I will," she hesitated, "and thank you for coming."

He left.

Rosa watched him walk to a waiting car from the window. The rain had stopped. The street lamp cast a shadow on his face. He looked back and waved with his left arm. He may have smiled. She nodded and raised her hand. The car drove away.

Rosa held the box and jiggled it. She was tempted to throw it in the bin. Shrugging, she placed it inside a compartment in her suitcase.

EPILOGUE

8 May 1945, V-E Day—London

A cheering crowd—dancing, singing, hugging, and kissing—had gathered outside Buckingham Palace: "We want the king!"

Joyous parents hoisted children onto their shoulders so that they could see the king who would appear on the balcony. Thousands filled Trafalgar Square, spilling onto the mall and all the way to the palace. More filled Piccadilly Circus. People hung from window ledges and stood on roofs. American sailors danced the conga with English girls. More that a million people were there, celebrating victory in Europe.

Representatives of the vanquished German government had signed surrender documents the previous day in Reims. Hitler was dead in his Berlin bunker, shot by his own hand, according to the wireless.

"Long live the cause of freedom! God save the king!" the prime minister intoned at Whitehall.

Peace had finally arrived . . .

Twilight filtered through the blinds in Rosa's in quarters. It was several days after surrender. She held little Sonny, two weeks old, born 23 April 1944—another monumental date. Sonny Joseph Emil Sander was his full name. "A bit long," she acknowledged. "But fitting, I think. I will tell him what I know about those men."

Jenny and Roman were with her.

"I cannot believe it is finally over," Rosa said in English, her new tongue.

"I know," Jenny responded. "Mingling in that crush of humanity, shaking hands, hugging, was . . . " she hesitated, " . . . bittersweet. We had a right to be there. We were part of the victory. We're guaranteed

403

a permanent home here or anywhere in the Commonwealth. We won't be stateless. Still . . . it was strange, interesting to observe but not be part of it."

Rosa had eschewed the celebration and stayed on base with little Sonny.

"Too many people . . . make me nervous," Roman said. "I look over shoulder, expect something bad, see people laugh." He shrugged.

"I felt half a pace behind, laughing a beat late, out of place—like a fish on a bicycle," Jenny observed.

Rosa laughed at the image. "What is next for you?" she asked.

Jenny glanced at Roman before answering. "We will stay with MI6. Here, on the continent, or somewhere else."

Roman nodded his agreement.

"I need to know what happened to Max. Is he dead or alive? I have to know!"

"I vill help," Roman said, as he took Jenny's hand.

"Back to the continent?" Rosa asked skeptically.

She did not have to explain. Rumors of murder on a scale so massive it defied comprehension—Nazi concentration camps, killing camps across Germany, Poland, and other conquered lands—trickled into London. If they were true, thousands of European Jews were dead. Nazi perfidy had infected every country it touched; none escaped the Nazi killing machine. Thinking of Germany in ruins, the millions of dead, made her ill.

"I have to go. What will you do?" Jenny asked.

"Take Sonny as far away from here as I can," Rosa answered without enthusiasm. "Thought I had it figured out. Sonny was torn. We planned to talk after . . . "

"Torn about what?"

"Normal life. He did not lead a normal life, not in Berlin and not after. Conflict and danger were his life for so long."

Little Sonny had fallen asleep. Rosa laid him on the bed.

"I know how he feel," Roman said. "You fight and fight. It get in your blood . . . hard to stop."

"You can," Jenny said, authoritatively.

"But if we stay with MI6 . . . " He shrugged, then smiled.

"Roman is right, even if the war is over," Rosa said.

"We'll be together—that's normal enough for me. Tell us how you plan to make your life normal." Jenny said dryly.

Rosa laughed again, realizing how good it felt. Jenny laughed with her; then Roman joined in, an unusual occurrence.

"See my parents in Havana. I feel like I hardly know them, and after that?" She shrugged. "My life is upside down again. We reunited after so many years apart . . . to have it end like this?" She gazed at little Sonny. "I have responsibility. And I feel Sonny's shadow, again, like a huge cloud above me. That is good."

In the weeks following, photographs in newspapers and newsreels on cinema screens of allied soldiers liberating Nazi death camps confirmed the rumors: Hollow-eyed, skeletal survivors, barely alive, flanked piles of corpses impossible to fathom. How many such death camps were there—dozens, hundreds? Einsatzgruppen, ghastly as it was, was but a drip in the ocean of vast, numberless dead.

European Jewry was on the verge of extinction. How many even remained? Were Jean, Alain, Catherine, and René alive? What about Sonny's friends Emil and Joseph?

. . . In the late afternoon of a summer day, Rosa, who had just finished work, found Michael Shannon waiting in front of the officer's quarters. They exchanged greetings.

"Let's take a walk," he said.

Little Sonny was at the base nursery.

"It is good to see you," Rosa offered.

"For me as well. Have you received your benefits?"

Rosa nodded. "Thank you."

"Good."

"I know there are thousands like me. Others have more pain."

"You are unique, 'a one off.'"

She smiled. "I like your English sayings. What is 'one off'?"

"One of a kind, special. That's what you are," he answered.

"Thank you, I think."

He laughed. They talked of Europe's new order and the horror in the wake of the old one. They talked of their plans and the future. Michael had found a home at MI6. Soon he would return to the Continent, but he could not divulge in what capacity. Rosa asked whether he had heard of a new organization—the United Nations—successor to the failed League of Nations. He had. Perhaps her fluency in three languages might lead to a job as a translator. It was in its infancy, but if it was located in America . . .

"If I can be of any assistance, I will."

"Thank you."

"I wish you the best. You deserve it." Michael gave her an address on a piece of paper. "Write to me when you are settled. Someday I will tell Sonny the story of how his father saved my life."

"I would like that."

They stood without speaking, their attention drawn to an airplane, its engines screaming as it took off. A group of soldiers ambled along the road ahead. There was no war to fight.

"You are a good man," Rosa finally said.

They hugged and said good-bye.

Rosa had a family and a life to live . . .

———

Palm trees shaded the street along the Havana harbor. The saltwater air felt good on her face. She searched the crowd as she walked down the gangplank, holding Sonny close. Then she saw them waving. She had never thought she'd be so happy to see her parents. She had rehearsed the words, but she was unable to say them through her tears.

ABOUT THE AUTHOR

Steven Muenzer is the son of parents born in Germany who fled to the United States at the end of 1939. World War II had begun by the time they left Holland on the *Rotterdam*, the last boat out. The author's exploration of their experience was the genesis of his first book, *Farewell Berlin*, a novel including some family lore. This work, *Rest at Journey's End*, is its sequel. Muenzer practiced law for thirty years before starting his writing career. He lives in St. Paul, Minnesota, with his wife Jeanne, a psychologist.